Tiny Righteous Acts

Parker Bauman

First paperback edition January 2020

Book design by Andy Bridge

Formatting by Jacob Hammer

ISBN 978-1-7344022-0-9 (paperback)

ISBN 978-1-7344022-1-6 (ebook)

www.parkerbauman.net

Dedication

To Steven, the rock to which this helium balloon is tethered, and to Zack and Jake, the pebbles.

Chapter One
They Just Keep Comin'

Like a good hookah, impunity is enjoyed by the men of Afghanistan. This much she knew. Representing beauties from Herat to Kabul, she had a good sense of what was coming. Another emotional earthquake—that's what.

I hope it isn't another acid attack. Lottie swatted the thought away and glanced out the window where the sun had scaled the blue ladder of sky, piercing the blinds with irritating optimism. Eleven o'clock would come, of course, with or without her approval. Time stopped for no one. It was neither sympathetic nor accommodating.

Across the street, her octogenarian neighbor four houses down, Miss Estelle, wobbled next to her red weenie dog, Oscar. *If she keeps feeding him table scraps, her wiener will become a sausage.*

And, on her small patch of terra firma in front of the condo, her landscaper, Mister George, all sweat and paunch, wiped salt beads off his soccer-ball-shaped head. A few forlorn gray strands crossed his forehead like arrows and pointed to his left eye, a magnified blue orb behind thick glasses. He looked up and waved, flashing teeth that had long ago surrendered to tobacco dye. Lottie waved back and smiled. Mister George had mowed, weeded, fed, and talked to her lawn as though it was his child for five years.

She glanced at the clock—10:54—heard the footsteps on the old oak staircase, a pathetic alarm system if ever there was one, and destroyed the better part of a pinky nail with a sharp incisor, sending periwinkle flakes of polish to the floor.

Seconds later, her assistant—not secretary!—bellowed, "Your eleven o'clock is here, baby."

"Okay. Thanks, Lou." Lottie glanced into the eight-by-ten mirror hung on the wall in her office, what she considered to be vanity's equivalent of a cheat sheet. One day, would she be less pale? Maybe less freckled? Less frizzy? Less whatever? She sighed. "Send her in."

The door to the office opened slowly, producing a mild waft of gardenias and a stunning woman à la Sandra Bullock, with hair the color of coffee without cream and Cleopatra-lined eyes. Beneath her eyes and across her left cheek, a scar, four inches, maybe, asserted itself.

The woman maintained her beauty despite the ostensible goal of a lunatic, no doubt, to diminish it, and her eyes rang familiarly hollow, lacking something. Life? Hope? Lottie had seen it too many times, especially in her female clients.

I predict a rape and a rejection. But I don't want to predict anymore.

"You must be Sadia." Lottie forced a smile, hoping the mood would tag along.

"I am Sadia," she lilted in a way that evoked images of the Hindu Kush and blue-burqaed women subject to the snappy whips of the Taliban. "Thank you meet me."

You have no idea how close I came to not. "Please sit down. You have the choice of sinking waist-deep into feathers or having no arms on your chair." Nervous laughter shot out of Lottie, the kind she thought was involuntary, the kind that was embarrassing. Why did she always try to be funny with people from other cultures? With everyone? It usually didn't work anyhow.

The beauty dropped into the overstuffed chair, sank deep into the down, and, after righting herself, crossed long, blue-jeaned legs with the finesse of a Rockette. The sun aimed its spotlight on her as if in interrogation mode, and Lottie got up and adjusted the shades. Sadia pointed up to the string of tiny white lights that hung above her. "I like."

"Thank you. It's supposed to make things better, happier." Lottie smiled broadly to drive home the point. Sadia might not have understood that, which was just as well. "Did Louisa offer you something to drink? Coffee? Tea? Juice?"

"She did. I fine." She looked down in her lap at her hands, which were entwined like one of those 3-D wooden puzzles.

"So tell me why you are here, please." Lottie pulled out a legal pad from the top drawer.

"I have fear to go back to my country. I want to stay America."

She doodled a frowny face on the paper, then a question mark.

"Okay. By the way, your English is very good. Please tell me your story. What country are you from?"

"Afghanistan."

"I see." Lottie steeled herself like a good girl, like a good immigration lawyer. "I understand." Already, she wished to reach across the desk and grab Sadia's hand, but refrained, being reminded of a colleague's sermon on boundaries. *Yes, boundaries. I must set them. I will set them!*

"Kabul or Jalalabad or…?"

"Kabul." Her guest wrapped her arms around herself tightly.

"Are you cold? Sometimes I blast the AC too high, though it's not so hot today?"

"I okay."

Knowing the interview was fraught with monsters waiting to leap from the shadows, Lottie slid between them the box of tissues festooned with corny but inspirational phrases. *Dream big! Be the reason someone smiles! Whatever you are, be a good one!* If only the decorators of the box had known whose nose they might reach, whose eyes they might dry, he or she might have printed: *Hang in there. It's gonna be okay. You are stronger than you think.*

Or even better—if the designer had printed realistic advisories like: *Are you sure you want to come here? The American Dream ain't what it used to be. Have you purchased your AR-15 yet? It's the American way.* Maybe she could do it herself and market to immigration attorneys. *Hey now! That's an idea. I could retire to a small flat in Paris.*

A nod and wet eyes materialized from across the desk. In solidarity, Lottie's nose began to sting and her eyes pooled. She chalked that right up to estrogen and empathy, her two biggest foes. Knowing that the needle of willpower and resolve wobbled around the Orange or Severe level, she put her shoulders back and pushed the tissues toward her guest. Sadia grabbed two. Lottie grabbed three.

"Please take your time," she said.

"This." She pointed to her left cheek. "My cousin, Abdullah, he do. I am pretty before, see?" She tapped her iPhone and flipped it around, revealing an even more stunning, pre-sliced Sadia.

"Oh, I think you're still quite beautiful. In fact, you may be more beautiful than before." *What am I saying?*

Sadia's lips quivered, and she vehemently shook her head, as if she wanted to wave a white flag at the whole situation. To be done with it.

This is going to be a tough one.

"Why did he cut you?" Lottie asked, though she could make a wild guess.

"He want to marry me. I no want to marry."

"So he cut you??"

"Yes." Tears fell from the dark eyes.

"Take your time," Lottie repeated.

Sadia sniffed. Sadia wiped. Sadia blew. Lottie sniffed. Lottie dabbed.

"My cousin want to marry me. I no want to. What he did to me." She wobbled her head again.

Outside the window on the streets below, laughter rang out cruelly. It wasn't uncommon in Lottie's lively neighborhood and certainly wasn't anyone's fault. But inside, sniffles and injustice and Third Worldness filled the room. She twisted in her fuchsia leather swivel, so chosen for its Venus message and subliminal power sensations, feeling powerless. She grabbed the Starbucks cup off the desk and threw it into the trash can.

It was one of the risks of having a home office in a neighborhood in an overly friendly city, of course. The inequality of things, the impolite and impolitic incongruity: *Thwack! In your face!*

"Do you want to take a break?" Lottie asked, though they'd just started.

"No, I tell you. Do you know about the laws of Afghanistan?"

"Yes, I'm quite familiar with them." She wished she wasn't. "I've represented several Afghanis." Thunderclouds formed in her head as the First and Third Worlds collided. *Smash! Bang!*

"Abdullah, he rape me." She pointed again to the four-inch welt on her cheek. "After he cut."

Lottie bobbed her head and scribbled on the legal pad, where she would rather write a poem or love letter: *Bastard!* Meanwhile, from behind the curtains in her cerebellum, doubts peeked: *What the actual...? Another day, another rape. And what the hell am I doing about it? Not much.*

Sadia wiped her nose and continued. "And because he rape me, I no good for marriage. I bring dishonor to my family."

Of course. Lottie knew too well that in Afghanistan, that wouldn't be the end of the story. Patriarchy was the gift that kept on giving. Sort of like herpes. And, of course, rape was never enough. It almost never ended there.

"My brothers Mohamed and Abeed kill me." She shook her head. "No, they…" She looked around for the words as though she could pull them from the air. "Want to kill me. I shame family."

Lottie couldn't help think about her own two older brothers. Yeah, they were a pain in the butt growing up, and she often begged for a sister, but at least she grew up safe, secure, and, most importantly, loved. She could still call on them, both firefighters and heroes, if she needed anything.

"It's unfortunately a horrible custom. And it's not just your country. Others do it too. And, it's certainly not your fault." Lottie said this out loud. Internally, however, a stew brewed. Yup. In cultures caught up in twisted rules pushed by certain influential imams, honor killing was the family's solution to dishonor. Ironically, one got raped, then, rather than killing the rapist, stellar human being that he is, the family would kill the rapee or victim. All in the name of honor. Probably the most effed-up set of customs on the planet.

Like a thoroughbred rearing up in the gate, Lottie felt the familiar adrenaline coursing through her veins, like she was hyped up on steroids. Again. Which couldn't be healthy, right? She imagined the endorphins logjammed at her synapses, potential blood pressure issues. And at thirty!

Honor killing! She stabbed the paper with black ink. *Rape. Abdullah. Cousin.* All ugly words, if you asked her, words that shouldn't be in her vocabulary. Her vocabulary should consist of words like *love, laughter, family, friends, Mardi Gras, Jazz Fest, crawfish.*

"So what did you do? I mean, how did you get here?"

"Marasta?"

"I'm sorry. My Pashto is no good. My Arabic is better."

"No Arabee." Sadia leaned over, grabbed the legal pad and pen from Lottie, and wrote M-A-R-A-S-T-A. Lottie ignited her laptop and googled it. Superimposed on the brown peaks of Kabul were the words:

Marasta! (Help!):
Afghan women's organization dedicated to assisting women in danger, helping them escape violence, and advocating
for women's rights by changing legislation.

The mission statement spoke her language—Feminese—and so she placed donating to it at the top of her mental to-do list. Right after the consultation.

"I see. So MARASTA helped you?"

"Yes."

"How did you get to it? Is it near your house?"

"*Na.*" No. "My little brother go. He don't know. He has seven years."

"Seven years old? I see. And because you needed a male to escort you, you took your little brother with you? Did you wear a burqa?" Lottie pulled at the collar on her dress shirt, feeling choked.

"Yes."

"Did you try to talk to your parents or to your brothers to change their minds?"

"*Na.*"

"Why not?"

"My friend same, and she tell family, and brothers put in Kabul River with…" She twirled her fingers around herself as though wrapping a rope or chain around her entire body. "Yes, she die."

"A chain? They wrapped a chain around her and threw her into the river?"

"Yes. Yes. Shain." She spun her hands around herself again.

Lottie could feel her mouth drop open and made a conscious effort to shut it. Unfortunately, a visual formed in her head, and she knew it would revisit her at an inappropriate time, like during sleep.

"Did you call the police after you were raped?" She put the "call me" fingers to her ears. At that, Sadia's eyebrows rose, but Lottie knew asylum officers would ask that obnoxious question and more. Best for her to think about it now.

"I no call police. They give me to brothers. To mother and father."

Lottie put up both hands. "I know. I know. I just have to ask."

"Please, miss, can you help me?"

Of course, she could. But would she? The fumes of patriarchy were fanned at her nostrils again. And they burned.

The phone buzzed obnoxiously, causing her to start. Could she handle the river of blood and tears that coursed through her office?

Chapter Two
A One-Woman Band

A minute after Sadia departed, Louisa Mae entered. "Damn! She was so pretty! And she smelled good too. Wow!"

"Girl, you act like you're leading brass down Bourbon, blasting freely and without apologies, a big old B-flat sousaphone complementing the upper registers of life and beating fast the drums of curiosity." It was a true enough description, Lottie thought.

"Huh? Don't use that poetry crap with me, please. I don't have a minor in poetry. Matter of fact, you know I didn't finish college."

"Sorry. And the minor was in literature, by the way. Besides, you're super smart, woman."

"Oh, sorry, baby. Was it bad?" Louisa Mae must've taken note of Lottie's red-ringed eyes and the strawberry patches on her skin, which often appeared when she got emotional—any flavor of emotional.

"What do you think?" Lottie looked down at her psychedelic skin and thought of what a field day Picasso would have had trying to capture her. Pink cubes with splashes of brown. A blue eye precisely in the middle of her triangular head.

Sure, Sadia had left the premises, leaving behind only the weak floral scent, but before doing so, in Frankenstein fashion, she transfused all her angst into Lottie's bloodstream.

"I'm okay. Just getting tired of this is all." The blotches began to subside, the epidermal disappearing ink performing well. Voilà!

Lou would have none of it, of course. "So do something else! You still have your mom and dad's life insurance money, right? Why don't you quit this stupid profession? Why not open an antique store on Magazine Street? I'll help you. It could be fun!"

"Nah. I'll figure it out." Lottie wiped her nose and twirled her hair up. It was always a battle, her hair, a regular Rapunzel war, and she was losing. She opened her laptop, triggering an onslaught, waking it from slumber as dings and whistles fired back. Tapping on her email, she glared at too much black and white and a daunting segment of unopened ones, the tiny empty boxes summoning her harshly.

One in particular caught her attention from a sender she did not recognize. "By the way, did you see this email?" She flipped the screen toward Lou, trying to reveal nothing but calm, almost boredom.

YOU BLASPHEME AND YOU DIE!

The emailer clearly had had a bad morning and wished Lottie the same, taking the time to employ ALL CAPS and yelling virtually at her.

"Son of a biscuit eater! Who the hell is that from?" Lou would soon morph into an F-5, Lottie knew, dispatching cows and trucks and houses into the air and destroying everything in her path.

"I don't know. It's from a new email address. Look." The ominous allahdefender@yahoo.com blared from the screen, an email with a low self-esteem, in Lottie's opinion, seeking attention.

"You better be careful, baby! Want to sleep at my place?" Lou's eyebrows formed a sharp V, digging in seemingly for a long haul, pure geometry at work, until Lottie gave a response.

"I'm good. Not even worried about it. Besides, I have bigger concerns."

She waved a hand and with one quick click deleted the threat. Loonies abounded, Lottie had learned the hard way, recalling an old boyfriend who'd once chased her VW down the street when she broke up with him. But she had no idea who this particular loony was or what he—or she, to be fair—wanted with her. Whatever the case, deleting such nonsense was her policy. If ever the police needed it, it could be retrieved from the cloud or hard drive or some such rarefied techie capsule that existed beyond her understanding.

For some reason that escaped her, Lou, satisfied with her answer, scooted back to her social media crypt and awaited another interruption. Outside, a truck desperately in need of new shocks and, judging by the sound, too big for her street squeaked by, most likely dodging pond-sized potholes.

Soon, Lou buzzed—they both got a kick out of the unnecessary form of communication, as she sat just on the other side of the door. But the buzzer, akin to a kazoo, lately sent Lottie into a Pavlovian frenzy, making her want to bark or run. What now? She cursed under her breath but remained steadfastly ensconced in her crate, ready to catch rabbits for justice, if need be.

"Hey, baby, Mohamed is here again. He says he has something for you."

~ ~

At last, a friendly face. She shut the laptop—that annoying facilitator of anguish.

The door creaked open, and a cloud of Brut trumpeted his entrance, the *zabiba* or prayer bump on his forehead beaming like a headlamp. She'd

15

tried to convince some of her friends that the symbol of a strong Islamic faith was not terribly unlike the ashes between the brows of Catholics on Ash Wednesday or the fish on the bumper of Evangelicals' cars. The brown spot signified devoutness, the skin bruised or marked from emphatically touching the floor in prayer. Christian Sudanese friends had warned her, "If you see the mark on the forehead, run." Of course, they had been persecuted by extremists in their homeland, but here in the US, she decided not to heed the warning, not to judge. She was a big girl, anyhow, and trained by her profession to gage the credibility of people.

Instead, she welcomed Mohamed, prayer bump and all.

After all, didn't he devoutly worship his god the way she did her Jesus?

"Hello, my *sadiq. As-salaam alaikum!*" she warbled.

"*Wa alaikum as-salaam.*" Mohamed smiled broadly, displaying khat-stained teeth that never took away from his handsome appearance and bubbly demeanor.

"How are you, my Sudanese Horatio Alger?"

"Eh?" His face corkscrewed.

"You need to google it. I will write it down for you. Horatio Alger was an Amreeki writer who wrote about boys from poor and humble beginnings who later became quite successful."

"Eh?"

"It's the personification of the Amreeki dream."

"Eh?"

"It's about people who start down here." She splayed her hand down low and then reached up high. "And end up here."

"*Ay-wa. Ay-wa.* Yes. Yes. I Amreeki, but I professor in Sudan. In Darfur. Not here."

"Yes, I know. You're brilliant! You were a professor of physics in Sudan, for heaven's sake, and I never went near a physics class. Don't worry, you'll get there again—teaching. You've only been here for three years, and your English is getting better and better."

Their relationship was lagniappe, a boon, a blessing. After a favorable decision by the asylum officer, who apparently didn't get the frightening *zabiba* memo, Mohamed and family entered her life with their own kind of armament: grenades of love and bombs of kuindiong—sweetened semolina—and even Arabic Scrabble. On two occasions, she babysat their precious twin toddlers, Zeinab and Ibrahim, who didn't appear to be the spawn of evil either, except in the form of poopy diapers.

"Thank you. Thank you." He bowed twice and, like the good Muslim man he was, did not shake her hand.

"How are Raaida and the kids?"

"*Alhamdulillah!*"

"That's great! Good to hear. And what brings you in today, my *sadiq?*"

Assaulting Lottie with a rat-a-tat of Sudanese Arabic, he spoked too quickly, his words too rumbling with all its Rs firing this way and that. She threw back a *bati-bati*—slow, slow—and gave him the universal sign for *slow down*, her hands patting the air gently. He began again, slowly.

"*Ay-wa. Ay-wa.* I. come…to…give…you…these." From behind his back, he produced a bouquet of daisies dipped in colors that might not be found in nature—bright blue, fuchsia, lime green.

Though they weren't exactly her speed, she didn't have the heart to throw them into the trash. "Ohhhhh. You didn't have to. Thank you!" She cradled them as though they were her favorites. "Would you like to sit down?"

"*La.* I must go pick up the twins from day care. Raaida at ingelesee class."

"Atta girl. Splendid!"

"Eh?"

"Never mind."

Out he dashed, as quickly as he had entered—a splash of sunshine in her downer of a morning—bowing to Lou along the way. "Bye, baby," Lou crooned, barely looking up from the computer.

Mohamed, Lottie reasoned, extended his appreciation beyond the meager sum he'd once paid her for representing him and looked like he would be forever grateful for his asylum in the US. She smiled, recalling the interesting gifts, the best he could do. Once, he gave her a pet crawfish that she dubbed Jacques, even though she could find hundreds in the ditches throughout the city; another time, a huge can of her favorite coffee—Community—though she could purchase it cheaply down the block at the Winn-Dixie. Now, she would admire the artificially colored daisies. Why? Because it reminded her of why she did what she did. Why she helped people.

She cracked her neck and thought of Sadia.

Glancing out the window, she saw Mo leaving and bowing to Mister George and extending his hand for a shake. Mister George seemed to recoil and didn't return the gesture. Not even a smile.

She calmly opened the French doors and hollered, "Hey, Mister George, can I see you for a second?" He put down the rake and made his way up the stairs, shaking the structure in his work boots.

The stairs boomed, then she heard Lou recite her usual "Hey, baby."

The door creaked open, and Mister George appeared and removed his Saints cap. "You rang?"

"Hi, Mister George." She ran over and gave him a big hug, in spite of the coolness toward her friend and the sweat running down his chin. He gave her a wet peck on the cheek in return. "You know you're like a dad to me, right?"

"Yes'm. And you're like my only daughter." A big grin spread across his face.

She stepped back. "But Mister George, I noticed that you didn't shake my friend Mohamed's hand. Why not?"

He hesitated, then blurted, "Oh heck, Miss Lottie. You know how I feel about those Islams. Why are you helping them anyway?"

"First of all—it's either Muslims or Islamic people. And Mister George, you know I help people who're in danger. It's my job. No, it's my calling. Mohamed will be killed if he goes back to Sudan. Killed. There's no doubt about it."

"Yeah, well, what about our safety here in this country?"

She was afraid he might break out an American flag and smack her with it. "What about it? You feel threatened by a man who was tortured by his government? Who escaped and came here just to be safe?"

"You know they're going to take over the country. Mark my word! Jesus wouldn't want you to do that, Miss Lottie. He is the one true Lord. He wants this to be a Christian country."

"Oh, Mister George. Jesus is not an American. He's not a Sudanese nor a Spaniard. He's not any nationality. Besides, he was from the Middle East and probably the same skin color as Mohamed, on the darker end of the spectrum."

And, though she was a Christian, she was pretty darn certain that Jesus would want her to represent people who'd been tortured or were hungry or fleeing certain danger. She made a mental note not to include Mister George on her extended guest list for parties; otherwise, he might very well thump a King James Bible over the heads of her more libertine guests.

No, sometimes the Venn diagrams need not intersect.

"Can you please try to be kinder to my clients?"

He fiddled with the salt-ringed cap, shifted, and scratched his head. "I'll try for you, Miss Lottie, but you know I won't like it."

"Thank you, Mister George. Much appreciated."

He muttered under his breath and left.

Lottie returned to her desk and splayed her fingers—little stubs of pink malaise stared back at her, a reminder to schedule a manicure for the next day—then opened her laptop again. Like a virtual siren, the deleted message folder summoned her. *O-pen me. O-pen me.*

What the heck. Curiosity won't kill this cat.

There, on the top floor of the email high-rise, sat the ominous message from allahdefender@yahoo.com. Lou sat like a guard dog just beyond the door. Lottie looked at the door and prayed she wouldn't come in. Then, as if in slo-mo, she finally clicked on the contraband.

Again, the threat appeared, and again she slammed the computer shut, but not before YOU BLASPHEME AND YOU DIE! floated up to join the other nonsense in her head.

Chapter Three
Find Out What It Means to Her

The events of Sadia's life flitted through Lottie's brain like the flying monkeys once had after she'd seen *The Wizard of Oz*, all fur and feathers. Annoying and wickedly aligned, the winged evildoers cackled hatefully, darted about, and swung through her psyche on vines of horrid facts.

Another gem smashed into a thousand pieces! She couldn't help it, couldn't ignore the stories that had assaulted her ears over the years, couldn't discard the fact that, in all her female clients' cases, the aggressors were males.

"I hate men."

It came out as more of a sigh than an exclamation, and whether it was true or not, she declared it aloud to no one in particular, unless you counted her cat, Franklin, whose gray velvet coat now appeared lavender in the morning glow. Unfazed, he stretched out front paws and commenced sharpening his claws on the armless patchwork chair, a collector's item from a Magazine Street furniture artist.

"Frank, stop! I paid a lot for that."

Rocking in her power chair, she looked up at the string of white lights. Sadia liked them. *A good addition, I think.* She considered the twinkling luminaries to be revolutionary in a law office—sparkles that transformed an otherwise cold and impersonal altar of confession into a hopeful space for immigrants. Paris or Mexico City or Marrakesh was the indisputable goal—not disco. If they could just forget about the bad and sad and disgusting things of the world for a few minutes, if they counted her an ally on a planet of enemies, then she would have accomplished something.

Ah, Sadia.

Of course she agreed to take her case against her best instinct, agreed to defend her before the mighty, if leery Uncle Sam, agreed to push down the VPTSD—vicarious post-traumatic stress disorder—but not until she had more details at Part Two of the interview two days after their initial meeting.

"He follow me long time," Sadia had said, and counted on her shaky fingers. "Six months. He chase me. How you say? Bother? Yes, bother my parents. I no like him. I no want him."

"So he raped you?"

"Yes, I am go from university. Kabul? University?"

"Okay."

"One day, he hide corner. I no burqa, he see me." She pointed two fingers to her eyes, then at Lottie's. "He grab me, put hand over mouth like this..." She covered her mouth with her hand, and Lottie's blood pressure began to gurgle simultaneously. "Then he grab his *salawar*, put on my throat." Lottie's face must've twisted sideways. "Sorry, his knife. But he no cut me first. He pull up my shirt and pull down my pants." After placing her head into her hands for a long minute, Sadia looked up again, and, with what appeared to be sad determination, said what she had to say. "He rape me. Then he take his *salawar* and cut me."

Lottie scribbled the details on her legal pad. *Salawar = knife. Raped first.* "Did he say anything to you while this was happening?" Again, she hated to ask, but it was her job. *My effin' job—talking to raped women.* She needed to create a detailed statement for the case, and sound bites were great for corroboration. Who could forget what her rapist said?

"He say, 'You *kusay*. This because you no marry Abdullah.'"

"I'm sorry. What is *kusay*?"

"Whore." Lottie's cell vibrated across the desk. She silenced it. *Kusay = whore.*

"Oh wow." Words sometimes stung almost as much as the acts. Almost. "What an asshole!" Lottie blurted, but followed up quickly with "Sorry! Very unprofessional. Please forgive my language."

Sadia smiled weakly and continued. "After, he pull his pants up. He smile like devil and then take up knife from ground and put on face." Tears returned to her black eyes.

Damn the torpedoes! Damn the boundaries! Lottie shot up from behind the desk and dispensed a massive hug. "I will take your case. It's okay. It's okay. Or it will be okay. I'll see to that."

Before she could take it back, she had birthed another daughter—or sister, really. One of many upon whom she would thrust her care—with representation, of course, but also trips to Old Navy or Winn-Dixie or Walmart, and friends, parties, and other activities. Helicopter Mom had another target.

~ ~

After the latest victim of patriarchy and ridiculous customs left her office, Lottie found herself zigzagging in socked feet, ruminating, pondering. She grabbed Frank and squeezed him into a soft sphere and squished each toe until a claw appeared. Much more effective than therapy or antidepressants, she found cat squeezing to be less expensive and without the drama of picking through her pretty awesome childhood looking for sharp objects or blaming her mother for her shortcomings. *Cat squeezing! I could open a therapy office and offer it. Rent out Frank. Then I could get a small apartment in Madrid.*

Never having felt the sensation before, she didn't wish to become the classic man-hater, become a female superhero with a Venus symbol bedazzled on a pink cape, emitting rays of inapproachability and danger, though she certainly felt like it at the moment. Perhaps she didn't despise the opposite sex. Maybe she would just keep both eyes open wide on behalf of her global sisters.

She pondered anew the exact number of female clients she had represented in the last year and the countries in which they were assaulted or raped, threatened, or enslaved, spit upon and such.

Let's see... She counted out loud, sticking out her index finger with gusto.

"One: Sadia, obviously the most recent one, from lethally patriarchal Afghanistan.

Two: Julieta from the exuberantly machismo El Salvador.

Three: Estela from Bosnia. Bosnia with its post-Yugoslav-war males dumped into society like dysfunctional robots."

What a sad monologue.

And this was only three—the tip of a very ugly and systemic iceberg. Each of these brilliant women and head turners sought refuge and protection because they were harmed by men, not women.

Unfortunately, the derivative rub fell into her lap. Not only did she have to craft great arguments in preparing cases before the Asylum Office and Immigration Court, but she struggled with the frustration wrought by her personal fruitlessness in changing a male-dominated planet.

Five thousand years or more of this baloney.

The second-classedness and discrimination, the abuse, the femicide was getting old. And sure, other women, like-minded men, and fabulous NGOs—nongovernmental organizations—sought to remove the cancer of gender inequality globally. Some even made headway. Unfortunately, though some tumors were surgically excised, the margins of gender carcinomas remained murky, unclear, and jagged.

That it drew purplish half-moons beneath her eyes—an easy feat with her transparent Saran-Wrap-like skin—and destroyed manicures, which were not only unattractive but expensive, infuriated her and only nourished the annoying preoccupation to do more.

But what can I do?

In her innards, just below her belly button, she recognized a calling to use her legal education to maneuver a system and assist people in the good ole US of A, but could she do something more?

Outside, the garbage men yelled, "All right" and "Go ahead" as the steel behemoth roared in practical cadence, accelerating, then squealing its brakes, accelerating, then squealing.

One thing she could do was avoid dating for the time being. *Yes, that's what I'll do! I'll go on a man sabbatical. Sabbatical implying temporary, of course. Let's not get crazy. But what else can I do?*

She shuffled papers around on her desk, stacking and restacking until each one aligned perfectly like a new deck of cards. In the ballroom of her brain, where Speakable waltzed gloriously with Unspeakable, images of female castration and child brides dallied, waiting to be penciled in on dance cards. And though she tried to push the images out, they winked and waved their embroidered handkerchiefs. After letting her imagination run wild (again) and entertaining a stale and humid ballroom full of homely loiterers, she finally arrived at the vicious conclusion that what she really wanted was to lob all-out revenge at the perpetrators.

That's right, R-E-V-E-N-G-E!

Eyeballing Frank, who had jumped onto the oversized chair, she spelled it out loud: "R-E-V-E-N-G-E."

And again: "R-E-V-E-N-G-E."

And again: "R-E-V-E-N-G-E," until Aretha Franklin's lyrical declaration came to mind, and she soon realized that the number of letters matched precisely. Like an insane projectile, she launched into a full-blown jig or probably something more akin to a seizure, her arms punching the sky and legs kicking in spastic delight.

"Hoo! R-E-V-E-N-G-E. Find out what it means to me! R-E-V-E-N-G-E. Find out what it means to me! Hoo!" She collapsed into a diabolical froth that made Frank start, thud to the floor, and scamper for the door.

From the next room, Lou hollered, "You okay in there, baby?"

"Yes, ma'am," Lottie effervesced.

And she was okay. In fact, she teetered on full-blown manic mirth, which frightened her a little but not enough to turn her second line umbrella inside out and stop the insane parade. At a minimum, male castration would be justified, but she could also consider worse fates for those who had the chutzpa to touch her girls and ruin their lives. She sat back down on what felt like her throne of devilry, spun a bit, let the idea lather for a minute, then put her feet on the floor, stopping suddenly.

What the hell am I doing? What is happening to me? she wondered, then prayed, and not entirely un-whole-heartedly, *Forgive me, God—not for the swear, but for the evil thoughts.* That such acts conflicted with her faith was a gross understatement. *WWJD and all, y'all, right?*

But Jesus wasn't a doormat, flipping out in the temple after all, overturning tables and barking at the money changers. And, on more than one occasion, while sitting on primary-colored chairs in Sunday School, she'd been instructed that it was righteous anger that Jesus brandished.

That's it. Righteous anger!

The thought spread like a balm on something, an ugly flame trying to blaze within, halting it, stamping it out before it grew into a legitimate and destructive wildfire.

But, if this were the case, wouldn't God smite them with a lightning bolt or a plague? No, that was way too Old Testament.

Furthermore, she reasoned, as she lifted her thumbnail to her teeth, didn't St. Augustine and Thomas Aquinas both theorize about the Just War? This much she learned in Philosophy 101 at UNO. And wasn't one component of a just war to seek peace in the midst of it? And was she not seeking peace for her clients? For herself? For the world?

Just war? Righteous anger? Yes!

Raising a fist into the air, she shook it at the invisible evildoers.

But going so far as to remove the genitals of a few men waxed extravagant, if gratuitous, and reeked of unbelief, not to mention it would land her in a dank, damp Third World prison where she would then ironically be raped and tortured herself. Then someone might have to avenge her assault and so forth and so on. It would be very much like a dog chasing its tail.

What can I do? Me? Me with parchment from an average law school? Marinated in a bizarre culture? Simmered in an overprivileged nation?

Her gaze darted around the office to the Louis Armstrong painting, whose eyes seemed to meet hers, up to the lights, dangling like streamers, over to the overstuffed chair, out the French doors where her neighbor, Mister Charlie, walked his retriever, the gorgeous beast stopping on each and every lawn and lifting a leg.

Lesser women had done more.

"Ha!" erupted from her diaphragm and into the cool air. She rocked back and slapped her knee.

This explosion of gaiety and revelation must have unshackled Lou from her Instagram cell, and she whooshed in with a vociferous "What the hell is going on in here? It sounds like you're losing it!" To accentuate the comment, she put one hand firmly on one curvy hip.

"No. I think I may have found it, Lou! I think I just may have found it!" Lottie smoothed an imagined and grand moustache and goatee above and around her lips, then fluttered fingertips together lightly as though the answer lay within her palms. She had found one answer, of that she was certain. Still, she wasn't sure if it was *the* answer. If she succeeded, she might not fix everything, but at least she might fix herself.

"Wait. What it are we talking about?" Lou asked. "I'm confused."

"Oh, dawlin'. I will keep you posted on what I'm thinking. No worries. I'll let you know. I just can't right now." She grabbed paper and a pen and began to doodle until Lou stopped staring at her.

Lou marched over to the window and looked out, waving at someone. "Okay, baby. Just worried about you. I'll be in here working on that Fifth Circuit brief, okay?" And, with that, the anthropomorphic brass band that marched in blew in the other direction, exiting less exuberantly than it had entered.

Trying to convert the ideas into a wild reality, Lottie blinked several times to jump-start her internal engine. She scrawled on the paper:

Women: Sadia, Estela, Julieta

Assailant Men: Abdullah, Miguel, Rifat

Countries: Afghanistan, El Salvador, Bosnia

Languages I speak: Spanish (fluent), French (fluent), Arabic (survival only),

Persian (spotty).

Funding: mine—life insurance and savings. NOT ENOUGH! Others? Lou? Other friends?

She opened the French doors and stepped out onto the porch, unlocking an odiferous vault, allowing treasures to float up to her nostrils on the warm breeze. The jasmine arrived as she had hoped and smoothed out the jumbled molecules of stress tightening her neck.

Magically, Lou reemerged, her Sicilian-inspired face tangled. She was not to be messed with. Her buxom frame could go from zero to Wicked Stepmother lickety-split. "What's going on with you? One minute you're angry, the next you're dancing like Cinderella."

At that moment, Lottie felt more like a CIA hopeful kicked out of Langley than Cinderella and made a horrendous attempt at concealing her mission. "Okay," she whispered and snickered like the demon she feared she was becoming. "Can you keep a secret?" Lou nodded. "Pinky swear, or I can't tell you. You can tell no one, because I could get in a lot of trouble for this."

Lou extended a dark pinky and Lottie a pink one, and they blessed the promise in one snap. Another nod arrived and accompanied Lou's jittery eyes. Lottie grabbed her arm and threw her into the wicker chair, while the banana tree leaves seemed to lean in closer to spy. And, though no one was around, Lottie bent down and whispered, "So this is what I'm thinking…"

Lou's eyebrows floated up and down like butterfly wings, brilliantly in concert with Lottie's disclosure, and a few gasps kept time. Then, as though hearing it all too, a blue jay docked on the balcony and protested at ungodly decibels.

Chapter Four
Peace Be upon You

Another two-cloud day anesthetized, the French doors flung open to welcome it and the jasmine. Rain, probably literally stopping a parade for this or that somewhere in the city, would arrive the following day, whereupon all inhabitants would don their rubbery and flubbery fleur-de-lis rain boots.

Lottie put down her copy of *The Feasibility of Girls Dressing as Boys to Attend School*—orange sticky notes protruding like fluorescent teeth out of its pages—and bowed repeatedly and unnecessarily to the Tulane professor of women's studies who shared her scholarship with the beer-swilling, fraternized masses less than a mile away.

She's from Central Asia, you fool, not the Far East.

In her research a week ago, when her brilliant idea first came to her, Lottie discovered that Dr. Fatima Hassan contributed her own ingredients to the pie of world peace: a cup of chopped equality, two cups of reason, three cups of education, several tablespoons of kind acts, and a zest of kindness.

"*Asalaam alaykum.*" Lottie whipped out the Arabic.

The doctor floated into Lottie's office, and Lottie imagined wisdom in her hijab-wrapped face.

"*Walaykum a salaam.*" Fatima pressed her hands into Lottie's. "So, you speak Arabic?"

"*Shwaya shwaya*. Little. *Poco poco.*" Why did she burp Spanish when she needed to speak Arabic? "But do you? You're from Afghanistan, correct?"

"Yes, Kabul specifically. My first language is Pashto. Second, Arabic. Third, English. *Pero, no español.*"

"What? Oh. Ha. Of course not." Anxious chuckles spewed out of her like sewage. "Well then, we have two in common, anyway. Sort of—except when I screw it up." She walked toward her desk. "Thank you so much for coming, Dr. Hassan. Please make yourself at home. Have a seat—no arms, or a steep drop into a sea of feathers," she offered, waving a hand at the two choices. The honored guest dove into the soft pool, the chair emitting a heavy sigh.

"So I am curious, though… Why did you answer my request? I'm just a nobody, and you're clearly a somebody," Lottie asked.

With hands in namaste, Fatima countered, "Oh, my dear. We are all somebodies. You must know this. And, I am honored to be invited, but please call me Fatima. I answered your request because I googled you and you look pretty good on paper too. I think we should know each other."

Lottie could feel her face going all modern art with swaths of red splashing across it.

"I must tell you that I read your thesis, *The Feasibility of Girls Dressing as Boys to Attend School*. It was quite good." She patted the tome.

"Why in heavens and earths would you do that? It's quite long."

"It's an area that speaks to my passions, you could say. And I am always in search of like-minded people, particularly women."

"I am very surprised that anyone not required to do so would make it through it." She waved one hand like a wand in the air.

"I am also acquainted with your credentials—a master's degree from

Yale, two international peace awards. The only thing missing is a Nobel nomination."

After a perfunctory knock, Lou sprang into the room toting a tray a-jangle with the teapot, cups, and saucers. "Here ya go, baby, I mean Attorney Fornea." She placed it on the coffee table, curved over like a comma, and backed away as though not wishing to turn her back to royalty.

"Thanks, Lou. You've met Dr. Hassan, right?"

"Of course. It's a pleasure." Louisa Mae curtsied, something Lottie had not witnessed heretofore nor ever wished to see again. She thought she detected a giggle from her distinguished guest as her BFF lingered near the door.

"Hey, Lou, can you leave us alone for a bit and then come back in when the others arrive?"

"Of course, baby."

Lottie burped up another guffaw. "My assistant is also my best friend, so please pardon her endearments."

"Ahhh. You are fortunate. I have been in—how do you say it—the Big Easy?—for a few years. It is lovely that people here are so friendly and comfortable with each other. It's very European, you see?" The professor removed her scarf of gold, folding it onto her lap.

"Of course. You are right. I am blessed. Tea, Dr. Hassan?"

"*Aywa, shokran.* With milk and sugar, please."

Lottie's hands complete with freshly painted Love Me True Red nails shook as she dispensed and handed over the tea. In the distance, a jackhammer hummed. A few streets over, a new sewer system was being constructed, and in a town where progress often moonwalked, Lottie assumed it would be a decade before the hum went on its way. As it were, it had almost achieved its own jazzy rhythm, causing her teeth to vibrate in merry measure at times. *Laissez les bons temps rouler*, right?

"So, Dr. Hassan," she began, interlocking her fingers to avoid making a snack out of her nails, "I called you in because I want to speak to you privately."

"*Tabaan*. Of course." Fatima took a sip. "This is very good, by the way."

Lottie eked out a smile. "First, let me say that I so admire your credentials, and I know a little of your story. I understand you're a war and rape survivor and somehow through it all have managed to convert that horror into something positive." The sage nodded but didn't tear up like the others. Lottie drew courage from this, but left the tissue box in default position—always at the ready—and continued, "I also know that you've given your life to help women." She rubbed her hands together, starting an internal spark though it was tropical outside. "That's why I wanted to meet with you. I'd love it if you could be on the board of a new nonprofit that I'm organizing." She exhaled, probably audibly.

And so it began. Lottie had dug down into her toolbox, chosen a capable wrench, and taken the training wheels off the idea. Now all she had to do was give it a good push and run alongside it. And maybe yell, *You're doing it! You're doing it!*

"Well, I don't know," Dr. Hassan began. "I'm on the board of at least two other nonprofits."

There it was.

Lottie could feel her shoulders plummeting and thought her guest could hear their thud. *But am I going to give up at the first hurdle? Did I surrender when I received a mediocre grade on my Successions Law exam, after plotting an extensive family tree and trying to make sense of all the begats and procreation and inbreeding? No!* She took a deep yoga-like breath, which hissed on its way out, and reminded herself that determination and initiative coursed through her Cajun blood as surely as cayenne pepper. She would not give up.

"Let me tell you about it first; then you can decide."

The professor smirked, perhaps at her persistence, and sagged farther into the chair. "What are the goals of your charity?"

The way she said it almost made Lottie second-guess the whole shebang for a second. Almost. But the adrenaline had kicked in, a shot of Red Bull, and propelled her to the front window, where she lowered the shades and shot back, "This is confidential, right?"

The good woman's eyes twinkled, and she pulled herself out of the feathered abyss. "*Tabaan,* my dear."

And with all the courage Lottie could summon, she leaned in and delicately divulged the sordid scheme, twisted thought, demented deal, then collapsed as though she'd just unleashed a thousand sins into Bishop Arceneaux's ear at the Cathedral, as though she had undergone an auricular ablution.

Invisible strings seemed to lift Fatima's lips slowly and symmetrically, and laughter, the deep, turbulent kind, followed. "I think we are two teabags steeped in the same vessel, my new friend!"

Chapter Five
A Cornucopia of Do-Gooders

A familiar banter kissed Lottie's ears and caused a smile to break free from a cage deep within.

"Girl, why you wearing that? Didn't you wear it last week?"

"As if I'm going to wear Chanel twice in as many weeks?"

"You are definitely over-Chaneling!" A snicker.

"Oh, be quiet. I think I've seen that Dolce & Gabbana before."

It was only a week after Lottie's meeting with Fatima, and already her scheme pipped its shell and neared hatching. The clickety-clickety of heels played a welcome percussion on the steps, the alliteration of her two colleagues, the infinitely stiletto-clad percussion duo, Jezebel Johnson and Anna-Maria Rodriguez. Both stellar attorneys à la Gucci, they could easily stomp a Milan runway with Kendall Jenner or Gigi or Behati. And though stylish, they were two formidable lawyers in two of the largest firms in the city. Often, they fooled their victims with highlights, lipstick, and au couture, then moved in with a bite of legal venom. Lottie pitied people who stepped on these coiled beauties.

"Oh anh. You have not," Jezebel said.

"Have too," Anna-Maria replied.

"Shushhhhh. You going to wake up the neighborhood."

"The neighborhood should already be woke!"

"We're coming, woman!"

"Okay!" Lottie shouted back through the French doors. Her neighbors had seen worse.

As they made their way into her dining room, a cloud of White Shoulders and Youth-Dew battled for the attention of her nostrils. Lou hugged her friends fiercely. "How y'all makin'?" she inquired before running to the kitchen to attend the gurgling coffeemaker.

"Just livin' the life in the Crescent City, dawlin'," Jezebel quipped.

"If it got any better, I'd be in heaven," Anna-Maria teased.

Lottie waved a hand. "Y'all come on in."

As for the remaining female, she would arrive soon enough. Isabella Francalangia, the only transplant in the group, hailed from Yale Law and had quickly become a Tulane Law professor. She ran the Immigration Law Clinic on campus and could often be found up to her perfectly sculpted Italian nose in intending immigrants. A Mother Teresa of aliens, she balanced the drive of the others with open arms and a big smile. As she was another impressive barrister, Lottie desperately needed her for the task ahead.

A kickstand squealed in protest outside. They looked at each other. "Isabella." After a few thuddy steps and a quick knock, she entered, wafting in patchouli and tie-dye. "Hey, y'all. Sorry I'm late."

"Did you ride your bike, honey?" Jezebel asked.

"But of course," she lilted in affected French.

Aside from her Woodstock-worthy skirts and snug tanks in chartreuse or oversized purple tees, had Isabella lived in France in 1910, Modigliani would have captured her. With skin the color of wet sand, a long and noble nose guarded by high cheekbones and which pointed to full lips, one could not help but stare at her, tie-dye or not. Of course, Lottie couldn't resist either, catching herself in the process, then over-apologizing just to add sprinkles on top of the embarrassment.

A perfect LSAT score didn't hurt her reputation either.

"Where's Emile?" Anna-Maria asked.

Rounding out the group of invitees was the only male—Lottie's best male and childhood friend—Emile Fontenot, a gay trombone player and LGBT activist famous for convincing the Louisiana Legislature to pass a law to install "Human" signs on bathrooms in establishments rather than the traditional "Men" and "Women" ones. He could be a bulldog of an advocate, savvy in the ways of nonprofit board functions and possessing an enviable savoir faire that Lottie lacked.

An "I'm comin'!" and thuds trumpeted his arrival, then the brim of a hat appeared. "Peek-a-boo, everybody."

Jezebel once-overed Emile's seersucker suit and boater hat. "Oh, I see you dressed up for us. Now I 'preciate dat."

"Hey, boo." Lottie kissed him on both cheeks.

Sitting at the dining-slash-conference-room table, they sipped coffee in mugs from Lottie's stay-cation: Audubon Zoo, Jackson Square, Buffa's, Spotted Cat. Lou had set them up nicely, she took note—then again, Lou always did. Taking a second, she allowed herself to luxuriate in the weird cacophony of different accents: Uptown, Ninth Ward, the East, New England.

Before she would spring this ridiculous idea on them, she paused, then cleared her throat. "I suppose y'all are wondering why I've called you here." A wave of nods went around the room.

"Well, I have the craziest idea. Heck, I don't even think it's legal, per se." This made the assemblage scoot to the edges of their respective chairs and glance at one another.

Taking a breath, she sucked in fortitude and exhaled. "As you all know, I represent some of the most violently abused women of the world, who have somehow managed to make it to this country in order to obtain political asylum." She twisted her fingers into a here-is-the-church-here-is-the-steeple pose.

"Okay, so here goes. Drumroll, puh-lease."

Emile rattled his fingers against the table.

"I would like to start a nonprofit that benefits some of my female clients and maybe even other females around the world."

Outside, St. Maria, three blocks away, rang her bells ten times. Lottie didn't know if that was a good sign or a bad one.

Jezebel raised a café au lait hand, jangling important baubles about her wrist. "Oh Lawd. Another nonprofit—that's all we need! That doesn't sound illegal at all."

Lottie put up both hands and chuckled in unattractive chunks. "Well, you haven't heard the real mission statement yet."

"Fair enough," Jezebel conceded. "Continue, please." The baubles rested.

Lottie cracked all ten knuckles in one swoop, another unsavory routine she'd picked up in recent weeks. Cracking. Nibbling. Eye twitching. But who's counting?

"Okay, so. So, okay. Here goes. All my clients have, at a minimum, been raped. Others have been beaten in addition to the rape. Still, some have been stripped of their womanhood vis-à-vis FGM." She took a swig of water, swallowed hard. "Even others have been splattered with acid."

If ears could wiggle, theirs would have. They were listening.

"Now in some cases, the assailants were never identified. However..." She let that word sizzle around the room like uttered lightning. "In other cases, we do, in fact, know who the perpetrator was—or is."

All eyes were upon her, and she counted it a very good sign. This was her big chance. Her big Mister-George-Bush-at-the-Trade-Center, Ray-Nagin-at-the-Superdome moment.

"These assailants"—her fingers scrunched quotation marks—"enjoy impunity in their countries, in their cultures. These thugs go on with their lives, go back under their rocks until they feel compelled to harm another woman."

"Preach!" Emile yelled beneath the boater, then took a big bite out of a buttermilk drop.

She breathed in encouragement.

"Yes!" Isabella chimed in and clapped hard, churchgoing-like.

Whirling with indignation and fury now, Lottie couldn't be stopped, a tornadic gust of righteousness. Her head felt helium light. Was her blood sugar dropping?

A voice of rationality broke the spell. "So what do you propose we do?" It was Anna-Maria, probably late for an appointment and wanting to move an impossible issue along. "You know the International Criminal Court—God bless it—can't do a lot. I mean, they indict for quote-unquote war crimes but never get to arrest the criminal."

"Tell us something we don't know. What do you propose?" Isabella appeared uncharacteristically histrionic.

"I propose that I—me—Charlotte Fornea—do something. I would like to seek revenge against these animals. I mean, it's not like my clients can do it."

Gasps suffused the sphere, followed by ricocheting heads. She had put it out there for the entire New Orleans human-rights who's who to see. Not an easy task. Most definitely a deranged one. Would someone report her to a higher authority? And if so, to which one? The FBI? The CIA? The ABA? The AILA? The BBB? *Or maybe they will simply commit me? I could use a good rest, after all.*

"Easy, girlfriend," Emile murmured and then coughed in staccato barks.

"Soooooo...you want to be a vigilante?" asked Anna-Maria.

"I get your frustration, but..." Jezebel warned.

Out of the light-trimmed windows, cumulonimbus clouds—regular visitors—moved in as if on cue. In a moment or two, they might deliver their own penal sentence: several inches of water, filling the city.

"Well, I, for one, would love to hear more. I agree with you, Charlotte. I think these bastards deserve justice. And, I am sick of it, me!" Jezebel spat, her perfectly threaded eyebrows needling toward each other.

"What kind of justice are we talking here?" Saint Isabella sputtered. "I mean, are we talking threats? Castration? Not...not...murder?"

Now Lottie took a turn at raising her brows, untamed as they were. "What? Me? Oh gosh, no! Although I admire what Saint Lorena Bobbitt did—peace be upon her—I could never do that."

A cupful of laughter spilled into the room.

"Girl, you had me worried there for a minute. I thought you were losing it, ya heard?" Emile took a sip from—appropriately enough—an Emile Fontenot's on Bourbon mug.

"I heard," Lottie replied. That they considered her capable of such acts puzzled her, though in truth, she was somewhat flattered. *Bond. Charlotte Bond.*

"Phew. I have to say, I was a bit concerned too," Anna-Maria threw in. "Not like I wouldn't blame you, but still..."

"Rats!" Jezebel growled, then looked around at the others. "Just kidding. I would never, ever think of doing something like that."

Rain rattled at the end of the block. It would arrive soon enough, thwacking them with its wet tail. Lottie figured she needed to move things along and save her distinguished crowd the agony of moving their cars to higher ground. Her driveway was high enough but was already filled with Mini Pearl and the other condo owner's Escalade, which was about the length of a Mardi Gras float.

"Woman, please explain!" demanded Lou, who had snuck into the room unnoticed—a rare feat.

A boom cracked above their heads. Lottie considered it for a second. "The kind of revenge I would like to exact against these guys is…" She paused for effect, but all eyes turned to the window, where the storm had officially arrived with all its wet bells and whistles—torrents of water, deafening thunder. When the eyes returned to her, she continued: "Humiliation."

Silence filled the room. A few heads tilted as cute kittens on YouTube would.

Jezebel cracked the quiet. "Well, that doesn't really seem like any kind of justice, you know, honey?" She rearranged the charms on her bracelet.

"It does sound harmless, doesn't it? But, stay with me…" And they did as all eyes remained on her, which made her feel self-conscious, and usually when that happened, she stammered, as if suffused with stage fright. She pressed on in spite of it. "The…the ramifications of the stunts can be extensive. Imagine being embarrassed in a country where males rule, where males must behave like cavemen and so forth. It truly depends on what the prank is. I think we can come up with a few whammies."

Another pause. The thunder boomed again.

It was Anna-Maria who broke the stillness this time. "Oh, I get it! I actually like it. It's like harming them without physically hurting them."

Nods seesawed about the table.

"I have to do something," Lottie said. "I…I can't take it anymore. I have to do this for me. I may have to quit the business otherwise." Knowing there must be a psychological diagnosis for her ailment, she toyed with names for her would-be self-imposed therapy. Vicarious absolvement? Vindictive immersion?

"That'll be the day," Isabella hooted. "You can't be who you aren't. This is where your heart is, helping torture survivors. Helping them obtain legal status. Helping them get set up. Embracing them. You ain't gonna quit." She replaced her Buffa's mug on the table and smiled sympathetically.

"Truth!" Jezebel huffed.

"Oh no? Watch me! If y'all don't help me, I'll just go become a tax lawyer or something prosaic like that. So hear me out." Would she really do that? She had no idea. Tax interested her about as much as vacuuming her car or emptying the dishwasher, but sanity concerned her more than anything. Her soul was thoroughly convinced that only this measure would cure her of endless frustration and VPTSD, and frankly, she wanted to sleep again.

Lottie got up, looked out the window at the storm, then turn back to face her colleagues. The rain roared now, so she had to raise her voice. "The official mission statement would go something like this: such-and-such organization's mission is to support, advocate for, and encourage females of all ages worldwide who have been victimized through violence or cultural or religious traditions." She folded her arms and cocked a hip. *Boom! Take that, world!* There it was, right in their laps, a big, fat, slightly demented but huggable baby. What could they do but love it?

Wanting to see who would rock her weird offspring, she scanned the crowd, bit her lip, and fiddled with the hem of her remarkably tight skirt, which featured a six-inch slit on the side. Isabella scribbled something on a legal pad. Probably: *she's crazy.*

But Jezebel slapped her knee and said, "Girl. I want in on this!"

The others exhaled and laughed in splashes, as if they had just witnessed something exciting. *Yeah, baby. Something exciting!*

The thunder rumbled like a bass drum. No one flinched, long accustomed to such brazen displays by the city's personal weather demons. "Well, that's why we're here, Jezebel. And, thank you for your enthusiasm. I would like all of you to be on the board of this esteemed nonprofit," Lottie insisted, albeit sarcastically. "And I propose that we keep the mission statement broad enough to encompass the intrepid task or tasks, as the case may be, that I have mentioned."

"So, you're serious, then," Isabella confirmed. "Are you saying that you're going to travel to these countries—most dangerous—to perform these little stunts?"

Little Bayou St. Johns formed under Lottie's armpits, and she wondered if she had forgotten to put on deodorant. "Pretty much. That's what I'm saying! And I need a great, slightly devious board to help me raise funds to do this. I'll contribute a large portion of my savings to it.

"This, of course, is highly confidential." She went around the room, locking eyes with each person. "And I assume because you're all still here, you're either interested or you don't want to go out in the storm."

The lights flickered, mocking her loss of steam. Louisa Mae stood in the back of the room and winked, then made the motion with her hands to go on.

"I do want this nonprofit to help women locally and around the world, and of course, we will conduct other operations like education and self-esteem workshops, etcetera. However, if I happen to, along the way, right a few wrongs or exact justice upon these unsuspecting creatures, Catwoman-like, then so be it." She twirled an imaginary moustache.

The air had warmed up with the number of 98.6-degree bodies squished into it, and the air conditioner countered with only a sad mist.

"So…once again, just to clarify or echo what Isabella asked: are you saying that you personally want to go and do something to these men?" Anna-Maria tried to ascertain.

"I do. I mean, I do! Yes! I am well aware of what this may sound like to all of you." Heck, she knew what it sounded like to herself: a disturbed hive of yellow jackets buzzing about in her brain. "But if you respect me, could you do it for meeee? I need this." Whining was not beneath her. She ripped her ponytail out of the elastic and shook her head. A headache began to assert itself.

Emile crept over to the window. Lottie joined him and looked out at the deluge. His mouth slanted slightly so that she couldn't quite tell if it were a smile or a frown. Since childhood, she knew that when Emile liked an idea, one dimple would form on the left side of his cheek.

Meanwhile, the potholes on her street had already morphed into little ponds. One time during a flash flood, a few mallards migrated over from Audubon Park and took up temporary residence in front of her condo. She sort of hoped it would happen again, being an ornithophile at heart, but at that moment, she only wanted to harness her brain and command it to rejoin her company.

Emile tacked back to the group. To her distinct pleasure, the dimpled harbinger appeared as he proffered, "I think we should take a vote, er, unofficially, of course." Heads dipped up and down in agreement, and a few snickers followed as if they were about to do something naughty, which, of course, they were.

"That would be great," Lottie quickly said before they could change their minds. "All in favor, raise your right hand and say aye." A human wave undulated around the circle as one by one, hands rose. "Ayes!" resounded, and beneath Lottie's sweat-soaked blouse, something curative began to seed.

Not knowing whether to laugh or cry, she squeaked, "Thank you! Thank you!" And whether they did it for her and her mental demands or for the women or for pure sport, she didn't know nor did she really care. These were good, good people. The brightest stars in a constellation of lawyers and activists. The kindest, the most complete packages of charity available. And she was immensely proud to have them on her team.

The rain had slowed, and in the distance, the sky flashed powder blue. She shot up a quick prayer: *Thank you, and help me to wield this power responsibly.*

Emile chirped as his dimple deepened. "Okay, dawlin'. You started this thing. Now tell us the next step."

"Naturally, we need to have a board meeting," Jezebel humphed. "Let's set it up soon so that this idea doesn't die." She rocked forward. "We need to choose officers, get the 501(c)(3) papers going to set up the nonprofit, all that jazz."

Failing to mention thus far the additional board member that she'd just recruited, Lottie jumped in. "So, there is one more board member with whom I have already spoken." Heads rose in expectation. "Do y'all know Dr. Hassan from Tulane?"

"Fatima Hassan?" Isabella asked, aiming her perfect nose in Lottie's direction.

"The same," she answered and hoped for a good response.

"Of course. We're colleagues. I collaborate with her on many issues,"

Isabella continued.

"Well, I've asked her to join us." Lottie smiled proudly and sat back down.

"She will be perrrrr-fect," purred Jezebel. "I used her once as an expert witness in an arranged marriage case."

"I heard her speak once at a rally," Emile offered his layperson two cents.

"So then it's settled. I would like to call a meeting next Friday afternoon, my place, say around noon. I will have jambalaya, crawfish bread, and Abita. Can y'all make it?" It was the best bribe she could offer. *No. Wait. I'll up the ante.* "Better yet, let's meet at Pierre's. My treat."

"Throw in the bubbly, and you've got yourself a deal." Jezebel always drove a hard bargain.

Pleased with herself, Lottie leaned back and beamed. Champagne wasn't cheap but was sometimes necessary.

"Deal." What could she do but abide? She walked over to lower the blind. The disagreeable weather had exited, and the sun ventured out, strong like her partners, resolute like herself. The flood turned into a trickling stream heading into the gutters.

The pumps must have been working hard. And that was a very good sign.

Chapter Six
An Auspicious Start

On Fridays when the sun is directly overhead, the weary disciples, their cloaks dragging the dirty and sticky and gravelly arteries of the Central Business District and French Quarter, make their weekly pilgrimage to the culinary sanctum that is Pierre's. The destitute who lack pertinent associations with the food messiah of urban professionals are abandoned in the sun to sizzle with the tar rivulets on the asphalt. With a red Sharpie, Lottie circled the review of Pierre's in the *Times Advocate*.

Luckily for her, her cousin Christa's boyfriend's father was the maître d' and was kind enough to let her dance before the Highest Order of the Savory and reserve the upper room for the first board meeting.

She considered it truly unfair—brandishing this weaponry of the scrumptious to loosen them of all thoughts rational either already expressed or forthcoming. And though they raised a chorus of *Ayes*, who was to say none of this philanthropic faction would back out and retreat to their cement cubicles of normalcy? Therefore, she shamelessly and additionally resorted to liquid armament in the bubbly iteration of Dom Perignon.

In fact, by tearing them from the prosaic and encouraging them to compose their personal magnum opuses, the notes of which to be fabulously orchestrated from several global loci, she might be doing another good deed in the process: unshackling them from convention. It was fairly common knowledge, even in the world of immigration, where the facts varied in each case, that routine could get on one's nerves. Her mom had taught her that idleness is the tool of the devil, and so, if you thought about it, she was actually doing them a prophylactic spiritual favor.

Her guests arrived timely, and who wouldn't as tantalizing wafts—Chicken Claiborne?—summoned the do-gooders up the stairs and into the paneled room that spoke of importance. The long, covered table invited with its Limoges china and native props: Mardi Gras beads and doubloons. The group moved in as an umbrella-less second line in single file, eyes expectant, noses working overtime, swaying to and fro, tracking the scents.

"My dear." Dr. Hassan led the way, approaching with a soft smile and a firm hug.

"I spoke with the chef, and he will be able to serve halal chicken just for you, my friend." Lottie sensed an indelible bond building between them, the kind that graces two of similar mind and ilk, though opposite in appearance. Fatima's head fully wrapped in a golden hijab called to mind the Oscar statuette, though she dazzled more.

In a Morse code of fashion, heel clicks drummed the arrival of the next two: the decked out and perfumed. Anna-Maria elbowed Jezebel as they stepped into the room. "Girl, please." They too embraced Lottie, leaving dueling scents on her freshly dry-cleaned suit.

"Hi, sweetie. I'm excited!" Isabella sailed forth next in cottonness and unadornment, and administered a buoyant kiss to her cheek.

"You really outdoin' yourself with this, dawlin'." The male caboose—Emile—trailed in, a Perlis, LSU bow tie seemingly illuminating his path.

After the precursory coquetry and banter, everyone sat—Lottie at the head and Dr. Hassan at the foot—or vice versa depending on one's view of the world and orientation to the river. A portly waiter with a stole of dark hair around his round head stood against the wall in formal attire, along with his partner, a tall and crow-like servant with a sharp beak, a black ponytail, and long arms for wings. A third waiter, who must've begun at Pierre's grand opening in 1905, shuffled in with determination and coughed in gargles. The other two graciously took him aside to straighten his bow tie and smooth down his field of gray hair.

"Mademoiselle, are you ready for the champagne?" The tall server spoke in a Cajun accent.

"*Oui!*" Lottie clapped her hands twice. "Dr. Hassan, what can we get for you?"

"Seltzer would be lovely." She lifted her glass happily.

"Right away, madame!" the shorter one declared and disappeared, while the giant popped the Dom and circled the table, distributing it generously and with great fanfare. The elder statesman shuffled toward the table in slow motion with a cloaked basket of bread. Lottie hoped the bread didn't get stale before it got there.

"Keep it flowing!" Emile sang.

"Yeah, you right!" Jezebel agreed.

"It's five o'clock somewhere," Anna-Maria insisted.

Isabella lifted her glass gloriously and Fatima did not seem put off at all by any of it, probably long accustomed to New Orleans's own religious tradition: baptism by booze.

Lottie found Lou slurping the Dom and pulled her aside. "Louisa Mae, can you do me a favor?"

"Sure, baby." She put the glass down.

"Would you stay soberish with me? We have a lot of work to do."

"Lottieeeeee. Oh geez. Okaaaaay. I just wish you had told me before so that I could have prepared mentally. Ya know?"

"Oh, honey. I'm sorry. I need a sober island in the sea of soon-to-be tipsy board members."

"Well, damn. I guess I'll have to have a beverage later."

Arms moved in time, ripping loaves, sawing butter, shoveling bread. Crumbs, the bread's offspring, spread across chins and rained on napkin-draped laps.

The board looked up and down the menus and emitted oohs and ahhs.

"What are you getting, Anna-Maria?" Emile wanted to know.

"Probably the soft-shelled crab," she said. "How about you?"

"Shrimp Étouffée has my name on it."

Naturally, the contrast of moments like these was never lost on Lottie—the irony of being so blessed while addressing the misfortunes of others. The thought stabbed her again, but like the many honed habits of the human rights attorneys, she had become adept at sweeping guilt into a corner.

"Whatcha thinkin' about, baby?" Louisa Mae was a damned mind reader. At least when it came to her.

"Nothing, honey," she fibbed.

Would she stumble upon the litter and detritus of First Worldness later and move it into a dustpan? Sure, but such makeshift relegation and compartmentalization was yet another tool necessary to exist in the West.

It was like flipping the finger at injustice. *Watch me have a good time and enjoy a shrimp po-boy! Watch me attend the Bacchus parade and dance in the middle of St. Charles Avenue!*

The penguined waiters moved around and took orders.

"I would like an erster salad followed by a big ole bowl of gumbo," Jezebel proclaimed.

Isabella chose wisely. "I'll have the drum, please."

Lottie decided on the duck and andouille gumbo and shot off apologetic vibes to her fowl friends in the Audubon lagoon. On this one occasion and only this one occasion, she was not at Pierre's to eat a lot, though she spied enviously some of the other entrées ordered. Gumbo would have to do.

～～

"Are we all set, Lou?" Lottie walked over to where Lou stood organizing paperwork and making notes and found her sipping something, but she didn't want to accuse, to awaken the bear.

"Yeah, baby."

Earlier that morning, she and Louisa Mae had wrangled the SMART board, dry erase, and computer into Mini Pearl and hauled it down to the culinary ambush long before the bar and restaurant workers began to hose down the sidewalks and streets. Now the room bombinated with forks and knives accosting the china and with lively discussions—"What the hell are we doing here?" "Will the Saints resign Drew Brees?" "They said it would be a lively hurricane season."—and two and a half men attending diligently.

As the sawing of forks slowed, Lou said, "Time to rock and roll." Resisting the urge to crack or nibble, Lottie nodded to the crow-like waiter to flick the lights, then tapped with a fork her now seltzer-and-cranberry-juice-filled glass. Like a black-and-white tulip opening, the two more lucid waiters retreated to the wall, the elder muddling behind and muttering something like "Huh? What are we doing?"

"So, here we are again," Lottie began. "First let me say how grateful I am that you all chose to come."

"We ain't here for you, dawlin'! We're here for the food," Emile interrupted.

"Yeah, you right about that," Jezebel said.

Everyone cackled. Even the penguins, though she knew they were probably long accustomed to such shenanigans.

"Ha. I don't blame you one bit." Lottie played along. "I'm sure that you have gotten acquainted with the illustrious Dr. Hassan, or Fatima, as she likes to be called."

Emile winked at the professor and did sort of a half bow in his chair. *Again with the half bows.* Anna-Maria and Jezebel smiled and dipped their chins.

"Oh, yes!" Isabella flashed incredibly white teeth.

"Good," Lottie said cheerily. "Please direct your attention to the screen on the wall." The tall waiter approached with a fresh bottle of Dom and refilled the flutes. She wiggled a finger about her laptop until large Garamond font—not too feminine, not too informal, esthetically pleasing and decidedly her favorite after going through the entire menu twice—appeared on screen atop the century-old plaster.

If the walls could talk...

But her mind swam in imagined conversations had in that very building—murmurings of how to beat Prohibition, who frequented Lulu White's brothel, whose sons had landed on the sands of Normandy, who honestly voted for Richard Milhous Nixon. And now she would add to the unspoken legends.

Reeling in her imagination, she pointed to the PowerPoint. "These are my suggestions for officers on the board of our organization, the name of which is to be determined in a little while." Behind her now-creased skirt, she crossed her fingers and hoped these ideas would not insult, slight, or mock anyone. She also hoped for zero hurling of tomatoes, but who could be certain in such circumstances?

CHAIR: DR. FATIMA HASSAN
SECRETARY: ISABELLA FRANCALANGIA
TREASURER: ANNA-MARIA RODRIGUEZ
PROJECT DEVELOPMENT: EMILE FONTENOT and JEZEBEL JOHNSON

If silence was tangible, Lottie could feel it, heavy and frightening and gripping. Perhaps it was only seconds, but it seemed like several minutes. She twirled on her pumps, waited for something besides the gurgle of the senior waiter to break it, and glanced at each face. They were thinking, she could tell. No smoke shot out of ears, but eyes blinked and brows moved in concentration.

Jezebel spoke first. "What the hell is project development, exactly?"

Thank you, Jesus. They speak!

"Well, it's actually the coolest part. You and Emile will help with the design of the actual missions. In other words, y'all will use your creativity to design the pranks that I will carry out."

A devious smile covered Jezebel's face, and she smacked her knee. This was a good sign, at least. Then from her lined lips, she said, "I *love* it! Uh-huh! Take that, you nasty bastards!"

The tall waiter elbowed his round colleague.

Capitalizing on the excitement, Lottie kept going. "I think you have, shall we say, a lot of passion, Jez, and Emile has been creating stunts for his own activism. The two of you are perfect." Emile's dimple deepened, and he dabbed his new partner.

"I say we meet at Pat O's," he suggested, and to that, they clinked glasses. The chubby waiter moved in to refill his flute, the contents of which rapidly dwindled. The older gentleman adjusted sharply the napkin draping his arm and straightened up, ready for action.

"Phew." Lottie wiped her forehead. "Okay, so how do the rest of you feel about the assignments?" She looked around. "Fatima, are you fine with this?"

She lifted her glass in salute. "I believe the assignments will work beautifully, like—how do you say—a fine machine."

"Great! Isabella and Anna-Maria?"

"Looks good!" said Isabella.

"Agreed!" agreed Anna-Maria.

Good, that's five of five. First hurdle jumped nicely.

"Well, that was easy enough. Now we must decide on a name for our nonprofit. I will work on the 501(c)(3) papers as soon as we decide on this." Lottie clicked around on her keyboard again and flashed her idea on the screen:

WOMEN AIDING WOMEN

(WAW)

"How does this sound for the name?"

Mediocrity sighed in huge black letters—font be damned. She couldn't help it—the name wasn't something on which she wanted to spend much brain petrol on. Frankly, she wanted to get on with things, to get to the meat—the mission statement—to talk about more interesting topics.

The alpine waiter swooped in and filled water glasses, his long arms flapping inward over the targets, his Adam's apple lurching above their heads. Lottie hoisted her glass to cracked lips and wished that she had reapplied the Mauve Magic lipstick. Probably fading into one orange blob.

It was what happened after hours of nonapplication, her lips disappearing into a sea of peach. A frightening prospect, if you asked her, though Lou always insisted she was a little too self-deprecating.

Her guests tilted and cocked heads and emitted a few *hmmmms* and *uh-huhs*.

Lottie imagined the gears grunting and shifting inside their craniums, trying to change the *ho-hum* into *kapow!*

No dimple magically appeared this time. Emile twisted his bow tie and scratched the thick black forest atop his head. By far the most creative of the group, he usually spat out ideas like a production line. Would he come through for her this time?

"Girlfriend," he said. "We have got to do better than that." He glanced at the others, apparently for approval, then squarely into Lottie's sleep-deprived and probably bloodshot eyes. "You're more creative than that."

"Shakin' my damn head is what I'm doing," said Jezebel, who really shook her damn head.

"Okay, I know. It's kinda blah, right?" Lottie's shoulders sank like a pair of scales.

"WAW is blah," Isabella teased.

Well, look who has a sense of humor.

Lottie took it as a positive and put on her big-girl girdle, fortified her innards for the creative tête-à-tête. Besides, this would be fun, right?

"You already know, girl," Anna-Maria chimed in and shifted to the edge of her seat, getting ready to launch into something. Creativity, maybe? "We have to make it more original, kinda sassy and all—like our mission. This ain't no ordinary organization, and this ain't no ordinary town. We don't do boring well."

And by boring, Lottie was pretty sure she meant that New Orleans didn't do normal—didn't do efficient great either, but that was a tale for another occasion. She imagined purple, green, and gold steam escaping her spicy friend's ears.

Behind the odd debate, the tall waiter's ears seemed to wiggle like radars, aiming at the chatter.

"Okay, okay. I cry uncle!" Lottie splayed two freshly manicured—and unchipped!—hands in the air. "I was just trying to move things along so that we could get on to the real work. I will now officially retract the name, and we can brainstorm about it."

Dr. Hassan quietly raised a hand. "I understand that everyone wants to give—how do you say?—props to this great city. However, let us make sure that we include the purpose of helping women in it also." Mutterings scampered across the white table. Lottie realized precisely then that English spoken with a Pashto flourish impressed, causing all to lean forward, elbows on tables.

"Okay, so who wants to start?" Lottie stepped over to the dry-erase board, whipped out the marker, and wrote in long squeaks:

NAMES: WOMEN AIDING WOMEN (WAW)

Then she drew an angry line through it.

"Well." Isabella held a half-ripped envelope in her hand. "I jotted down an idea." She glowed with something like pride. "I thought because we're helping women and because we're in NOLA, we can call it NOLA GIRLS." Heads went up and down in uncertain pacification as Lottie scribbled on the board:

NAMES:

WOMEN AIDING WOMEN (WAW)

NOLA GIRLS

"No offense, dawlin'," Emile ventured. "But I still think we can do better than that, though that's a nice name." Lottie could tell from his cadence that the Dom Perignon had kicked in a little, softening the assault.

"Let's see." Anna-Maria stepped up to the creative plate, ready to swing. "How about Y'ats For Justice?"

Lottie added to the list.

NAMES:

WOMEN AIDING WOMEN (WAW)

NOLA GIRLS

Y'ATS FOR JUSTICE

The crow shook his long black ponytail in furtive disagreement.

Nosiness. It's what's for dinner in New Orleans.

She winked at the waiter and smiled, for who knew if he could be the one to offer the best idea?

"Hmmm," Jezebel huffed, "that may be a bit too informal, ya heard? Besides, who the hell knows what a Y'at is besides Y'ats?"

Isabella and Anna-Maria swung and missed.

On deck stood Emile, waving with aplomb and imagination. After all, he had been the chairperson of the NOLA Nutjobs for several years. The Tutu Parade that rolled through gasping conventioneers on Royal Street with floats festooned with sparkly trans folks, his conceit. Ditto the Bring Your Cat to Work Day—which ended in much yowling and sneezing, and even produced a few fights and scratches, but raised thousands for pediatric aids. Emile was the Einstein of Entertainment in a celebrator-chocked city.

Maybe he could save them with his brilliant right-bending brain. He stood with poise and grasped both suspenders. "Well, it isn't my best work, but I understand that we want to move things forward." Clearing his throat, he took a swig of what appeared to be a Sazerac, which he had discreetly switched to somewhere in the course of the event. "I think because we shall be based out of New Orleans and we are looking for justice for the women of the world, I humbly suggest NOLA Justice for Women, or perhaps Love from NOLA. I understand the gravity of the situation and didn't want to put too sarcastic a spin on it."

"I adore both of these titles," Lottie said. The beanstalk and the sphere smiled and nodded. Even the air conditioner seemed to squeal in delight.

She scribbled quickly.

NAMES:

WOMEN AIDING WOMEN (WAW)

NOLA GIRLS

Y'ATS FOR JUSTICE

NOLA JUSTICE FOR WOMEN

LOVE FROM NOLA

In Pashtoglish, Dr. Hassan offered, "I do also. And what I am thinking, you see, is to put a parenthesis around the LA in NOLA. Then, you see, it would read NO(LA) Justice for Women. In this manner, it will present to the public that there is, in fact, no justice for women. And we are going to right that! Right?" If anyone should be able to rant about women's rights or the lack thereof, it was Fatima, Lottie expected.

She immediately drew the parentheses, stood back, and examined the latest development,

NO(LA) JUSTICE FOR WOMEN

and let the idea float around the room like pixie dust until it settled on each head of her compatriots, then watched as satisfied smiles spread from one to the next. Could it be that Fearless Fatima had dubbed their collective newborn? She had to admit that though the title was the least of her concerns, it now tickled her heart.

"No Justice for Women?" Emile's eyebrows rose into an arch and—

miraculously—his left cheek concaved into a beautiful pit. Perhaps gold dust sparkled across his cheeks also. "NO-LA Justice for Women! It could totally work!"

"Ooooo, I like dat, Dr. Hassan!" Jezebel clapped her hands, launching into the air her wrists and the tolling of her bracelets.

"Great collaborative effort! Yeah, you right!" Anna-Maria raised her flute in salute.

"I like dat too," concurred the round waiter, whose pants resided just south of a well-endowed waist, a forlorn belt cinching it like a sausage string. His less loquacious, skyward colleague nodded heartily.

"I think Emile's idea augmented by Fatima is wonderful and genuinely captures the essence of who we are," Lottie said. "All in favor, say aye!"

Ayes resounded from her colleagues and the waiters, the sum of which well exceeded the quorum. Even Lou agreed.

"All against, say nay." Not even the elder waiter, who cupped one ear, trying with all his octogenarian might to pay attention, uttered a word.

The sweet potato cheesecake winked at her, Lottie was certain. But it was the bread pudding that won her affection with its praline-liquored hugs and brown-sugar kisses. Again. Resistance retreated faster than the British had from Andrew Jackson and his stew of pirates and ragtags in 1815.

"If any of you are still with me—er, mentally, that is, what we need to do now before we leave is construct a mission statement for NO(LA) Justice for Women." She let the fresh nomenclature swirl on her tongue like the first sip of Clos du Bois on a hot day, enjoying its context and relevance, the way it felt at home in her mouth.

"We're here!" Lou burped. Lottie shot her a look like: *Really? You partook of the secret weapon, didn't you?* Though who could blame her for not resisting? This was Lottie's baby, and it was she who needed to attempt to stay sober during the pregnancy. "Attempt" being the operative word.

"Us too!" said the Danny DeVito-esque waiter.

"Everyone else?" Lottie asked. "If you can handle the mission statement, raise your hand." All hands went up, Anna-Maria's swaying a bit.

Emile, clearly inspired by the stealthy Sazeracs, jumped in. "Darlin', I thought you already had one. You mentioned it when we met at your office. Don't you remember, ya heard?"

"I heard. I mean, I do remember, but that was just my quick and brainless attempt at something broad enough to legally—sort of—accomplish the real assignments."

Jezebel jingled a hand. "Can you read that one again, the one from that meeting?"

"Of course." Lottie blanched at its simplicity. "To support, advocate for, and encourage females of all ages and all nations who have been victimized through violence or cultural or religious traditions."

"So, if we add the name of our organization to it, like this." Isabella employed air quotes for emphasis, her Buddhist bracelet softening the gesture. "'NO(LA) Justice for Women's mission is to support, advocate for, and encourage females of all ages and all nations who have been victimized through violence or cultural or religious traditions,' then, I think it works! I mean, it covers the operations totally."

Lottie went back to the dry-erase board and recorded the first stab. Fatima lifted a right hand. *Ah, the right hand, so important to my Muslim friends.* "Indeed, that is quite inclusive. Do you think we could either omit or combine some of the words?"

"I thought of that, Fatima, but couldn't pick one thing that I thought should be omitted," Isabella countered, her Ivy League education in attendance, no doubt.

"I see what it is you are saying." Fatima seemed to capitulate. Lottie decided not to interject and stood expectantly and in admiration. She looked forward to the brainstorming of this brain trust of NOLAJFW.

"I love it!" said Anna-Maria.

"Yeah, you right!" Jezebel attempted a fist bump with Emile, whose big paw bypassed her and dropped into his lap.

The new chairwoman, Fatima, spoke again, and all heads tilted—including the three waiters—from one end of the table to the other. "I have been on several boards before, and I shall now provide my opinion…" A cliffhanger, Lottie thought, and inhaled. "I kiss it!"

This could only be a good kiss, right? Not at all like the Al Pacino *The Godfather* venom. Lottie asked, "And this is good, correct?"

"Oh, yes, *habeebee*. I bless it. I like it." Between declarations, Lottie managed to wave to the Crow and had him fill her thirsty flute with the champagne. After all, she had refrained like a responsible beast and now deserved a sip. Or a swig. Or a guzzle. Fatima said, "In point of fact, as chairperson, I am now going to call on a vote. All in favor of the proffered mission statement, say aye?"

Once again, the ayes surged through the stately room. Lottie wished she could harness the energy and with it spin the earth, fuel the masses—forget solar, this was something more powerful, cleaner, lovelier.

Lou approached and dispensed a hearty hug, which was the only way she operated. "Baby, looks like it's happening! You see, now you can take care of this and get on with your life."

"Meeting adjourned," Dr. Hassan said.

"Ah, but first…" Lottie clapped her hands twice. "A board that second lines together stays together!" With a stretch of one long wing, the lanky waiter reached into a utility room and flipped a switch. Then it began, the rattle-tattle of the snare followed by the root-a-toot-toot of the trumpet, inviting all to grab a napkin and form a line.

Lottie's cheeks burned from smiling. She jumped in as with one hand on the hip in front and the other waving the white napkin, all seven attendees, plus the waiters—even the elder—shook, swayed, and shimmied to "Joe Avery Blues," one anthem in the Republic of Crazy.

Chapter Seven
Burqa Schmurka

A map of the world stared back at Lottie with accusing, pastel eyes and braced itself on the cheery wall as an unwilling participant in her deeds. On it, three bright pushpins stood fiercely and beckoned her. A few days back, she had carefully positioned the primary-colored stickers on cities in North America—Central, really—Europe, and Asia.

One pin pricked more than the others, even going so far as to visit her dreams. The royal-blue one sang a siren's song from the vast expanse of Asia. It rose stalwart and dignified, like a miniature soldier, in the center of the Hindu Kush, and more specifically, in the mysterious metropolis of Kabul.

As in Afghanistan. As in home of the *shalwar-kameez*-wearing, Toyota-pickup-driving Taliban.

The hair on her neck shifted as she zeroed in on the tiny harbinger, on the spot where hell typically broke loose—and perhaps literally.

With an acute awareness of the status of women in that volatile cauldron, she still chose to push the blue pin precisely into the black circle.

She grabbed Frank and held him like a newborn, an act that produced a grunt and a sleepy look, his pupils struggling within yellow irises. "Tough, buddy. This is the cost of your rent." And it was. Nothing could squash a surge of adrenaline faster than assaulting her kitty with hugs and kisses. She took a deep breath and massaged his pink pads.

Breathe, Lottie. Breathe, girlfriend.

The others would be along shortly, and she called out, "Lou, do you have the water boiling for *shai*?"

"Girl, don't use that Arabic crap with me!" she barked back. "The answer is Y-E-S, and I bought a Randazzo's king cake, ya heard?"

"Okay, and sorry. I need to practice my Arabic more." Actually, Arabic wouldn't do for the first assignment. What she really needed was a Pashto phrase book. Pronto. "I take that back. I believe tea in Pashto is *chaay*."

"Tea in what? Oh Lawd, I can't keep up." The clanging of cups being placed on saucers rang forth from the tiny kitchen like cranky church bells from a twisted belfry. That it was her grandmother Helen's china wasn't a good thing, and she instantly regretted asking her spitfire BFF to handle the task.

Lottie mindlessly rearranged a vase of irises—purple and gold, of course, for LSU allegiance—then dropped into the swivel and lit up her laptop with one swift stroke.

YouTube videos of Kabul summoned her right away. Before she got distracted by one of her six thousand thoughts, she punched in the search. One in particular raised her eyebrows and made the strawberry hair on her arms stand fiercely.

WOMAN ATTACKED BY MOB FOR BURNING QURAN

Above the caption, a freeze-frame of a bloodied woman's face filled the screen. And as surely as Lottie knew that her fair skin would collect more freckles in the sun, she knew that the woman had probably not even touched the Quran, much less burned it. False accusations soared across Afghanistan like poisonous arrows, quickly destroying their targets, usually females. This poor soul was just one more.

She looked up at her ceiling and shot up a quick prayer.

Lord, I don't know why you allow some countries to fall apart while others prosper and why some people are persecuted while others aren't, but I would appreciate if you could comfort this woman's family, unless, of course, they are the perpetrators. Amen.

Unfortunately, it was not the time to dwell on the relentless riddle that could, if she let it, send her into certain despair.

"You want me to cut up the king cake?" Lou yelled and didn't wait for an answer. "Huh? Baby?"

"Sure, dawlin'. Be careful. You might get the baby, baby."

"Very funny. If I get him, I'm sticking him right back in there."

Lottie popped over to her email and gawked at the mass that had accumulated in the last twelve hours—a horrid, techno Jenga game, each piece waiting to be pulled out without crashing the computer.

Five waited—like trapped gas—from Immigration, three from her cable service, six that appeared to be viral bombs, and two from United Airlines, which she promptly opened—those veritable black clouds of flight confirmations to Kabul loomed among the others.

Who flew to Kabul, anyhow? Apparently, Charlotte Alice Fornea did. Unless she chickened out, of course.

There was still time to back out, and for a millisecond, she also wondered if a CIA file had been opened with her name emblazoned on it in Sharpie black. Her associations and acquired languages certainly could be misconstrued as terrorism potential by a pencil-pushing neophyte looking to score points within the Agency.

Add to that now—a flight to Kabul.

Outside, Mister George fired up the leaf blower, its roar vibrating her eardrums like the drill at the dentist's office. She lifted the window and frantically waved both arms, beckoning her devoted helper. After chasing a cigarette butt around for far too long, he looked up and silenced the vulgar beast. "Morning, Miss Lottie! How you doin', dawlin'?"

"Good, Mister George. How are you? How was your weekend?"

"Let's see. I went to bingo at Saint Ignatius on Saturday night, won a hundred bucks!" He cracked a big smile. "Bought a bunch of crawdads with it. Then on Sunday, I passed by my nephew's lake house, and we had a crawfish boil. Oooo-weeee, we passed a good time, *cher*!"

"Action packed, I see!" She laughed.

"How 'bout you?" He laid the monster on the grass and slowly straightened.

"Pretty good. Saw Kermit at the Howlin' Wolf on Saturday night. Too much fun!"

A gargantuan chuckle erupted, one befitting his amplitude. "Never too much, right?"

"Right." She winked. "Hey, Mister George. Can you do me a favor?" Across the street, two dog walkers with their respective black and yellow mutts stopped for rear sniffing and a chat.

"Anything, Miss Lottie!" She knew he meant it.

"Would you mind not using a leaf blower? I mean, just because my yard is so small, and I believe that the magnolia leaves can be raked pretty easily into a pile."

"Ah geez, dawlin'. I'm sorry. I will not bring this stupid thing with me next time."

The dogs moved in a circle and entangled their leashes.

"It's just that the sound is so loud, and I have some people coming over for a meeting."

"Oh, a meeting, hanh? What kind of meeting?" And just like that, there it was. The snoopitude that he employed at his peril of her aggravation.

She wouldn't bite, of course. "I'm afraid that's confidential, dawlin'." Neither flake nor crumb would fall from her lips, especially her upcoming soiree to Afghanistan, which just might send him leaping off the Crescent City Connection.

"Confidential, hanh? I gotcha." He waved her off with one thick hand and picked up the rake.

Behind him, a minivan pulled up and spilled its contents onto the curb. Fatima, Isabella, and Emile descended on her sidewalk like an international rock band—and not unlike the Spice Girls or The Black Eyed Peas, each one uniquely their own. Mister George cast a gimlet eye on Fatima, from the top of her scarved head to the bottoms of her covered legs.

He tipped his Zephyr's hat automatically but continued to eyeball her as she passed. When he noticed Lottie eyeballing him eyeballing her, he began to push the rake around in circles, creating a sad and crunchy current of magnolia leaves.

"Talk to you later, Mister George." Lottie shook her head, hoping that her disappointment showed.

Grumbling something about "not having time for this nonsense," Lou set up the table in the living room. Lottie ran in and attempted to snatch the tray from her, trying to salvage her MawMaw's only bequest. Though Lottie had little in the way of inheritance and though she was seven when her MawMaw died, she still wanted to preserve what little she had.

"I got it, Miss Thing!" Lou humphed and placed the tray on the barge-board coffee table, on top of an old *Gambit* that featured the late Allen Toussaint on the cover.

The door creaked, and Emile's beautiful face appeared followed by Fatima, loosely veiled in chartreuse and violet, then came Isabella, unadorned and glowing, as always. Before long, the balance of her creative equation entered the fray in designer fashion.

"*Asalaam alaykum.* Howdy. Hey, y'all. Where y'at?" Lottie greeted. It was a great title for a chick lit novel, but at least she covered all the bases. "Come on into my den of equity. Get it? Den of equity?"

"Haardy har har," Jezebel sniffed.

After pouring the *chai, shay,* or whatever it was, and ripping apart the king cake, they got down to business—just the six of them, with Fatima leading the way. "In our last meeting, we loosely discussed Lottie's upcoming and brave adventure to my homeland and, how do you say, her plan of attack? So today, I think it is important to go over some things before her embarkation thereof."

The four others scooted to the edges of the lounge chairs and sofa.

"So, now, if it is okay with y'all, we will go through some Afghan ground rules that will save you from probable death."

Lottie hoped and wished that she was joking, but something told her she wasn't. Plus, the "y'all" didn't befit a woman of her background and stature, nor the conversation, but God bless her for trying.

Fatima pushed back her hijab and began. "I teach such things at university, you see." Everyone stared at her, eyes large and full of something, maybe awe, maybe fear. Lottie wondered if they were breathing, and she reminded herself to do the same. Even Lou sat in the back of the room, big black eyes zeroing in on the professor.

"The first thing you should know is when you meet a man, do not, I repeat, do not shake his hand. Do not touch him. Though you are an American, or because you are, you may not be given much slack." Heads nodded, as if they understood. "In fact, it is best to even avoid the eyes."

Lottie asked, "The eyes?"

"I mean, you should not look directly into the eyes of a man. Or you will be seen as Western, which you are, of course." She laughed. "And Christian! Which is one and the same with being Western. These are two characteristics, if you will, that are not welcome in my country."

Fatima continued, "You may associate professionally with males, but you must make sure that you do nothing offensive. Do you understand, Lottie? This is imperative." Dr. Hassan glared so strongly into her eyes that she thought she might change her mind right then and there.

"Um, Dr. Hassan?" Lottie squeaked. And shrank. "What else would be offensive?"

"Well, you see. Everything I just mentioned. I want you to practice not touching the men and so forth."

They all knew, she figured: the whole "burqa" or "hijab" thing. This was the image of Afghanistan that had garnered the most notoriety in the Western press: the smacking by religious police on uncovered legs—even by centimeters—of baby-blue-burqaed women in Afghanistan.

"So, do I have to wear a burqa? A hijab? What's the difference anyway?" She knew; she just didn't know if her colleagues did.

"Okay, my dear. So, a hijab is really the head scarf, like I wear here today." She waved her hands around her bright head scarf like a model on a game show. "The burqa, on the other hand, is what you have seen in the news. The scary-looking light-blue thing that makes you look like a ghost." The corners of Fatima's mouth ascended, while everyone else's descended.

"So, which should I wear?" Lottie sputtered.

"Dear, I'm afraid, for complete safety, you should wear the full, gorgeous, baby-blue burqa." Sarcasm leaked from her speech, but Lottie still detected a degree of sincerity in her voice.

"Really? A full burqa?" And she wasn't kidding when she posed the next question. "How will I see? I don't know if I can honestly function with my eyes covered." Claustrophobia, an old friend, sat in the rafters of her cerebellum, feet up, waiting for its next assignment.

"You will be able to do it!" promised Fatima. "Then, you shall have empathy for those who are forced to do it."

"I have empathy already. That's why I defend them. I don't think I need more."

Ignoring her, Fatima continued. "So, I brought this." She reached into her satchel and pulled out a package wrapped in white cotton. Unwrapping it delicately, she produced a light-blue object that might have been a tent and shook it gently.

A *whoosh* fanned the air, and Lottie thought the collective air was being sucked out of the room and into the lungs of her colleagues. She surveyed the group as "oooohs" and "ahhhhs" splattered about.

The first thing Lottie noticed was how elegant and, yes, beautiful, it was. Its satiny fabric, probably nylon, surprised her as she'd envisioned a much heavier broadcloth or canvas. Additionally, embroidery adorned the skull cap (if that was what it was called) and trimmed the lower front. Regrettably, she spotted the mesh, the dreadful screen through which fully burqaed Afghan women viewed the world. If ever there was a symbol of misogyny and patriarchy, the screen mesh was it. After closing her eyes for a long second, she eyed the skull cap and wondered if her thickly maned, gargantuan head would fit it. She heard it was one size fits all.

"Now, my dear, if you would try this on, please…just to see how it feels."

She froze.

"Go on, dawlin', you can do it!" Emile encouraged.

"Go, girl!" cheered Jezebel. Claps and whoops and hollers reverberated off the walls.

Her hands rattled as she held the cultural symbol that got such bad press. The front, to her surprise, was shorter than the back, and this observation prompted more questions. "What happened to the rest of it? Isn't the front supposed to reach the ground also?"

"That's what I thought too," Isabella agreed softly, as though afraid to speak.

"That's the impression one gets from CNN etcetera, but truly, the front comes down only to here," Fatima gestured toward her waist. You see? One has to grasp the outer edges of the burqa to cover oneself."

"Do I wear my hair up or down?" It seemed irrelevant as no Afghan on the street would see whether it was clean, dirty, shorn, long, curled, or straight.

"This is up to you, you see. Whatever feels comfortable. When you go to Kabul, the temperatures can reach thirty-seven degrees, in Celsius, of course." The gawkers looked down at their fingers, counting, then up at the ceiling as if a magic calculator would appear and convert it to Fahrenheit. Luckily, Fatima saved them the excruciating task of using the left side of their brains. "Ninety-nine degrees. That is the highest it goes."

Lottie wiped her forehead reflexively. Subtropical New Orleans she knew. But—and this was a big but—her fashion was limited to tanks and shorts or skirts—without stockings. If she wore a cardigan, she could throw it off without a thought, exposing her slender pale arms. If she exposed her bright white arms in Afghanistan, she might very well, one, blind someone, and two, ignite a rage-filled bomb. Traipsing around Kabul in the full weight and heat of the burqa did not excite her. Well, it would just have to excite her soon enough.

"But because this only goes up to my waist, does that mean I can go commando underneath?" Lottie snorted—the snort always a rude and uninvited visitor. Thankfully, everyone laughed with her. Everyone except Fatima.

"Commando? I do not know the meaning, I am sorry." Of course she didn't.

I'm such an idiot!

"Sorry!" She insisted, "I was trying to be funny, but it was stupid." Another snort slipped through. Surely she could see a shrink about this abrupt and involuntary bodily function. Hypnosis, maybe? If it could help smokers, it could help her. Or perhaps she could start a group: Snorters Anonymous. "It means to be without clothes. Or underwear. Or...I'm sorry."

Now Fatima chuckled, but of course, she didn't snort. "Well, that just might get you stoned, but it might be worth it to see the faces of the men." She grabbed Lottie's arm and bent over in laughter.

Glory be, the professor is funny.

And Lottie knew then—or hoped, rather—that her new friend would become even more of a sister to her—one she could both laugh with and slay the beasts of injustice. Fatima actually got her.

"How do you say it? No worries?"

"Yeah, you right!" said Lou.

Fatima gave her a high five. "Because I brought this also." She drilled into another bag, an enormous L.L.Bean tote with her initials, FH, scripted on the side—the woman was full of Western surprises—and dug out a pink tunic top and what appeared to be black pajama bottoms.

"Ah well, that answers that question," Lottie sighed. When she overheated, she sometimes broke out in a rash—a gorgeous rosy raised one—that highlighted the constellation of freckles already inhabiting her pale body. Not that anyone would be able to see it, mind you! She would just have to find a way to scratch beneath the layers—count them: two and three—and without revealing her pajama-clad body to men desperate to see even a freckle.

Jezebel began furiously fanning a manila folder. Anna-Maria loosened her silk scarf. Emile wiped his brow. Isabella shifted in her chair.

"Baby? You sure you want to do this?" Lou asked, totally trying to rain on her James Bond—or Jane Bond—moment.

"Girl! I got this!" she lied. "Okay, so can I just try on the burqa first to get a feel for things, then I can try the shirt and pants on later."

Fatima nodded. "Allow me to demonstrate." Holding the garment by the headpiece in one hand, she slid the other under and managed to swoop it over her skull as if spreading a sheet over her head. Shifting the grate into place over her eyes, she morphed into a pastel ghoul. Then, in one move, she pulled up on the top and yanked the blue beast off. "Now, your turn."

"Okay. Here goes nothin'." Lottie mimicked the professor, dousing herself in fabric. Unfortunately, the screen rested precisely over the back of her head. Her eyes stared into a blanket of blue. Beginning to flail and fumble, she felt caught in a web. She heard someone jump up and then footsteps. Many arms moved tugged and twisted the burqa into place until the mesh sat in front of her eyes. "Phew," she joked and looked around at her helpers. "Peek-a-boo. I see you!"

Next, grabbing the sides with her hands, she pulled the right wing up across her chest like Dracula, then followed with the left. Fully cloaked now, she scooted around in a small circle to assess movement. Not too bad, though admittedly, her heels clashed with the ensemble.

But how would she lift objects? Access her purse? Her camera? Tools?

"Fatima, how will I use my hands when I need them?" Surely, Lottie's spasmodic movements would trumpet *Westerner!* to the Pashtun masses.

Fatima chuckled. "You will find a way."

Lottie put her hands together and looked up, the ceiling now divided into a hundred boxes or more behind the screen. Prayer was her answer to all challenges. It was her lifeline, sometimes literally.

But would God protect shenanigans?

And why did shenanigans begin with "she" anyway? Another term created by males, no doubt, just got real, if it wasn't real before.

The manila folder ignited her fingertips and demanded to be opened. Within it, typed in neat, benign English, was the following:

TARGET:
Abdullah Dawoud
Five-eight, salt-and-pepper hair, hazel eyes
Age: 35
Profession: Spice Merchant
Speaks only Pashto

CONTACT:
Ishmael Mahmud
29 years old
6'0" black hair, brown eyes
Education: Bachelor of Linguistics, University of Chicago
Profession: Interpreter/Tour Guide
Religion: Covert Christian (convert from Islam)
Fluent in Pashto, Arabic, and English.
And her favorite part:
Please memorize and destroy before arriving in Kabul.

Double-O Seven, move over. Enter the Cajun, redheaded, freckled, man-loathing human rights agent. Thank you very much. If only Fatima could produce a poison-dart-spitting pen to tuck in her pajama bottoms. Or Maxwell Smart's shoe phone.

"Do I have to eat this paper?" Another attempt at a stupid Western joke. Would it bring tomatoes or giggles? Nothing. Absolutely nothing. She slumped, the blue tent deflating with her.

Fatima didn't miss a beat. "Oh, you must eat it, my dear," and grabbed her cloaked arm again. In staccato chuckles, the others followed.

The fabric seemed to get heavier, and beneath it, she struggled to find oxygen. She yanked on the headpiece and tried to pull the burqa off in one fell pull. Unfortunately, she slapped around beneath, looking for an exit, finally finding the door and crawling out, her hair rising with static.

Yeah, baby. Light and air flooded her senses. Good to be back. Back in her coddling, if underappreciated, world.

"So are we all on board with Lottie's assignment?" Fatima canvassed the board members, each one producing wide eyes and halting nods. "And you, Lottie? Are you ready?"

Lottie saluted and slapped her heels together, which might not be culturally accurate, but it was all she could think of under the circumstances.

Chapter Eight
You Can Take the Girl Out of New Orleans

Shades of melancholy. Ombrés of lassitude. Lottie had plenty of time to dust off her poetic facility as the Emirates Airbus began the approach into Kabul, and these were her first impressions looking out the window. Somehow, she snagged a window seat and was therefore able to preview the world she would soon enter and consequently give her nerves plenty of time to gear up for her ultimate demise.

From ten thousand feet, the land didn't look so frightening, but a forlorn brown dominated the view—sepia punctuated by henna. Mountains. Houses. Businesses and roads. It was as though God himself shook a giant sifter of dirt over the metropolis. In the background, the Hindu Kush winked seductively, their tempting frosted peaks aloof to the struggles below.

Guilt stabbed her—guilt coming from the US's participation in the destruction of Afghanistan, necessary or not—first in battling the Soviets, then searching for the six-foot-five bearded guy. And now the US had become as permanent a fixture as the mountains or the Kabul River.

Dizziness chased the guilt and gave her brain a good thwack, then a familiar undertow of adrenaline threatened submersion. "Whoaaaaa," she said out loud to no one.

Baby, just breathe. You know how you get worked up, Lou said in her head.

Dang. Why didn't I bring Lou? Why didn't I bring anyone?

She surveyed the passengers, looked at the flight attendant—a white scarf covering only one side of her head—and located the emergency exits. *Window exits are the closest. Just follow me, everybody!*

If she could just inhale the recycled airplane air and hang in there for ten more minutes, she would stand on the rocky ground of an exotic country, undertake a crazy adventure, one that, if she lived to tell it, she could someday share with her grandchildren—if she gave up her recent man abstention, that is, and the way she felt, that was a big if.

The thought of turning on her flats and getting out on the next flight out to somewhere else—anywhere else—tantalized her. She could certainly chuck the whole lot of silliness, and no soul would blame her. That she even landed in Kabul would be evidence of courage—or madness, depending on one's viewpoint.

Who am I kidding? I ain't goin' anywhere. She had taken a huge step toward healing, albeit a pretty dramatic one, and had come too far—geographically and psychologically—to retreat back into normalcy. She would survive. She just knew it.

The floral hijab in which Lottie had incarcerated her curls now rested on her chest like a sad bib. She rubbed her eyes, then glanced around the airplane and noticed a small flock of females with covered heads, even Western-looking ones with fair skin like Lottie, all covered.

Shaking the American right out of her head, she repositioned the scarf back over her tangled mop, which protested greatly with several radical strands trying to escape imprisonment. Educated at the School of Fatima, she wouldn't dare exit without her head covered. In fact, the full-burqa bequest winked at her from the tote beneath the seat in front of her, a fabric fiend, waiting, waiting to smother her.

"Bzzzzz. Ur-qu. Bzzzzz." Something in Pashto and Urdu squawked through the intercom.

Passengers began shifting, buckling seat belts, crumpling up bags of potato chips and juice boxes, shoving purses and carry-ons beneath the unforgiving seats, putting back on shoes and socks—and belts. Approximately twenty or so women including Lottie occupied seats on the flight. They began to resecure head coverings, wipe off lipstick and eye makeup, and strip off anything that might be misconstrued as a temptation to the opposite sex.

She attempted the same.

In the bottom of her tote sat a package of makeup-remover wipes, and not unlike an acrobat of Cirque du Soleil, she contorted her body sideways and managed to wrestle out a couple of the sheets and run one across one eyelid, then the other. She used the other wipe to smear off the remaining evidence of an overindulgent and infidel Western life that covered her face and lips. A swipe of Forever Pink lipstick appeared forlornly on the wipe. A swath of surrender!

Commanding her brain to join her, she slapped one cheek, then the other, widened her eyes. She pinched her arm, inwardly squealed, then reminded herself that she was in Seat 23A on Flight 772 to Kabul.

The landing gear thundered down and wing flaps buzzed, magnifying the drama that she would try the entire trip to compartmentalize in some fictitious mental drawer. The wheels smashed against the runway and caused her heart to jump, and in one collective mass, everyone lurched forward. A child's toy slid cockpitward; a bottle of Pepsi rolled in the same direction. The pilot pumped the brakes a few times.

Laden with an obese purse, disheveled carry-on, and uncomfortable camera bag that constantly slipped off her shoulder, she wobbled down the way-too-skinny aisle behind a rotund woman in a full black burqa, and for a second feared that she had mistakenly just landed in Saudi Arabia. Just to be sure, and in a half-lucid state, she bent down, glanced out a thick window, and shook off the thought.

As she descended the metal stairs, the heat slapped her about the face and her head felt as though it was on fire. A shot of jet fuel flew into her nostrils and sent a current of nausea through her, and droplets of sweat dripped between her breasts, landing squarely in her Victoria's Secret excuse for a bra. Nevertheless, she squared her shoulders.

Showtime!

~ ~

"Hey, you. Dees way! Dees way!" A male airline employee wearing protective headphones waved Lottie toward a yellow-painted path that led to a door where another man beckoned passengers. Insecurity shot through her as the male guarding the door scanned her from the top of her disingenuously wrapped head to the bottoms of her Tommy-Hilfiger-Marshall flats.

An interloper is what I am. A fake. A redheaded phony. Does he realize it?

Once inside, two lines formed, one seemingly for Afghan citizens and the other for people like her. Interlopers.

Lottie moved into the "other" line—for she certainly was an "other"— where the Western-looking passengers stood and wobbled and looked down at passports and paperwork.

Were they interlopers like her? *Let it go, Lottie. Let it go. Rumination be gone!*

Taking a deep breath, she stood behind a man in a suit and tie and judged him to be an *Amreeki*. "Hi, where are you from?" Nothing ventured, nothing gained. Maybe she could make a friend on the trip.

He mumbled something in a language unknown to her and mentioned a word that sounded like "Hungary," but she wasn't sure she interpreted it correctly, and even if she had, she didn't speak the language, and who cared anyway? Beneath her blazer, she *shvitzed*.

Finally, Lottie arrived at the booth and, with not a little tremor in her right hand, slid passport and paperwork to the man in uniform behind the glass. She smiled but would not look him in the eye as instructed by Fatima and thought about how the opposite was true in the States, an insult.

Focusing on the clock behind the man, then down at her twitching fingers, then to her right side, then to her left, she began to tap her fingers on the counter, then clasped her hands together, forcing them to stop.

After what seemed like hours but could have been only seconds or minutes, the officer stamped and scribbled in her passport, then slid it back. Still refusing to look at him, she figured he could have had two heads. She had no idea. And she certainly wouldn't be able to identify him in a lineup.

Gaining her footing on knees that felt like limp spaghetti, she sucked in a lungful of air-conditioned atmosphere and surveyed her surroundings. To her right and down an uncomplicated and austere hall walked men in *shalwar kameezes* and *pakools*, the kind of hats she saw on CNN and Al Jazeera. She also saw a few women draped in long shirts or tunics and flowing pants and swaddled heads, though none of the garments appeared too binding and awful, especially when compared to the blue basket into which she would soon leap.

Noticing a flock of women entering a door that she hoped and prayed led to the ladies' room, she floated toward them. It was the one place, after all, that females attended in pairs or trios or quartets. She quickly punched in "bathroom" on her Google Translate.

"*Tashnab? Tashnab?*" She blurted it out.

Almost alarmed, they nodded and pointed.

Inside the six-stall restroom, women stood at the sinks, shuffled in and out of the stalls. Some who went in burqaless emerged fully clad in the now-familiar blue garment. She was thinking how dense she probably appeared, gawking at all the action, when a small girl wearing a bright orange headscarf and her black-hijabed mom approached.

"You *Amrikaayi?*" the mom asked with lipstick-free lips.

A spluttering fool, she answered, "Um. Me? Yes. I am American," and patted her chest.

Is it that obvious? Are there no gingers in Afghanistan? Are freckles banned? Or do I exude American naïveté? Or worse—arrogance?

"*Zama num Lottie de?*" Lottie extended her right hand.

"Lot-tay," the mom said and gently took her hand. "Meetra." She patted her chest. "Sahar," she pointed to the girl, who had now zeroed in on the curls Lottie could feel escaping from her hijab.

"You want to see?" Lottie chirped, and the girl's amber eyes widened to the size of yo-yos. Without hesitation, Lottie unwrapped her hair and bent over, shook out the mop, and flipped her head back up, Beyoncé-style. The eyes grew to Frisbee size, so Lottie continued, "You want to touch?" and bent down to the little one. Tiny fingers dug into her locks, and the girl looked back up at her momma as if to say, *Can you believe this stuff?*

Apparently, by now, Lottie had attracted an audience, because when she looked around, several women stared at her. But they also smiled warmly.

A troubling thought waited backstage in her mind, peeking from behind the velvet curtains of her cerebellum, an eager understudy to reason. *Am I exposing myself? Will these women spread the word about the American in the restroom in their American-wary country, easily identified by freckles and hair the color of wild geraniums?*

Remembering the baby-blue sheet in the black hole of her tote, the limited advantages of it now came into focus. Not knowing what else to do and near the exhaustion of her meager stockpile of Pashto, she smiled and pointed to the stall. The throng smiled and stared and stood frozen until she excused herself and entered an empty stall with all her baggage, not an easy feat for a nervous American with weird hair.

Unwrapping the hijab, she tugged on the burqa until the famous symbol of oppression—or was it anonymity?—came rushing out in a torrent. Strangely, the adrenaline fizzing throughout her veins began to subside, and she found herself in an unfamiliar place: in the moment. Granted, it was a strange moment, yet she was fully present. She, Lottie Alice Fornea, born of Bettie and Jake Fornea, from New Orleans, Louisiana, was in a bathroom stall in the Kabul airport, and she was okay with that.

Her breath—hot and heavy and blocked by the wall of blue—shot out of her

mouth and directly into her nose, like steam rising. Unfortunately, a ponytail or bun was not an option, given the design of the cage, so she could also look forward to her thick hair resting on her neck in the heat.

Who designed this sadistic schmatta? I would like to have a word with him.

Struggling to position the screen precisely over her eyes, she twisted, turned, and moved the fabric. After a hefty match, she won, managing to center the garment in its proper position. The skullcap, if that was what one called it, was snug, not allowing ample space for her unusually large skull. A headache, she was certain, would be forthcoming.

Then there was the matter of her eyelashes, which smashed against the screen. Fortunately, she remembered the cheap pair of prescriptionless glasses buried in her bag, and fumbled down beneath the burqa until she found them. She threaded the spectacles under and upward until she reached her eyes. Fatima taught her this little trick. The lenses would mercifully stop her eyelashes from smacking the screen.

Through the mesh, which made her vision multiply like a 3-D movie without the proper glasses, she would hopefully and carefully find her way out of the restroom. It was empty then, and she didn't want to contemplate where the women had gone or what they would do. She simply wished to move out of the bathroom and become like so many other women in Kabul: invisible.

A sensation of solidarity coursed through her body. *Have I become like my Afghan sisters?* She swished away the thought. *Not exactly. I get to leave. I have the Holy Grail of travel documents…a US passport. A hearty* Ma Salama, *and I am outta here.*

Afghani women could not leave and were trapped, often without education, or pregnant at a young age from an arranged marriage. And God help them if they fell in love with the wrong person, the unapproved man. A love marriage simply wouldn't do.

Ah, but how she longed to get to know them all, to reach out to them. To have real discussions with every female in the country. Because—because she knew that she knew they were beautiful humans. Oppressed, yes, but beautiful too, somehow soaring above the pointlessness of the times. Poets and artists, teachers and mothers, engineers and doctors, Lottie had Afghan lady friends in the States and felt a kindred spirit with each one.

Of course, there were the anomalies, those who fell upon or constructed a path out, but those fortunate daughters usually had progressive parents—still conservative by US standards, those who saw their female offspring as gifts, not curses, and saw them as potential contributing members of society. Those who educated their daughters.

Thinking about moms and daughters made Lottie think of hers. Her apple didn't fall far from her momma's tree. Bettie had virtually adopted all strays, discriminating against no one. She'd invited Nigerians from the church for dinner, Central American workers for lunch, everyone for Christmas. And now, Lottie modified it slightly—*okay, greatly*—by seeking retribution for immigrants who couldn't do it themselves. Just remembering her mom made her heart expand but also ache. Killed in a freak car crash along with Lottie's father when Lottie was only twenty-two, it took Lottie several years to absorb the shock of her mom's death. *You did good, Momma. Thanks for what you gave me.*

Aiming the mesh screen toward signs in Pashto and Urdu with universal symbols above them, Lottie managed to find the baggage claim. Her contact—operative?—Ishmael was to be there, holding a card emblazoned with her name in Pashto, which looked like Arabic, which she knew. English was unacceptable as it might arouse suspicion of many varieties and from many different sources, all nefarious.

An attractive guy of twenty-something with hair the color of freshly mined coal and eyes cloaked in Ray-Bans stood out among others who were more middle-aged, salt-and-peppered, and modestly paunched. He gave the impression he was looking for someone different looking—as in the American.

He surveyed her, and nod and raised his hands as if to say "Are you Lottie?" She nodded behind the blue and directed her careful steps toward him. Trying to move gracefully and not trip over her burqa, she glided gingerly toward the man. As she got closer, she noticed a Pashto sign that she thought spelled Sharlot.

"Charlot? Charlot Fornee?" the man asked with the CH coming out like cha-cha.

"Yes!" Lottie blurted through the fabric, creating a perfect circle of steam from exhaling.

"Ishmael Mahmud!" He didn't extend his hand.

Fighting the urge to squeal *Oh my gosh! It's you and I'm here!* she nodded like a good ghost.

"Come. Let's get you out of here." He grabbed her—rather roughly, she judged—and yanked her toward the door.

Exiting into the tacky air, she must've missed the step down and toppled in one huge mass of amateurishness into what appeared to be a taxi sign. How she wished she had practiced walking more! *Note to self and Fatima: practice walking in burqa.*

Ishmael barked something at her, and, judging by his tone and accompanying sneer, she interpreted it to mean something akin to *You stupid cow, why can't you be more careful!*

She whirled the face mesh around full circle and noticed men laughing at her and nodding at Ishmael as if to say, *Ha, you weak man. Can't you control your woman?*

Feeling the blotches collecting on her cheeks and spiraling down her chest, she knew the tide of embarrassment was rising and was immensely glad that the jokers couldn't see it or the fear in her eyes. *Score a point for the burqa!*

Ishmael kept a firm grasp on her arm, practically dragging her, and she was certain a bruise would declare itself within a day. Trying to free herself from the vise, she twisted and jerked like a powder-blue Gumby. Giggles turned to guffaws as the men doubled over and elbowed one another. Some of them shouted in her direction, slurs that didn't sound very nice at all.

And what else did she hear? So much for devotion and protection from her contact, as he joined in the snickering and also fired off an apparent curse in her direction. And did he lift a hand to her too? Behind the mask, it was difficult to be sure, but she thought she saw his arm rise in jest toward her. Was it just for fun? She began once again to doubt her purpose in the Afghan capital.

They stumbled to an old Toyota sedan, some hue of green in its former life, Lottie half tripping, then righting herself repeatedly. He threw her into the front passenger seat, the skin of which was bandaged by duct tape, and saluted the men who continued to loiter and gawk as if it were an occupation.

When he jumped into the driver's seat, Lottie snarled with the same undercurrent of outrage that fueled the crazy trip to begin with. "Hey, what's the idea?"

Ishmael, if that was really his name, glared back at her.

Chapter Nine
Drop and Roll

"Shhhhh!" The black-haired man next to her who was supposed to be Ishmael snapped and threw the car into first gear, which made it jerk and sputter and exit the baggage claim area with great fanfare. As they made their way onto the main drive, he began to laugh uproariously.

"I'd like to ask what you think is so funny," Lottie demanded, not that she was exactly in a position to do so, but if she was a wiser person, she wouldn't be in this predicament in the first place. "I want you to know that the United States State Department is aware of my presence in this country. They will follow my every move."

"And? Do you think that it will approve of your little ruse? Do you think it can protect you? Nothing can save you now. Ha."

She swallowed hard, her throat rocky like the surroundings, and swung the checkered viewfinder downward to locate the door handle, then at the side of the road. A swift exit might be necessary, James Bond-style, though she had no idea what she would do after leaping to what? A broken leg? They passed a long stream of commercial stalls, a market, perhaps. Lottie could see cages of something—chickens?—and stalls of fabrics and spices. On the side of the road, mostly men walked. Why? Because they could. Occasionally, she spotted a woman sporting the same outfit. *We coordinated!* she thought weakly, trying to cheer herself up. Her stomach had already leapt from the vehicle in a fit of complete discombobulation.

"Relax, silly," her alleged contact urged. "I'm just—how do you say?—yanking your chain." He glanced over at her and winked.

She unshackled a covered arm and pressed the fabric to her chest to absorb perspiration. "Oh, funny, riiiggghhhhtttt. I get it." Glancing at him through the aperture, she allowed herself to breathe. "Do you have air-conditioning, by the way? You mind cranking it up for this sweltering, silly woman?"

"Not at all." He smiled and reached down to blast the AC, but all it did was puff weakly.

Even from behind the screen, she could see sparkling well-maintained teeth, as in Afghan movie-star teeth. Good dental hygiene, she inwardly applauded but didn't lower her guard. Not yet. "So, why did you throw me around like that?"

"Oh, that?" He tilted his head back and laughed.

"Uh, yah, that?" Beneath the stifling burqa, her shoulders relaxed just a little, as they had been clamped around her neck, thanks to this joker. She took another deep hot breath.

The sun shot through the windshield like the weather judge and executioner in the process of administering punishment for a prior crime she may have committed. She turned toward him and tried not to be obvious, but when one's vision is reduced to a two-by-four-inch window, one has to be obvious. And frankly, she didn't care whether she was conspicuous or a bump on a log.

His hair glistened with gel and formed one smooth tidal wave of black, so dark, it was almost blue. A cropped beard resided just below a strong nose and accentuated his chin, which was neither prominent nor absent. He sported blue jeans and a short-sleeved Polo from which well-nurtured biceps yelped.

"I had to put on a show for the locals. They know me. I told them I was picking up a cousin who had relocated to Dubai." He put one hand on the steering wheel with swagger. "They're all cavemen. I had to have a little bit of fun."

"Some fun," she huffed. "I'll probably have a bruise tomorrow."

"I'm sorry." Still, he smiled. It was the thing about the opposite and more distracting sex that crawled under Lottie's skin and made her itch in irritation—the not-taking-females-seriously thing. She had just displayed obvious aggravation to this guy whom she had just met, and what happened? He smiled. *Oh, isn't she cute when she's mad? She'll get over it.* She reflected on this while they rocked and rambled around the rutted roads, renewing silently her fast from men.

"So where are we going? And when can I take this, um, garment off?"

"Not yet," he said with a laugh. "Soon enough. I am taking you to a restaurant, then the hotel."

"Speaking of restaurants," she said. "How am I supposed to eat under this thing?"

"With your mouth, of course!"

"Very funny."

"So…you take the food with your hands under the fabric and bring it to your mouth."

"Great. Can't wait." In her jet-lag fog, which was quite thick, she had forgotten Fatima's eating lesson on how to maneuver the meal into her tented mouth. Fatima demonstrated how to grab the food with her right hand and creep it up the underside of the front, then insert said food into her mouth. Did one miss at times? Absolutely. But a few tries at it would paint her as an experienced and less conspicuous burqafied eater.

"And obviously, no burping! Or—you know—out the other end! Eeeek." So, now this guy was the Jim Carrey of Afghanistan. She suppressed a giggle but knew he couldn't possibly detect it under the miles of fabric.

"Well," she played along, "who would know who burped—or you know—out the other end? Besides, I have a long history of throwing my voice."

"Throwing your voice?"

Ah, she had him, finally something he did not understand. She swelled with pride, though he could not see that either. "Ventriloquism. Look it up."

"Ven-tril-o-kwaz?"

"Oh, forget it. I'm hungry."

～～

The Toyota coughed its way into a dirt parking lot in front of what appeared to be a native-style restaurant, designed to give foreigners the real deal, the true culture. Lottie didn't know whether to jump out or wait for Ishmael to open the door—another bit of information she should have gotten from Fatima. In the US, women had dealt with the chivalry matter in one of two ways: allowing the guy to be a gentleman, and not allowing a date to do squat. And this was in Afghanistan to boot.

Well, this was certainly no date. Still, her belly and brain said to sit still and wait. Taking his sweet time, he turned off the engine, which coughed a few more times for good measure, then sauntered around the car, examining each inch as though it were a late-model Maserati. *Good grief,* she thought. *I will dissolve into puddletude soon.* She blotted her upper lip, not that she had anyone to impress, or, for that matter, anyone she would be allowed to impress.

A headache loomed like a thunderstorm—in the distance and closing in. This might have been caused by a) jet lag, b) the skull cap squeezing her oversized skull like a lemon, or c) both. Some combination of the two was most likely the culprit. Finally, her gentleman caller realized she was waiting for him to open the blasted door and did so—without apologies.

Following him into the restaurant, she ran smack into a cloud of cumin and garam masala that traveled quickly enough through the nylon and up to her struggling nose. Her stomach approved with a growl, and thankfully, the gurgle didn't travel beyond the fabric and into the ears of the diners. Or Ishmael. As if he needed further fodder.

With a healthy dose of swagger and an equal waft of cologne, he walked briskly before her, and she followed, trying desperately to appear obedient and submissive, which wasn't difficult considering the head-to-toe cover and a world view from behind a wobbly grate. Maybe she was being a bit paranoid, but she preferred to blend in. And live.

"*Psssst. Psssst,*" she hissed from behind the screen.

Ishmael turned around, his face corkscrewed.

"I can barely see where I'm going. Can you slow down, please?"

"Absolutely," he whispered back and winked again.

The restaurant was packed with about ninety percent men, some in traditional Afghan garb and others in button-downs and pants, and the balance, women in full burqa and hijabs, tunics and billowing pants. How she longed to wear only the latter. If allowed, she promised to be a good girl, never complaining again about a scarf sliding off her head. Unfortunately, the board agreed that total anonymity was the safest way to operate in a country where a gang stoning could break out faster than you could shake a rod against her covered ankles.

"Right this way!" She assumed the maître de' said as he extended an arm. They followed, Ishmael first, then her.

Small tables and chairs filled the place just like in the good ole US of A, and Lottie was a little disappointed that they wouldn't be sitting on an Afghan rug in crisscross, apple sauce fashion. Large posters of the countryside and Afghans in cultural clothing decorated the walls, and a curtain separated what appeared to be the kitchen from the dining area.

"Would you mind ordering for me?" she asked, aiming the face screen at him.

"Not a problem." He looked down at the massive menu. Were he in her hometown, she might do the same, except order jambalaya or étouffée.

"Mantu. Kabuli palaw. Shish kebab," he recited with what could be pride, but she thought it sounded like an awful lot of food.

Within a half hour, a series of male waiters in *shalwar kameez* delivered the steaming plates in rapid fire. Lottie froze, a blue Christmas tree, she figured, lacking only tinsel.

Which hand is it again? The right? The left? Due to the mist looming in her brain and the impending headache, she couldn't remember.

What did Fatima say? *Let's see. In Islam, one uses one hand for clean activities and the other in the bathroom. Um.*

Now sitting there for her final exam on Islamic culture, she would get a big fat "F." She would have chewed on her nails, but she didn't even know which hand to choose for that. It could be considered clean or unclean. She didn't know which and didn't want to risk it.

"Dig in!" Ishmael commanded and picked up a kebab with his right hand, and his lips parted, not to eat, but to grin broadly, apparently appreciating her dilemma.

"Okay." She said a quick and silent grace, then, just to confirm—she didn't trust the jokester—she glanced at the other eaters, who were using only their right hands also.

"This looks great!" Relieved and starving, Lottie quickly followed suit and grabbed a kebab with her right hand and threaded it under and up, up, up through the tent to her mouth. Yet another advantage of the burqa: it offered a cover for slobbering.

Devouring sweet lamb beneath—and she didn't eat lamb, normally—she intentionally chewed with her mouth open. Why? Because she could. She even hoped that spinach resided precisely between her teeth. Sauce on the chin? Not a problem.

"Good, yes?" Ishmael asked.

"Oh my goodness. Makes you want to slap your grandma." It came out in her momma's accent—à la the great state of Mississippi—more Southern than Y'atty.

"Slap your grandma? That seems quite disrespectful. You must respect your elders!" Ishmael spoke under his breath and shook his head.

Got him! "Oh, it's a joke. It's said in the South, um, in the US, that is. It means that the food is delicious."

"You Americans have an interesting sense of humor." He said it as a couple squeezed past the table, the woman fully covered in blue and the man in Levi's and a T-shirt—not fair, but it was what it was. The woman aimed her mesh at Lottie's and nodded. An act of solidarity, perhaps? Or was she in danger? Lottie couldn't tell from that gentle gesture and sadly would never know. And what could she do anyway?

"What? Oh, likewise!" She wouldn't let Ishmael punch without a counterpunch.

After the lamb, she dove into a bowl of kabuli palaw, rice mixed with raisins, carrots, and beef. Surprisingly, the jet lag did not affect her appetite at all, and free from fabric encumbrances, she might have eaten the entire bowl solo. Ah, but the burqa—formidable foe of eating women—hampered her, which, if she was dieting, might have been a good thing.

Shoveling rice into her mouth with one hand while moving the fabric out of the way was an art, she supposed, one she might not master in only five days. She failed to notice right away that a small pyramid of rice had accumulated on her lap, trumpeting an amateur under the blue.

What hand should I use to scoop it up? Because technically, it is both cleaning and eating.

"Excuse me, Ishmael? I have a question." Lottie leaned over and whispered, noticing the smell of an unidentifiable spice in his cologne, "What hand do I use to collect the rice that has dropped into my lap?"

He rubbed his chin for effect. "I would go with the right and just put it right back in your mouth. Don't worry. You're looking good! Besides"— he looked around—"I don't think anyone is paying attention to you." She surveyed the patrons and agreed. The men sitting together—who were many—were busy shoveling their own lunch into their mouths as if they had to hurry. The burqa-anonymity thing seemed to be working.

"You see?" he said and launched another gorgeous smile. That he was attractive—quite—annoyed her. Why couldn't she have a homely contact? One with stained teeth or a pot belly? It was a distraction for sure, one she didn't need. She had a goal on which to focus, and at the moment, it was simply retrieving food from her lap. She looked back down sadly, raked it up with her fingers, then shoveled the rice into her mouth.

He leaned back in the chair, clasped his hands behind his head. Besides being attractive, Lottie noted, this guy, this Ishmael, was confident, and from what she could tell in the two hours spent with him, he also oozed a quiet humility that he didn't display in his prior ruse of pushing her around. All her exes assaulted her universe with hooks of cockiness and jabs of arrogance. Rare would be the find of a confident man without cockiness. *Not that I'm interested,* she reminded herself. *At this point, I pretty much dislike them all.*

The latter thought made Sadia's face flash through Lottie's mind like a compelling film in slow motion. Her beautiful face. Beautiful, even with a scar diagonally branding her left cheek. The cut of a knife. A jilted and angry man. A tattoo of patriarchy and impunity.

Erasing beauty was the goal of the offender. Instead, Lottie thought, it only enhanced it. Sadia's good looks couldn't be erased. Especially since arriving in the United States, where she blossomed further. *The bastard! Ha! He tried to ruin her but only bettered her life. Well, he will learn about vengeance soon enough.*

"You okay?" Ishmael whispered. "I think I lost you."

She faked it. "Yah. I think I'm just tired. Would you mind taking me to the hotel now?"

NO(LA) Justice for Women had paid for single rooms for the two of them. Ishmael would stay in the adjacent room, far enough away not to make a pass at her and close enough to keep her safe. Lottie had been assured by Fatima that he was a good man. Trustworthy and God-fearing and all about Jesus. And Fatima assured her he wasn't looking for an American wife. That he did not wish to leave Kabul, enjoyed his Afghan life, and ran a profitable business.

Ishmael came around and pulled back her chair. How refreshing! Lottie hummed and let the moment sink in. He might be able to give lessons to the guys in the States. This time, he helped her into the car far more gently and waited until she bundled the full burqa into it, thankfully. He turned the key, and the Toyota yawned to life. A cloud of dust enveloped them as they sped away.

Lottie grabbed the grill of the face mask and pulled it back from her face. "Ishmael, I don't know if I can do this. I mean, this…" She flapped the blue wings more like an angry wasp than a happy butterfly and rolled her eyes beneath the glasses and the prism. It was true. Between hearing her own breath—which was why she didn't scuba dive—being visually impaired, sensing certain cortisol spikes, she didn't know how much longer she could last. And it was only day one—the third hour of day one.

"As soon as we get you into the hotel, you can rip it off, I promise." He glanced over at her. Inspecting his eyes as best as she could, she thought she saw genuine concern. "I just think it will keep you anonymous, and that's a good thing for an American. Trust me."

"Okay, but I think I'm hyperventilating in here. Could you please turn on the air conditioner?" Drama was not beneath her under the circumstances, and technically, she wasn't even in danger. Yet.

He fumbled for the dial, trying to quickly appease her—Charlotte Fornea, the whining and spoiled American—and put the air on high. She positioned the screen over it and blew up like a frosty balloon.

~ ~

The garden was lovely, just as Lottie imagined. She had seen photos online and also knew the reputation and history of Hotel Serena in its exotic locations around the globe. Kampala, Kigali, Kabul. It was a five starrer, Islamic in design, with byzantine paths flanking a long column of rosebushes. A fountain bubbled in the center.

She paused and smiled.

"Beautiful, no?" Ishmael gleamed. She could only nod.

This might become her newest favorite place on the planet to reflect, and she was torn between staying right there, entrenched in the smell of roses and near the spray of the fountain, and running into the hotel and stripping down to her freckles.

"So, just to be clear," he said, breaking the spell. "You will sign in as your authentic self."

"Huh? Oh, yes, I'm checking in as Charlotte Fornea with my US passport…"

"But if anyone asks…"

"I am Susan Baker, a freelance reporter doing a story on the city's welfare after the withdrawal of most American troops."

"And I, madame…"

"Are my guide and interpreter."

Legitimate. Fatima advised that once inside the lobby of the hotel, she could shed the burqa. The hotel was an oasis in a desert of bedlam. She would be safe.

Her steps quickened as they approached the entrance, and if she could've skipped without tripping in her encumberment, she would have. "I'll be right back," she chirped and glided toward the ladies' room. After running into a stall, she stripped off the offender, letting it fall to the ground, an act which sent her glasses flying into the other stall. She reached across and grabbed the spectacles. Unconcerned with hygiene, she cared only about sanity. Then she reached up toward the ceiling, stretched, and inhaled.

Standing motionless for a good thirty seconds, she inhaled air that was an odd combination of lavender and Lysol and then quickly rolled the objectionable blue into a ball and stuffed it into her tote.

Thank you, Jesus! She inched her way to the mirror to see what remained of who she was. Wishing to splash concealer and makeup over her freckles, she let it go, figuring that Ishmael would want to get some rest.

When she reemerged, Ishmael was leaning against a pole, looking at his cell phone. "Okay, ready!"

"One second," he mumbled, then looked up distractedly.

Then something weird happened. One side of his mouth rose slightly, then he looked directly into Lottie's eyes as though she were an exhibit, which she supposed she kind of was, and then just as quickly redirected his gaze to the wall clock behind her. Puzzled as to why he could break the rules but she couldn't, she asked, "This is okay, right? I mean… Fatima said that I could remove the burqa once inside the lobby."

"No. I mean, yes! Of course, it's okay." He raked one hand through the lawn of black hair and glanced down at his Nikes. She wondered what exactly had come over this brazen stud of linguistics.

They shooed away the porters, and he maneuvered his suitcase and Lottie's suitcase and tote, as well as the camera bag under his arms and over his shoulders until he resembled a tree burdened with square fruit.

"Hey, I can help," she ventured, but he shook his head and wobbled to the elevator.

On the third floor, he collapsed in front of room 323, grabbed his bags, and dropped them in front of 325. "Okay, good night. CHar-lot."

"I thought we were going to debrief tonight. Ya know, talk about tomorrow?"

He rubbed his eyes and continued to avert them from hers. "I'm a bit tired. I'll see you at breakfast," he spluttered, then ran into room 325.

Lottie cocked her head and mentally revisited her earlier behavior. Clearly, she had offended him.

Rules, blasted rules, always evaded her. Even when she was a wee five-year-old in Sunday School, her teacher Miss Annabel, picked her up in her tiny preschool chair and carried her in it to her parents to report reprehensible behavior. In tenth grade, Mrs. Fitzmorris, her chemistry teacher, made her move to lab during class because she couldn't master the art, and it really was an art, of not talking.

Well, life presented many rules. Eventually, Lottie would either grasp them or perish by them.

Chapter Ten
Windows to the Soul?

At 3:20 a.m., the clock radio sang out unintelligibly. Was it jazz? Funk? Maybe an alto was belting out a tune on WWOZ? Lottie rolled over and smacked it. It continued. She rubbed her eyes and seriously considered brewing a pot of coffee and chicory before her clients started climbing the stairs and banging on her door. She tried to block out the sound, but it continued. Only…in Arabic. Not only that, but it grew louder.

I am dreaming. She sat up, blinked, and faced the window. It was dark but through the open blinds, she saw the sun's promise.

Lā ilāha illā-Allāh. There is no god but Allah. *Allāhu akbar.* Allah is greatest. *Allāhu akbar.* Again. *As-salatu Khayrun Minan-nawm.* Prayer is better than sleep.

That's it. I'm dreaming. She continued to rationalize, pushing hair out of her face, rubbing her eyes. Doors opened and closed, and she heard the shuffling of feet and the murmuring of voices, male voices. She felt the cool sheets, which could only belong to a hotel, with their bleachy scent and crisp status, and stared at the elaborate armoire in the room.

Then, she remembered.

No, I am not dreaming. The flight, the Hindu Kush, the brown landscape tiptoed through her sleepy head. Afghanistan? Yes. *That's it. I am in Afghanistan; more particularly, Kabul. I am in a chilly five-star hotel in Kabul.*

Ishmael? Ishmael. She met a man named Ishmael. Yes! He was her guide and interpreter. *And he's attractive.*

What she believed to be the clock radio and tunes from New Orleans turned out to be the *Azān*. It was mesmerizing even before sunrise, though she preferred to hear it much later. She rolled over and placed a pillow squarely over her head.

At 12:00 p.m., a similar scenario repeated itself: the blasted radio blared again, and this time, the sun screamed from the window. *Afghanistan. Kabul. Ishmael.* She ran down the list. As she did so, a loud knock shook her. "CHar-lot! CHar-lot! It's Ishmael." She shot out of bed, seized a thick robe from the closet near the door. Through the peephole, she confirmed it was, in fact, Ishmael, pacing outside her door; she removed the chain lock, and cracked it enough to look at him.

"What's up?" she asked and scratched her head. Her sleep breath reeked and rose to her nose. She placed a hand over her mouth.

"We were supposed to have breakfast, but you wouldn't awaken. So, now I'm back."

"Oh. Sorry. Why aren't you at prayers?"

"Shhhh." He looked around, up and down the hall.

"Okay. Give me a half an hour, and I'll be ready," she croaked.

Shuffling back into her hotel room, she slumped into the wingback by the window and let the sun beat up on her. By speaking without a filter, she had just blown another rule. Her stupidity astounded her sometimes. If she wasn't careful, it could cost Ishmael his life.

~ ~

Eating burqaless in the hotel restaurant was a treat, for she only had to select a scarf that she hoped would accentuate her blue eyes. Choosing the Monet Water Lilies scarf sufficed. Beneath it, a simple tunic and pants would do. Though this trip was fulfilling a lifelong dream as well as settling a beef, she dreaded donning the Dome of Domination again and having to view the market and the people through its porthole. Nonetheless, she resolved to follow the rules this time. She would not endanger herself or Ishmael by making stupid mistakes.

Over Tandoori chicken, they laughed about the muezzin awakening her twice. Ishmael seemed lighter, and she would wait until the conversation lulled to ask him about the abrupt exit last night. After the unobtrusive waiter slipped in the delivery of halwa and tea, she jumped in.

"Hey, can I ask you something?"

"You just did!" He was so proud of his American-style joke. *Hardee har.*

"Ha. So did I offend you last night? You kind of ran away." She looked into his eyes and noticed this time yellow flecks within the caramel. Butter, maybe? What would caramel be without it, after all? Only brown sugar. Under most circumstances, looking a man in the eye would be a no-no in Afghanistan, but they were surrounded by Westerners and Easterners, and she was a journalist, after all, and he her interpreter, so she went for it.

He stuck a fork into the halwa and twirled it. "No, madame. You didn't offend me."

Her shoulders relaxed. "Phew. I thought maybe I did something wrong."

He flashed perfect teeth, then looked onto his lap as if more answers rested there. "I was just…" The waiter came by with more tea. Ishmael ignored him. "I was simply enchanted by your beauty."

Putting both hands over her mouth, she tried to stifle a massive smile but knew her eyes would betray her anyway. After an American-looking guy—all smiles and bravado and self-assuredness—bumped into the table and apologized, she managed, "Wow. You're kidding. No one has ever given me a compliment quite like that." And it was true. Guys in the US gave her compliments like maybe "nice legs" or "beautiful smile," but never uttered anything amounting to this.

He continued, looking up and down, slightly embarrassed or shy, she couldn't tell. "And even in the States, to be honest, I just had never met anyone with your coloring, your hair and your eyes."

Full embarrassment circled, wanting to land, and in order to avert a splotch fest on her skin, she chirped, "Why, thank you! That's really sweet." Now she looked away from the candied eyes—at the table, at her lap, at the food—probably to the point of ridiculousness and wished very much to change the subject—and fast—back to the project at hand. After all, this was the last place she would allow the opposite sex to redeem itself.

It wasn't necessary.

"But anyway, that's all, and you're not here to be complimented and such. You have a mission." He stuck a forkful of halwa in his mouth and launched a crooked smile.

She could only cough and nod.

After the meal, they headed back into the garden, where they sauntered and retreated under a ficus, its umbrella offering a modicum of comfort from the punishing heat. She inhaled and stretched out her arms and surveyed it—nature harnessed by man, meant to be a sliver of heaven. Rumi, the Persian poet, drifted through her mind:

Out beyond ideas of wrongdoing
And rightdoing there is a field.

I will meet you there.

For a good ten minutes, they sat on the cast iron bench beside one another. Unfortunately, and with the help of the man sitting next to her, she was on a mission, one dubbed by the crew back in New Orleans as Operation Justice for Sadia.

Ishmael broke the stillness. "You seem far away."

"It's just… It's just so beautiful here. It feels like one of my soul's homes. Do you know what I mean? Like either it has resided here or it wishes to."

He surveyed the landscape and smiled as though satisfied. "I do. I really do. Of course, we *are* in a garden. It's supposed to be beautiful."

"True enough," she conceded.

"As you know, it's different beyond these walls."

"I do. I mean, I do. But can we just stay here? Forever?" Part of her wasn't kidding.

"I would very much like this, Char-lotte. But that's not why you came. To stay inside walls."

"You're right. You're right! I was just being dreamy."

"Gardens will do that to poets."

"What? How do you know that I'm a poet?" No one, not one, had ever referred to her as a poet—even the poets.

"Well, 'poet' can describe a certain personality, right? One who appreciates beauty? Feels things more deeply than the average man or woman? Didn't Gibran say, 'Poets see the whole' or something like that?"

Gently filling in the blanks, she recited one of her favorite Gibran verses. "Poetry is the understanding of the whole. How can you communicate to him who understands but the part?" Floating now on poetry and the garden and a scented, really good-looking exotic man, she commanded her soul to return to the role at hand.

Looking like someone up to something, Ishmael managed, "But, just to be honest, I googled you." He folded his arms and smirked.

"Oh, yes?" She didn't know whether to be flattered, nervous, or flattered and nervous, and prayed quickly that nothing too damning showed up.

"Several chapbooks of poetry?" Now he gleamed.

"Well, literature was my minor at the University of New Orleans, and I published a little poetry. But don't worry—I won't quit my day job. Ha." A little laughter followed.

"Well, that's good, because we have work to do."

Ishmael dug into his backpack and produced a file containing a close-up of the assailant. The target was quite handsome. Like the devil, probably. The first features to leap off the paper were his eyes, the color of nickel, standouts in a collection of blacks and browns, and they actually appeared kind, which infuriated her further. He also modeled the common thick beard and moustache, black with a drizzle of grays. Around his head sat a black-and-white-checkered keffiyeh, and he sat crossed-legged on a small rug in a hovel of pinks, reds, violets—folded fabrics. A merchant, she guessed.

"Abdullah?" she sniffed.

"Yeah. And listen. Just so you know, he hangs out with the warlords and Taliban creeps."

"What shall I ask him?" Lottie asked, already getting nervous.

"Well, you are a reporter telling the Americans how Afghans feel about the troops leaving, right?" he said matter-of-factly.

"Right."

"So, as your interpreter, I will ask his feeling about it and the future of the country. You just take notes."

She shivered violently at the thought of confronting Sadia's abuser and shook her head as if she could shake the whole idea away.

He nodded. "I know where he sits in the market. When do you want to leave?"

Rumi and the garden would have to wait until later. "Just let me grab my burqa," she said.

~ ~

Through the grilled aperture that she wished never to grow accustomed to, she could tell that the market was the happening place in town. Overwhelming her senses, golds and blues and reds jumped out, roasted lamb and vegetable scents assaulted, voices and bells beckoned. Stalls stood, one after the other, full of clothing, spices, fruits, and vegetables, rice, household items. Like a loyal and old friend, the Kabul River snaked alongside it, its flinty water dead in contrast to the life in the market.

Her stomach jerked and blue nylon dragged as she and Ishmael walked beside each other on the dirt path. As much as she had practiced, she must have appeared amateurish; but no matter, she was an American reporter, after all, if anyone asked. They passed several booths of merchants clad in *shalwar kameezes* and turbans, sitting beside or standing before their wares. In singsong Pashto, they beckoned.

Ishmael stopped abruptly in front of an ancient man encircled by bins of rust and orange and brown spices. The vendor smiled broadly with his remaining amber teeth. She could tell with a sideways glance that it wasn't her man and whispered, "I thought he was a fabric merchant?"

"Shhhh. He isn't. Our guy is two stalls down. Pretend to be interested in the spices."

She nodded and moved her viewfinder around like a nervous radar and pointed to a burlap bag of small seeds—coriander, maybe. Ishmael said something in Pashto and nodded, then handed the octogenarian cash. The merchant shoveled the seeds into a brown paper bag and handed it to him.

The next stall presented tchotchkes for the home, pain relievers and other items, like a drugstore. Lottie's adrenaline raced around beneath the sea of blue, turbulently, a cruel riptide. Her feet—swollen from the heat and stuffed into the flats like Vienna sausages—floated on electricity.

Jesus! Please don't let me faint. She prayed rotely as Ishmael gave her the "go" sign with a firm nod. They inched along, their behavior professing an interest in everything. Soon, the pinks, reds, and violets came into view.

Then, he—the target—appeared in her viewfinder.

Whether it was anger or anxiety didn't really matter, as either manifested itself in the form of a boneless body. Thank the Good Lord, he couldn't see her expression, which featured large, blinking eyes and lip biting. Behold! Another point for the burqa! Hiding ridiculous habits, facial tics, rolling of the eyes.

Ishmael said something in Pashto, which elicited a nod and a fiendish grin, so enamored the beast must've been to be interviewed by an American reporter, especially a female. The idiot said something.

Ishmael smiled and interpreted. "Ah, he wants to know…if you're American, why you are wearing the burqa."

She held up the edges like a bat and flapped. "Tell him that I wish to experience what a traditional Afghan woman does."

The knucklehead bowed happily, then murmured something in Pashto. Ishmael said, "He says it's good for a woman to cover."

Lottie was too nervous to give her knee-jerk, feminist response. In this guy's country, she would let it slide. Then she laughed internally. *As if I would say anything to him. Ha. I would end up in the river or be stoned.*

Ishmael presented the fake questions perfectly, just as they had discussed. Basic questions, like how an esteemed vendor such as himself felt about the future of Afghanistan, and in particular, Kabul. "He says that he thinks Kabul and all of Afghanistan has a great future."

Lottie brought up her right wing and scribbled in a tiny notebook. Then, she turned to Ishmael and asked him to hold the notebook and swung the camera that locked her further into the burqa around front. Holding up the camera, she gestured like a mime. Could she take his photo? For the story?

"Of course," Ishmael responded.

Holding up the camera in front of impaired eyes, she zoomed out to catch the kaleidoscopic material. The vendor grinned a tacky smile with khat-stained teeth, and she bowed and curtsied and made a hand gesture beneath the burqa that would make her momma blush.

Ishmael said, "*Ma salaama.*"

"*Ma salaama,*" replied the reptile. Then he asked something in Pashto.

"*Newsweek!*" Ishmael blurted out as they walked backward out of the booth, then turned and quick-stepped toward the river. Lottie's face would not be remembered, of course, but Ishmael's might. And this guy was a gangsta with turbaned gangsta pals. She liked this Ishmael and wanted him to be as protected in Afghanistan as Sadia was now in the States.

When they were about a block away, she held up a hand. "High five! Step one completed!"

Ishmael gave her a high five but grabbed her covered hand and held it for a few seconds.

Through the thin nylon, Lottie felt something she wished she hadn't.

~ ~

Before step two of Operation Justice for Sadia, Lottie had two days to see the sights. Did James Bond take sightseeing breaks? Probably not.

Seeing the Darul Aman Palace topped her list. It sat on the outskirts of Kabul like a defeated monarch, heavy head in lap. Thankfully, the US had little to do with its destruction. Instead, Afghanistan's own famed mujahideen destroyed it as they fought for turf in the mid-1990s. Ishmael would be the perfect companion as an accomplished tour guide, great interpreter, and feast for her eyes—what she could see of him, anyway.

They waited until noon prayers to leave.

The Toyota burped along a paved road leading to the palace, air conditioner cranked up to its fullest potential, of course. In the distance, a large structure appeared atop a barren hill. Even from a distance, the building appeared to be gnawed on by a giant rat, its corners jagged or missing. The formerly splendid cupolas were reduced to metal framework.

"Why do you want to see Darul Aman anyway?" he quizzed as they jostled. "Why not visit more beautiful sites, those more intact?"

"Valid question," she answered through the tent. "All my adult life, I have heard about Darul Aman from different sources." Looking out the window at the browns along the way, she continued, "It symbolizes not only Afghanistan's lost grandeur, but also its hope."

"I'm listening." He smiled.

"So, Kabul and Afghanistan cling to life by their fingernails. That the structure stands at all is a miracle."

"Ummmm. If you say so…"

"Hear me out. Darul Aman's stubbornness to not collapse entirely inspires me. From the expats I've formed close relationships with, I derivatively formed a vision of a restored country. One with human rights for everyone, especially women. And this great edifice will be restored one day. Mark my word!" She wondered if he could hear her smile.

"Well, I suppose you are an optimist, then?"

"Not exactly, but in this case—sure. I think I happen to be a mere poet who sees symbols wherever I go. Ha." It was true, if a little odd.

"You are mad!" He threw his head back and laughed.

"Mad? As in crazy? Maybe." She laughed. "I just have a vision of a beautiful, fully functioning Afghanistan."

Ishmael stopped the car and turned toward her. His eyes danced. Delicious and caloric candies. Dancing.

She looked away.

~ ~

Across rocks and rubble, they climbed to the entrance, Ishmael gently supporting her arm. Ocher weeds rose between the stones and reminded her of overprocessed hair. Ahead, defiant arches stood like determined sentinels. Hope must be protected, she imagined.

The only inhabitants, a handful of pigeons, flew up and away in protest. Her own breathing—which hissed hollowly against the nylon—and the flapping of wings were the only sounds. When they reached the structure, Ishmael grabbed her hand and weaved her through a colonnade like a schoolboy. She followed but intentionally loosened her grip until he released her hand. Beside them, bullet holes and graffiti festooned the interior walls.

"Bad decorator." Lottie laughed and tried to envision its former glory.

A cloudless sky stretched out above them as they stood in the interior courtyard. Again, as in the garden, they remained silent. Silence seemed to come naturally to them, which in her mind spoke volumes in a loud world. Or maybe it was an unspoken respect that they shared for the space, for the country, for each other? She knew that Ishmael could provide her with encyclopedic information, yet they both chose quiet.

Footsteps on the rocks broke up the quietude. That and the beatboxing of her heart. With Kalashnikovs drawn, two soldiers approached.

~ ~

"I need a Xanax," she said out loud and in English.

"Let me handle this." He patted her hand and probably said something like she did when pulled over for speeding. Something like: *Good day, Officer. Is there a problem?*

Overcooked noodle legs. Hyperventilation. All arrows pointed to a panic attack. She tried to suppress it. Beneath the fabric, she squeaked, "Jesus."

The guards' respective eyebrows were in the down mode. Not good. She winced. What could she and Ishmael have possibly done wrong? Were her ankles showing? No, impossible! What else could she possibly put on? She thought through her attire. Tunic?—check! Voluminous pants?—check? Socks?—check. Shoes?—check. Burqa over the whole lot?—check.

In Pashto, a discussion flamed. Ishmael's hands were out as though he was trying to reason with them. Or plead for his life? *My God. What have I done?*

Beneath the identity thief, she inhaled in and hissed out. The guards looked over at her and barked something. She did it again. Again, they looked at her. *This is it. This is the end.*

Ishmael said something, and the three encasements of testosterone busted out laughing. He pointed at her. *Great. I am the butt of more female jokes.* Her body seemed to relax, at least.

Within a few minutes and after more exhausting Pashto babel, the guards slung the Kalashnikovs over their shoulders and walked away. Ishmael came to her. Lottie collapsed onto a bench and said nothing. She'd be damned if she would continue to be the brunt of jokes again, by golly.

"What the hell was that about?"

He shrugged and flashed beautiful teeth.

"Well?" She folded her wings and humphed.

"Yo, chill. Isn't that what you Americans say?"

"Well, sometimes…but again I ask, what the hell was that about?"

"Mind your manners, Miss CHarlotte!"

"Pleeeeease?" She was not above groveling.

"Oh, that? They just said that next week, reconstruction of the palace begins and wondered if I knew it and that it would be closed. Happy?"

"Not exactly. They looked pretty scary. And angry."

"Could that be your imagination possibly?"

"Well, yes. I suppose so."

They began the dusty and rocky trek back to the Toyota, which sat forlornly beneath a new coat of grime.

"Can I ask you something?" he asked as they bounced along the road back into Kabul's belly, his café au lait face behind Ray-Bans.

"You just did?" *Touché, my Afghan friend.*

"When I grabbed your hand, why did you release mine?" She looked down through the hot screen into her steaming, layered lap, wanting to dig a hole through it and the bottom of the jalopy. "I know that you're here on business, so to speak, but I thought I felt a connection."

"Look, I appreciate your obvious interest, but I don't need a relationship at this point in my life." She paused and shifted in the cramped seat. "And I certainly don't need one across the world with an Afghan man." As the emphasis on *Afghan* left her nylon-filtered mouth, she regretted it, but there it was, out there like the dust and the heat and the patriarchy.

"Oh, I see. You think that we are all animals here. You put us in one big—how do you say?—bubble. We all want to dominate women, right?"

"I didn't say that. It's just that if you're steeped in your culture, how can you not be affected by it?" She deemed it a fair question.

"Wait a second. Aren't you a human rights activist? And isn't the core of human rights giving everyone a fair chance?"

Good point, she admitted, but this was Afghanistan, not Germany, not Japan, not Sweden. A country of men that was spawned by Taliban and mujahideen remnants. Afghanistan was an epicenter of patriarchy from which misogyny rippled.

"Well, yeah, sure. But anyway, even if I did sense a spark, I wouldn't start a relationship with a man across the world in any country. Better?"

"Sure."

Silence imposed itself again, only this time as a very awkward companion.

Chapter Eleven
Spreading the Word

The walnut and cherry trees seemed to welcome them as though waving thousands of shimmering leaves like tiny hands. Not to be upstaged, the apricot trees joined, shaken by the earth's warm breath. Water gurgled and coursed down a marble channel that ran from top to bottom of the man-made beauty, dropping several feet at each tier. Fountains sprayed and danced cheerily within every landing, inviting onlookers to splash in their coolness, though no one dared.

"Welcome to the Gardens of Babur, or Bagh-e Babur, as we like to say," Ishmael said in an overly professional tone. The sight, though, gave Lottie pause as her eyes scanned it. It was much more structured than City Park back home.

"Madame, these gardens were built by the Emperor Babur in 1528 AD." He waved one quite impersonal arm, releasing another bouquet of spice. Bergamot came to mind. She had smelled it once in a sumptuous triple-milled soap and loved it. Around the massive site, tourists posed for photos on steps and in front of trees and fountains. Meanwhile, Lottie and Ishmael were trapped in a stalemate, and she wondered how long it would last and whether it would ruin the operation.

And this, my friends, is why you don't get romantically involved with someone at your workplace.

Ishmael continued in an affected accent, as if to erase all traces of the West. "It was personally designed by the emperor himself. His full name was Ziihir ad-Din Muhammad Biibur." He pointed to the far end, his nose pointed upward and eyes away from hers, even if they were screened. "That, as you can see, is the mosque." She nodded pathetically, a mountain of blue, melting beneath the ambitious sun. "The mosque was built by Shah Jahan, who also commissioned the Taj Mahal."

It was difficult to concentrate amid Ishmael's cold shoulder—ripped as it was in an Apollonian way, but what could she do about the standoff? Certainly, lightning bolts struck her when the guy—this Ishmael—intentionally or accidentally touched her, but electricity alone did not a relationship make, and she was determined to honor her fast, trying as it may be. Distrust of men ordered her activities of late and fed her moods, and she couldn't, with one wave of a hand, rid herself of it.

It wasn't Ishmael's fault, so unaware was he of her sabbatical, and judging by his profound good looks, he probably hadn't faced rejection much either. Throw into the mix a conversion and freshly minted preference for Christian women, and he had a dire situation, one in which his odds of finding a sweetheart had dwindled exponentially. Add to all that the bonus of his probable interpretation of the "jilt" as an affront to his manhood.

Tomorrow would be the planned attack, after which Lottie would sail forth from Afghanistan on the 3:00 p.m. flight. She desperately needed Ishmael to be on board—the plan, not the flight, that is.

Gliding along in blue, Lottie felt like a phantom of nothingness. A nonentity. An erasure of a life. Then again, other blue nonentities dotted the landscape while their partners walked about in free-flowing and cool pants and even Wranglers, and she could leave the erasure behind when the plane took off. The temperature toddled around 90 degrees Fahrenheit, and the layers of clothing and sediment of anxiety added to her personal temperature that registered as hell.

"How long are you going to act like this?" There it was. She threw a stick of dynamite at the impasse and waited for it to detonate.

"Madame, I have no idea what you are talking about." He pulled it off poorly, this Adonis of Afghanistan, tantalizing tour guide. "Look, my aunt asked me to help you out. For her, I do it." He folded his arms dramatically, causing his biceps to advance unfairly in the battle. At an excessively attired disadvantage, Lottie couldn't even bat her eyelashes at him to make him laugh.

"Your aunt? Who's your aunt?" She adjusted her burqa and aimed it at his eyes, acutely aware of the danger. Ocular Kryptonite is what it was, his eyes.

"Well, I'm not going to tell you now. You've been so difficult." He turned his back to her, but Lottie could see his shoulders shaking.

"Oh, please. I promise to be a good girl!" she begged, muffled by the fabric prison.

"Hmmm. I don't think you really want to know. I can barely hear you." He shouted away from her, out into the impressive expanse. A couple turned toward them curiously and leaned into each other to comment, their small boy's big eyes gawking at them. Shouting English probably wasn't heard too often in those parts.

Lottie rolled her eyes, blew a thick sigh into the blue, and blared, "I saaaaaaid, I promise to be a goooood girl. Okay?" Then she grabbed his shoulders from behind and shook him. "Please tell me!"

"Fatima Hassan. You might know her. She is a professor at Tulane." He said it while hurling a pregnant smile at her, then stood back and waited for it to sink in. That took a few seconds, her mind treading in confusion.

"What? Your aunt is Fatima?" Lottie rubbed her chin with a covered hand and scanned him head to toe. "I mean, she never told me."

He shrugged.

Wow and wow.

Did this change the game? Probably not. Maybe. She didn't know. This beautiful creature whom she'd rejected as soon as the wheels touched the ground was related to a woman Lottie trusted literally with her life, just as she currently did with him. That Ishmael was Fatima's nephew gave him a bucket of credibility. That he not only got into the University of Chicago but excelled there gave him a barrel more of it. His position as a Christ follower and progressive spirit further appealed to something deep within. *Fast, Lottie, fast.*

On a branch nearby, two turtledoves alighted, their wings whistling alarmingly as if to warn her about love and commitment. *Run away! Run away!* That fluttering had always puzzled her. Alleged symbols of peace, when they flew, they screeched of acute fear instead of calm. Mates for life. Was that even possible?

"Yes, Miss CHarlot, I have visited your fair friend and your fair city. The French Quarter. Audubon Park. I even considered getting my master's degree from Tulane but decided to come back to try to contribute to my country."

A noble cause. That Lottie respected most of all and didn't know if she could do the same were she in his position. "Very, very cool," she muttered through the screen.

~~

Lottie was ready for the muezzin call this time. Armed with her own arsenal of prayers, at 3:23 a.m., she unfurled the tangle of sheets, then rolled in one awkward movement down to the bedside, where she knelt, three-quarters asleep.

If you can't beat them, join them, right?

As she prayed on a regular basis, especially when she needed help, she didn't feel the need to officially commit to the five-times-a-day prayers. Mind you, she wouldn't roll out a rug and go through ablution, and her prayers often featured requests more than anything else, but at least she sent up some form of communication throughout the day—while in traffic, when remembering a sick friend, while appreciating the sunset over Lake Pontchartrain.

In her predawn mist, she beseeched God for protection, common sense, and his blessing in the endeavor. *Why should he bless it, though? Is it a righteous act?*

She wouldn't dare allow herself the luxury of that declaration, as something about it felt presumptuous and unholy. But could she deem it a half-righteous act? Or better yet, a tiny righteous act? A little something that she could physically do—as the hands and feet of God—and on behalf of her scarred and deflowered friend forced to leave her home?

Justice witnessed firsthand was what it was. Justice about which she could report to Sadia, not to mention the kind that might throw a wet blanket on the bonfire of anger within her.

From the time Lottie could utter *Dear God* or *Dear Heavenly Father* or *Dear Jesus*, she was taught that in order to approach the Creator, the only holiest of all entities, she had to first clear the air, confess imperfections before even thinking about entreaties.

Dear God,

I've done a lot of wrong in my life. Please, please, forgive me. Like, I can be self-righteous, Lord knows—I mean, you know. I can be rebellious, mean-spirited sometimes. Please help me to do better.

Please be with Louisa Mae back home and all my dear friends and family members.

And, um…what I am about to do, can you please forgive me for that too? I don't want to make excuses, but I kinda feel like I am righting a wrong.

In Jesus's name, Amen.

Preemptive or advanced forgiveness. Was that even allowed?

The world, of course, witnessed righteous acts regularly, without realizing it. God using people to enact justice, to right a wrong. The organization that busted up brothels in Thailand and rescued young girls came to mind. Another example: the nonprofit that redeemed slaves in Sudan—it was controversial, but not to the rescued.

And obviously, Sadia had already been "redeemed" and settled safely in the US, so Lottie once again questioned the excessiveness of the plan. *No. I don't wonder—I pretty much know it is excessive.* But it wasn't like God was against justice—it was just, in the case at hand, Lottie wasn't an officially sanctioned court or law enforcement officer. On the contrary, she was a rogue human rights attorney and women's rights activist who was fed up.

Sleep did not return after the prayers. But the jitters did. She tried to be still—to imagine safe success.

Peeking out the window and beyond the protective cement barriers that guarded Kabul Serena, she saw again men in turbans and tunics shuffling into the nearby mosque. A few Taliban types fed into the swarm, and she prayed she didn't bump into them later.

A light tap on the door shook her—hard. Had they discovered her? She prayed she wasn't worth missing *Fajr*, the predawn prayers. She grabbed the robe, peeked through the hole, and exhaled. Ishmael. What did he want at this hour? She cracked the door. "Hi," he whispered. "I can't sleep. Can I come in?"

The unorthodoxy and danger of the moment—simple but not so simple—gripped her, and she glanced quickly up and down the hall. A single man and woman together in a hotel room would render a quick stoning in the streets. She envisioned being buried up to her freckled neck and facing a fierce mob armed with rocks. No matter that she was a "reporter." She didn't think for one second they would take the time to inquire before administering a summary judgment of death.

"Okay, hurry." He entered quickly and slowly shut the door. The click was louder than she hoped, and within seconds, other doors opened and shut too. The men were returning from prayers.

"What in the world?" Lottie whispered, forcing Ishmael's eyebrows to descend. "Another American expression." She pushed back a curl. "Can I make you some tea?" She grabbed the pot of the hotel coffeemaker and filled it with water. "So, what's up?" She feigned more control than she had. "You gettin' nervous? I know I am."

He dropped into the generic chair by the window and looked down at his bare feet—long toes frothed with a few dark hairs stood out—then fiddled with his terry-cloth robe, which, thankfully, covered everything. The coffeemaker gurgled to life.

"Yeah. I guess so. I was just thinking if they find out that it's me, they will kill me." His soft eyes seemed to awaken and dart about, which twisted her heart. It was true, and she knew it.

A couple of male voices thundered outside the door. Why weren't they back asleep already?

Ishmael held up a hand and shushed her.

Chapter Twelve
The Guilt Alone Will Kill You

For several minutes, they froze in place. Lottie even refused to exhale.

After the brief postprayer banter, the voices separated, then disappeared altogether.

"What were they saying?" she whispered while visions of *let's drag them out and stone them* danced in her brain.

"They were talking about a business meeting later. That's all." He looked out the window and rubbed a stubble-free chin.

She walked sock-footed over to the coffee pot, her legs regaining a modicum of feeling. After pouring two cups of water, she pinched the tea leaves and dropped them into the cups, then dropped a chunk of cardamom in and followed up with two scoops of sugar. A YouTube video had prepared her for this tea-making moment, though she didn't expect it to arrive predawn. She delivered a steaming cup to him, but he placed it on the adjacent table, then stabbed his fingers into his dark-as-midnight hair.

"What have I done to you, my friend?" She said it in a low voice and hoped he didn't hear her.

But he did. "I don't know. It's not you. It's me. Maybe I'm not as brave as we both thought I was…"

Guilt sat on one of her shoulders and joined selfishness on the other. "I'm so sorry."

Crazed by her own idea of vengeance, she had made and continued to make insane choices. Worse, she enlisted innocents in her scheme, when it was clearly her own mental issue.

Justice, as it turned out, did not always have to be enforced—it was optional. The damage to Sadia had already occurred, the knife already sliced. It wasn't as if Sadia could have stopped that cruelty. And wasn't starting over in the States with so much promise the best revenge of all? Wasn't it sufficient?

The sun again teased with grays and pinks. In a couple of hours, it would morph into a solar warlord, as threatening as any radical. Ishmael gazed out the window, and his reflection looked empty—no, defeated.

"You're right, Ishmael. This is stupid and unnecessary," she whispered and placed her hand on his slumped shoulder.

"I'm the one who should be sorry. Please forgive me." Shame radiated from him just as guilt did from her. He wouldn't even look her way, this brazen and proud Afghan man reduced to what? A mere mortal?

"What have I done?" Lottie sputtered and shuffled around the carpet in fuzzy socks of red and green left over from Christmas—not the sexiest, but they did the trick. For being in such a sweltering locale, the room was downright arctic.

Lottie returned to him and replaced her hand on his shoulder, ignoring its unpolished nails and the electricity running through it. *Look at us, two very human humans in our hotel robes—not so brave after all.* His long copper fingers tapped his knees as if banging out a tune, and she could tell that his engine still revved in contemplation. Neither touched the tea.

The clock radio read 3:50 a.m. when he jumped out of the chair. "No. I'm going to do this!" Standing up straight in his robe, shoulders squared, he appeared darker against the bleached fabric. "This is what I want to do.

What he did to her was awful and what men get away with in this country is not right. We've got to start somewhere. That's why I came back—to change things." He looked down at her jumble of hair, then at and into her sleep-deprived eyes. "My aunt told me that she was quite beautiful."

"She still is." Her stomach twitched. What was that? No way could she be jealous; it wasn't possible, nor would it be justified. Lottie resolved the matter once and for all. Besides, any iota of a chance was erased when she jerked away from Ishmael at the palace or when she proclaimed her unavailability. Frankly, any contemplation about it at all was ridiculous anyway. She stood tall and tightened the belt on her robe, then looked down at her merry socks. "Are you sure you want to do this?"

"Yes." He grabbed Lottie's shoulders and moved in close, so close that she could inhale his morning breath, which didn't bother her one bit. Closing her eyes automatically, waiting, she heard a hearty "High five!" then opened her eyes, observing his hand awaiting hers. She gave it a good slap.

At noon, when others filed into the mosque for the *Zuhr*, they marched in the opposite direction, upstream from the Devoted, toward Ishmael's office down the block. The stone exterior managed to keep it somewhat cool in the midday oven. As soon as they entered the two-room space, Lottie closed the door behind her, threw off the smothering garment, and placed a basket of pears and apples on a chair. On his desk, she spotted brochures offering tours of the city and countryside and Ishmael's business cards. She couldn't help but wonder why a graduate of a fine university was tour guiding when he could probably be president of Afghanistan, but immediately admonished herself for such a smug thought. *It's not like I'm the managing partner of Baker McKenzie, the famous immigration law firm.*

They worked side by side—first at the computer, then the printer, which enthusiastically shot out a large stack of colorful fliers. In silence, they gathered the contraband, then stuffed all of them except one into his briefcase. Lottie folded the single sheet, then placed it beneath the fruit in the basket. Taking a simultaneous deep breath and blowing it out, they looked at each other and held the gaze for many seconds before she threw her "uniform" back on and they left the office.

Ishmael knew of a building in the bosom of Kabul with roof access. It was nearly vacant due to prayer time, save for an elderly janitor in the lobby pushing a mop in small circles. They nodded in acknowledgment, then glided toward the elevators. Inside the elevator, Lottie looked over at Ishmael as best as she could manage and admired his handsomeness in the *shalwar kameez*, which he hadn't yet worn in her presence. The elevator button dinged, and they exited onto the twelfth floor, then dashed into the stairwell leading to the roof.

Pushing open the roof door, they marched into the sunlight, which began to bake her immediately. She lifted the burqa, let it sit atop her curls, then grabbed his arm. "Look, I just want to say thanks and…it's been a pleasure getting to know you. If you ever return to the States, look me up." This time, she meant it.

"I will." Ishmael hugged her fiercely, then slowly pulled back. The caramel weapons looked her in the eyes, and she felt tears stinging. *Great, Lottie.* "You ready?" She nodded weakly as he pulled the stack of leaflets out and handed half to her.

They had to act quickly before someone decided to come on the roof after prayers, to smoke a cigarette or escape an overbearing boss and before

Lottie chickened out.

"On the count of three," she squeaked. "One... Two... Three!" Leaning over the edge, they released the papers, which twisted and turned and floated slowly to the ground, carried like petals by a rare and divine breeze. A few clumped together and spiraled downward.

Men, women, and children dotted the streets then, prayers having ended. All looked skyward, searching for the origin of the confetti as they pulled back from view. When the papers stopped floating downward, the recipients began to pick them up, reading them, showing them to other bystanders.

Ishmael and Lottie exited the roof—blue and white blurs—and ran down the long flight of stairs to the lobby. She re-covered with the burqa, and he led her by the arm through the crowd on the street. He grabbed a leaflet off the ground, admiring his handiwork, showed it to her aperture, then let it fall back to the earth.

ABDULLAH DAWOUD IS AN AMERICAN SPY
HE WORKS FOR THE CIA

Beneath the accusation, a colorful glossy photo of Abdullah appeared, arms wrapped around a US soldier. Murmuring spread in the streets like a wildfire, ablaze with distrust and anger. Some recipients of the paper shook fists in the air; others gasped. The few burqaed women present gathered, their heads leaning in toward each other. A conservative man sporting traditional Taliban gear—turban, *shalwar kameez*, a long beard—grabbed the paper from a small child. He waved over other similarly dressed men and headed in the general direction of the market.

Lottie found an adolescent and handed him the basket, while Ishmael said something in Pashto like "Brother, will you please bring this basket to the man on this paper." Ishmael pulled out the sheet and pointed to

Abdullah. The boy smiled and held out his hand. Nothing was free in Afghanistan, so Ishmael dug into his pocket and pulled out an afghani and placed it into the dirty hand. Beneath the lowest apple in the basket, they hid a greeting card of sorts that read: For Sadia. *Alhamdulillah.*

They would never know if the recipient got the message, but they knew the crowd did. Ishmael firmly grabbed Lottie's arm, and they ran around the corner and jumped into the sad but faithful Toyota, which would take them to the airport.

Chapter Thirteen
Brief Debrief

Louisiana from twenty thousand feet used to look like a fine and verdant boot with long marsh appendages reaching out into the Gulf of Mexico and interspersed with hundreds of inlets and clandestine waterways where pirates like Jean Lafitte would hole up and hide their booty. The marsh itself was a wild hodgepodge of thick grasses and grand cypresses, inhabited by coyotes and beavers and mink or nutria and any kind of shorebird one could imagine. This was until the state sold its own marshy soul to benefit the rest of the oil-grubbing US and allowed the construction of pipelines, which gnawed on the wetlands with their salty teeth and continue to do so to this day. Salt water devours marsh grass, and marsh grass is the glue that binds the wetlands, and as the salty tide munched on the wetlands, the state also lost a wonderful buffer from tropical depressions and storms and hurricanes. Enter Miss Katrina, Miss Category Whatever circa 2005, heading straight for the nibbled-on toes of the "boot" and which sailed in without any natural bulwark to stop her aggression and voilà! You've got yourself a real problem. So when Lottie flew over her homeland, she saw what appeared to be a moth-eaten sock where a strong and solid boot should be. She wanted to stitch it up with the yarn of remorse and sew up the wetlands with hard work and freshly planted marsh grass, but rebuilding that toe at this point was almost beyond hope.

All this Lottie contemplated as she flew over it again and the airplane approached Louis Armstrong International. The mourning of Louisiana's coast mingled with an acute desire to enter a hyperbaric chamber to decompress from her initial voyage into the burqa world, and by the time the wheels skidded onto the stunted and more-like-a-driveway runway, she had disrobed of patriarchy, stripped off misogyny, removed anything designed by angry men who manipulated a world religion to retain control. Anything beyond her elbows and knees went *salaam* and *adiós*. She even went so far as to remove her watch, necklace, and earrings, stripping off any shackles of fashion, be it Eastern or Western. Anything deemed unnecessary, just shy of being obscene, Lottie wanted gone. If she could have deplaned buck naked, she might have. Granted, she was swapping one sweltering place for another, but this was *her* sweltering place, *her* humid hometown, *her* sticky comfort zone. Here, no one cared whether you covered your arms or your eyes, and in some of the wards, they didn't even care if you covered your derriere. Especially on Bourbon Street. Especially during Mardi Gras.

Forced by languishing security guards to circle the airport several times in her blue Dodge Ram pickup—black-and-gold Saints flag flapping from its snout—Louisa Mae made it a point to express her distinct displeasure to Lottie. The pickup in the pickup was a must because its bed was the size of a small Central American country, able to accommodate a heap of luggage. They agreed that Mini Pearl might be inadequate.

"I'm sorry, dawlin'. Immigration gave me a hard time about traveling to Afghanistan. Imagine that! Can you say redheaded terrorist?" Lottie spoke into her reignited cell phone, trudging through the undercarriage of the airport, across waves of hotel-shuttle-generated diesel fumes, stacks of taxis waiting expectantly, and strands of frustrated drivers forced to revolve around the airport like cars on a Ferris wheel.

Lou assaulted the bags and lobbed them into the back, then wrapped Lottie in her strong arms, causing Lottie to expel a *whoosh* and gasp for air. Ironically, Lou's hugs deflated her lungs while actually raising her endorphins, because they were the best on the planet. Lottie had missed her best pal and inwardly berated herself for not bringing her to Kabul, imagining the two of them in burqas tripping and giggling about it and mocking patriarchy and scoffing at peril. A South Asian Thelma and Louise, or Louisa, as the case may be. Better yet, Lou might have distracted Lottie from the temptation embodied in Ishmael—strong and well-kept body and soft eyes—which threatened her resolve more than the Taliban.

"Oh. My. Gosh!" Lou's voice reached an upper register that she usually reserved for such excitement, though, if you factored that in with her Italian tendencies, arose with great frequency. "I can't believe I just picked you up from a flight from Afghanistan. Hell, I'm not even sure where that is! You so crazy, girl." She adjusted her rearview and turned down the radio, which blared a Journey song on the Good Times Rock-n-Roll station. "And damn, you look good! In spite of traveling across the world. How is that even possible?"

Lottie knew the question was rhetorical, but managed a less than enthusiastic response anyway. "Thanks, sweetie, but I am exhausted."

"Baby, you can sleep when you get home, ya heard? I had the cleaning lady come by and put fresh sheets on the bed and clean the place up. It was a mess, by the way." Lottie thanked her and looked forward to a thorough shower, washing away with suds any and all memories of nylon, then getting between cool sheets, if she made it that far.

They joined the throng of vehicles slogging along the airport circle, then sped onto the access road, merging with other Louisiana-license-plated and Saints-stickered cars. "Hey, baby. Look..." She smacked the horn at a taxi that almost forced her off the road and held it for a good five seconds. "Jackass! What an idiot!" then returned to Lottie without missing a syllable. Lottie nodded faintly, too fatigued to be bothered with it. "I been thinking. If those emails continue, I am going to contact the NOPD. In fact, I may do it anyway." Struggling to keep her eyes open, Lottie could only nod again and wave an unenthusiastic hand. She guessed that Louisa Mae had had some time to chew on that thought while she was gone. Lou was fuming—downright in flames—not uncharacteristic when she entered protective mode, which could be both good and scary. "You know, I know people." Yeah, Lottie knew that. Lou was connected, all right—to a colorful array of other "watchful" types and definitely had, as her people liked to say, *amici*.

Within fifteen minutes, they pulled up to the condo and ran up the exterior stairs and dropped the bags just inside the front door. Lou promised to be in touch and said something about a manicure, jumped back into the pickup, and hobbled down the warped street. The condo swaggered with bleach and Pledge and an unidentifiable scent that Lottie could never achieve when she cleaned. She puttered into the kitchen, opened the fridge as she automatically did on the rare occasions that she had the place professionally cleaned. The refrigerator shelves reflected like mirrors, and the egg container was no longer painted in egg yolk. Too tired to fully appreciate it, she wobbled to her bedroom, where she found Frank sprawled across the bed, pink pads up, gray tummy facing the ceiling.

"Kitty!" Lottie purred in that ridiculous articulation that owners use to address their pets. "Mommy missed you."

She rubbed his belly, which spread out like a flattened water balloon, appreciating the sedate softness and watching the fur make weird designs as she went against the grain. "Kitty?" Frank was a talker who always responded to Lottie's touch with at least a squeak; that he didn't respond was highly unorthodox. Maybe he had sympathy jet lag. "Frank?" She smiled and scratched under his chin and along his whiskers. When he still didn't respond, she stared at his chest until she saw the sweet rising and falling of his breaths. *Thank you, God. But still…*

"Frank!" She shook him again and stared wide-eyed at the gray clump while her blood sprinted from her big head to her big feet and back again. Finally, he lifted his head weakly. "Hey, buddy. Are you okay?" she muttered maternally, which finally produced a faint meow. Something was wrong, and her gut told her that she should contact the vet right away, that it wasn't just a cold or a bug, nor was it kitty lethargy. "Please God, fix my kitty," she half prayed and half screeched.

Punching Doctor Cat's number into her cell phone, Lottie paced as one could only after traveling across the planet: like a zombie, but with limbs still attached. "Hi, this is Lottie Fornea. Something's wrong with my cat, Frankie. He's super lethargic. Well, I mean more than normal. He's four. Eating? I don't know, I just returned from a week of traveling. Right now? Okay, great. Thanks."

She ended the call. "Come on, kitty. We're going to the doctor," she whispered then carried his limp body into the tidy and dust-free living room and placed him into the carrier like a porcelain doll, an act that normally would've produced claws of revolt. In a mist of panic and jet lag, she strapped the carrier into the front seat of Mini Pearl, threw it into Sport mode, and dodged potholes the size of moon craters all the way to Tchoupitoulas Street, where Doctor Cat's one-story building sat two blocks away from Doggie Plaza, an upscale doggie day-care facility. Even ablur, she thought nervously, *if they here can coexist side by side, why can't we?*

The techs convinced Lottie not to follow Frank into the examination room. Doctor Cat would do a full blood panel and examination and call her later. The female veterinary assistant only offered, "He don't look so good." Lottie smiled miserably and thanked her, though she thought the editorial unnecessary and unhelpful.

As though on automatic, Mini Pearl sailed down the smoother Tchoupitoulas, turned right on Nashville, left on Magazine, then right into the parking lot of Audubon Park, where Lottie stumbled out of her and shuffled on over to her peaceful place—a stone bench across Bird Island. Situated in the swampy lagoon, it was aptly named because it served as a rookery for flocks of migrating birds, most notably orange-beaked whistling ducks. It was a place where she could just be herself, or just be, didn't have to necessarily think about anything, though, with her jumbled thoughts, often did. And just for such drive-bys, Lottie stored bird seed in the trunk, which, in the humidity and if not dispensed quickly, would sprout into sunflower and corn and millet crops. The rattle of the seed bag signaled in Pavlovian style to the ibises that descended en masse, while mallards with their iridescent heads and funny mannerisms sailed forth and waddled over. The singular swan motored toward her and honked and hissed for treats and even tried to nibble on her shoe. "Hey, stop, you!" Alerted by Ducks & Co., turtles followed in the murky water, approaching from all directions, little submarines with two-holed periscopes. Normally, this symbiotic relationship, this caring for her fellow creatures, nursed her emotional wounds, but this time, she couldn't get Frankie off her mind.

Dear God, please don't let him die. He's so sweet. Please don't take him from me. Her OCD kicked in hard until she was sure she sounded like a short-circuited robot as she rocked and threw seed mindlessly to the birds and repeated *Dear God, please don't let him die. He's so sweet and such a blessing.*

Please don't take him from me. Not yet. An ibis moved next to her with his colleagues and reminded Lottie of old Eastern European businessmen at the market. Each cocked his or her head and with one crystalline blue eye, spied the bag in her hand. "Oh, okay. Here ya go, sirs." They took turns snatching seeds from her open palm with their comma beaks and toddled back and forth on Jurassic Park feet. One side of her mouth lifted briefly, but quickly sank again.

Sleep chased Lottie like the birds, pecking, squawking, tempting. She found herself half crying, half sleeping until she nodded, then caught herself, then nodded again until she stopped, and everything got weird.

She approaches Ishmael inside the palace, where he stands shirtless and ripped inside the formerly glorious structure with a baby swaddled against his firm and hairless chest. With one hand, he supports the bundle; with the other, he shields it from the nagging sun like a good daddy. She smiles at him and floats inside his soft, smiling eyes.

She reaches up to adjust her burqa, but instead finds a bridal hijab, white and pearly and gorgeous, covering her red hair. On the bottom half, a pair of Levi's jeans hugs her hips tightly. She reaches for the baby, and Ishmael hands over the bundle. She lifts the fabric, which is baby blue and nylon; inside, she sees Frank, mouth open, blood trickling out of the corners.

Lottie startled and jumped up, shaking and wiping water from her eyes and drool from the corners of her mouth.

Back in difficult reality and on an equally unforgiving bench and surrounded by feathers and seed, with tingling fingers she punched in a text to Lou. *Something is wrong with Frankie. Please pray! He's at...* But midsentence, the phone chirped and displayed Doctor Cat's number. "Hello. Yes, this is Lottie Fornea. How's Frank?" She jumped up, generating a white plume and a squawking cloud skyward. "What? Rat poison? Are you sure?" Lottie ripped into her thumbnail, which had just grown an astonishing millimeter, oblivious to her latest attempts at femininity and a no-bite policy. "Can you save him?" She gulped, now a buoy in a turbulent ornithological sea, the birds having decided it was best to follow her. "You induced vomiting, Okay… Oh, thank God. When can I get him? A day or two? Okay. Thank you so much!"

Thank you, God! Elated by this gift, Lottie blurted out to her entourage, "Come on, y'all, Frankie's going to be okay!" They tottered and waddled deliriously behind her, an unusual second line, back to the bench, where she threw a celebratory handful to the flock and likewise to the turtles, who still waited patiently in their hilarious queue in the water. Even the usual whiff of biodegradation smelled heavenly just then.

Lottie texted her best human pal while throwing seeds and dried fruit out into the murky lagoon *They said he must've gotten into rat poison, but he's going to be okay.* With each of Lou's suspicious texts, Lottie could see her throwing Sicilian arms into the air, wanting to take someone out. The conversation went something like this:

Lou: *But do you even have rat poison?*

Funny, Lottie had never thought of that, so fuzzy was the state of her brain from the trip and the Frank emergency and the unintentional nap. Had she once, years ago?

Lottie: *Gee I don't know I don't think I've ever purchased any maybe Mister George did he likes to take care of me LOL*

Lou: *I don't like it something is fishy*

Lottie: *What do you mean?*

Lou: *I think someone poisoned Frankie intentionally (angry emoji attached, eyebrows down, red face)*

Lottie: *Seriously?*

Lou: *Yeah seriously*

Lottie: *Nah cmon I think ur being a tad paranoid anyhoo you wanna come over tonight for drinks? I'm exhausted but i would love to talk to you*

Lou: *Sur, baby*

Lottie: *KK see you soon*

~ ~

As the curtain to lucidity lifted and Lottie's brain attempted a strong performance, she could see that Lou had a point. She never had a problem with rats because (a) she had—*has*—a cat; and (b) had an exterminator who came regularly. Like most felines in love with their significant human other, Frank often brought her gifts d'amour: mice, sparrows, and, on one very rare occasion, a rat. Never had she purchased poison—didn't even know where to purchase it or what it might look like on the shelf—nor did she know anyone who had. As it turned out, cockroaches were the pest du jour—*toujours vraiment!*—in New Orleans, full-time natives of her soggy town, who would fly at you kamikaze-style if you tried to thwack them with your shoe or a rolled-up newspaper.

So then, what could have happened? Maybe Mister George had taken it upon himself to pursue extermination, taking the time to go to Walmart and purchase it, then strategically place it in a spot where the disease-carrying, swear-inducing rodent was spotted, scuttling and scampering on her hardwoods. However, and this was a big however: though no Einstein, Mister George wasn't a dummy either. Surely he would have realized that Frankie could get into it as well as any rat.

And if what Louisa said were true—that someone, in fact, tried to poison Frankie, that someone intentionally put it in his Friskies, then what on earth would the motive be? Her frontal lobe worked overtime, tap dancing, shuffling, and soft shoeing, and had just about moved into a full-blown jazz tap complete with wide arm circles, a mental Lindy Hop, when Lottie connected the poisoning with the "blasphemy" emails—the ones she'd dismissed so cavalierly. She had put on a brave face in front of Louisa, though she needn't; she could display all her freckles, warts, and wrinkles to her friend, and she wouldn't judge or tease. Maybe the brave face was to convince her. Maybe now Lottie would give more attention to the emails and investigate allahdefender@yahoo.com.

She flew home in Mini Pearl with the jitters tailgating her, glad it was only a half mile away, and trying half-wittedly to avoid death by potholes, the wide-mouthed, sharp-toothed monsters lying in wait for Pearl, the same ones that morphed into mosquito condos after a heavy rain. *Got Zika? Got malaria?* Still overcast from the trip and the Frank trauma, Lottie scuffed up the old but sturdy steps to her condo, eyes wide open, scanning the roots and stems of her small world for clues, or worse—predators.

In an unusual fit of caution, she flipped the dead bolt behind her and whisper-shouted, "Hellooooo. Hellooooo." She removed her well-traveled flats, the tread worn bald by adventure, and placed them quietly on the hardwood floor, then slid around in her socks. "Hallllloooowwww." She peeked in corners, under the sofa, behind her desk, but discovered nothing out of place. She grabbed the broom from the utility closet in the hall, tiptoed into one bedroom, then the other, flipped up bed ruffles with gusto, and expected what—a very skinny perpetrator? A few fossilized fur balls and dusty tumbleweeds reminded her that no cleaning person was perfect and also that she must sweep when she turned off her detective switch. She then moved into the cozy-living-room-slash-office-lobby, slapped at the burlap curtains, and lifted them, happy to find no one or nothing lurking.

Like a kung fu champion, she kicked and chopped the shower curtain in the bathroom and discovered nothing but a sparkling and bleachy tub.

Satisfied with the absence of other fauna, Lottie reentered the bedroom, her best temple and the one place on the cockeyed planet where she could be grateful for her good fortune and stare at her pretty things and almost forget Evil. Almost. She locked the door and fell face-first onto the fluffy comforter, admiring the smell of fabric softener, thankful again for Lou's gift of the cleaning lady. Her eyes, pregnant with sleep, gave birth.

Weird. She woke up back in Afghanistan. In Kabul again. Wait. Kabul but also in New Orleans. Jackson Square surrounded her, but also downtown Kabul with *shalwar kameez*-wearing men on mopeds swerving down dirty streets. Women in blue burqas formed a dance line in the Square and kicked in synchronization like the Rockettes. Ishmael was with her again, and she held a baby—this time of human form—with beautiful walnut skin and hair the color of wild cherries. She rocked her back and forth, sang a lullaby to her in Arabic. This must be heaven, she thought. *It has to be.* She swam in Ishmael's eyes, feeling more love than she could ever recall. More love than Bettie and Jake gave her, more than past loves. She leaned forward to kiss him, squishing with love the bundle between them. Something soft rubbed against her legs. She glanced down and saw Frank weaving between her and Ishmael's ankles. He purred softly and looked up at her with amber eyes. She leaned over and scratched under his chin. The happiness seemed present yet eternal. Someone knocked loudly, but she couldn't find the door, couldn't find the big wrought iron gate to and from the Square. Or was it a curtain door that she sought? The knocking grew louder.

"Coming!" Lottie heard herself shrill, still floating in rapture colored by her own subconscious crayons, and must've found the door or curtain—

whatever it was—because Lou was in Jackson Square with her—no, she was beside her on the bed.

"Baby! You okay?" Lou pushed a springy coil out of her face and stared at her with those midnight-colored eyes that always shook with emotion of some variety. Lottie was certain that she was a fright for the senses with certain bedspread wrinkles traversing her cheeks and coordinating with the circles and pillows under her eyes and with an arid mouth that made her tongue stick to her gums.

In Lottie's mind, three images lingered from the dream and vied for cerebral center stage: Ishmael's delicious smile and embrace; the baby that had to be hers given the red hair; and a healthy and contented Frank. Lou's natural question wanted to butt into her fantastical thoughts and succeeded. "Whoa. Yeah. I'm okay. I think. Good dream." Lottie smiled as though she had consumed too many Sazeracs and nursed a love hangover, but her condition didn't require a Bloody Mary. If anything, she wanted more of *liquor d'amour*. She wiped her eyes and forced herself to recall exactly where she was and who she was. *I am Lottie Fornea, daughter of Bettie and Jake Fornea. I am in my bedroom, in my condo on Leontine Street. My best friend, Louisa Mae Fiorini, is with me.*

"Who is Ishmael? You called out to him. Sorry. I could hear you through the door. I couldn't get you to open it."

"Sorry. I don't know. Wow. Crazy, right?" Lottie counted it a blessing that Lou apparently didn't know her Afghan operative's name and rubbed her head, which still blurred with the hurdle of time zones and divergence of cultures, not to mention a certain ill feline and his condition, but nothing of it could make her forget the dream. In it, she felt wrapped in indescribable warmth and still did, and she wondered if Ishmael thought of her at all. Probably not. The trick would be hiding the impossible infatuation, which was what it was, from her friend, who knew her better than she knew herself.

"Let me make you some chicory, ya heard?" Yeah, Lottie heard and even listened and watched Lou disappear from the bedroom, and something in the process made her miss Frank too, because she knew he would pad after her and meow and grunt and beg for a scratch. Lottie lay back down and hugged her pillow, still consumed by love, or at least love imagined or concocted or fantasized. Within ten minutes, Lou returned with a steaming mug of coffee with cream and sugar. "Just the way you like it...tan and sweet, like your men!" Lottie shot her a look, wondering if her telepathic switch was in the On position and Lou was interpreting her every utterance or lack thereof. "I know. I know. No men currently. I gotcha. Just jokin', baby!" Lou spoke the latter nervously, and rarely did she say anything nervously, which meant that deep below the surface, more gurgled.

Lottie took a sip and blinked, deeply tucked within the fluff and comfort of her festive sanctum. "This is good. Thanks, boo." She turned slowly and surveyed the apricot wall, the large oil painting of Mardi Gras Indians dancing in feathers and beads and sequins on a foggy Mardi Gras morning. She smiled at the fringe on her Roman shades, which jingled with silver-ball borders. "There's a crack on that wall." Lottie pointed at a four-inch crack on the far wall zigzagging just above the painting and threatening to swallow it. It happened regularly, the paint and plaster expressing anger at their below-sea-level existence with all its shifting accoutrements.

Lou nodded sadly. "Baby, he's gonna be okay. The doctor caught it quickly."

"But why would anyone hurt him? He's the sweetest cat ever." Lottie could feel the wheel of emotions spinning again and landing on sadness.

Her eyes began to fill like the streets of Nola after a shower, and her nose began to sting at the tip. Lou ran to the bathroom instinctively and grabbed a yard of toilet paper and threw it at her. "I mean, I feel like it's my fault," Lottie blubbered. She grabbed the streamer and dabbed her eyes, then blew her nose. "If you want to hurt me, then hurt me, but don't hurt one of God's innocent creatures! What kind of sicko would do that?" She spun the wheel again. *Vanna, I'll take Anger.* The very emotion that Lottie was in the process of attempting to alleviate or even eliminate completely by taking crazy trips ten and one half time zones away foamed up, thick and rancid and able to destroy all forms of life in its path. She didn't like it, but there it was. Again.

Like the others, she would slay this beast too, brandish legal weaponry this time to ensure that the stalker first made new "friends" at the infamous OPP and, after trial, check in to the posh Angola "hotel" where he would don stripes and join a modern chain gang or become a litter-removal expert, spending his remaining days trudging along the steamy and weedy highways of South Louisiana with a personalized pokey stick. The difference here being that Lottie no longer only vicariously experienced cruelty, it had arrived in her city and her town and right on her doorstep. No matter that she didn't yet know who the perpetrator was. With Lou in her corner, she would find out soon enough, and when that happened, Lottie would pursue justice in the old-fashioned, if boring, law-enforcement manner. Meanwhile, she would try to calm Lou down, try to preempt her from pursuing the wrong kind of justice; not that hers was perfect, but Lottie did not want a body to turn up on the banks of the Mississippi either.

Speaking of her Category Five friend, Lou reassured, "Don't worry, baby. I already called my friends at NOPD, and them. They gonna find him." It was the "them" part of that equation that scared Lottie.

"Yeah, well, I'm going to go back into the emails and my cases and try to piece things together too." Lottie sniffed and blew her nose in a long honk. Even then, in her vaporous head, she tried to run through clients who would use emails referencing Allah. And was that even allowed by the Quran and the Hadith? Lottie knew that images of Mohamed weren't sanctioned, but could one have an email address with Allah in it? Of course, when Mohamed received the Quran and the scholars recorded the Hadiths about his life, it was passed along orally from person to person and not by digital messages between electronic devices that store data.

"You want me to stay here tonight? Me and Mr. Glock?" One beautiful black eye closed in jest, but Lottie knew it was a sincere offer.

"Oh gosh, no! You know I hate guns. I have a baseball bat for just that reason." Teased as the adopted one by her four siblings, she was left behind on hunting trips because they feared she would alert the deer and boar and bunnies and even the frogs. "Nah, I'm good. I will lock up thoroughly and keep my car keys by my bed. If I hear anything, I'll press the panic button, which will dissuade our friend and alert the neighbors. No worries."

"Yeah, well, too bad. I'm gonna stay. You are so tired, you won't hear anything. You didn't hear me knocking." She grunted and got up. "Besides, this is where I crash when I've had a few too many. You have that bedroom just for me, right?" Her smile was as irresistible as her rancor. All of her, in fact.

"Okay. Suit yourself. You know where everything is, right?" She did, and Lottie kept a stash of Lou's most treasured indulgences in the kitchen. It was all good. And secretly, she felt much safer with her personal bodyguard close. Minus the Glock. Lou disappeared into her own space, but not before Lottie made her promise not to retrieve the gun from the glove compartment of the pickup. Even the thought of a weapon in the house made her nerves flare, and that in and of itself would prevent the night of good and sound sleep of which Lottie felt worthy.

A clock shaped like an upright piano and engineered to plink the first few chords of Professor Longhair's "Big Chief" upon each hour lit up the room. Ten o'clock. Lou was in the living room nursing a Cuban cigar and a snifter of B and B, watching Jimmy Fallon. Her laugh, which sounded more like the barks and howls of a rabid wolf, filled the air along with the fragrant smoke. Strangely, the smell didn't bother Lottie, as the closer the smell, the closer her friend. The closer the protection.

When Lottie awakened, the sun smiled and the clouds danced and Frank was curled up in the crook of her arm. How long had she slept?

~ ~

Emails towered Lincoln-Log-like on Lottie's laptop, an unwelcome welcome back to reality, a ticker-tape parade of responsibility and annoyance and stress. Still, she managed to knock them down one by one with swipes of the Delete button—an annoying and unnerving endeavor—and search for clues about the poisoning scum of the earth. Frank coiled on his throne, wheezing softly, as though nothing had happened. He'd needed only one night at the vet, and now, a day later, seemed on the mend. Still, she couldn't stop looking at him between screenward glances. Outside, Mister George was back at it, mowing the twenty-by-twenty square that posed as a lawn. She would interrogate him later too, as she would everyone else, quizzing him about suspicious comings and goings.

Asalaam Alaykum read one subject line and made her left eyelid twitch. The sender, who was unknown to her, clearly spoke *alarabiya* like she did. Lottie examined the address—seeker@yahoo.com—and with one quivering finger, clicked on it with justifiable hesitation.

Dear Crazy Lady, it began, the words making her right eyelid join the other in spasmodic percussion. Yeah, she was crazy of late—in an Indiana Jones-James Bond sort of way—but this dude could win a blue ribbon at the annual Poisoning & Other Cool Ways to Spook People Conference. *Who do you think you are, creep, for calling me crazy?*

Lottie fidgeted in her power chair, torn between valor and disquiet, her best and worst natures duking it out. Someone once said courage is doing something even when you're scared; well, she must be a redheaded Superwoman, because she had a constant case of misfiring synapses and a generous helping of cortisol. But the flips in her stomach and eye dances were all for naught, and Lottie soon exhaled audibly, unaware she had even been holding her breath. Something like a *Feeeshhhhhh* came out and caused Frank to stir.

There on the screen in beautiful black-and-white Times New Roman probably 12 point—heretofore much too prosaic for Lottie—the message read: *I just wanted to say HI and see if you made it back safely. How are you doing anyways? Sincerely, Ishmael.* He even included a selfie sitting at his desk trying to look professional, but with a smirk that belied anything serious or work related. Lottie laughed, and recited to Franklin the old adage, "It's just what the doctor ordered," an utterance that absolutely did not impress him, and he resituated himself into a fine and perfect "O" on the chair.

In the adjacent "lobby," which was nothing more than her dining room, Lottie's confidante, fellow festival slayer, and bodyguard stayed close—an Italian-American sentinel with a New Orleans accent and a nice left hook. Lou formidably kept guard behind her desk, and currently complained at high decibels to the copier repairman. "I'm telling ya, the damn thing don't work! I don't care who did what. It ain't workin'." Forcing herself to breathe slowly, Lottie reminded herself that everything was okay. Actually, it was more than that with the receipt of Ishmael's email. Certainly, the message was antiseptic and not emotionally charged at all, but Lottie viewed it as evidence in print that he'd thought about her at least once.

He thought about me. What does that mean? It doesn't mean anything, just that he was concerned and is a good and decent human.

Lottie got up from the desk and walked stupefied over to the window, closed because of the heat and humidity, and looked down at her old friend Mister George, who edged the lawn manually and carefully as though it were Versailles. The smell of freshly mowed grass rendezvoused with the lavender aromatherapy candle burning on her desk, and massaged the disquietude within. It was a pure and wholesome visual and triggered a middle-American part of her hidden beneath all the Cajunness. She smiled at the simplicity of the mowing patriot, green confetti shooting out from the machine, baseball cap snug on his head. Then, as though her brain didn't wish to give her a break, Lottie recalled his opposite, the quite un-American, Isis-following miscreant who sent her foul emails and poisoned her kitty.

Lottie shook her head, trying to reconcile the events and people of her life, and headed back to the laptop, where at least a hundred emails yet awaited her. A few spams later, she saw the one that she sought—or dreaded, rather—the one from Frank's probable attacker. The sender allahdefender@yahoo.com leapt off the screen with suffused anonymity and caused her also to jump too as though he could reach out through the screen and grab her. "WEEEEEEEZY!"

Within seconds, Lou stormed into the office like Chuck Norris, all much ado and ready to karate-chop something or someone. "What? What?

Is it him?" Lottie nodded, leaning against the window. "Open it!" her superior officer commanded. With a tremble and not a little curiosity, not to mention unkempt fingernails, she obliged.

The same thing will happen to you, if you don't honor the one true God.

The words sizzled and crackled and misfired, then got jammed up at Lottie's synapses like cars on Poydras before a Saints game, wishing but not achieving their goal. Hoping she had misread or imagined what she had just seen, Lottie read it again, this time out loud.

"The same thing will happen to you if you don't honor the one true God."

High up above her in a fleeting cloud, Lottie heard Lou mumble, "Bastard! I'll fix him," then watched her turn and pace the small space, past Frank, past the coffee table, slapping a fist into her palm. After a few smacks, she returned and grabbed Lottie by the shoulders and looked into her eyes with her black pinballs darting about in white. "It'll be okay, dawlin'. I promise you." Lou said it trying to pacify, but then lasered a hole in the distant wall.

"It will be okay," Lottie repeated, while her stomach lurched in disagreement.

Her mind reeled with potentialities. The NOPD, FBI, and maybe even the CIA would helicopter her soon enough, demanding access to her files, her computer, her life—pathetic shenanigans that it was. That Lottie visited Afghanistan recently was no small matter either. *Oh, man.* She cringed.

On top of all that, the attorney-client privilege would bind her up like a few Lucky Dogs. With cheddar. Lottie's good-natured and already tortured clients did not deserve to have the unspeakable disclosed to anyone else in the government. USCIS under the mighty umbrella of DHS or Homeland

Security was plenty.

Asylees often experience a secondary form of torture—albeit emotional—by the US government in its effort to thoroughly vet them. After revealing to attorneys with great trepidation and fat tears stories of electroshock or rape or feet beating, they then had to endure hours of "nonadversarial" interrogation by asylum officers, and frequently, their cases in the days of xenophobia ended in denial. Next, they were booted to Immigration Court, where they enjoyed an honest and proud butt whoopin' by a bona fide and black-robed judge and an overworked and underpaid government attorney. And though they spoke the truth—often through a garbled, phoned-in interpreter—and raised a right hand, they experienced flashbacks of their former governments, and shook and quivered. A third round of cross-examination might just render self-immolation or a one-way ticket home, its slower equivalent.

Now, Lottie might have to battle the feds and locals like she would the malfeasants across the globe. With vigor and creativity.

~~

Long drizzles of Spanish moss swayed from the twisted arms of the ancient live oak and to the breaths of the bonfire. No matter that it was a crisp eighty degrees that welcomed to Lottie's backyard the board of NO(LA) Justice for Women. They came fearlessly, the festive do-gooders, and jitterbugged with debilitating curiosity, so silent the past month had been with reports from her—away masquerading in the land of Rumi and Khattak. Refusing steadfastly to communicate with anyone except Lou, Lottie did it to avoid an acute acceleration of nerves that one of them might trigger.

Melting daiquiris in Styrofoam cups appended to hands like frozen prosthetics. Crawfish waited—heads and tails up—on the *Times Advocate*'d folding table, while fireflies sparked in the azaleas and Ligustrums not unlike the embers dancing far into the night sky. On this evening, before Lottie would debrief on what Ishmael and she accomplished in Kabul, they would gather for what she dubbed The Burning of the Burqa. Adamant about this opening display, she assured them of zero utterances, zilch syllables, nada words until she incinerated with great glee the pastel two-man pup tent, the greatest symbol ever of the oppression of women and from under which she beheld the sights of Afghanistan.

Admittedly, after her jaunt into the Hindu Kush, Lottie clad herself in as little as possible, just shy of a woman of leisure on Airline Highway, choosing spaghetti straps and shorter skirts. A knee-jerk reaction? Perhaps. But in her contrarian and feminist mind, she was purifying her soul of the toxins she'd ingested—or wore, rather. Lottie literally wore patriarchy and, not wholly unlike William Wallace in Braveheart, wanted to scream *FREEDOM!* upon arrival in the sticky streets of her hometown.

"C'mon, girl," cried Jezebel, sucking on a straw, the interior of her lips stained in blueberry blue.

"Yeah, the suspense is killing me," declared Emile, who unsuccessfully attempted to cool off with a miniscule battery-operated fan. Everyone nodded in anticipation.

"All right, y'all," Lottie caved and slurred. "Raise your daiquiris for a toast, please." She lifted a large Hurricane daiquiri, half-finished and rubberizing her joints.

The group followed suit, cheering in unison, "A toast!"

"To the women of Afghanistan unable to pursue an education without being shot or beaten, to those raped and then killed in the name of honor, to those maimed in the name of love, to…" A rocky froth inhabited Lottie's throat, and her eyes stung. She struggled to continue, "To a beautiful country and lovely people."

They slapped Styrofoam together, and just about everyone wiped an eye or two.

Funny thing, life. Emotions too. Both pranksters enjoying their own hilarity, they reveled in good and practical jokes and snickered at the ensuing hoopla. Sensitive folks like Lottie were enslaved by them, responding unpredictably and embarrassingly. Whenever she stored anger or sadness in a show of bravery or, practically speaking, to be able to function, it almost always bit her in the butt, insisting upon attention at the most inappropriate time. If negative emotions were the earthquake, then misplaced emotions were the tsunami. Think Thailand.

"On that note…" Lottie regained momentum and cleared her throat, removing the boulders. "In honor of the women of Afghanistan and even the men who support them, I hereby burn this Dome of Domination." She lifted the blue subject out of a Macy's bag, balled it up, and dropped it into the flame, watching within minutes its disintegration into a few strands of charcoal.

The All-Knowing Lou hugged her with the force of a thousand women. Emile too. Fatima kissed her on either cheek, then the forehead. She aimed her mahogany eyes toward Lottie's pale ones, which no doubt had now been invaded by scarlet waves, and then clasped her face in her hands. "My darling, you did a noble thing and you were very brave. Your coconspirator, Ishmael, gave you the highest praise." The mere mention of his name knifed Lottie's heart and caused a torrent of sobs, a cruel waterfall coursing down her numb and mascara-run face. She had to sit and spun around to find the picnic table. She could feel the eyes of the others upon her, probably wondering if she too had been assaulted in Afghanistan, probably wondering what horrible fate befell her there.

Collapsing on the bench, Lottie accepted the silk handkerchief of Emile, way too symbolic of defeat in her opinion, and blew. Blowing with the ferocity of a barge horn bouncing off the Mississippi less than a mile away, she alarmed a green anole, which leapt from a banana leaf, causing it to spring up. Her guests fell over in uproarious laughter, which in turn made her explode with the same—a delicious, healing mirth. Lou plopped down next to her and began her routine of powerfully scooting her larger derriere into her, Steel Magnolias-style, until Lottie fell onto the patio. "Owwwww," she whined with much rum encouragement.

"Poor baby. Now can we eat?" asked Jezebel, whereupon all descended on the long table drenched with damp newspapers and a heap of steaming and scarlet crawfish and spicy red potatoes and cobs of corn. Like machines, they ripped into the crustaceans, a human assembly line twisting off heads and sucking the juice, pulling out the precious meat and discarding the shells into individual piles that would later become badges of consumption.

It occurred to Lottie a little late that they had an awful lot to be thankful for. "Hey, do y'all mind if I bless the food?" Many *ers* and *ahs* followed, and one by one, heads bowed. Between sniffs, she said, "Dear Lord, thank you for my safe return. Thank you for the people of Afghanistan. Please watch over them and guide them into a better situation, one with human rights for all. Thanks for Ishmael who…um…showed me around so well and made me feel safe. Please keep him safe. Oh, and thanks for the crawdads. In the name of Our Lord and Savior, Jesus Christ, amen."

"Dawlin', are you gonna tell us or ain't you gonna tell us about your trip?" Emile inquired and bit into a new potato, hot juice trailing down his arm.

Lottie scoured her hands with a Handi Wipe and, like a witness before a Congressional committee, began with how monumental the task felt from ten thousand feet, as daunting as scaling the frosted Hindu Kush below. Continuing with all her senses going numb, she tried to describe the feeling of floating off the airplane, in a queue with the non-Westerners, probably as intimidated as she was. Was she veiled at that point? Veiled, yes. Burqaed, no. What was it like to tour Kabul anonymously, a mere remnant of a person, stripped of her Cajun identity and tangerine curls, long legs, thin body? It was hindering, smothering, weird, on the one hand. On the other, it was unusually freeing to a certain degree to enjoy obscurity behind the blue curtain, to be the fly on the wall. How did she see behind the screen? Very carefully. Imagine progressive glasses, trying to find the small prescriptive circle, and aiming it at what you wanted to focus on. What was Ishmael like? Extremely helpful, quite courteous, selfless at the end of the day. She omitted anything that might flag a budding romance or fleeting attraction. They didn't need to know that. Heck, she didn't need to know it either.

What happened after she dropped the leaflets? It was impossible to know, though it didn't look too good for the fabric merchant. Ishmael would try to stay abreast of the info but would have to be extremely cautious in obtaining it. Ishmael's life, after all, might be endangered. Most likely, Abdullah would be tried according to Sharia law. If they determined him to be innocent after questioning several witnesses, he might not suffer any consequences except in the so-called court of public opinion. Which might not be pretty either.

Did she feel guilty? It just didn't sound like sweet, humanitarian Lottie. That, she had to think about. The most immediate sensation indicated otherwise. After all, Sadia told her she really did see Abdullah with US soldiers. Perhaps he was just taking brag photos, or maybe he was a spy. Lottie would let the locals decide. At any rate, she hoped she had just dynamited away part of her mountain of anger and man detesting.

"Any other questions?" Lottie proffered, then moved that they continue to discuss the next assignment.

The fire died down until it reminded her of a bed of molten lava spilling up from the bowels of her emotional core, sizzling with the fragments of an interesting page in her life. The sugary smell of Gambino's petit fours and unmistakable odor of crab boil blended with the fire's smoke until an exotic, voodoo-like air enhanced their intoxication.

"Emile, why don't you present it?" Fatima offered, melodic accent making the simple question dance.

In skimpy tank and shorts and, for some reason, sans fedora, he jumped up and emphatically placed one hand on his hip. "Well, we thought that because you traveled across the world last time, maybe you should remain in the Western hemisphere this time. How does that sound to you?"

It sounded wonderful, Lottie admitted, so exhausted was she—physically and mentally and emotionally—from her soiree in Central Asia and into another world entirely. "Tell me. Will I speak French or Spanish there?"

"Spanish," he announced. "And"—he glanced around at the group with a half grin and wide, moss-colored eyes—"you will still be in the same longitude."

Lottie clapped and sat precariously and loopy on the edge of the bench, somewhat relieved about the announcement, though internally trying to review what countries were situated within their time zone. Truth was, even a month after her return to Louisiana, her body still nursed something, not jet lag but perhaps its landlocked cousin, lackadaisicalness, along with a desire to bury her head precisely beneath a pillow. An effusive talker, Lottie had no desire to speak to anyone. Even with Lou, words didn't spring forth from her otherwise chatty lips. Lou had inquired extensively as to the source of the newfound reticence, but Lottie could not give a reason. Give her time, she implored. It would all be okay.

Regardless, in one month, she would board another flight, this time to El Salvador.

Chapter Fourteen
¿Como estas?

She dove into the deep end of her mind again as she looked out at the streets of the Quarter. Steam fingers reached up through Decatur's freshly scoured sidewalks as they did each morning, the ancestors of the Choctaw and Saint-Dominguens and Spanish and French, no doubt reminding them they would not relinquish this colony again to the Americans.

The sun trumpeted its imminent wrath as the board, still with sleep in their eyes, squeezed into a sticky corner table at Café du Monde. Just opposite the entrance, a tall black saxophonist in Wayfarers opened his case with two clicks and without fanfare and removed the instrument that mimicked in brass the Mississippi with its sharp twists and turns. Soon he would blow "Amazing Grace" or "Nearer My God to Thee" or "St. James Infirmary"—slow stuff at first—until the tourists truly awakened and snaked in the line in front of him. Later, when the street workers and tourists and businessmen awoke, he might blast "When the Saints Go Marching In" or "Basin Street Blues" or "Take Five."

The whiffs of coffee and chicory and fried dough danced awkwardly with the occasional and unmistakable wafts of urine left by naïve tourists or wild fraternity brothers or desperate homeless people or all of the above. Beset among throngs of tourists identified by lanyards and name tags and dramatic straw hats, the board awaited the delivery of mountains of beignets dusted like the Alps with sweet snow.

Carrying legions of coffee mugs full of café au lait or hot chocolate or tea on wide trays, slender Vietnamese waiters and waitresses marched around like ants transporting many times their body weight. The joint remained somewhat subdued for 8:00 a.m. on a Saturday, with only the clinks and clanks of the traditional white dishes ringing in the assembly line inside.

They removed elbows to clear a path for their tiny attendant, who set down the burdened tray with nary a grunt or ooooph or apparent broken nail. "Six order ben-yay, three café au lait, two hot chocolate, right?" She scanned the group from behind a curtain of black bangs, trying to figure them out, Lottie guessed. "You tourist?"

"Dawlin', we all from here!" Emile sang, his chest visibly puffing.

"Where y'at?" Anna-Maria added. Jezebel waved, bangles a-jangling. Isabella rendered a soft smile.

"Even you?" She nodded toward Fatima, who sported a water-colored hijab and could have been mistaken for Monet's muse or Da Vinci's Afghan Mona Lisa.

Delighted rather than offended, Fatima smiled. "Even me." The waitress shook her head, stuffed a couple of Mr. Jacksons into her pocket, and scampered away.

Again, the professor led the charge of the questionable army as a gentle general, a soft-spoken leader in a battalion of y'atty rancor. Handling the square donuts with great care, she tried with earnest and crooked smile not to dust herself in confectioner's sugar. Lottie could not manage the same, but accepted her fate after hundreds of trips over a lifetime to the tourist mecca. After the consequent and collective cleansing process with everyone rinsing hands with wipes and even a few dips of digits in water glasses,

Fatima handed her the manila folder with the contact.

Designated Operation Justice for Julieta, it contained the following:

Contact: Sergio Marquez
5'6" black hair, brown eyes
Sixty years of age
Education: Columbia University, BA English; MA English
Profession: Professor, Novelist
Fluent in Spanish, English, and Portuguese.

"I believe you know this contact." Emile winked.

"Indeed!" Lottie noted. "He was a surrogate father to me when I lived in El Salvador as an exchange student." She grinned like a proud daughter. She still loved "Papito," her nickname for him.

The folder also contained the name of the assailant and breaker of the human spirit, the gross offender with whom she couldn't wait to tussle:

Offender: Miguel Lopez
6'4" black hair, black eyes, scar above right eye
Thirty years of age
Profession: Police Officer
Fluent in Spanish; broken English.

Her eyes ran down the curriculum vitae of her newest bull's-eye, seizing the first—*At least I am fluent in Spanish*—then catching the profession of which she was already aware but missing line two in the first scan. Bouncing back to it, she gulped. "Six-four? Really? Oh my. I guess I...um...forgot that little—though not, ha—piece of information. I'm going to have to be very careful with this one." With a rather obvious tremor, she chuckled.

"As opposed to Afghanistan?" Jezebel leaned back, her threaded eyebrows rising. "Hmph." Her voice carried above the saxophone, which had just begun to paint the air with "Autumn Leaves," though they rarely fell in Nola-Town.

"Anna-Maria, would you like to discuss the itinerary?" Fatima tossed it to the oddly toned-down style guru, who sported only a Saints tee and shorts and who currently dipped a napkin into ice water, then dabbed her chin with it.

With one raised, sculpted finger, she began as though addressing a CEO. "Okay, here we go. You are ticketed on Avianca El Salvador Flight number 919, approximately two weeks from today. It is a direct flight out of Armstrong to San Salvador."

This would be a piece of cake with unimpaired vision.

Chapter Fifteen
Baila conmigo

In a cultural display typical of Central Americans, the passengers on Avianca El Salvador 919 applauded with great enthusiasm and repeated signs of the cross as the wheels touched down at Aeropuerto Internacional Monseñor Óscar Arnulfo Romero. This would be neither Lottie's first nor last foray into San Salvador, the capital of the smallest Central American country, and despite State Department warnings to the contrary, she foolishly felt safe visiting. A sweet tether in the form of a sixty-year-old man bound her to the tumultuous land at the cinched waist of the Western Hemisphere, to the terra firma that packed a powerful punch with its moody volcanoes and proud people.

First on her to-do list was gleeful surrender to the Pacific's saltwater sirens. She would smother herself in sunscreen to thwart impending freckles, rashes, and their nasty ilk, stretch her teaspoon-size swimsuit over her frame, and conquer the surfing hotspots before clocking in to the official unofficial assignment.

Could it be that she was developing a rhythm? Her own cadence in the underground world of requital? Sightsee, then attack. A little diversion followed by a little justice. *Mo' fun, then mo' revenge.*

Lacking still the trench coat and shoe phone, she nevertheless felt a curious case of smugness rising in her chest, an unwarranted dose of pride in her belly, having pulled off the Afghanistan affair without incident. Fleetingly, she fantasized over becoming the Joan of Arc of women's rights, summoned by the Creator to lead her sisters to victory, yet forced herself into giving up such foolery that she—a humble if thoroughly confused servant—was called to do, which she was in the process of doing.

Sergio would soon retrieve her from the airport, where, thankfully, no wardrobe alterations were required, no covering of limbs and *cabeza* with sky-blue blanket necessitated, no donning of mighty screen behind which to view the world. Years back, when she invaded his homestead as only a true and naïve and spoiled Yanqui could, they established a father-*hija* relationship. Over many plates of beans and rice and huevos rancheros, they, along with her adoptive *madre*, Victoria, discussed, among many other things, Lottie's taste in men and whether El Salvadoran ones would fit in her Venn diagram.

"Lattie!" Her ears tweaked from the general direction of the lobby, which was jammed with small taquerias and tiendas selling toiletries and chips and neck pillows, and she enjoyed the music in the pronunciation of her Salvadoran nickname. "Lattie!"

Whirling around to find him, she spotted a hand waving frantically behind rows of limo drivers brandishing handwritten signs and vendors hawking peanuts and chips. Then she spotted the man attached to the hand, a man who might have doubled as a retired running back for the NFL, with curly graying hair and a still-black moustache. Several years had passed since she had seen him in person, and FaceTime, as of yet, anyway, did not feature the most satisfying sense—touch—and did not bestow physical hugs between its subscribers.

She dropped her bags and entered "attack hug" mode. Used to her nonsense and having lived through it before, he braced himself by slightly spreading his legs and bending his knees.

"¡*Ven aquí!*" he shouted and opened his arms.

"¡*Papito!*" she squawked and launched her best armament, a heat-seeking, full-frontal monster hug, nearly knocking him down. The assault released a blast of cigar tobacco from his thick moustache, the signature scent waltzing in her nostrils, resurfacing with sweet memories.

"Charlotte Fornea!" Not unlike that guy in Kabul, he pronounced her name with the CH of "church" or "china," singing one of her favorite melodies, an old flamenco song complete with castanets—music, as they say, to her sometimes yawning American ears.

With smiling cocoa eyes, he scanned her top to bottom and back again, then commanded, "¡*Déjame mirarte!*"

She spun—arms wide—a sixteen-year-old again, and let her skirt flurry in the air-conditioned air. He slapped his head—a little too hard, she thought—and barked, "*Dios mío*, how you've grown into such a beautiful young woman!"

"¡*Muy amable, Papito!*" She grabbed his arm, he lifted her bag, and they sailed down the long corridor, which could have been Anywhere USA Airport, stuffed with fast-food restaurants, expensive watch and menswear stores, and makeup shops.

"English, *por favor*," he begged as they jumped into his old Volvo station wagon, which whined of better days, something he'd had when she'd entered his life. Lottie could see that they would settle into Spanglish, as she needed to reawaken her Spanish, and he rarely had a chance to practice his *inglés*.

"Papito, you still have this car? Why don't you invest in a new one? I mean, you are a famous writer! For cryin' out loud, you're a Nobel Prize nominee."

"*¿Por qué?* This is a great car. *Se llama Nellie*," he defended.

"*¡Claro!* I remember." Recalling that, she laughed and thrilled at the prospect that another eccentric named a car besides her and Lou. Alas, she divided the world into two kinds of people: those who named inanimate objects and those who didn't and enjoyed fraternizing with the former. "And she is a good girl."

Lottie put her hands up to him—The Man, blankin' Nobel prize nominee, speaker of her second language, extraordinary human, finest stand-in dad ever. He had grayed until his loose curls resembled a Brillo pad and his belly was now a small boulder, but he still looked like a movie star to her and could not shed that image no matter his age.

With more than one click, he started the Volvo, which had faded from its original lemon-yellow hue to that of a dying sunflower, and they headed northwest on the tree and billboard-lined Autopista Comolapa toward Colonia Escalón, on the other side of the city.

With the windows down, her coils lifted divinely, and she thought they must've resembled red streamers merengueing frantically to "Bésame Mucho" on the radio, which still sported dials. "*¿Dónde está Victoria?*" With one hand trying to catch curls, she yelled, her senses defeated by bliss. She hadn't heard from her Mama Dos lately, though they were Facebook friends.

A beauty reaching five-two on a good day and with a raven's nest of hair—probably grayed somewhat—and hazel eyes pinched at the edges like a feline's, she too was a stand-in parent, hugging Lottie from afar when her heart broke or she stressed over an impending court battle. Victoria was a brilliant and creative person in her own right, turning earth into art—a *milagro!*—firing clay into vases, jars, and platters, and her work was the buzz around San Salvador. As a lanky and weak sixteen-year-old, Lottie dragged back to the States a suitcase stuffed with bubble-wrapped bowls—one fruit, one decorative—and vases—one bud and one large—and one ashtray into which she still placed her jewelry, all stamped with the insignia VMG (Victoria Marquez de Garcia).

Pointing to the side of the road where a Papa John's flashed capitalism in neon letters and with its green umbrellas, he roared, "Ju see. We have a lot of *restaurantes americanos* here," then waved one hand emphatically to the other side, toward the red-and-white awnings of a TGI Fridays.

"*Claro*, Papito. But do tell me, how's Victoria?" By the time she got it out a second time, she sensed him avoiding the topic, and her stomach dropped.

Then, as though she had just unplugged him—and the Volvo—he took his foot off the gas and slowly turned it to the side of the road and in front of a Subway sandwich shop. He threw it into Park, then looked at her with his moustache drooping like a dead caterpillar. "Ju see, I didn't want to tell you." *Please, dear Dios, what?* "We lost her, Lattie." He looked down at his khakis and back at her with swimming eyes, searching eyes. "We lost her six months ago. It was cancer of the breast. *Recuerdas* she had it a few jears ago?" Lottie nodded faintly, her head buzzing at a high frequency, not wanting to hear more, but wanting to hear more. "Well, ju see, it came back. And so, the monster came for her, and I could not defeat the monster. There wasn't a damn thing I could do! There wasn't a damn thing I could do for my *bonita* Victoria." He slammed the steering wheel with both hands and pressed his forehead against it. Tremors followed and led to a full-fledged quake.

Lottie had never seen him cry—in El Salvador or in New Orleans when he had visited, not that there was anything to be heartbroken about then. Victoria was in remission, and life arrived wrapped in a big bow.

Suddenly, she felt unsettled. And helpless. Sliding over, she wrapped her arms around him—him, her adopted papa, childless, unless you included the lost souls he made his own, like her. And who was she anyway? Just a stand-in? Yes, though at that moment, she could have been the closest thing he had to family, to offspring, and now she was there physically, and her arms were capable and great at hugging, if nothing else, and she squeezed him as best she could across the console and stroked his head.

When he pulled back, bereft of breath, Lottie managed in sniffs, "Oh, Papa. Why didn't you tell me? I wondered what had happened. I kept asking, but you never responded."

A young boy resembling Mowgli from *The Jungle Book* and selling red roses approached her window, and she said, "No, gracias," and waved him away.

"Of course I no respond! I did not want to worry ju, my beautiful *hija*." He retrieved a crisp handkerchief from his back pocket and wiped his eyes, his sweet face now blotchy with loss. "But, I am okay. Ju see, life is *maravillosa*, even when it breaks you into a *millón* pieces. I can never ever put the puzzle back together again, but that doesn't mean that the puzzle wasn't gorgeous and still is *actualmente*."

He wiped and blew, then looked directly at her. "Of course, the piece missing is the most precious of all, but even its absence is a reminder of the beauty and the risks one takes in loving another human being. We must embrace life, even when our puzzle misses a piece."

"Oh, Papito. That is beautiful." Torn between the poetry of the moment and missing Victoria herself, she wanted to adopt his philosophy, to digest it and put it into practice, and to look through whatever lens he viewed the world. And viewed love. Or at least the approach to it. Throw caution to the wind, as they say. Perhaps he was contagious and could infect her with the disease of carefreeness and open-heartedness and *alegría de la vida*. Pre-self-vaccination, she had all the symptoms, but players and schemers and cads and rakes had helped immunize her and forced her to fill the syringe with guardedness and hurt and suspicion.

Papito put the car in Drive, and they coursed through the belly of the city, to the western outskirts, Lottie quietly refamiliarizing herself with what she had not seen in a *millón* years. Along the way, as they passed two particular electronic billboards, one in the Centro, where most businesses headquartered, and the other in the perimeter but in the path of commuters, he pointed and said, "There!" and "There!" She smiled big, knowing.

Up and up and around and around, they wound in a steady ascent, and a rotogravure of memories flicked through her brain: sixteen-year-old Lottie in the backseat of the Volvo as they returned from *al mercado* or *el cinema* or *la universida*, Sergio and Victoria in the front, her Jean Patou flirting with wafts of ripened mangos and weird mameys and warmed grass. One final turn and they pulled into a long stone driveway that led them to a two-car garage. The grand bungalow rested in the arms of stately pines and firs and hemlocks, and she could have sworn that it smiled too, remembering her.

"Oh, Papa. I remember! It's been so long."

"Jes, and do you remember that it is only a small drive to the *universidad*?" She looked at him, trying to call up knowledge probably flushed or thrown out or forced to the back of her mental attic to make room for newer memories, then shook her head. "*Pues*. It is only thirteen *kilómetros* from here. I will take you there, if you like. Or would you first like to go to the beach? Or would you like to rest?"

"No rest necessary! Would you mind if we do the Pacific first? Then tomorrow, I can sit in on your class, if that's okay, Professor? May I?"

"*Cualquiera, señorita.* Whatever you want."

She untied her sandals, which, though she wasn't a Roman citizen, ran up her calves with many crisscrosses, and let her feet greet one digit at a time the cool Spanish tiles. Gliding to the window, she leaned out and inhaled as much as she could. The pines and guava and sapote triggered a poetic nerve, and she swore they tried to reach into the open *ventanas* with proud, verdant fingers and succulent fruits. Lifted by the scent, she couldn't help it. "Oh, Papa! Maybe I should stay here. With you? Like, forever?"

He eased onto a stool next to the mahogany table that was festooned with several pieces: a ceramic vase the hue and patina of oxidized copper, the top molded into a lily; a small bowl in the shape of a heart but tricolored in blue and green and black and melting like a Dali, and a small white dog, primitive and about the size of a jigger. He picked up the vase affectionately and rubbed it with his thick fingers. "Char-lot, we both know this is no place for young ladies, *particularmente* American ones. Did ju happen to look at El Departmento de Estado website and travel warnings?" Of course she had, and bowed her head, back in the principal's office at Sherwood Forest Elementary, bracing for a *grande* lecture. "Jes, ju know! To top it off, the MS-13, Mara Salvatrucha, has taken over the country. The gang members are in—how do you say?—bed with the national and the local *policía.*"

Lottie sank, well aware. But couldn't she dream? Dream of staying safely in this beautiful country? A comfort zone but for that criminal element. Dream of picking breakfast off the tree, a large and ready papaya, which she would cut in half, then scoop out its one hundred seeds, while letting her feet cool on the tiles that did the same for the house? Couldn't she?

"And let me remind ju why you are here, in case ju have forgotten.

Remember what they do to women." He put his hands together and lifted them toward the sky. "Aye aye aye. Ju know that there is femicide here. That the murder of women is not given any attention." Yes, she knew that too. "So, *bastante*! Enough!" he spat in his authoritative tone, which she had witnessed only once before, and that was when an El Salvadoran guy ten years older hit on her at sixteen.

"Besides, maybe I should come live with ju!" He winked at her, and she watched the black brush above his lip rise and fall with laughter.

Now that...that was an idea.

⁓ ⁓

Immersing her torso in a tub of Banana Boat would be more practical than the long-winded and contortionist task of slathering. In the art of the slather, one could never reach everywhere, could never overtake the essential spots unless and until one had a significant or even insignificant other: a slatherer. To slather the slatheree. In all honesty—and she tried to be that, honest—next to the opposite sex, the great flaming orb in the sky was her greatest foe. Occasionally, she had trysts with it, an intermittent solar significant other, thinking she could out-fool it, play sunscreen and umbrella games, out-slather.

Papito, on the other hand, effortlessly and proudly wore his native skin with the grace of a Pipil king from the original Cuzcatlan empire that dominated western El Salvador back in the day. "Lattie! *Vamos!* The water will be dried up by the time we arrive."

She slathered her feet, the last frontier, and emerged greasy and spotted, her least favorite state. "Papito, should we bring the boards?"

"Ah no, *señorita bonita*. The last time, remember? You wiped out and bruised your—*como se dice?*" He pointed to his rib cage.

"Ribs."

"Oh, *sí.*"

She grabbed her left side and slumped. "Ouch. True enough. But can we at least go watch the surfers? What's that's place called? La Libertad?" One side of his mouth lifted, and his moustache piggy-backed with it. She imagined that he thought she might be more interested in the surfers than the waves, but as she was right in the middle of a bona fide opposite-sex crisis and subsequent hiatus, this was untrue.

When she failed at her first real attempt on the pipeline, cool surf music playing in her head and waves slashing her about like a water noodle, she hung up her board, which was technically Victoria's, who had surfed since toddling. Taking lessons from a lithe native with hair down to his waist and a smile that would outshine the tropical sol that day, Lottie allowed him to lean over her, arms around her waist. He practiced his English on her so that he could one day venture to California and Hawaii: "Squat! Stand! Balance! Spread your *pies!*" What was his name again?

"Ricardo. Did you keep in touch?" Bingo. What a mind reader.

The doors to Nellie protested as they opened, squeaking as though they wished to go to car heaven soon but weren't allowed. "No. For a while, but as the years went by, we grew apart, and I believe he got married to another *gringa*. If I remember correctly, a Southern Californian, a really good surfer." Lottie slammed the door and looked out the window, trying to conceal a memory-induced smile.

They headed almost directly south along the Carretera al Puerto de La Libertad, the noon sun thrashing the peeling roof off the Volvo like an angry master. Mimosas and wild vines hugged the road affectionately, occasionally giving way to juice stands and papaya vendors and kiosks hawking hairbrushes and Band-Aids and *chiclet*.

Within forty minutes, they had arrived at the Punta Roca Surf Resort, where a large rock jutted out of the water, threatening surfers literally with their lives, and palm trees clung to the soil adjacent to the rocky beach, holding on for dear life.

With a sizzling cigar snug in his bite, Papito waved at the locals, who magically opened the gate when they spotted the old Volvo, some shouting "Sergio!" and others yelping "*Profesor!*" He extended a hand for high fives, so she did the same, slapping bronze. Clearly, he was well-known and welcome at one of the most esteemed surf spots in Central America, and Lottie felt a swell in her chest that she wished would linger forever.

In flip-flops, she waddled behind her more adept Salvadoran counterpart, over lava-colored rocks until they found a smooth surface on which to rest their bums and watch the silhouettes gliding gracefully over water. Several surfers navigated the curvy water, some cha-cha-cha'd up and down long boards, while others drilled through the wave tunnels on shorter ones, sometimes touching the water gently with the tip of a finger. All were braver than she was and, of course, tanner.

Meanwhile, her head luxuriated in salt air and her blood pressure took a much-needed nap. Clinging to her gigantic straw hat, the size of a small hut, with one hand, she clutched a piña colada with the other.

Then, like flies to *semita*, several locals began to buzz around them, guys with strong accents and magnificent bodies, chiseled by battling the waves until they resembled copper Cuzcatlan gods, biceps and six-packs yapping at her. They chatted in Spanish with Papito, not realizing she was fluent. "*¿Quien es tu amiga? ¿Ella es de los Estados Unidos?*"

"*Es mi hija adoptada*, Charlotte," he barked.

"*Hola*," she greeted and blocked the sun with one hand.

"*Hola,*" they replied in unison with big grins.

She couldn't quite understand the fascination unless it had to do with being a biological rarity in the same vein as a freak show, like the bearded lady or the man with a tail or Siamese twins. *Step right up! Come and see the redheaded, freckled woman. Witness the blue in her eyes! Watch as the sun scorches her skin.*

Her ears tingled like tiny radars, and her eyes smized behind her fake Ray-Bans while Papito fielded questions like a pro.

"No, she's not available."

"No, she won't date any of you!"

"If you wish to date her, you must first go through me."

Finally, he roared his famous "*Bastante!*" by which he settled issues right then and there and frightened the poor *hombrecitos* into profuse apologies and *adióses.* He then smoothed his moustache like a pet, but she could see the lines around his dark eyes crinkling.

"Wow, Papito. That was protective, eh?" He jerked with laughter as she leaned back on her elbows.

After a few moments listening to only the chatter of the waves and the *Oyes!* and *Hombres!* of the surfers as they propelled their bodies through the wet playscape, he leaned over and asked, "Well, because you know I care about you, I must ask: is there a man in your life?"

Ishmael's bright smile against olive skin popped into her mind, and she figured she might turn all shades of pink and red. But what with the sun doing a number on her anyway, perhaps Papito wouldn't notice. "There is the idea of someone, but he's a long-distance interest. Let's just leave it at that." There wasn't a lot to explain to him anyway. How can you say that you have a crush on someone literally around the world? One day when she was daydreaming, she looked up the longitude and latitude of Afghanistan, and lo and behold, the latitude was about the same as good ole NOLA. But who was counting?

"Well, okay, but you seem to have a glint in your eye." He radiated at that declaration.

"Oh, good grief, Papito. I'm wearing sunglasses!"

"This is *verdad*—true, but your glint is on your face too."

"Nothing to see here. Moving right along." Pulling her hat well over her face, she allowed herself a brief vision of Ishmael and might even put it on her to-do list to do it again later.

"As you wish!" He rubbed his hands together. "*Por todos modos*— anyways—are you ready for our little assignment?"

Ishmael left as abruptly as he came, unfortunately, and she slid her hat back up and sunglasses down and winked.

"Ju will be Susan Baker, no?"

"*Sí*. I will be the journalist Susan Baker." The crowd interrupted them with a roar, and she looked back out at the water, where a surfer tucked into a big wave with great finesse. "Wow. ¡*Mira!* Papito!"

"¡*Dios mío!*" he shouted and stood up, clapping. "Bravo! Bravo!"

Lottie joined him, and the trove of spectators on the shore who emitted "oooohs" and "ahhhhhs." The surfer emerged from the inner loop victoriously, then dissolved in the blue calm.

"Now, where were we?" She sat back on her towel. "Oh, yeah…so I will be the journalist, but I won't necessarily interview this creep, right?"

"No, *amor*. You merely have to seduce him." He smiled not unlike Dr. Evil from Austin Powers fame.

"Oh, yeah, that. What if he's not into the Heath Bar Crunch look?" She looked down at her freckles, too many to count.

"The what?"

"Never mind. What's the name of the bar again?"

"*Se llama* California." Her admirers walked by, demonstrating great bravery or stupidity, she couldn't tell which. Again, Papito raised an eyebrow, and again, they scattered.

"Oh right." She took a big slurp of her piña colada.

"Ju must be careful, Lattie. Dese guys don't play. They are *muy* powerful."

"Of course, Papito. But you will be close by, right?"

"Of course." He swatted at a horsefly. "*Bastardo.* Now, tell me about your young lady for whom you do this. Ju must really care for her to do this. To risk your life, no?"

Squeezing the viscous white paste out of its tube, she rubbed her hands together and spread it down her thighs, not unlike spackle on Sheetrock. "Oh, what does it matter? She's just one variable in an invisible subset of society."

"But you seem to care about her a lot, *preciosa.*"

"As you can imagine, she is a beautiful indigenous woman, was a maid for someone, and that someone raped her repeatedly. Of course, because that someone was a police officer, there was nothing she could do but run. Now, you and I are exacting justice on that someone." Her legs now alabaster, if she stood and posed, she could easily be mistaken for a marble sculpture.

"She means a lot to you, though."

"Yes, she does. I mean, of course. Then again, they all do. That's the problem. That is why I'm here. If I can't change the culture, if I can't change the laws, then by golly, I will change the verdict. See?"

"Yes, *amor.* I see. And I am happy to join you in dis endeavor." Adjusting his fedora, he looked the part of a Nobel prize nominee, a data point that made her swell.

"So, Papito. The guys at the hotel are going to help us, right?"

"Yes, my love. They know this creep, and they hate him." He swatted another fly. "¡*Bastardo!* And…they hate what has become of our country. What it allows to happen to women. They are good family guys."

"Oh, man. I hope I don't endanger them too."

"We are all willing *participantes, amor.* And we are sick of it, like you."

She looked directly at him. "Are you sure? I mean, I'm so grateful!"

He leaned over and kissed her on the forehead, no doubt getting a hefty mouthful of sunscreen. "How do you say…it's all good?" With that, he rumbled, and this was the Papito she remembered so well, rife with guffaws and thunder. So much life in one body.

A few surfers and tens of freckles later, they packed up and bid *adiós* to the surfers, who continued their discomforting voyeurism, and headed back into Colonia Escalón, to a refuge of coolness and a beckoning lounge chair on the deck.

Chapter Sixteen
Monkey Business

The primatial criminals must have had a blast lobbing mangoes or cacao bullets, or whatever the heck they were, at the shingled roof of Lottie's temporary abode, the results of which were thud, thud, thuds every two minutes. The offenders were howler monkeys, who, as she recalled, were pelleting scoundrels.

Known as one of the loudest mammals on the planet, just behind sperm whales, for their howling as the name implies, they could also give an MLB pitcher a run for the money. The two-minute thing was a rough estimate. She actually had no idea how often they fired their missiles; it could've been every five or ten minutes or even twenty. But it felt like two. The result: a prematurely awakened *señorita*. A rooster conspired with the furry dastards and released his delightfully alarming cockle-doodle-doos as though sleep was a bad thing.

Too excited to sleep anyway and very little jetlag, Lottie succumbed to the natural alarm clocks and slid into the bathroom to splash water on her face. Bags threatened like little dark clouds under her eyes, but it was what it was. She whipped her hair into a ponytail and shuffled to the kitchen, where she found Papito making coffee.

"Blasted monkeys!" she cursed as she hugged him. "Well, I guess it's better than the drunken partiers that walk down my street early in the morning. Ha." At least this was natural in a non-homo-sapiens way. People, in fact, paid good money to hear the howlers, packing flights to Central America and going on monkey tours.

Of course, he offered a smiling "*¡Buenas días, querida!* I have made you your *favorito*, huevos rancheros and sliced cantaloupe."

With a screech, she yanked a chair and slumped into it. "*Gracias, Papito. ¿Y tienes café?*"

"*Sí, claro.*" He poured the dark brew into a *San Salvador es para amores* mug and shuffled over.

"Is that Old Spice I smell, *señor?*" She pointed her nose ceilingward and took a deep sniff.

"Jes, ma'am."

"It reminds me of my dad, Jake." She smiled and remembered and thanked God for the odiferous coincidence.

"Oh, jes. I remember *tu papá.*"

"It's so weird that both of you wear the same aftershave: my two favorite men on the planet."

"Well, jes. Victoria loved it, ju know." Now he looked down at his coffee, and she took the opportunity to dispense another big hug. After all, weren't hugs medicine for the soul's flu, instantly reducing its fever? "Thank ju, *preciosa.* Thank ju."

Swigging her joe, she eyeballed him head to toe. "Wow. You must've woken up before the monkey terrorists. You look so nice." And he did—starched shirt and pressed khakis, freshly shorn cheeks with the most famous male cologne ever. It must be what Nobel nominees did. Early bird and all.

Outside, the cock continued his encouragement to get on with the day, while the monkeys must have rewarded themselves with a nap.

173

~ ~

At 7:15, Nellie transported them to the *universidad*—chugging uphill like the Little Engine—where they met with the women's rights group on campus. That Sergio Marquez mentored the flock was no small deal, as having such fame in one's corner made the ladies straighten their spines and throw their shoulders back.

Addressing groups of ten or more wasn't Lottie's worst fear—shout out to drowning in the ocean—yet she wasn't a fan. Still, she agreed to be the "guest speaker," hoping that by doing so, she would contribute even just an iota to the women of the small nation.

"How do you help women's rights as an immigration attorney?" a petite brunette with wide-rimmed glasses asked from the first row.

"Well, we have developed an area of the law that provides for domestic violence victims from other countries to apply for asylum. In my practice, I have developed a microniche of helping foreign domestic abuse survivors. I have even represented several from your home of Central America."

"But didn't the law change? I thought that DV survivors couldn't ask for asylum anymore," interrupted another woman, knowing more than most Americans do about US law.

"You are correct in that the attorney general of the US issued an order that allegedly changed the law to omit domestic violence as a grounds for asylum." Lottie couldn't leave it at that, though; it just wasn't in her nature. "However, many of us continue to represent these women—and men. Some have even won since the attorney general's order. We keep pushing on a case-by-case basis to change the law back to where it should be." Praying that she wasn't getting splotchy, she took a deep breath and exhaled, then looked around for more questions.

A male with a beautifully coifed pompadour held up his hand. Lottie nodded. "Is there anything *afuera*—um, outside—the practice of law that you do to help women's rights?"

Looking down at her fingers, she sputtered, "Um…where do I begin?"

Chapter Seventeen
Do Creeps Like Redheads?

At noon, they arrived back at home for siesta—a habit that Lottie wholeheartedly wished the US would adopt, especially Nueva Orleans, where the culture more closely resembled Central America than America anyway. On the other hand, her hometown folks needed no reason to stop or pause or even slow, speed not being their most prominent characteristic. On the other, other hand, why shouldn't the city fully embrace its own slothfulness and take it to the next level? *Resurrect the siesta! I say.*

Hot air drifted into the open *ventanas*, delivering with it wafts of life: the acridity of a neighbor's trash burning, which Papito despised, some unidentifiable animal's dung, an equally unknown floral scent, and coffee. Relieved to discover that even the howlers took a siesta, Lottie put a mask over her eyes and lay on top of the made bed and fell soundly asleep.

At 2:00 p.m., Papito came in and shook her, though he needn't— excitement and anxiety kept her precisely on the edge of the bed (figuratively speaking), at the ready. She jumped up and went to her suitcase stuffed with props. She laid out her uniform for the night: sequins on top of sequins on top of fishnets, and closed the door to dress.

But what if the creep didn't like redheads? The thought churned her former calm, but she immediately employed her well-worn thought-replacement technique to quell any impending alarm. *Should he dislike redheads, I will simply purchase a blonde or brunette wig the next day and postpone my departure until another day,* then return with the different hair color tomorrow night. *No big deal, right?* Immediately implementing plan B to reduce the hiccups of anxiety, she began the deep breathing learned at NOGA (New Orleans Yoga) slowly exhaling like a leaky tire. *Psssssssssssssssss.*

"*Querida,* you okay in there?" Papito barked from the other side of the door, true concern in his voice.

"*Sí,* Papa! ¡*Muy bien!*" It wasn't totally true as she tried to wrestle the cortisol into submission, but it would be soon enough. *There now, even that is a positive thought.* Already, she was on the upswing, even with wobbly legs.

At 5:00 p.m., she squeezed into sequins not wholly unlike a Lucky Dog shoved into its casing. Her pinkie nail got caught up a few times in the fishnets, but she finally managed to stretch them over her legs. *Oh, baby. If my momma could see me now.* Then, as if she signaled danger to the neighborhood, the howlers began to warm up, a discordant orchestra of furry instruments. Finally, she stepped into golden spikes that lifted her to beyond Heidi Klum's height. Savage hair? ¡*No problema!* With four products and a long-suffering blow-dryer, she tamed it.

When she exited the bedroom, Papito whistled like a construction worker. "Very funny," she said. "You don't seem so bad yourself, though certainly not pimpish enough to be seen with the likes of me." He looked rather distinguished in crisp shirt and tie, she noted, and she surveyed him dramatically, then whistled back. Within minutes, they would be at the after-work hangout frequented by the offender, whom she had dubbed Señor Slimebucket. The thought pumped her with a fresh shot of adrenaline. *Psssssssssssssssss.*

With hands at *diez* and *dos* o'clock, Papito drove even slower than before, and she wasn't sure if he was nervous on her behalf or his. It was dangerous business, after all, to disrespect policemen in El Salvador, let alone humiliate them. She applauded his bravery while berating herself for involving him.

Past the houses, bicycles, and cars, they coasted downhill, bidding the monkeys *hasta luego*, and finally parking a few blocks from California, which gave them time to split up and avoid being identified as a pair. Susan Baker preceded him with the clicks and clops of stilettos and all the finesse of a Clydesdale. Awkwardly yanking and tugging at the short sequined dress, she commanded herself to relax. *Pssssssssssssssssssss*. If the flaming hair didn't give her away, the inorganic mode of walking with spastic legs would. A mother shielded her little girl from Lottie, no doubt identifying her as a hooker, a prostitute, a lady of the night (or in this case, twilight) and a pathetic-looking one at that.

~ ~

The front of the club sported military-looking types, buff and camouflaged, that stopped mid-discussion and assaulted her with their eyes. *"Hola, caballeros,"* Lottie squeaked. Parting the testosterone with her estrogenic chainsaw, she entered the murky club, which displayed a genuine disco ball à la the 1970s and blue lights. It was already stuffed with people, maybe because it was the end of the workweek. Smiling, she again commanded herself: *calm down, you got this.* But inwardly, a war erupted. *What if he's not here? What if he doesn't like me? What if he has already picked up another dame?* She scanned the joint as though looking for a friend—tables first, then the bar—when she spotted an enormous guy in a police uniform sitting at the end, near the waitress station. *Bingo.*

Shaky at best, she clicked and clacked and wobbled over to the convenient and empty chair next to Señor Slimebucket. When he turned, she noticed the scar above his eye and thought about calmly exiting the premises, but when she glanced back at the door, she saw that Papito had already entered, playing well the part of a middle-aged businessman just stopping in for a drink.

Like a good yogi, she exhaled slowly. *Psssssssssssssssssss.*

The beast of a man said, "*¿Quiere sentarse aquí?*" He slid the chair back gently like a real gentleman and smiled, revealing one gold tooth that caught the glint of the disco ball. Cigarette breath—her least favorite—shot out of him when he spoke.

"*Segura,*" Lottie said in a breathy tone, internally chuckling at her poor rendition of an easy pickup. "What are you drinking?"

When he replied, "Whiskey," she said, "I'll have what he's having," just like they did in the movies. Climbing onto the stool, she prayed her skirt would not inch ceilingward and tried not to yank it. She didn't need or want to blow her cover with this dude, him being a cop in a country run by them.

"*¿Es americana, sí?*" She nodded and winked and tried to play a tough guy, like she had been around the globe a million times. When the whiskey arrived, he threw down a few US dollars—the currency du jour of El Salvador—and leaned over, his breath shooting toward her cornered nostrils. "*Pero, ¿habla español?*"

She smiled, tried not to get nauseated, and forced herself to blink. "*Sí,* but do you speak *inglés?*" He revealed the gold tooth again and a mouth full of mercury, and in an amalgamation of broken English and rusty Spanish, they continued to talk, her revealing her in-El Salvador-as-a-journalist story, leaning closer and batting her lashes like a frenetic butterfly. And holding her breath when she could.

"Ju know, I *amor* redheads."

"¡*Suerte la mía!* Lucky me."

Julieta and her destroyed innocence jumped into Lottie's brain, so she squared her shoulders and downed a full glass of water to dilute the next few hours. The bartender slammed down two more whiskeys, and her head whirled. Señor Slimebucket pushed the jigger of bourbon in front of her. Making a big deal out of swinging her legs and singing "Wheeeeeeeeee!" and spinning around on the barstool, she tried to spot Papito in the process. Midloop, she spied him, and he nodded and winked. He sat with two other gentlemen, who seemed consumed by cigars and conversation. "Take it easy, *bebé*," Señor Slimebucket said.

"*No estoy* working *ahorita!* I'm not working now!" She threw her hands up and waved them like they were in the midst of a party, which they sort of were, though a sick and twisted one. "Wooohooo!" It was true—she wasn't working per se, unless, of course, you included in her job description destroying rapists. Indulging in a brief fantasy, she imagined her ideal CV:

PhD, Justice Administration; Dissertation, Creative Acts of Retribution

MA, Locating Elusive Creeps

Bachelor of Arts in Communications, Minor in Disguises

Invading this internal event came the notion of the IRS and all its bureaucratic bells, whistles, and alarms. Lottie hoped and prayed that NO(LA) Justice for Women would never be audited, but if it was, she certainly had to document the trips as true women's rights adventures.

Was that the only reason she'd made sure to speak to Papito's Derechos de Las Mujeres club at the university? Of course not. Nonetheless, the meeting was well documented, and the students, female and male, thrilled to hear from a bona fide immigration and human rights attorney. If only they knew…

She continued to nurse the whiskey and down the water, while Gold Tooth slammed them back, one after the other. Lottie knew she had to make her move soon before he passed out. "Hey, big boy." She leaned in, making sure to make eye contact and bat her tarantula lashes. "What do you think about us? *Nosotros.*"

"*¿Nosotros?*" His eyes did a little cha-cha-cha. "*Me gusta.* I like it." He rubbed a sweaty brow and winked at her.

"What do you like?" Lottie gulped. "I mean…what are you into?" He shrugged and pointed a grimy finger into her chest. "Me, huh?" She glanced back at Papito, who nodded again as if to urge her onward in this Iwo Jima of pranks. "Well, I'll tell you what I like…" Smiling, she whispered into his ear, making sure to exhale a big, long, bourbon breath into it.

"Oh, jes?" He put his head back and let out a choppy bark, a laugh she had never heard from another human and that made her flinch. "*Pues, seguro.* Sure."

The disco continued to spin, and Spanish rap music boomed from the huge speakers flanking the dance floor. She couldn't see how the two correlated—two genres and decades clashing—but was in no position to judge. A skinny young man with slick hair pulled a round woman in too-tight tights and balancing atop platforms onto the dance floor and placed two thick hands squarely on her rump. Likewise, Señor Slimebucket pulled Lottie by the hand until her thighs ripped from the vinyl seat, and she wobbled onto the nosebleed spikes. Throwing a last imploring glance to Papito—who quickly emptied his wallet onto the table and looked as though he was saying his goodbyes—she exited with the target into a sunset of uncertainty.

Chapter Eighteen
¿Dama o caballero?

The sunset urged romance, but Lottie refused to either honor its request or participate in its pheromonious shenanigans. In watercolors of violet and rose, it ushered in a nice night for *guanacos,* and she imagined fire pits soon to be lit and guitars soon to be strummed in backyards soon to be beneath stars.

Getting into a police car with a drunk *policía* had never been on her bucket list, but she had made a commitment to Julieta and to the women of the world and mostly to herself, so get into the police car with a drunk *policía* she did. Surveying her chariot for the night, she took note of the requisite iron grate that rested behind her overproduced hair, the kind you see in cop dramas or Denzel movies and not in person, thankfully—it separated her grimy partner for the night and her from the backseat, where would-be criminals (or victims!) would sit. Señor Slimebucket patted the seat next to himself and flashed gold. She giggled and, against her better judgment, slid over—so close that she swore she smelled hell or at least what she imagined it to be: cruelty and lust or cruel lust or lusty cruelty. And sulfur.

"Please, God, protect me from my own stupidity," she murmured, pretty sure that God had tired of her recidivism, tired of dispatching angels down to attend, wings aching, halos fading, tired of arguing with his emissaries. *Yeah, it's Lottie again. Yes, she's foolish. I know. I know. I'm hoping she will wise up. How old is she? She's thirty in earth years. I know. I know.*

Examining the ceiling, which featured what looked to be a knife cut surrounded by dried splatters of a red liquid, she tried to convince herself that it must be red wine, splashed by a cabernet-smuggling offender. Glancing out the side mirror, she saw Papito, who had just exited and slapped a few loitering officers on the back along the way.

Señor Slimebucket put on the sirens—for fun?—and they sped away crazily and hopefully not toward her demise. On her mental keypad, with all the attending thumping and clicking, she typed out the headline:

CUERPO OF REDHEAD FOUND ON SIDE OF ROAD

Policía dice que the body of a lanky and freckled woman, described as muy fea, was found on the side of the Highway to Hell. "I have never seen hair like that before," La Policía, Eduardo Diaz, dijo. "It was like, how do you say? A rojo Brillo pad."

It was a sad and yet fun fact that when faced with deadly force, Lottie concerned herself more with her appearance than with the danger itself. Yes, she sometimes swam in the shallow end with others, and she was okay with that.

Within minutes, however, they arrived at El Presidente, where Slimebucket ushered her out of the car eagerly and sloppily, as though he couldn't believe his great fortune, a *gringa* voluntarily entering his lair, snagging her upper arm with his chunky fingers and wiping what could only be drool from the corners of his mouth. The key to room 303 hid in her miniscule and gold-sequined purse, along with a tube of Baffling Beige lipstick—not her color, but a necessary prop—and her cell phone.

"Right this way, *mi amor*," she coaxed, as in two-step fashion, they sauntered through the lobby, arm in arm, one step forward and two steps back and vice versa.

"Oh, *síiiiiiii*," he exhaled.

Along the way, Lottie spied two of her coconspirators, so identified by the single white rose stuck to the lapel of each. One was the regular desk clerk for the night; the other, the concierge. Tapping away on computers, the two, in Gucci-looking suits—lean, crisp, and lovely—looked up. "*Buenas tardes, señor y señora*," they said and glanced at her, then at each other, their dark eyebrows floating with anticipation.

Slimebucket didn't notice and gripped her waist like a vise as they zigzagged toward the elevator. "Dis is going to be fun. Oh jes." A glittery salmon in the grasp of a grizzly, she feared an acute attrition of sequins. Meanwhile, her heart jigged spasmodically, and she kept glancing around, searching for Papito or another life preserver.

Hunter and prey, they twirled primitively in the elevator as his mouth roved around her neck, slurping and breathing like a wild animal and making several attempts to descend to the depths of her uninteresting if underqualified and now-splotchy chest. Wishing desperately for a bottle of Windex, she wanted to squirt the both of them, ridding licker and lickee of the Eau de Toilette of Evil.

When they made it to Room 303, she said with great Marilyn Monroe finesse and tarantula-leg-eyelashes aflutter, "Tsk, *amor*. Do you remember what I like? Do you remember what I asked you to do?"

With a howl from his *boca* and a guzzle from his flask, he responded. "Okay, *amor*. Give me *un segundo*, okay?"

Lottie swiped the key, and he barreled into the room, a glob of desire and alcohol spilling into another opportunity to brandish his sadistic wares. She, on the other hand, froze—a human ice sculpture on the thick, shagged carpet in the hallway until the door clicked shut, then turned to spy Papito peeking from around the corner. One of the men from the lobby pretended to deliver a bill at 309 just doors away, shuffling papers and sliding one under the door.

They huddled together for a good minute in the hall, excited, snickering low, not really talking, just giving Señor Slimey time to change. Finally, nodding to the two, Lottie whispered, "Ready?" Papito and the *muy guapo* desk clerk saluted.

Lottie rapped on Room 303 and said "*¿Estás listo?*—are you ready, darling?"

From behind the door came a feral growl, followed by a "*Síiíiíi.*"

The lock clicked, fumbling ensued, and when the door opened, a figure neither quite male nor totally female appeared and caused her lips to lift and a snort to escape. In scarlet corset and black garters, stood a drunken blonde, hairy knees knocking, legs toddling in size-13 high heels.

"Darling. You remember. You know what I want. Walk to me, *amor.*"

Apparently, Belle Époque rang and someone answered, a vile someone whose image within minutes would appear around the world on Instagram and locally on two digital billboards. Too debilitated to notice the hotel employee and coconspirator down the hallway videotaping, he agreed to walk like a runway model toward Lottie.

It was truly more like a wobble than a walk, but Miguel Lopez, repeat rapist of her beautiful Julieta—and God only knew who and what else— had become Margarita, the Queen of San Salvador.

When he finished his runway stomp down the hall, he lunged at Lottie, hands wide open, fingers extended, targeting her breasts as though they were tiny lightbulbs and he would unscrew them. Lottie moved back until he fell face-first onto the ground, then reached up as though his life depended on it.

"*Amor,*" she whispered. "Thank you, thank you, thank you. Now you must go, *amor*, back into the room and get into the bed, and I will meet you there." The scarred, six-foot-four, platinum-blonde dudette and resident oaf ping-ponged from one side of the hall to the other until he smashed into the door and spilled into the room. Lottie expected him to pass out before she even made it off the third floor.

When the door slammed shut, she looked back and saw Papito and the male-model-slash-hotel-clerk waving to her violently. "¡*Venga!*" they urged and not a little panicky.

She ran to meet them, a blur of heels and glitter, sequins trailing down the hall like breadcrumbs à la Hansel and Gretel, and the three bolted down the stairs and out a back door. After bowing over with laughter, the clerk bid them *adiós* and reentered his reality, while Papito and she jumped into Nellie, who faithfully waited curbside and blasted in burps and chugs out of the parking lot.

Through the streets of San Salvador, past lit sedans full of revelers and commuters, Lottie and Papito arrived a block from the digital billboard to which Papito had pointed earlier and parked so that craning their necks would be unnecessary. Darkness had descended on the town, just before they would deliver a grand view of one of Evil's imps. Crickets and cicadas sawed their wings eagerly, magnifying the moment and their effort with a din of chatter.

Papito looked at his watch. "Almost time!"

Within seconds, a larger-than-life-size Marilyn with frothing chest hair and a nasty scar appeared in red corset and garters, wobbling down the hall like a drunken runway model. For thirty full and hilarious and beautiful seconds, he toiled on black stilettos and looked directly at the camera with dark and lustful eyes, revealing every inch of his face. At the end of the video, in bright lights and large font, appeared the words: *Miguel Lopez, El Oficial de la Policía Nacional Civil, ¡Es Muy Bonita!*

A roar of laughter split the old Volvo as the pair, the older and wiser, and the younger and definitely more foolish, the *profesor* and the *gringa*, the *papito* and the *hijita*, enjoyed the first fruits of their silly and vindictive labor.

"*Oye*, this tree of mischief will produce more fruit, ripe and delicious." He spoke as though reading her mind and in his signature metaphorical mode. "Bananas of extreme social fallout. Apples of work consequences. Oranges from the patriarchy in which he participates!"

"Will you keep in touch and let me know what happens?" she queried—after all, who knew what the true ripple effects would be?

"You know I will, my *hija*."

"And…you know where to find me. I will be just there, across El Golfo de México." With glittery nails, she pointed to what she thought might be the general direction of New Orleans. Of course, she could not stick around to witness it firsthand due to the flight out first thing in the morning, the leap back to her quasi-ordinary reality of New Orleans.

Detection of who carried out the feat would be nearly impossible. At least, Lottie hoped so. They had covered themselves with layers and layers of complication and anonymity. Papito knew people. Many people. Good people.

And Lottie suspected that *la policía* wouldn't help Señor Slimebucket investigate, as in such a testosterone-fat community, who would risk association with the newly minted, out-of-the-closet, trans *policía* or *transgénero*? Embarrassment by association should shut down any request. Once it was out there, only God could help him, and that wouldn't happen, Lottie hoped, though she was certainly in no position to say what

God would or wouldn't do, having just perpetrated her own extravagant, if complicated, version of sin. Papito, she prayed, would be safe in a world where creeps and criminals had a way of surviving and fighting, just like kamikaze cockroaches would survive nuclear war.

They drove to the second billboard and did the same thing: park, look at his watch, look up. Again, the dark disaster of a woman appeared: intoxicated, blonde, unsteady. Again, the words appeared. Again, they laughed to the point of tears, but this time, Papito erupted louder and longer. Lottie thought maybe because he had just witnessed too much in his lifetime. Too much corruption. Too much police swag. Too much abuse—especially of women. "Aye aye aye," he said between eye wipes. "I sure wish Victoria were here to see this! Ju know?"

"Aye, Papito. *Es possible* she is giggling in heaven, no?" She leaned over and gave him a hug, then produced her cell phone and tuned in to Instagram and Tumblr and Twitter and Facebook and YouTube, where the same comedy had already unfolded before thousands. "Look, ten thousand views on Instagram. Let's see what they're saying!"

What a babe!

What a fruitcake!

He won't last in the Policía. Ha! Serves him right.

Someone is out of the closet. Ja ja ja.

"¡*Sí sí sí!* Okay, *mi amor*, we must get going!" he insisted, and she agreed. The last thing they needed was for Gulliver to wake up and track them down. They were but Lilliputians in an insane Lilliput. "He could squash us!" He turned the key, Nellie sputtered to life, and they flew back up the hill, toward home and at least one more promise of justice.

Chapter Nineteen
¡Too Close for comodidad!

The smell of *carne* and plantains on the grill should have thrilled Lottie, but the knots in her tummy wouldn't allow it, twisting as though an invisible force tightened them, which, of course, it had. Dallying with Evil had consequences, and those consequences begat more consequences, and those consequences begat more and so on.

When her nerves jumped up and pranced around, Lottie couldn't eat, and if she couldn't eat, she just might have digestive issues, her stomach mimicking a disgruntled volcano. Add to that being in a foreign country, and she might have a bona fide intestinal blooper or stomach snafu or colon clusterfudge. But, with all that was going on both within and without, of course she couldn't eat! Because of this and in order not to worry or offend Papito, she might have to resort to a method from her childhood: the Stirring of the Veggies, or in this case, the *carne*. She smiled, thinking about how she fake-ate as a kid when her momma demanded she stay at the table until she tried her broccoli or green beans or asparagus. Stirring until the vegetables appeared at least half-eaten, she would pass each time. Or until she wore her mom out. Looking back now, she figured her mom always knew but let it slide anyway.

All that Lottie really required was a bucket of vino—then, then, she would calm down. To this end, she had already begun that task, seizing a glass of fat Chilean chardonnay. A chorus of various species began to lift her in song, with the glass frogs woggle-woggle-woggling and the crickets tweetum-tweetum-tweetuming. The mountain's soft evergreen arms also drew close until her soul melted in its arms, an old and familiar lover returning to rescue her.

It was, in fact, all good.

Lottie had tackled another apprentice of Beelzebub, and in her gut, where hornets nested and scorpions sometimes crawled, their comma tails threatening, she knew this was a necessary component of her already complicated life. Necessary—not optional. Something, again, she must do. Consequences or not.

Her second father loaded a tray with steak and plantains and raised it above his head, showing that he could still lift like a twenty-two-year-old. Behind him, the tangerine moon loomed so close that she thought she might be able to reach out and steal the man in the moon's nose and say, *Gotcha nose! Gotcha nose!*

"Ju must eat," he commanded beneath rising moustache and crinkling eyes. "It will be great, and you and I will be fine."

The moon and mountain and concert of animals convinced her stomach to settle enough until she capitulated and stabbed a steak unenthusiastically and placed it on her plate.

"So, I'm thinking..." she announced between bites.

"Oh, Lord, help us," he teased. "That is always a dangerous thing. *Ja ja ja!*" A small yapper dog yapped down the street, and a diesel-fueled car clacked by, part of the concert.

Putting down a forkful of steak, she said, "No, this is a good thing. So...I was thinking..."

"You said that already. *Ja.*"

"You—maybe coming to live with me? In the States."

To this, he shook his head until his salt-and-pepper curls bounced vigorously like Slinky coils. "I appreciate that, *amor*. But this is my home, and I am not leaving."

"But you said—"

"I know what I said. But I was just kidding, *amor*. I shall stay here. My life is full."

"But you could teach literature at Tulane. How fortunate they would be to have you! And Victoria isn't here. I would love to take care of you."

"What's to take care of? I am a grown man." His moustache pointed south.

"Okay, maybe I'm being selfish. Maybe I would just love to have you around." Lottie fluttered her lashes—false eyelashes still secured, tarantula legs waltzing, up and down, up and down, one-two-three, one-two-three. "Pleeeeease."

The moustache pointed north again, this time aiming for the stars and the intoxicating moon and toward heaven itself. "*Pues*, since you put it that way, I will think about it. It could be fun for a while. Though, someone needs to stay here and fight for justice."

"*Pero*, Papito, you have trained up a whole batch of young people dedicated to that cause. You have treated women equally and taught others to do so. Just please think about it. If you left, you would leave quite a legacy. Wouldn't it be fun to come and relax and let me pamper you for a while?" He gazed beyond her as though he could see that gumbo of a city, with its lumpy streets and drunkards and second liners and maybe, just maybe, himself in the middle of it.

After eating at least half her steak, which wasn't so bad after all, and drinking entirely too much wine, Lottie bid Papito *buenas noches* and collapsed atop the mattress, the scent of pine and guava and papayas singing a sweet lullaby.

Sometime mid-night, she stirred and shuffled sock footed to the open window, the mountain siren summoning her and offering unadulterated Goodness. *Oh God, how great is your creation.* She whispered, her breath a vapor in the cool air. Then she remembered a Bible verse put to music when she was a small child; she had learned it in Sunday school and now it reemerged, as God would have it, in timely fashion: *You will go out in joy and be led forth in peace. The mountains and hills will burst into song before you, and all the trees of the field will clap their hands.*

Softly clapping her hands with the oaks and pines and banana trees, she noticed her phone awakening too with the usual flashes and blinks and vibrations. Nowhere in the Bible did it say that the field of cell phones would clap their hands. Against her better judgment and in a half-asleep and highly emotional state, she chose to read a few more Instagram comments. It was the usual twaddling as before, some comments threatening him, others ridiculing, still others defending his right to dress however he wished. Lottie scrolled sleepily and stopped at one that made her want to run and awaken Papito, yet even in her half-conscious state, she knew it wasn't right and hesitated. He had worked hard as a writer and a professor and now as a coconspirator in a most dangerous prank.

You redheaded bitch, I will find you. You better sleep with one eye open. Along with the comment, Miguel Lopez posted a photo of himself, lips smudged with Luscious Red lipstick, lumpy scar pointing to his descending eyebrows. Had someone awakened the angry fiend?

Psssssssssssssssssss. Beginning yoga breaths automatically, she glanced at the glowing alarm clock. 3:31 a.m. Well, she didn't give a hoot what time it was, she was not going back to sleep. Danger's cold shower had just doused her, causing her to blink repeatedly and twirl this way and that like a lawn sprinkler. She ran to the light switch, flicked it on, ran to her suitcase and flung it open, ran to the window, looked around, this time for Evil, not Goodness. No one around, she confirmed and forced herself to exhale once more. *Psssssssssssssssssssssssssss.*

Like a frequent-flyer nutjob, she threw more items into the suitcase, exhaled, and returned to the window, which now didn't reveal trees clapping at all. Instead, the oaks and pines, banana and papayas seemingly stood with arms folded and peered ominously at her standing there in the scrap of a sequined outfit. The crickets and frogs screeched at high decibels, and the moon had moved along as though it were frightened too. She repeated the process: mindlessly refolding the items in the suitcase, exhaling, and returning to the window. She morphed into a robot and would remain so until Papito woke up. She hoped that his sweet smile and strong presence would calm her.

The hour and twenty-nine minutes until he awakened passed as in dog years. At 5:00 a.m., he finally knocked, and Lottie replied, "*Entra*, Papito."

"Oh wow. Are ju awake already?"

"*Sí*, Papito. I couldn't sleep. I'm very sad about leaving you and yet excited about returning home." Well, it was partially true, anyhow. She glanced out the window. It was still dark outside, and she wished the sun would go ahead and rise already. *Evil shrinks in the light. Evil runs from the light.*

"We must leave in *una hora* if you are going to catch that flight." He flew out of the room, gray hair a-jumble, wrinkled pajamas sagging, the great writer! Lottie jumped into the shower, which she had been too afraid to do while he slept. With the shower scene from *Psycho* rolling through her head, she jumped in and stood under it for a full minute, rubbing soap over her numb body as fast as she could.

~~

Thankful that he couldn't see her hands shaking as they raced to the airport, Nellie pushing the outer limits of her motor, Lottie willed herself to smile. He said, "Ju are very quiet. Ju do not wish to leave Papito?"

With an exaggerated frown that mimicked a circus clown, Lottie pushed down the guilt foaming up in the back of her conscience like bile. "*Sí*, Papa." She vowed not to tell him about that threat or the other one back in New Orleans, because the best gift she could leave him on this departure was a worry-free life, full of the simple pleasures of constructing a great plot or mentoring other, eager writers. Papito had no business accompanying her on this adventure beyond the borders of San Salvador, beyond videotaping a drunk, cross-dressing *policía*. She couldn't give him Victoria, but maybe, just maybe, she could leave him in peace.

"*Dime*—tell me—about your forthcoming novel. Everyone wants to know, of course. Can you? Tell me?" She loved that the whole literary world awaited her adopted dad's work.

"*Pues,* it's about a certain couple, a young and poor and handsome—*ja ja ja*—writer in love with an up-and-coming potter, the most beautiful woman ever in the history of the planet."

"I see. I wonder who that can be." She propped up her chin in her hand.

"And ju see, the writer bought a piece of her pottery each week—which nearly broke him—just to get a glimpse of her, this glorious woman."

"Ah-ha."

"In the end, it was worth it, though."

"*Claro*—of course." Smiling, she inwardly steeled herself for drop-off and looked in the side-view mirror to make sure they weren't being followed as they arrived at their destination.

The airport, a nettled nest with cars flapping in auricular bumbles, spawned diesels belching odors that one could taste, doors slamming, people yelling and hugging and crying, *las policías* waving everyone around in irregular patterns. The sun stayed in bed, hiding beyond its clouded quilt. Her palms dewed like the petunias flanking the gardens in front of the airport.

Papito whistled "Vaya Con Dios, My Darlin'," deliciously clueless, and pulled up at the departure area. They had prearranged his quick departure to get him to the *universidad* in time to prepare for his 8:00 a.m. class.

Kissing Papito on both cheeks and squeezing tears out of him like a sponge with an *hasta luego*—no *adiós!*—hug, she scanned the parade of rattling cars, passengers, and drivers, as well as the airline agents attending. No sign of the expectedly livid, scar-sporting, and probably hungover Miguel Lopez allowed her shoulders to loosen, and she finally exhaled the breath she seemed to have held for the entire car ride. Papito chugged away exquisitely in Nellie, a national hero disguised as a regular José.

After snaking through the long security line dotted with soldiers and being interrogated about the contents of a small tube and convincing the inquisitors that it was, in fact, moisturizer—SPF 95—Lottie reassembled herself in that humiliating 9/11-inspired ritual that passengers must go through after passing through the Arc de X-ray—replacing belts and shoes and pride—and headed toward the end of the concourse to get a semblance of exercise. When she arrived at Puerto 30, her turnaround point, she stopped and purchased one last cup of El Salvador *café*.

Much in the way gravity pulled her feet to the ground, a newborn held by an adoring couple drew her over involuntarily, with its black down peeking from its swaddle and its tiny yowl, some maternal fiber in her coming alive.

Along with a throng of onlookers, she allowed herself to relax finally, seeing that it was T minus ninety minutes to liftoff. The scent of baby lotion was interrupted by a cloud of nicotine, and before she could turn and assess, she felt a familiar and firm grip on her arm and a sharp cold poke in her back. The gripper hissed in her ear, "*Hola, preciosa.* Remember me?"

Chapter Twenty
A Slight Hiccup

Bourbon and anger burned Lottie's neck, and she felt a sudden urge to regurgitate, and hopefully would do so on his black Adidas, which was the only part of him she could see.

"*Hola*, creep," she snarled out the side of her mouth, not turning around. *Like he has the market on being tough?* She felt a ripple of courage—or stupidity—surge through her, which, under the circumstances, she considered to be a rare treat and more advantageous than panic.

An orchestra of chaos spewed from the intercoms as Spanish and English announcements guided excited passengers to their departure gates. Nueva Orleans wasn't yet among them.

Señor Slimebucket pulled her slowly backward out of the mesmerized crowd and continued to shove what felt like a *pistola* solidly into her ribs. The crowd ignored them, probably mistaking them for another amorous couple, entwined by choice. Glancing around stiffly and not wishing to trigger the trigger, so to speak, she surprised herself with fortified knees and a stiff spine.

Unfortunately, with a firearm pointed at her vital organs, it was not the best time for psychoanalysis. Perhaps she would later reflect on this sudden and newfound courage and unorthodoxly calm and steady legs.

And how—pray tell—had the elusive Señor Slimebucket gotten past security? Of course he would have flashed his badge and bravado, would have passed around his swagger and testosterone; but she had hoped that by now, word had spread like the native poison ivy across El Salvador and that the national police were allergic to it.

But here they were.

He pretzeled Lottie's arm snugly behind her back, which she was certain would bruise like a Salvadoran banana. "Smile, *preciosa*," he commanded.

"*No problemo*, creep." He probably flashed his gold tooth proudly at passersby, and she tried to lift her lips while her brain racked with ways to escape. Would-be passengers floated distractedly past them, suitcases following obediently, heels hammering the tile. Surely, someone would look her way and spot her imploring eyes and fake smile.

At last, an elderly woman à la Mother Teresa, with gray hair pulled taut at her nape, looked directly into her eyes. Lottie lifted eyebrows and mouthed, ¡*Ayúdame!*—*Help me!*—but the *abuelita*—grandmother—only smiled and offered the obligatory *buenas*—hello.

"Ow, you're hurting me," she grunted between clenched jaws.

The response: a rattling breath that sounded like a perverted engine coming to life, revving up for a supremely sinister event.

Smoldering in his brain's transmission, she imagined, were notions of rape. Also murder. And possibly dismemberment.

Just when she could feel anxiety trying to reclaim its proper place, its legally established easement in her wiring, threatening to ignite and render her totally insane and consequently useless, she heard the intercom sparkle with a beautiful message:

Now boarding, Avianca El Salvador Flight 627 to New Orleans at Gate Doce—12.

Miraculously, they had just cha-cha-cha'd past Gate 20 in descending order, toward the baggage claim and the exit. A round man with a rolling suitcase slammed into her shoulder and spat, "*¡Permítame, señor y señora!*" First of all, she wasn't a *señora*! Secondly, Lottie didn't even know if she wished to become a *señora*! And thirdly, of course, if she did, it wouldn't be to Señor Slimebucket, her scar-bearing, stenchy captor. How dare a complete stranger make such an assumption and declare her marriage to the idiot to whom she was momentarily attached? *Another inconvenient analysis, Lottie.*

Willing herself back to the present, not that it was a good one, she noted she was still alive, still able to think, still able to fight. That said, Gate 12 would come and go, as would Avianca el Salvador Flight 627 without her, if she didn't do something fast. Up ahead, she made out the lively amoeba of passengers gathered dutifully around the gate. They clutched and glanced down at boarding passes and cell phones, and lifted carry-ons.

"You'll never get away with this, creepo," she stammered, now feeling the familiar electricity rising from her toes, making its way to her cerebellum.

"What a *deliciosa* treat ju will make," he growled into her curls. "Did you see *la pelicula Silence of the Lambs*? Tastes like *pollo!*" He sounded as though he wore an evil grin, as if he were drifting into another level of consciousness. She swallowed. Sand. Her throat was a desert.

A small boy sporting a big-boy haircut with a zigzag razored onto the side of his head and staring down intently at an iPad tripped into Lottie, which caused the parents, laden with bags of El Pollito, to apologize profusely, then scold the child. Unfortunately, they failed to notice the hostage situation unfolding right under their *narices*. The grip on her biceps tightened when they scraped past the gate, she ocularly imploring her New Orleanians. *Who dat and help me!* A tall woman with a slicked-back ponytail, who might've been a supermodel, leaned into her equally handsome man. A troop of teenagers of both sexes, high on life and hormones and probably on a school or church trip, bent and slapped and swarmed around two unfortunate female chaperones, charged, no doubt, with thwarting nature.

"Don't even think about it, *preciosa*," he seethed, steering her, the marionette, past the gate.

About that instant, two thoughts rose from the ferment of agitation below. The first: *God didn't put me on this earth to become a victim, at least, not like this, and not now.* And the second: Oprah—who in many minds was the closest thing to God on earth—said never let an assailant take you to a second location. She would never let him take her out of the airport. Mind you, she might die trying, but she would at least put up a fight.

Though Lottie wasn't left dominant and, in fact, rather spastic in all things left, she mumbled, "Damn the torpedoes!" and cocked her left elbow up, pretended to wipe her forehead and then released it with all that her 120 pounds could muster. The bony dagger shot into pure muscle but was enough to cause him to release the grip.

Lottie shrieked, "*¡Terrorista! ¡Terrorista! ¡Tiene una pistola!*" and pointed at him, then bolted toward the gate, the supermodel and the hormonal teens looking back as much as they could. This alarm, of course, caused most around him to drop to the cold tile, except for one intrepid and balding man who lunged at him and tackled him by the waist. With one swift move, he wrangled her ex-captor's arms behind his back and whipped out a pair of handcuffs. As she backed into the crowd at the gate, trying to blend in, she noticed that, rather than struggle, Miguel Lopez apparently chose to lie still on the ground. This confounded her until he let out a "BWAHAHAHAHA" just as a Stephen King character would and cut the air and her mind with the terror of which he had been accused.

After the brouhaha, the crowd at the gate resumed a sloppy queue, and Lottie gathered enough wherewithal and moxie to remember her ticket and passport stuffed into her satchel splayed over her chest. While she fumbled with befuddled fingers, she felt an electrical shock on the back of her skull, which made her rub it. Turning slowly, Lottie saw a look she might never forget: eyes the color of sin seared hers as Miguel Lopez focused his final look on her before being whisked away.

Out of habit, she made a point to *psssssssssssssss* again, but it didn't help. Wobbling onto the airplane with limp legs, she collapsed into the window seat next to a rotund gentleman sporting a severe comb-over and who unfortunately took an immediate interest in her. Normally, strangers weren't strangers to her, but if she could not formulate a cohesive sentence, then how in the world could she speak to a nonstranger stranger, as it were?

Her row mate attempted a civilized conversation between bites of *semita de piña* (pineapple-filled tart), wiping his mouth, and, while still housing the confectionary in his ample mouth, began the preliminary *¿Habla español?* Pineapple mingled with a regrettable body odor to further exacerbate her already under-siege stomach, and, God forgive her, but she shook her head vigorously, a gesture that caused him to turn to the person on the other side and give it another go.

Through the scratchy and double-paned airplane window, she witnessed airport security still surrounding the unusually complacent rapist. Realizing that cobwebs of corruption and connectivity entangled the country, ensnaring the innocent like random flies, she knew he might darn well be immediately released, though they still held him in cuffs. Perhaps they staged a cruel show of honor for the trusting and the media and human rights organizations. Would her ruse render a disruption in the creep's little fraternity with fellow officers? Or...or...would it backfire in her face and produce even more creeps who would eventually seek her out, even across the El Golfo?

The thought of being the fly in the web, legs twitching futilely, thorax wriggling desperately, made her momentarily regret her actions. *Well, Lottie, did you think it would be all Mardi Gras and Jazz Fest without any hitches?*

The airport professionals appeared to huddle in conspiracy, while Miguel Lopez glared at the airplane with nastiness—such evil—evil piercing what? *Goodness? Heavens, no!*

She really didn't feel well—physically or mentally—but would have to deal with that on some unlucky therapist's couch. Automatically, of course, she prayed, but could only manage *Dear God.* The gargantuan and friendly neighbor dropped a napkin and leaned over to attempt pickup, his gut migrating mercilessly onto the armrest. He tottered and shimmied until the entire row seemed to shake, finally giving up and crumpling back in his seat. Lottie leaned over, picked it up, and handed it to him, offering a weak smile. It would just have to do.

From a cluttered cubicle in her brain, far from the water cooler and the window office and on the desk covered with old memos to self and to-do lists, she retrieved a positive thought: El Salvador is too proud, too patriarchal, too homophobic, and, by deduction, therefore must be too cross-dresser-phobic. It would never ever accept a man dressing as a woman, and definitely not within the roster of the National Police. "Testosterone R Us" is its slogan. "Patriarchy Forever!" its motto. "Muscles and Guns" its theme.

Thanking God, Lottie leaned back and closed her eyes, breathing through her mouth to avoid the bouquet of fruit and BO wafting from her greater and friendlier neighbor. The *clunk* of the cabin door closing made her legs regain feeling and her breathing renormalize.

When she opened her eyes and looked through the periscopic window, she blinked twice to check her vision. The security huddle had dispersed, and the muscle-bound, formerly restrained creep was standing free as a jaybird, flailing arms at gate agents and pointing toward the airplane. Shoving aside a female agent, he raced toward the Jetway. *Psssssssssssss.* Her eyes woggled from the male flight attendant in the aisle to the airport and back again. Then the blood left her body as a female flight attendant banged on the cockpit door.

Dios mios. Gulliver has awakened, and I am still a Lilliputian.

Chapter Twenty-One
God Sometimes Helps Fools

Gray curls swelled from beneath the captain's hat like a great surf as he emerged from the cockpit, giving him the appearance of a thinner, darker Mark Twain, ready to do business. *Never argue with a fool!*

His hat nearly touched the ceiling when he stood, and he leaned over toward a petite blonde attendant, and, after some discussion, looked out the peephole of the front door and scratched his head. The blonde pointed repeatedly toward the airport, then mimicked banging on a door. She picked up the phone handset and said something to someone on the other end that Lottie couldn't decipher. Was it him? Was it the gate agent?

"*¿Qué pasa?*" her seatmate wished to know, leaning over to get a better view and squishing her in the process.

"I…I don't know…" she managed, but really wanted to say *leave me alone! I can't think.*

Her cranium began to pulsate, a gross of firecrackers exploding within, fuse lit by the creep, and she was uncertain of exactly what was happening, only knowing that a violent man just outside the airplane door was seeking an audience of one: her.

Her sticky-handed and odiferous friend belched, then released with a grin, "*¡Perdóneme!*" She smiled weakly and rubbed her biceps like the dickens, shivering so from the over-air-conditioned cabin, the tiny vents blowing like a Category Three into her hair, and from the situation unfolding in the Jetway.

"Ladies and gentlemen, we have to address *un poco problema*, and then we will be underway. *No se preocupen*—don't worry—it is not mechanical." Lottie heard it, but she didn't hear it, floating as she was above the entire scene. *A little problem?*

Back in the web, she was the fly again, wriggling frantically, legs caught in silk, unable to escape, unless, of course, she opened up a can of Cajun crazy, ran down the aisle, and cracked an emergency exit, which would detonate an inflatable slide down which she would go, and that wouldn't do her much good as the spider and his spinneret waited just on the other side of the fuselage.

Bottle rockets soared. Her thorax ached.

Just for fun, Lottie turned and looked at the rear exit, contemplated the mechanics of the window exits just two rows behind her. Her seatmate rubbed his belly and said, "*Dios mío. ¿Qué pasa?*" She ignored him and closed her eyes tightly, trying to summon the courage to pray. For the first time in forever, she could not, though she had heard that in such times, Jesus could actually intercede for her. She hoped so.

When she looked back up and into the airport, she noticed that the agent appeared to punch a code into the door panel in order to let the creep in, an act that would allow the insatiable and bloodthirsty Señor Slimebucket to drag her by her red curls out of the web.

M-80s exploded.

Sinking into her seat, she yanked out the safety information card from the seat back in front of her and used it as a screen. Hiding her inconvenient hair behind it wasn't an easy task, so she sank even lower until she became an angular clump and smaller version of her former self. Big Man next to her stared. The woman next to him stared too. She knew that, like a hairy periscope, her mane rose above the card.

A *rump rump rump* thudded the cabin door. *Please don't open it... please don't open it.* She focused on Mark Twain, willing him not to do it. Another *rump rump rump* hit the cabin door, and she envisioned the creep's thick, disgusting fingers curled into a fist. *Please don't open it.*

What were probably seconds felt like twenty minutes at least, as she continued to dwindle into nothingness in Seat 19A. Finally, the pilot shook his head and returned to the cockpit, slamming the door behind him. The petite blonde picked up the intercom. "Ladies and gentlemen, we are now going to get underway, so please prepare for takeoff. Store all items beneath the seat in front of you and turn off your cell phones."

Please. Prepare. For. Takeoff. Four beautiful words. Probably the best four she had heard in her life and which combined like sweet symphonic notes to make her heart sing. Or rest? Or dance? She leaned over to her flight companion and blurted, "Please prepare for takeoff! Please prepare for takeoff," and leaned in farther and kissed his sweaty, pineapple-smeared cheek. Smells be damned! Overflowing perspiring flesh? Not a problem. Even if the flight was an hour and a half, she could handle it.

The engines whirred to life and blocked out whatever her new friend said in *español*. She leaned in and laughed and shrugged, indicating a false *no comprendé*, then dug into her satchel and pulled out a box of Tic Tacs to share, hoping he would accept. The jet began its glorious pushback, the emancipating and deafening engines shaking them violently.

Inside the airport, Lottie could see a levitating Miguel Lopez, spit flying from his lips into the face of airline workers. He turned back to the airplane and pointed two fingers at his black eyes, then right at her in an *I'm watching you* gesture. A male flight attendant asked her to push her bag under the seat. She happily complied, then turned to the window again, curled her fingers in a wave, and mouthed the words, *Buh-bye*.

Having effervesced from the dread, a gurgling stew out of control, she leaned back and luxuriated in safety—safety within the confines of a stiff and finite Avianca El Salvador seat—but safety nonetheless. Within ten minutes, the jet climbed steeply, the Aeropuerto Internacional Monseñor Óscar Arnulfo Romero and San Salvador becoming smaller and smaller until the clouds blanketed the city and the current source of fear.

Mark Twain entered the right side of her brain, puffing on a pipe. *It's not the size of the dog in the fight that matters; it's the size of the fight in the dog.* She gave herself a firm slap on the back, and her astute and new BFF rumbled with laughter and gave her a pat too.

Chapter Twenty-Two
Don't Mess with the Feds

Being a vigilante, if only a self-proclaimed one, was becoming exhausting. And while the satisfaction of forcing possible justice into an impossible situation rose within Lottie, the years taken from her life by the stress of doing so must've amounted to several. A gray hair waved brazenly from the shag of red on her head. She looked into the mirror at the hair and plucked it with as much energy as she could muster. Puffy semicircles gathered like storm clouds beneath her eyes, a sure symbol of the tropical storm brewing in her life. Two fence posts formed between her eyebrows.

Alas, her life in the Big Easy was not so easy, she laughed, and worse, the difficulty was voluntarily inflicted. Still, she couldn't stop her vengeful escapades. It was as if an uncontrollable and vindictive gremlin had seized her.

After convincing Lou not to join her in El Salvador, assuring her that Papito and his allies were sufficient protection, her best friend was kind enough to stay at the condo, ensuring a clueless but safe Frank.

That same healthy feline was currently in the preliminary stages of coughing up a hairball, gagging and hovering over her favorite Pier 1 rug. "Not on the rug, Frank!" She lunged at him and, in one well-practiced gesture, scooped him up and swung him over to the hardwood, where he succeeded in his disgusting quest. "Oh, kitty. I know. It's okay." She scratched his head and launched his feline motor into a loud rumble. "I know, baby. I know you want to go outside, but I just can't let you. Just give me some time to straighten out this whole mess, and then you can." He meowed loudly, and Lottie tried to appease him again. "I'll be back, boo. I'm just going to take out the garbage." Lottie greeted Lou as she passed her desk. "Hey, sista! How you makin'?"

"Just working on a few naturalization applications. You know, the usual." Lou chomped on a wad of gum, freely and uninhibitedly. One of the perks of working for your best friend.

"I'm just going to take out the garbage. You remember the garbage?" Lottie teased.

"Don't give me that crap! I took care of your cat while you were running around the globe, Miss Thing!"

"Point taken." Lottie knew better than to push it with Louisa Mae and shuffled past her toward the kitchen, where she gathered the stockpile of empty Abita cans and yanked the garbage out of the can.

Opening the back door, she was assaulted by Sweet Olive-infused air, and her nostrils danced in thankfulness. With a Hefty bag in hand and murmurings of the near miss in El Salvador in the back of her mind, she dropped the bag into then, almost missing the large object dangling from the crooked arm of the oak. Not knowing whether to laugh or cry—either being appropriate in the present state of weirdness—she pulled down the noose-hanged blow-up doll. Curiously, the female-shaped balloon wore a poorly crafted black burqa, duct-taped by some idiot onto her plastic body. Even in pranks, testosterone rules—were it estrogen, it would have been crafted more carefully.

"What a joke." She laughed as she untied the poor fake woman, lifted the burqa, and read a warning, Sharpied in large block letters: YOU'RE

NEXT.

"Yeah, right, dude. Whatever." Unable to gather concern from her now much-worldlier frame, she knew one friend who could. Lou's dander and blood pressure would certainly escalate quickly upon full disclosure of her newest friend and victim.

Throwing the doll on the ground for a second, Lottie spread her arms out and reached for the sky. She wouldn't let the beautiful sensory overload of the intoxicating weather be ruined by some amateur. Beyond the Sweet Olive, a distinct smell of crab boil wafted over. Her next-door neighbor must be boiling crawfish, and she wanted some. Would it be rude to invite herself over? *Jamais en Louisiane!* Never in Louisiana! She briefly contemplated shouting over the fence, but thought she should bring the evidence inside to preserve it. How could she hide it from Lou?

"I dub thee Gertrude. Now, we just have to find a place to hide you." She picked up Gertrude, stuck her under her arm, and carried her up the stairs and into the condo. Throwing the doll stiffly into the pantry and forcing the door closed, she hoped that Lou wouldn't discover the puffy intruder. Then, after pouring a large glass of Toasted Head, she raised it and declared, "Here's to you, Gertrude, Queen of the Blow-Ups, ruler over the inflated kingdom—sorry, queendom. May you never be real."

An hour later, Lottie decided to go ahead and hit the panic button with her bestie. Tugging the doll, who protested with squeaks and hisses, from the pantry, she presented her as though it was a gift.

"For you, my dear."

Lou responded as expected. "What the hell is that? Is this some kind of a joke?"

Lottie raised the burqa and revealed the stupid admonition and swore she could see a scarlet tide rising on Lou's tawny skin. *Here we go.*

"Lottie! Where did you find this? And when?" On the Louisa Mae scale between one and angry, this registered a solid ballistic. Her dark eyes seared Lottie's, igniting the uneasiness that only Lou could.

"Outside in the back, um, hanging from the tree." The idea of a feline shield entered her mind, and she grabbed the cat and held him between herself and her infuriated girlfriend. It wasn't that Lou would hurt her—because wouldn't that defeat the purpose?—but she did possess the ironic ability to scare Lottie when all she wanted to do was defend her. "I wanted to have a glass of wine first, darlin'." Frank purred, of course, and Lou scratched him under his chin, falling for it. "Besides, look at her. She looks so innocent. I named her Gertrude after my aunt." Lottie went over and tried to force Gertrude to sit, which was impossible as it was not the task for which she had been designed.

"And why the hell you gotta name everything?" Lou scolded. Thankfully, a laugh escaped, and she commanded, "All right, give me a damn glass of wine too!"

~ ~

The FBI did not find the caper nearly as funny when Lottie reluctantly called them a day later, the unfortunate Gertrude deflating more and more with each passing hour, making her look old and wrinkled rather than young and, well, puffy. Now Gertrude's covered and withered head rested in her own lap in the chair, as in a yogi pose, a mountain of fabric rather than a life-size doll for a lonely man. Ironic that the ostensibly Muslim man, the mystery stalker, utilized a sex toy to illustrate his point of Allah's will in her life.

Ah, but isn't life full of ironies? Case in point: a jazz funeral. Even the term was oxymoronic. Ditto on the decorated potholes, filled with plastic flamingos or, in December, Christmas trees. Even more on point, a waspy thirty-year-old jet-setting around Third World countries, hopefully—but not certainly—exacting justice to regain sanity in her life. Rather than sitting back and enjoying lattes and Instagram. And Mardi Gras parades. Now that was irony.

"Girl, don't touch it anymore!"

"You're right. All my criminal training, which was limited to one class under the fine tutelage of Judge Spalding at Loyola Law School, tells me to not reinflate Gertrude and slather my own DNA and fingerprints all over her disappearing body."

Wise decision.

It wasn't that Lottie had anything against the FBI, per se, she had just begun to distrust most feds, namely, immigration officials: USCIS, CBP, ICE. Perhaps she clumped all federal authorities into one heap.

When the feds finally arrived, through no fault of their own, they fired questions in semiautomatic fashion. Why hadn't she called them sooner? Who would do such a thing? What was the significance of the burqa? And was it technically a burqa or was it a hijab? Why did she speak Arabic during this terroristic age and in this quasi-anti-Arabic country?

Lottie answered, "I suspect the suspect to be a silly scoundrel, but all the people I know are really nice, so I have no idea." Mentally, she patted herself on the back, proud of the alliteration; but back in reality, the agents appeared annoyed.

A stiff thirty-something female agent with a bob haircut shifted in the dining chair, her federal-issue suit masking her probably tiny waist and her thick panty hose squeezing her probably toned legs. She scribbled something into her small spiral notebook, then glanced at her more junior, and Ryan Gosling-looking, partner. Did they roll their eyes?

"I'm sorry." Lottie couldn't help herself. The bob cocked her head and lifted one side of her lips. "Okay, okay. I'll try to take this more seriously." And she would. If she didn't respect law enforcement, why should they protect her? And who knew when she might need them down the road.

The assailant, the jerk—or, to be fair, jerkess—was an amateur. Lottie was almost embarrassed for the stalker. Wasn't she even worthy of a real and more creative hoodlum? One who could produce a better effigy?

Ryan Gosling spoke. "We're going to have to take the doll in as evidence, okay?"

"Oh, no. We were just getting to know each other." Internally, she slapped herself, but it did little good. "See how relaxed she is? And by the way, her name is Gertrude."

"Miss Fornea, do you or do you not want our help? Besides, this could be a national security issue. This person could be connected to a terrorist cell. So knock it off." And just as when the principal scolded her, she snapped out of it, straightened in her chair, and cleared her throat. Rather obviously too.

Puh-lease, a terrorist cell? And spending time on little ole moi? I don't think so.

"You don't mind if we have a look around, right? Inside and out?" the female asked.

"Of course not. Please, can I get you a Co-Cola or something?" There now, see how cooperative she could be?

"We would also like to question your secretary."

"Um, it's best to refer to her as my assistant, if you don't mind." Lou would kill them, then her, if they titled her incorrectly. Forget terrorism, Lou-ism, was more of a threat to world security than Iran obtaining a nuclear weapon. More of a threat than Kim Jong-un and Trump going at it. Lottie was glad she didn't have to be there for the questioning.

"Do you have any other employees?"

How she wished. Along with a weekly housekeeper.

Well, there was Mister George. Sweaty, weed-whacking Mister George with his obsessive-compulsive, if overexuberant, landscaping. "I have a landscaping guy, but he's technically not an employee."

"Okay, then, let me rephrase the question. Can you give me the names of anyone who has access to your office or a key to your property? Employees or independent contractors? Better?"

My, but Miss Bob could be sassy. Perhaps her job didn't excite her anymore. Perhaps she had a crush on younger Ryan Gosling-like G-man. Perhaps she had been jilted by him. Also of interest, Lottie detected a New York accent. *Maybe she's angry about being exiled in Louisiana, the northernmost Caribbean state. And who could blame her?*

Lottie shifted. The chair felt aflame as she dealt with Miss Sassy Bob. "Just me, Louisa in the next room, and Mister George, who comes about twice a week."

"Can I get full names and contact information?" The female pushed the pen across the note as though it weighed a ton, then released an audible sigh.

A wave of empathy splashed over Lottie, causing her suddenly to feel sorry for Agent Regrettable Hair. It wasn't like she was unattractive. She just needed a little tweaking in the coiffure department. And what if she did hate being stuck in the Land of the Idle, her New York engine revving up futilely stuck in the bayou mud? Who could blame her? Lottie was certain that busting a drug ring in the Bronx or throwing Wall Streeters into white-collar prisons trumped dealing with a feisty and confused New

Orleanian.

Lottie vowed to befriend Agent Grant as she identified herself. "By the way, I just bought a king cake. Would you like some?"

The ice began to thaw. Her mossy eyes smiled. "I thought you'd never ask. I mean, I did see it on the table when I passed. Is it Randazzo's or Gambino's?"

"Gambino's this time. We switch it up. Equal opportunity and all, right? Just remember, though, if you get the baby, you have to buy the next king cake and invite us over." Lottie rose and headed toward the kitchen.

"Yeah, I learned that tradition the hard way!" A glacier melted and flooded the office with a potential and newfound friendship. Boundaries dissolved way too easily in the Big Easy.

When Lottie entered the next room, she found Lou fake filing, which she was known to do when the conversation in the office interested her. "Oh, Lawd. They wanna talk to me. Me?" She absentmindedly stacked papers on top of the open file cabinet. Lottie gently took the papers and looked into her eyes, which seemed to flit spasmodically. She put the papers down and cut pieces of the purple, green, and gold cake.

"No worries, babe. It's just procedural. You're not a suspect. You might think of something that I couldn't. And it will help them track down whatever creep is doing this." Lottie heard whispers in the next room, FBI lingo, no doubt. The clock on the wall ticked loudly. The smell of sugar and cinnamon from the king cake rose in delicious defiance.

"But what about my past? Will they learn that I smoked pot in high school? Or that I like to shoot my gun at the range across the lake? Or that I have, you know, connections?"

Lottie shook her head. "No, dawlin'. Don't worry. I don't think you'll interest them too much. No offense." Lou cracked a weak half smile, a good effort given by one getting ready to be interrogated by the feds.

"Here, take these with you." She shoved two plates into Lou's hands. "And just be yourself. They're going to love you!" Lottie winked and slapped her on the butt.

"Yeah, right," she grunted.

~ ~

Fake filing. It wasn't just for assistants. Lottie stood at the cabinet near the door with a pile of scratch paper in hand at the ready, should the door open. Frank looped his velvet body through her legs, knitting one and purling two. She imagined her ears turning like satellite dishes to the forbidden conversation.

"I mean, yeah. I smoked a few times. Are y'all gonna arrest me?"

"No, Miss Fiorini, we won't arrest you. We have bigger catfish to fry." Agent Grant attempted humor. This was a good sign.

"Oh, I love catfish, fried or grilled. Ya heard?"

"What?"

"Oh geez. I'm sorry, baby, I mean, ma'am. It's just an expression here. People say 'ya heard' after saying something, dat's all. Heck, I don't know where it came from. Oh, geez. I'm talking too much. Okay, I'm going to shut up now." Lottie envisioned nuggets of perspiration beginning to form under her friend's arms and across her dark forehead and wished that she could be in there to hold her hand.

The expressions on the agents' faces had to be scrunched-up mugs of confusion. Lottie had already concluded decisively that Agent Grant was alien to the Crescent City, which, if you thought about it, would be like landing on Mars. Ryan Gosling, or Agent Spotansky, as he identified himself, was more difficult to read. The way his Rs curled up at the end of words like "there" and "our," indicated roots in the Bayou somewhere, but other than that, no clues to nativeness presented themselves. Had he rid himself of Y'attyness in Quantico? Either way, Lou would perplex them, local or not, as she did most people.

Explaining the city's patois and foibles to Yankees would be nearly impossible and sometimes produced condescension on their part, spoken or not. Lottie hoped they didn't look down upon Lou, because, like a pig to truffles, she could sniff it out. And that wouldn't be pretty. Then she might get arrested.

Muffled voices seeped through the crack in the door. Lou fidgeted, no doubt, and her Sicilian eyes must have been jittering. "Miss Fiorini, you say that you stayed here the past few days, correct?" A pause. "Did you see anyone or anything unusual?"

"Let me see. Please, y'all go ahead and eat the king cake while I think about it." Another pause. "Okay, so a few people came by."

"Did you recognize them? Were they clients?"

"I didn't recognize them because they were new. They just wanted a consultation, but I told them the attorney was out of town and to come back in a week."

"Do you remember what they looked like?"

"Let me see." Soon, she would crack her knuckles. "One was a young African woman. Tall. Skinny. Very pretty. Another was a Muslim man, around fifty years old or so."

"How do you know he was Muslim?"

"Because I've met many Muslims, and he wore a skull cap. I think it's called *kufa*. No, wait, *kufi*. Oh geez, I don't know. And, he had a long beard, which is, you know, like they dress when they're devout."

Oh no she didn't.

"Devout, huh?" the male regurgitated.

The female jumped in. *Kapow!* "So, you've met a lot of Muslims, you say? Why is that?"

Lottie clenched her hands and looked ceilingward. *Oh, God. No. Crazy people are crazy people. Who cares what religion they are?*

Obviously, use of the words "Allah" and "infidel" and the distasteful replica of a burqa were clues pointing to the fastest-growing religion in the world, but delivering the "M" word to an agent of the organization that was hypersensitive to it was akin to presenting John the Baptist's head on a silver platter to Salome.

"That's because Ms. Fornea has represented several clients who are Muslim." Lottie knew that that statement would beget many more questions about Muslims, but for some reason, rather than get into the specifics about her Muslim clients, they moved the interrogation along quickly. Maybe they would return to the matter at some point.

"Did he speak English?" Silence. Maybe she nodded, maybe she didn't. "Did he say which country he was from?"

"I think it was Pakistan." Lou coughed.

A cardinal pecked at the window next to Lottie, where she had spread a few sunflower seeds.

"Can you describe him?"

"So, like I said, he seemed around fifty or so years old. He was about my height. Oh, I'm five-nine, by the way. He had a belly, wore a crocheted skull cap, had a salt-and-pepper beard. Light brown skin. Dark eyes."

"Did you happen to get his address?" Silence. "Okay. Anyone else hang around here? Anything out of the ordinary?"

"Not that I know of."

Shuffling ensued. "Okay, Miss Fiorini. Thanks for your help. I'm sure your friend and colleague appreciates your help, and so do we. We will follow up soon with y'all, if that's okay." Unnatural, it was, when a Northerner used y'all, but hey, at least she tried.

Lottie skittered across the room to the desk and tapped the computer to life. The door opened, and, with eyes rolling skyward, Lou emerged followed by the interrogators.

"We have a lot to go on right now, Ms. Fornea, but what we really need to get is a copy of your files."

Oh geez. Here we go. Lottie took a long deep breath. "And I would like nothing more than to give you copies of my files. However, according to the Code of Federal Regulations, I can't do that. They are confidential."

Her new buddy, Agent Grant, spoke first. "Ah, but Counselor, you know that for the safety of the country, and in this case, for you also, we are authorized to take a look at the files. Terrorism will always trump confidentiality."

They have a point.

In court, she might lose the battle. Still, it killed her to turn files over and breach a promise made to her clients, especially when lives were threatened. And who knew what the government, which admittedly could be sloppy with its files, would ultimately do with them, even when the crisis had been resolved? What if info leaked to the respective countries that endangered her clients?

Of course, she knew which names they would single out. It certainly wouldn't be the Christian ones.

Then again, weren't these agents the employees of the taxpayers? And wasn't she a taxpayer? "I'm sorry, y'all. I just can't do that. If you really want the files, you're welcome to get a warrant."

The agents looked at each other a long second, then Ryan Gosling spoke. "You do realize that this is to protect you. It's not just about terrorism." Lottie nodded. "Very well."

Ending in a good place, they shook hands, and Lottie even sent them on their way with more king cake. She hoped and prayed that neither got the baby.

Chapter Twenty-Three
Monkey Business

From the office window, Lottie and Lou watched the feds as they drove away in the way-too-stereotypical black Ford sedan. That Lottie was the object of a federal investigation did not surprise her. What did, however, was that it wasn't regarding her recent trips abroad. Neither Agent Gorgeous nor his female counterpart asked to see her passport or travel records. This, of course, was a very good thing, for if the FBI caught wind of her new hobby, it might just tell its annoying sibling, the IRS. And that would be the end of NO(LA) Women for Justice. So many women had been victims, and, if she could swing it, she might avenge more. To that end, Bosnia, purged of many Muslims and reeling in post-Yugoslav-war abuse and Sudan, the Mother of all Radical Islamic Countries, loomed brazenly in the balcony seats of her brain.

"Girl, I was so nervous," the usually unperturbed Lou said. "I hate that."

"What—getting interrogated or getting nervous?" Lottie joked.

"Both, I guess. I need a drink."

"But it's only noon! Come to think of it, though, that did wear on my nerves too, dawlin'. Want to go over to the Monkey Business for a second to debrief?" Lou nodded weakly. Lottie had never seen her look so vulnerable, and she supposed that hanging around the feds would do that to a person who prided herself on avoiding them for so long.

"Mind if I check my email first?" Lottie sat at her swivel and scrolled down the usual lengthy queue of emails. She stopped and paused.

"What? Is it him?" Lou got the wild, possessed look in her dark eyes again.

"No. It's just from my friend Ishmael." A broad smile took over a large portion of Lottie's face.

"Oh, yeah. That guy. You like him, don't you?"

"What? Oh, yeah. I mean, he's okay."

"Lottie, I've known you for your whole life. I know when you like someone. As a matter of fact…"

"What?"

"Oh my gosh. You don't love him, do you?"

Outside, the neighbors were talking way too loud. Lottie glanced out the window, where the sun went undercover behind a trio of puffs.

"Well, that's kind of impossible, right? He's eight thousand miles away."

"Yeah, but you have a funny look on your face. Besides, I thought we were fellow man-haters these days. What happened?"

Through a nagging smile, Lottie tried to defend herself. "For the record, I have never been a man-hater. I just hate what some of them do to women. And…and I hate the societies they've created to oppress women." She swung back and forth on her fuchsia throne.

"Well, that's fair. Still, you look kinda funny, like you're in love!"

Lottie knew that at a minimum, she looked like an idiot. Like there was a village missing her. Her cheeks flamed, and she couldn't do anything about it. Worse, she didn't *want* to do anything about it. Independence R Us, right? Maybe it was just that he was across the earth. Hidden in a tiny office in the middle of the war-torn country in the middle of the Hindu Kush. Remarkably too, a very, very long-distance relationship delivered zero vulnerability. Zero. Couldn't she then, after all, let herself dream about him a little bit?

And drift off onto a magic carpet she did. She could see his bronze face, feel his cut arms. Only, for some reason, this time, she saw him in New Orleans—walking with her in Audubon Park, biking along the Mississippi, eating muffulettas on Decatur. How foolish. But, hey, it was her script to produce, and she would write it as she saw fit. A pinch on the arm crashed the fantasy, sending her right back to earth and her office chair. "Owwww!"

"Let's go," Lou muttered and grabbed her by the arm.

~~

If bars were supposed to be dark, then the Monkey Business fulfilled its mission. Entering from the sunlight into the abyss rendered them blind, though they had developed an embarrassing adeptness for feeling their way to the long and sticky bar. Lou grasped Lottie's hand and tugged her through the chair-and-table maze as though reading furniture braille. In a sense, it was a bizarre comfort zone for Lottie. She had cut her drinking teeth there, back in her UNO days, when her frontal lobe had yet to develop and her hormones led her to guys they she shouldn't have. As she grew older (not necessarily wiser), she questioned the attraction of the venerable drinking establishment. Maybe it was the three-for-one drinks served on Tuesday nights that originally lured her? Or the biweekly ladies' night that attracted her and her friends? And the gents who followed the ladies like they were Pied Patricias?

The bartender delivered two cosmos without fanfare, and she and Lou reflexively lifted glasses. "Here's to surviving interrogation," Lottie toasted. They clanked and sipped. "You're not really going to let that bother you, are you?"

"No, but man, I just hate dealing with cops…especially the feds. Locally, I'm okay. I know a few people, you know?"

"You? Nah. You have zero connections. Right? Anyways, dawlin', it's all going to be okay. They are so not interested in you. No offense."

"Yeah, but I hope that your problem goes away soon. That's starting to creep me out. I mean, I was probably there when the guy dropped it off."

An icky awareness of self-centeredness saturated Lottie's head just as the vodka was in her blood. Not once through this stupid ordeal had she ever considered Lou and her feelings. "I'm so sorry, Lou. I've only been thinking of me me me throughout all this. Are you okay? Do you want to stop working for a while and stay away from it all? My treat!"

"No way. I won't leave you." She raised two entwined fingers. "Together always, right?"

Lottie did the same. "Through thick and thin! Good and bad! Sort of like a marriage, only better, right?" They fist-bumped and then laughed—the kind of giggles inspired by Grey Goose. "Remember when we became blood sisters? What were we, like twelve?"

"Yeah, something like that. You were such a wimp!"

In their prepubescent glory, Lottie and Lou had hidden in the woods behind Lottie's house in a special camp-like area that they cleared and claimed as their own. It was where they tried cigarettes, where they told creepy stories. Lou brought the needle and Lottie flinched at first, but then bit her lip and let Lou poke. They rubbed tiny index fingers together, sealing their friendship forever.

Remarkably, after only one cosmo, Lou declared her ability to return to the office, even her desire. This pleased Lottie, who couldn't wait to return to her desk and her computer perched on top of it. It was Thursday, or weekend's eve, in NOLA and in the rest of the US, the beginning of revelry that should, in theory, not begin until the following day.

In Muslim countries far away, though, it was already Friday, a holy day, the Day of Jumu'ah or Day of Prayer, which meant that Ishmael might be more available to communicate with her. Without telegraphing his conversion as a Christ follower, he carefully navigated the world of faking it, sometimes attending prayer services and praying to Christ instead of Allah. Maybe he was skipping it just then. Businesses would be closed, he would be more relaxed, and she might be able to—oh, maybe—Skype with him.

Lottie assumed her eyes sparkled at the thought, and was grateful for the darkness. She spoke in her most serious tone. "Yeah, we should get back. Lots to do."

"Lots to do? Yeah, right! Don't think I don't know what you're up to." Okay, so she couldn't hide anything from Lou. Not even in the dark. "Just be careful, all right, boo? I don't want you to get hurt."

"*Tabaan!* Of course."

"And don't use that Arabic crap with me!"

"Oh, yeah, that." She grabbed Lou's hand, yanked her up, and ushered her through the beer-soaked jungle.

~ ~

The shock waves began in her brain, specifically where lovely things were stored, and traveled down her lesser-endowed chest through her long arms and down to her fingertips. Responding to Ishmael's email which, by the way, merely read *Hey, how are you? I was just thinking about you and your beautiful blue eyes,* made her shiver with an unidentifiable emotion. And no, it wasn't love as Lou suggested. Whatever it was, however, possessed all of her. Every inch of her five-nine-ness, all her innards, all her soul. Not even Lottie's recent carousing into another country could engender such commotion. Like live wires, her fingers zapped as they tapped in the response, which consisted of two explosive words: *Oh, hey.*

But then something extraordinary happened.

By some miracle of technology which she had no desire to understand, and from almost directly across the globe, from a laptop glowing in the darkness of the Afghan night, lit only with spotty electricity at best, came the *bing* of a Skype request. It was from a username she did not recognize, Believer, but she had morphed into a ridiculous chance taker lately, so what was one more risk? She clicked Accept and leaned way back in her chair to brace herself.

Within seconds, Skype chimed with its bizarre, space-age ring. It was Believer. The mysterious caller, as Lottie hoped, was not so mysterious. She trembled while the computer did its thing, and before her vodka-subdued eyes appeared one Ishmael, his caramel eyes dancing like a small child's.

"Hallow," he began, and she inexplicably began to laugh. Correction, guffaw. This man, who sat so far away, made her smile. Unabashedly. Curiously.

Finally, she managed, "Oh. My. Gosh. It's you!"

"Indeed it is." Blackness loomed behind him, and she hoped only goodness as well.

"Oh. My. Gosh." she squeaked, then chided herself for her idiocy. "So, how are you?"

"I have been so good. I can't reveal all that has happened recently because of you know. You know?" He rolled his eyes toward the ceiling, and she thought his voice quivered.

Dear God, how she knew. How he had occupied the top of her prayer list. How she worried like a mother about his safety. Conversion was love, but conversion was also death. The Taliban, capable of anything, invented new forms of torture each day. It was as though its creative juices flowed solely to that cause. Why not direct it to improving infrastructure? Planting a garden? Designing new threads to wear? Grooming themselves?

And the Taliban was just one potential enemy. Warlords abounded. Families who would destroy in the name of Honor. And even society at large. The majority of the general population had been brainwashed by malicious and long-winded mullahs because of its inability to read Arabic, the original language of the Quran. Unable to read the instruction manual for their lives, most found themselves at the feet of the religious leaders and their radical interpretations and whims. If the mullah said "Jump," the congregation might ask "How high?" If a mullah said "Stone," the locals might ask "When?" or "Where?" And if a mullah declared a person to be an apostate, then guess what? He was. And what happened to apostates or infidels? Death. By any mode. Just like the Clue board game, murder could happen in a variety of ways. Colonel Mustard in the library with an Uzi? Miss Scarlet in the kitchen with a rock? Not a problem.

But at that moment, he was safe and sat before her like Adonis behind a desk and screen. She would never understand his interest in her, but would enjoy it while it lasted. Interestingly, now that he sat in front of her, she didn't know exactly what to say. What she did know was that her flesh was the color of a pomegranate. She could feel it. Must her emotions be so obvious? Her skin a canvas? She felt like a human mood ring, telegraphing each emotion with a spectrum of reds.

"So," he continued, "how are you?"

"Oh, me? Well, I'm doing really well, you know? Up to my usual shenanigans, you know?"

"Oh, yes. I do know about your—how do you say—shenanigans? I participated in some, remember?" And for a moment, she was back in the Hotel Serena in Kabul, looking into his concerned eyes.

What in the good Lord's name have I done? Ishmael, Papito: two innocents dragged into danger.

"No worries, Lottie Jan." Jan, a term of endearment used in Afghanistan and throughout Persia. Its meaning: dear. She could get used to that.

"Okay, phew. So, I didn't get a chance to tell you, but I went to El Salvador to do similar work. Do you know where El Salvador is?"

"If I don't, then I didn't get my tuition's worth at the University of Chicago." He revealed all his bleachy white teeth.

Oh, yeah, that. "Good point. Sorry, Ishmael."

"Things are getting crazy around here, if you know what I mean. But, can you say my name again?"

"What? Oh, how come?" And what did he mean by "getting crazy"? The idea made her uneasy.

"I like the way you say it. I want something to think about later."

The mood ring turned a shade of strawberry. By the end of the Skype session, she might cover the gamut of fruits. "Um. Okaaaayyyy. Ishmael. Ishmael. Ishmael. That should hold you for a while!"

"And speaking of a while, I have to get going. It's not good for me to be on so long."

"Okay, sure. It was nice seeing you, if only in the video sense."

He looked around him as though someone might be approaching, waved quickly, then whispered, "Bye, Lottie," then disappeared from the screen. But hopefully not from her life.

And just for the record, she liked the way he said her name too.

~ ~

"You done in there? We have work to do!" The shouting preceded the banging. Lou could be that way—no, not productive—jealous. Though a man eight thousand miles away should be no threat to their thirty-year friendship, Lottie still cut her slack. No one was perfect. Louisa's weird jealous and possessive manner appeared occasionally, though she must know how much Lottie loved her, couldn't imagine life without her, and would never let a man come between them.

The other idiosyncrasy that had puzzled Lottie for a couple of decades was Lou's secrecy, as though she was an operative for the CIA and the fate of the world rested in her hands. Lottie didn't know if this was culled from her Italian ancestry and lifestyle, centuries of Sicilianess inculcated into a twenty-first-century broad. Lottie wanted to tell her that nothing she did would really shock her, yet even when she went to the grocery, it was like she wouldn't say what she was going to purchase. Woohoo, a big mystery, buying a loaf of bread.

"Girl, calm your jets!" She gave it right back to her. "Okay, what's so important?"

"We got work to do." She shoved a schedule under Lottie's nose. But it was a Thursday afternoon, which, in New Orleans, was considered Friday Eve, and celebrated as such. What on God's green earth could be happening?

"Don't forget. We have a board meeting tonight. You know…your bright idea for a nonprofit? We have things to do."

"Didn't I just return, though?" She looked around the room pretty much like Dorothy had when she landed in Oz, and she clicked her heels together for effect. "I could swear I just returned. Why is this happening so soon? Did you schedule it?"

"No, baby. You did. Don't you remember? You wanted to 'debrief'"— she made the nasty air quotes—"while everything was fresh."

Oh, yeah, that. "Can I cancel? I'm really pooped. I thought maybe you and I could go catch a movie or something."

"But, baby, a lot of people probably rearranged their schedules so they could come."

Lottie hated when Lou was right. And noble. "Of course, you're right. I just feel like relaxing for a bit."

"So do it now, baby." Lou stood there for another second, boring her dark Sicilian orbs into Lottie. "Oh, crap. You still thinking about that guy, aren't you? Son of a gun! I knew it!"

Having a best friend who knew her better than she knew herself could be a liability. "Yes. Actually." No sense in hiding it from the soothsayer. Weird, though, how a nagging thought now interfered with the elation that first flooded her when she saw him on the screen. She couldn't shake it.

"You okay, boo? You don't look as happy as you did earlier. If he hurt you, I will go to the Hindu mountains myself and kick his butt!"

"Hindu Kush."

"What? Oh, whatever they're called." Lou waved a hand to wipe away the mistake. Lou also had trouble remembering geography and the proper names of places, which Lottie happened to find adorable.

"Nah. It's not that. I think he's in danger."

"Oh, crap! Dang, I already said that."

"I'm just worried."

"I wouldn't be surprised. It is Afghanistan, after all. What happened?"

"Nothing, really. It's just he had to get off really quick, like someone was coming, and as you say, it is Afghanistan and he is a Christian convert and he did help me with my selfish, stupid caper."

"Baby, we been through this before. Anyone who has helped you—Ishmael, Papito, the workers at the hotel—they did it because they feel like you do. They want to make things right in the world."

"I know, but it was my idea. I could've just sat back here in good ole New Orleans and minded my own business, but nooooo." Lou put her hand on Lottie's shoulder, offering some degree of comfort. Lottie rubbed both cheeks with her palms. "If anything happens to him, I will never forgive myself."

"You know what? Nothing is going to happen to either of them. I too have intuition, ya heard, and it tells me that everything is going to be fine."

Lottie so hoped she was right.

On the feeder suction-cupped to the window a sparrow landed. He dug around for his favorite seed, then looked up, directly at her.

Yes, it would be all right.

~ ~

She would have to move fast, enlist her nonsecretary friend to help her with the board meeting. In less than two hours, the mishmash of humans would come barreling in with all their foibles and jewelry. Just the thought made her smile and shook her momentarily out of the worry. Food was what they needed, and fast. Who could they call? Restaurants dotted the neighborhood like freckles did her skin, prolifically. In the wider metropolitan area, the choice was overwhelming.

"Lou, can you help me with something?" Her put-out best friend stuck her head in the office. "Would you mind, pleeeeease ordering some food for the board meeting? I know you don't like to do that, but could ya? Would ya?"

"All right. I'll do it." *Glory be!* "But, I get to pick." Lou put her right hand squarely on her right hip.

"No worries, dawlin'. And thanks."

And off she went, out to order Lord-knows-what from Lord-knows-where. The last time Lottie entrusted her with the task, she ordered all her favorites: jambalaya, seafood platters, the works.

This bounty might hurt the pocketbook, the very one that had become dependent on marriage and employment cases, both scarce lately. She couldn't exactly charge asylees a hefty fee, could she? Still, it was necessary; and delegating the errand to Lou gave Lottie a much-needed moment to herself. Again, she needed time. To worry. If she could actually get paid for worrying, she would be a rich woman, having become such an expert at it. Maybe she could lease her abilities out to those without the time to worry, she was so good at it.

She played a little game where she called it constructive thinking, but in the end, the result was the same: frazzled nerves, deep lines between her brows, more imbibition. It was like a haunted amusement ride she could not get off. She would go through one spooky scenario to another, try to invent a solution and fail, then repeat. The bogeyman in this scenario was the Taliban and other iterations of it. On the ride, a bearded, turbaned man would pop out, grab Ishmael, and drag him before the masses. Lottie would rack her brain trying to think of a way to get back into Kabul, rescue him, and get him—and her!—safely out of the country. But then the ride would make another loop, her trapped in the seat, and the Taliban monster would pop out again from behind a curtain.

So what could Lottie do about Ishmael? What if he really was in trouble? It was, after all, her occupation: rescuing people. The problem was she never actually physically brought them to the US. If they could get here, then she could help them obtain political asylum. Big whoop. It was a constant source of frustration for her.

"I ordered fried chicken," yelped Lou from the next room. Not the healthiest of choices, but it was a risk worth taking. The board would appreciate it anyhow.

The board! Lottie remembered—Fatima was on the board. Fatima was Ishmael's aunt. Therefore, Fatima might have information about the aforesaid Ishmael. That idea alone was enough to get her off the scary ride. Yes! She would simply inquire about the state of Ishmael, and Fatima would reassure her.

Outside, the banana leaves stroked the window seductively, keeping a gentle rhythm with Frank's snoring. Across the street, her elderly neighbors got into their vintage Buick and puttered away. Married for fifty-one years, those two. And with a buzz and a growl, Mister George fired up the blasted weed-whacker again, though she had asked him repeatedly not to. He had a knack for beginning projects the day of events at the condo, especially board meetings.

Lottie wondered if he stayed around just to get a peek at Fatima in her hijab, then later complain to her about how the world was turning "Muslim." With her help. It must be his only exposure to a real live, genuine Muslim. Up close. In the flesh. Perhaps in the vein of an animal in the zoo? And did he take the time to get to know her personally? Not a chance. He was educated at the School of Conservative Talk Radio, true, but sometimes the way he looked at her made it seem as though he was actually attracted to her. Could that even be possible?

Lottie looked down at him, her de facto uncle, navy-blue work pants sagging below a well-tended belly. How blessed she felt to have him around, incessantly buzzing around, but still… As only those of his generation could, he brought to her an old-school, homemade-quilt level of comfort. She felt loved and safe with her flannel-clad friend constantly on her lawn. She waved and watched him whack away at the narrow curb and the one weed that stood bravely near it.

Lou brought in a slender stack of mail, the real, hard-copy kind, most of its brethren having given way to emails and the internet. Lottie fished through it, past the tide of junk. No, she didn't want a new sofa. No, she didn't have any items to donate to Bigger Siblings.

At the bottom of the stack, something odd awaited. It was white and rectangular, with her address handwritten in cursive. Could it be a real, bona fide letter? She hadn't seen one—not a card, but a letter—in several years. Who on earth would take the time to handwrite a note to her?

Los Estados Unidos was written on the bottom line in curlicue, singsong handwriting. *Papito!*

She ripped it open, and a newspaper article fell to the floor. "Louuuuuuu!" she screamed and ran to show the contents to her.

Chapter Twenty-Four
Noticias buenas

"What now?" Lou barked.

Lottie shouted the headline from the front page of the *El Salvador Times*:

"TRAVESTI ALTO FUNCIONARIO DESPEDIDO DE LA POLICÍA NACIONAL!"

"I don't understand *Spañol*. What does it say?"

Lottie didn't have the heart to tell her that no one understood *Spañol*. "It says 'Cross-Dressing Top Official Fired from the National Police.'" She turned the paper to face her pal.

"Is that the guy?" Lou looked at the photograph beneath the headline, where a stiletto-wearing, blonde, and sequined Miguel Lopez balanced awkwardly in black-and-white.

"Yes! Too bad it's not in color! You should have seen that corset. Gorgeous."

Lou grabbed Lottie by the shoulders and began jumping up and down, a measure she reserved for exceptional news.

"We did it! We did it!" They shouted and bounced and shouted until Lottie wondered if the ancient homestead would handle such enthusiasm. They might just land on the first floor if they weren't careful. Frank scurried by like a fat gray rat.

"I know! Thank you, God! I can't wait to tell Ish— Oh, never mind!"

The timing of the *fabulosa* news about the haute couture scoundrel could not have been better. She could only attribute it to God's perfect timing. In no other way could the pieces of the puzzle have landed in place to make it possible—on the same day that Ishmael called and she commenced worrying, and on the afternoon of the board meeting, where the eager members would certainly want news of success.

Success! Like a piece of chocolate, I will savor this for a while.

When she reentered her office, she noticed the residual contents of Papito's envelope lying mid-rug. She hastened to picked it up, and a smile stretched way beyond its intended width. It read:

Querida,

I could not be more proud of you! You did it! I wish that I could see your face as you read it! My beautiful hija, joyous and full of light. I thought that you might prefer a hard copy of the report, rather than a cold and easily forgotten email. I relayed the information to the men at the hotel too. They were very excited.

As you can imagine, I am up to my old tricks, teaching, writing. Life, querida, is good, as Dios would have it. And don't worry, no one has bothered me since our little expedition. And if someone ever does, I will come to visit you! As you Americans say, "If the heat is too hot, get out of the cocina!"

You are always in my corazón,

Papito

And just like that, Lottie was in the process of experiencing a day she would always remember, much like the day she passed the Louisiana Bar Exam or when the Saints won the Super Bowl. She would remember the way the air felt, damp but with promise, the scent of the candle on the end table—pine like the loblollies of Louisiana, the beat of the banana leaves, slow and lovely.

Lottie would place that one tiny and righteous act in El Salvador in her mental accounting, and in the success column. But would she be able to put the others there also?

〜〜

Lottie wondered if they did it for effect—the carpooling and tumbling onto her lawn, a tangle of badass human rights activists unfolding in front of her, a flock of do-gooders frolicking on terra firma, stacked with good will and high IQs. It would look powerful if it wasn't so dang amusing.

With apologies to the Charlie-in-the-Box, they magnificently resembled the Isle of Misfit Toys: Fatima, draped in yards of fabric, arm in arm with Emile in seersucker and bow tie; the *Vogue*-cover-worthy couture twins with baubles and jangles and hoisted atop shoes Lottie couldn't afford; and, rounding out the odd confluence, the patchouli-doused, hippified Isabella. Together, they would make a Broadway cast blush or the United Nations salivate.

When the misfits decamped from Isabella's minivan, festooned, of course, with rainbows and ERASE bumper stickers, Mister George stirred the rake. Once again, his eyes bore a hole into Fatima's hijab and added another target to it this time: Emile's persnickety attire. Never mind that they were all about excellence and integrity. Lottie just shook her head.

After the talented, if chatty, mob made it to the stairs, she watched Mister George gather up his barrel of landscaping tools and head toward the shed out back, his task complete, whatever that may have been. She made a mental note to discuss it with him later, to ask him about his curious and miraculous materialization when the board met.

Upstairs in her tower, though, her lips tremored with the secret she would guard until later, when she would release it in super cool, CIA-debriefing fashion. Just below the surface, it gurgled like a wellspring, fresh water that would quench their expectations, that would bandage their bleeding hearts.

"Lottie Jan, how are you, darlin'?" Fatima asked with an embrace.

"Great, actually! I missed you."

Lottie's friend cupped her face softly in her hands.

"Well, do tell, girl!" erupted Emile and presented her with two air kisses.

Anna-Maria and Jezebel got in queue to hug her. "Whaddup, ma sista?" Anna-Maria started.

"Patience! In due course, I will fill you all in." She literally couldn't stand it and knew that the lifted corners of her mouth would powerfully betray her secret.

Louisa high-fived and dispensed hugs all around, then directed them into the boardroom, which doubled as Lottie's dining room or vice versa depending on the day. Or on some days, the table was stacked with court cases to be assessed, to be assembled, fat files awaiting attention. "Willie Gee's will deliver the chicken soon, y'all!" Lou wielded her wand, trying to fight off the drooling guests.

Emile presently manned the makeshift bar, fashioning martinis for each thirsty philanthropist, while twaddling filled the room, New Orleans news circulating from one to the other, a rattling streetcar of gossip or truth. "I hear there's a new Mardi Gras krewe. It's going to be another all-female krewe called Medusa, I think." "I don't care for that name at all. It evokes a scary image." "Did you see the new development going up on Magazine Street? Is it going to be a restaurant or a bar? Or both? Not that we need either! Ha-ha." "O-M-G! I can't stand the mayor! He drives me crazy."

Lottie was La Conductora of this cacophonous orchestra. She had collected each instrument—every one distinct and necessary—polished each one, gave each player first chair.

It was music to her ears.

A soft drizzle misted the windows but didn't douse the enthusiasm cracking the plaster of the room. The meeting would be held indoors, as a regular deluge was forecasted—the usual not-to-be-messed-with rain, cars moved high atop lawns up and down the block. WWOZ was locked in on the radio, and Momma Sugar, a sultry alto, ushered in the jazz, while the Live Wire trumpeted the whereabouts of local musicians.

A rap on the door pierced the din, and Lou opened it, revealing a young Creole man in a black button-down embroidered with a brazen red "Willie Gee's" on the pocket. He entered, a large foil-covered platter filling his hands. Beads of mist decorated his cropped curls. "Is it bad out dere?" Lou asked.

"Not yet, but they say it's coming."

Ah, yes. The proverbial It of New Orleans precipitation. Any explanation of it would be gratuitous, as everyone knew. He placed the tray in the center of the table. "I'll be right back with the rest."

Like crawdads crossing the road to get to the bayou, they scratched and clawed their way to the table, elbows launched, mouths watering. There was no need to ring the chow bell. The adorable delivery guy returned with another platter of an odiferous something—greens, probably—then left.

"Y'all grab a plate and sit on down. We have lots to discuss!" Lottie didn't have to tell them twice, for such were New Orleanians' appetites for all things fried, particularly chicken from the renowned Willie Gee's.

After each wiped his or her chin and pushed the plates forward, Lou collected the dishes, then brought out the belt-busting and magnificently layered doberge cake from Gambino's. And so as not to face the wrath of Lou, Lottie brought out the coffeepot and mugs.

When everyone had taken a slice and stirred a joe, Lottie cleared her throat and tapped her spoon on her coffee mug. "I have a bit of good news to share with y'all." She let that germinate for a few seconds just to tease them, starting out slow and making them beg. Yeah, it was cruel, but it was also fun. "But you gotta show me your excitement! If you wanna know, I want you to applaud!"

Thankfully, they went along with it, and whoops and hollers and claps shook the room. "That ain't good enough, ya heard?" They clapped louder and pumped and spun with their fists in the air. "There, that's better."

"So, I have here in my nail-challenged hands..."

"Gurl, I told you to stop chewin' on yo nails," blasted Anna-Maria.

"Let her finish!" blurted Jezebel and slapped Anna-Maria's arm.

Lottie flapped it in the air and let the crackle permeate the room. "The San Salvadoran newspaper, *El Salvador Times*!" She unfolded the article and flipped it to face them. "I present...the front page. Tah-dah!" The first page revealed the upper fold with a photo of the bewigged Miguel Lopez and the headline. Smiles began, then stopped. Heads tilted. Faces scrunched.

"What the hell does that say?" Jezebel pointed a fierce fingernail to the paper like a dagger. "You know I don't speak Spanish." The others nodded in agreement.

"Is it good news?" Emile leaned in. "It's gotta be! I mean, look at him. Or is that our guy?" He launched air quotes around "guy" as it left his mouth.

"Kids! Patience. Patience." Lottie slowly went to a chair and sat, savoring their enthusiasm. "I shall read the headline to you. It says, 'Cross-Dressing Top Official Fired from the National Police.'"

Real, bona fide, enthusiastic applause erupted.

Dr. Hassan said, "How wonderful," her licorice eyes smiling under her scarf.

"Oh. My. God," Emile exclaimed, his one dimple morphing into a crater.

"This is major!" Isabella jumped up, all five-four of her, and approached for a close-up.

"I can't believe it!" Jezebel sang. "You did it, girl!" She bounced up and clapped and began to do the Wobble, a dance Lottie had enjoyed on YouTube of an NOPD officer jigging with the locals. Anna Maria joined her for a brief hip shake until they fell back into their chairs.

"We did it!" Of course, it was a team effort, and Lottie would never deign to take all the credit. "And let me just say too that I could not have done it without Professor Marquez. He helped so much, and also the two hotel employees. It was a true team effort."

"So, what will happen to him? To the perpetrator, I mean…" It was sweet Isabella who asked, concern sprinkling her voice. A familiar wave of guilt ran through Lottie—she who defended the Persecuted now creating another member. It was an emotional roll of the dice, a siesta from more sainted deeds.

"Hopefully, he will stop molesting women," Lottie offered.

In the background, Dr. John banged out "Big Chief" on WWOZ, while the raindrops grew fat and played their own percussion on the roof.

"But, if you have a real, legitimate concern, let me assure you, one thing I have learned—and you also probably—is that evil is resilient." Lottie paused to let it sink in before guilt would. "So, if this man does not ask the public for forgiveness for all his crimes and change his ways and then peacefully coexist with his people, I suspect he will find another way to survive. Maybe cross the border into Honduras or Guatemala and reinvent himself?" This seemed to satisfy her internally, and she hoped she wouldn't second-guess the operation. Her constant inner conflict was greater than any outer one. No one was harder on Lottie than Lottie. "Besides, he wasn't acting kindly when he savaged Julieta and caused her to flee her home and come to a foreign country, right?"

As though struck by flint, Isabella's eyes sparked. There was the look Lottie enjoyed—and needed. "Yes! Of course! You're right."

Lightning flashed fittingly, and Lottie began to count silently to see when and where the otherworldly bowling ball would strike the pins. When she arrived at four, thunder shook and cracked. Anna Maria dipped her fork back into the doberge, slicing it like royalty, and revealing all six decadent layers. Emile sipped his Sazerac in one slow, savory move. "Any word on the jerk in Afghanistan?" He leaned back in his chair and ran one hand through the wave of black. "Did the crowd rip him to shreds?"

"Yeah, did you ever hear from the contact?" Jezebel asked.

"I did hear from him, but he didn't reveal anything. Probably because it's too dangerous. The government ostensibly monitors communications, especially with people who have been in the West."

"So why did he call? Just to keep in touch?" A big smile slid across his face. Ah, but Emile knew her too well.

Okay, Pain in the Butt, Lottie thought. "Actually, yes. Just to keep in touch. We bonded." She tried to stifle the twinkle that wished to appear in her eye by blinking, then glancing back at the paper. "Professionally, you know?" Frank had made his way in and softly wove through the sea of legs under the table, undisturbed by the human invaders.

Anna-Maria smiled profoundly from the other side. "Fatima, perhaps you received some news about the gentleman? I mean the assailant, not Ishmael." Thank you. More coverage.

Fatima cleared her throat and sat up. "Actually, I did hear he was being prosecuted by the government. He will be given a trial, but he has many connections, and he is a male. Unfortunately, he will benefit from the broad blanket of immunity spread across the land. If we had said he insulted the Prophet—peace be upon him—or converted to another religion, he might have then and there been stoned or immolated."

Jezebel shook her head. Anna-Maria clutched her pearls.

"Well, we don't want him to die. We just want justice for Sadia." Lottie twitched and folded the newspaper article.

"Agreed, my dear. No reluctance on my part." Fatima must've been able to read her mind, to gage the uncertainty. "Sadia will not be able to return to her home because of him, and her family will try to kill her in the name of honor."

"And how about your nephew—is he safe after all that?" Isabella asked. The radio oozed the first notes of John Boutte's soulful rendition of "A Change is Gonna Come." Lottie froze.

"Well, I believe he is for the time being, but Ishmael is at constant risk because he converted to Christianity. As a moderate, more progressive Muslim, I have no problem with it." She placed her hand over her heart. "But the fanatics in Afghanistan might want to stone him or behead him because they consider it to be apostasy. As they follow the Quran to the letter, they will enforce its penalty for that, which is death."

"Excuse me, please. I have to go to the restroom." Lottie couldn't get to the bathroom fast enough. Her legs liquified as she made her way to it—just feet away. Her stomach wanted to expel the fried chicken. She collapsed on the cold toilet seat into a mess of tears. *Oh, God. Please please please protect Ishmael.* It was all she could utter, all she could think about. She repeated the petition, then stood and looked in the mirror. A map of the world in red amoebas stared back at her, with Africa prominently featured on her right cheek, Australia situated on her chin.

A rap hit the door. "Baby, you okay?"

"Yeah, Lou. I just have an upset stomach. Be right in." Lottie sat back down, grabbed a *Harper's* magazine, and fanned her face. After the strawberry patches settled down, she reemerged, hoping her feelings for Ishmael weren't written across her face in fruit-colored poetry. Most of all, she certainly didn't want to reveal to Fatima that she had a monumental crush—even if geographically problematic—on her nephew.

Fatima approached first, a human Valium, and placed her hands on Lottie's face. "My dear, you are doing the right thing. Ishmael will be fine." Then she winked—whatever that meant.

Jezebel came over and gave her one of her glorious hugs for which she was famous. The rest followed.

"Sorry, y'all. I didn't mean to turn this into group therapy." Lottie laughed through blackmailing tears. "Can I get anyone a drink?" Four lifted glasses.

"I got this, dawlin'!" Emile jumped up and went over to the tiny bar to work his magic.

~ ~

By the time WWOZ had switched over to the Rhythm Room show and everyone—except Fatima—had consumed at least one more adult beverage, Lottie felt blotch-free. They chatted nonsensically for a good half hour, but the meeting was not over. Items on the agenda, such as budget, donations, etcetera, still had to be addressed.

"Lottie Jan, are you up to finishing the meeting?" the chairman asked.

"Of course! Piece of cake and all, right?" The cosmopolitan flowed through her veins, a gentle river—the Pearl, maybe. "Can we skip budget and donations, though, y'all? I'm getting a bit tired and bamboozeled. Get it? Bam-*booze*-led?" They nibbled at her poor attempt at levity and hardy-har-harred. And that was only because they were in the same state of mind.

Fatima smiled, indulging the infidels. Again. "That is fine. Why don't we discuss the next project, then?" She pulled out a file from her brilliant Afghan satchel and set it on the table. "Emile, you are the one true musician. Why don't you give us a drumroll, please?" Emile thumped on the table as though he were in U2, taking the opportunity to perform. "Presenting… dat DUMMMM…Operation Estela!"

The feasters applauded and banged the table with fists, a little too exuberantly, in Lottie's opinion, but such was the way of alcohol and board meetings.

"Bosnia, eh?" It wasn't as if Lottie didn't know what the possibilities were, which countries would be attended to, etcetera. She was just eager to know which one it would be, which time zone it fell into, and what risks were involved. She thought she could handle Bosnia and certainly Bosnian men, with their towering statures, dark eyes, and slender noses. Actually, they were quite handsome and most industrious, though many were scarred emotionally by the Yugoslav War. Therein lay the problem. Many men suffered PTSD and consequently were candidates to abuse their women.

"Bos-nee-a! Bos-nee-a! Bos-nee-a!" the Fruit Loops exclaimed and banged in sync again.

Fatima tried to gather the unruly crowd into a semblance of order. "Okay, gentleman and ladies."

Jezebel held up her hands. "Hey, fools, that's enough! Let's hear what Fatima has to say." Silence spread quickly across the table, and Lottie thought no one in his or her right mind wanted to deal with Jezebel. Dr. Hassan bowed her head in acknowledgment and handed Lottie the file.

She flipped it open, though in truth she already knew who the assailant was, as he squarely and permanently resided in the Creep file in her brain. Estela had, like so many others, become family and carved her way easily into Lottie's heart, and Lottie was admittedly and overly maternal with Estela, even more than with the others. The fact that Estela's boyfriend had beat the stuffing out of her and left her for dead, and laughed like a hyena while doing it, really chapped her fanny. Moreover, he'd left her with a little souvenir: a hysterectomy. Something to remember him by, Lottie supposed. In short, she would do just about anything to exact justice for Estela, but fortunately or unfortunately would again limit it to a prank, so that she wouldn't have to bear the guilt of killing another human, even if he was a scumbag.

CONTACT: Murad Rakić
Gay male, Five-eleven, brown hair, brown eyes
Age: 30
Education: Associates Degree in Business
Profession: Secretary
Fluent in Bosnian, German, and English

ASSAILANT: Rifat Turković
Six-five, black hair, brown eyes

Age: 40

Profession: Auto Mechanic

Fluent in Bosnian, broken German

Quirks: outrageously homophobic, into kinky sex and playing dress-up, misogynistic (and all the other ICKS), loves to dance

"Good Lord." Lottie laughed nervously. "They just keep getting taller and taller."

"I'm going with you!" Louisa Mae declared and almost threw herself out of her body doing so.

Lottie approached her gently, the only way to calm her down. "I told you, I have to do this alone, babes. The guilt of someone else, especially you, getting hurt would kill me." Lottie winked at her and looked around the room at the others, who had increasingly become accustomed to Lou's volatility and charm. "It will be okay. I tell you what—let's take a trip to Paris just for fun, maybe in six months." The thought of strolling the Champs-Élysées must have enticed Lou, because she let the matter drop. For the time being, anyway.

In the midst of the solemnity of the moment, the door opened and closed, revealing a soaked and sloshing Mister George. He removed a dripping Saints hat, the fleur-de-lis hanging forlornly and sacrilegiously. "Goodness, Mister George! What are you doing here?"

"Um. Miss Lottie, I'm so sorry to interrupt your, um, meeting." He couldn't take his eyes off Fatima, though Lottie could tell he tried. "I was just driving by and noticed that your car is on the street. It's starting to flood a bit. Would you like for me to move it up in the driveway?"

"That's really sweet of you, thanks. But really, you couldn't have just called me."

"I didn't think of that." He seemed a bit embarrassed or something. She couldn't put her finger on it exactly.

Lottie got up and fished around the kitchen counter, then threw him the keys. "Thanks again, Mister George."

After he left, Emile threw out there, "Well. That was weird."

"Lawd. I'll say," agreed Jezebel.

"Who knows?" Lottie said. "He's getting up there in age, you know?"

Ten minutes later, a wetter Mister George reentered and stood in the doorway, dripping. He took off the soaked cap again and wiped his head, smoothing the small feather of gray. "Would you like to join us for a drink, Mister George?" Lottie asked.

He glanced at all the half-empty glasses. "What, like alcoholic? Miss Lottie, you know that the Lord doesn't want me to drink alcohol."

"Right. I forgot. Sorry, Mister George. Fatima doesn't drink either." He nodded at Fatima, forcing a half smile. "Well, would you care for a piece of doberge cake and a cup of coffee, then?"

"Nah, I need to get on home, Miss Lottie. Thank you anyhow." He replaced his cap and nodded to everyone. "Y'all have a good night."

After he left and splashed down the stairs, the table burst with laughter. Maybe it was the alcohol. Maybe it was the odd nature of the visit. Either way, the entire episode puzzled her.

Chapter Twenty-Five
What is a Sarajevo?

Sarajevo had been robbed when the world declared Paris as the City of Light. At least it seemed so from row twenty of the Lufthansa behemoth. Below Lottie, a sea of lights awaited, waves of amber and white, while the river Miljacka's dark curves flowed through her center like a mystical sea serpent. Trebevic supervised grandmotherly from the southeast, quilted under blacks and greens, and illuminated minarets pierced the skyline, directing the faithful to mosques, their smooth and rounded roofs sprinkled about the city, while steeples pointed the faithful to their God.

Among the exotic metropolises of the world, Sarajevo slyly evaded her geographical conquests. Even the name Sa-ra-ye-vo rolled around on her tongue like a splash of Courvoisier, spicy and luxurious, tingling her senses and intrigue. Understandably, the chess match known as the Yugoslav War boggled the US population's minds. And though she was a small child when the Serbs attempted a thorough cleansing of Bosnian Muslims, forcing them to wear white armbands à la the Holocaust, because of her profession, she understood the players—Bosniaks, Serbs, Croats—better than others in her hometown, shy of maybe a Tulane or UNO or Xavier professor. It was her job to exhaust the subject that drove so many Bosnians from their homeland and into the once-welcoming arms of the United States of America. The confusion of the typical US citizen, however, was only exacerbated when the former Yugoslavia separated. Maps had to be redrawn, old globes thrown out or relegated as antiques. Ask the average American if Yugoslavia still existed, and he or she might say yes.

Unfortunately, Lottie didn't speak much Bosnian. It was one language, like its country and its former country, that got away from her. The few phrases she could utter, she attributed to Estela's crash course. *Draga*—darling—was her favorite. Ordering a beer or taking a cab, looking for a restroom or saying *havala ti*—thank you—was not beyond the realm of possibilities either, and she certainly hoped she wouldn't revert involuntarily to Spanish, as she was in the habit of doing when she struggled with a new language. She wouldn't be surprised if *Una cerveza, por favor* came spewing out of her *boca* in a café.

"You go to my Bosnia," Estela said with twinkling eyes when Lottie informed her of the trip. Another beauty, she was as tall as Lottie but sported Clairol-ed blonde hair.

"Yeah, you know, I became really interested in your country after being your lawyer." Lottie also attributed her sojourn to the internet, to the sparkling photographs of Estela's beloved home popping up on her feeds, visual temptations that lured her to punch in her AmEx digits and hit "complete purchase." This was not totally untrue, as Sarajevo began its fruitful attempts to court her long ago, delivering its dance card in white gloves.

"But, *draga*," she explained to Estela, "you can't go back to Bosnia, at least not until you get your US citizenship."

"I know," Estela replied, having paid attention, a rarity in this age of ADHD.

"Do you remember why?"

"Yes. It's because it says to US that I am not afraid anymore…not afraid of returning to Bosnia."

"And do you remember what will happen if you go, other than just being in danger of the jerk that beat you up?"

"Yes. Immigration can take my green card away from me because I don't need the protection anymore."

"You got it. Good job, *draga*!"

Curiously, and she informed Estela of this, a "green" card has absolutely zero trace of the green that it once did. No chartreuse. No lime. Not even moss. Just a blasé off-white. Yet the world still referred to Permanent Residence Cards as green cards. Go figure. At least it sounded better than Boring White Cards, and it was easier than spitting out the multisyllabic "Permanent Resident Card."

The board debated hotly whether Estela should be told of the project, but Lottie argued and successfully convinced otherwise. Such knowledge might put her client and friend in further danger, and to do that would defeat the original purpose of gaining asylum for her, wouldn't it? No, Estela need not know anything other than that Lottie was a Bosnian-dictionary-toting *američki* in her hometown.

And just as brightly as the luminescence of the capital city, the promise of justice sparkled below, though the exact ramifications were yet to be determined.

～～

Hoisting her monster suitcase—dubbed, for no apparent reason, Doug by her friends—off the belt with her less than muscular arms, Lottie managed to roll it over to the inspection station like the Eastern-Euro-invading boss that she was. She couldn't help the size anyhow, as this was uncharted geographical turf for her. And because it was autumn in Sarajevo, and she was a Southerner devoid of weather-appropriate dressing sense, she couldn't decide what to bring. Therefore, she brought everything. The Bosnian sisters tried to help her weed, but pulling things out of Doug was apparently more difficult than putting things in.

Lottie declined assistance from a member of humanity with a Y chromosome, who flexed arms the size of her waist, and though she knew her biceps hung about like pathetic, half-full ziplock bags, she could manage. Who needed a man when she had her bad mamma-jamma self? This was a debate to have with said self later, she noted.

Okay, she had to admit. They—men, not luggage—were sometimes lovely to look at—especially when packaged in bronze skin and white teeth and came with a dreamy accent. But for the time being, she needed to reel in such foolishness and look for Murad.

A bleached, lubricated head appeared in the distance. Attached to it were slender but strong-looking shoulders, which were attached to flailing arms. Lottie flailed in response, not caring if she cast her freckles and blinding white skin upon the masses. Already she could tell she would like this guy. Responsively, her stilettos, of which she was not anatomically or fashionably worthy, moved faster and clicked the floor until they produced a gypsy rhythm like two delighted castanets. Doug wheeled before her, a small country on wheels, while Bosnian—she assumed—singsonged from the loudspeakers, along with English and German. She approached her gorgeous coconspirator as if she had known him for years, and tackled him with a big American hug.

In point of fact, Murad was Estela's cousin, though Lottie had met him neither in the States nor in Bosnia. She obtained—or perhaps stole—his contact information from the affidavit he wrote in support of Estela's case. Like the other spectators, he, on several occasions, had witnessed Rifat's brutality to Estela. But, unlike others, he was more than happy to tell the world about it. It could have been because, just before Estela gathered up her clothes and fled, Murad even tried to stop it, an act that put him in the ICU at the hospital. Since then, he had gotten buff and strong, waiting for the best opportunity for some semblance of retribution. For Estela. For himself. Enter Lottie and her similar short-term goal and little plan, and he was more than willing to coconspire.

"*O moj Boze!*" Murad proclaimed, then jumped up and down and clapped as if she'd just delivered a delicious surprise, which may have been the case, but she wasn't sure. Lottie thought it could mean *Oh my God* or *Oh my gosh*, but wasn't sure of that either. Some things sounded universal, in syllables, anyway. This was just one.

Like a pair of soldiers about to embark on a common mission, they latched arms and advanced toward the exit. The automatic doors flung open and produced a *whoosh* of frosty air that hit Lottie squarely in her face. She pulled her coat's belt snug.

"Girl, you brought a coat?" His first full sentence—question, really—in English came out without a trace of an accent. Impressive. "It's not that cold."

"I know, *dragi*, but I am from a subtropical climate." Ever since Lottie learned the zone, she loved announcing it, trying to make her life sound somewhat exotic. "I'm like a magnolia. I wilt in cold weather."

"Let's see." He counted on his fingers. "It's only around forty-five degrees in Fahrenheit."

"Oh, yeah. I guess I do look wimpy." She popped her collar as they walked into the cool air. The brisk temperature and golden lights made her feel at once nostalgic and wistful, longing for something—for what, she wasn't sure. Had she believed in reincarnation, she would say that her soul had definitely lived here in a prior life.

Murad took Doug and wheeled him or it and lugged her laptop bag over his capable shoulders. "I can't believe you're here!" He bumped a hip with Lottie's. She couldn't believe it either and reflected happily on how Americans had not yet discovered—and consequently, invaded—this jewel directly due east of Florence, just across the Adriatic. *Good for me, then!* She would guard the secret forever as, once the Yanks came in, so did baseball caps and bellies. And McDonald's. Best to leave it pristine in all its Turco-Islamic splendor. "And you're tall. Actually."

"So are you, darlin'." It was true enough, though she was taller than him perched on four-inch nails. But she hoped not to be outdone by Bosnia's beautiful women, one of its main attractions. Tall like the Dinaric Alps bordering the west coast, radiant and olive-skinned, they could easily overshadow her wan Anglo-Saxon skin any day. This might be a tough one to pull off. She flinched at the thought of making herself attractive to another oaf who probably had a hankering for Miss Universe-worthy Bosnian beauties. Thankfully, she brought a brunette wig just in case and would discuss other hair options with Murad later.

After strapping Doug to the roof, they jumped into a sparkly, baby-blue Smart car, whose brilliance made up for its size. "Go small or—how do you say—go home?" He stifled a guffaw with his hand, as though something was wrong with it. Surprisingly, for two taller folks, they fit mostly adequately into the contraption. "Where to, *Gospodica* Lottie?"

"I'm a bit hungry. Do you think we can eat before we hit the dance floor?" It was a small request, though, honestly, she couldn't wait to dance with a man who didn't want to grab or rufi her.

"*Burek*, then?"

"My fave."

Murad pressed the gas pedal as though Sarajevo would run out of *burek*, which it just wouldn't. In like a thousand years. Lottie clutched the tiny strap next to her ear in the speck of car on the multilane road leaving Sarajevo International.

~~

The *thump thump thump* of the disco alone could've shot her back across the pond to New Orleans like a redheaded flare out of a cannon. She didn't know how they did it, how they kept moving to the deafening music, the beat growing faster and faster and faster, the psychedelic spotlights spinning berserkly, bouncing off the ceiling and dance floor, where it seemed hundreds jumped up and down and moved their rumps. It was a far cry from Clive's back home, where the pool table often doubled as the dance floor, and New Orleans' signature boogie-woogie music way outlasted the '50s and was as daring as the natives got.

But she aimed to please her host, who currently ricocheted between her and others like a blonde ping-pong ball. Besides, the gesture was not entirely altruistic as it was one of Rifat aka The Coward's favorite pickup spots. Apparently, he was the rufi king of the joint, often slaying his victims with his favorite love potion rather than relying solely on charm. This was probably accomplished with the help of silent bartenders who, according to Murad, he palled around with and overtipped with large *markas*.

"Is that him?" Pointing with her chin while she bopped her head side to side was no small feat, but she managed to aim at a taller-than-Bosnian-tall dude pushing his way through the crowd toward the bar, high-fiving along the way.

Murad was head-banging and pogo-sticking violently to yet another EDM beauty with indecipherable lyrics. "Yeah. Yeah. That is him." He huffed and bounced away.

Lottie kept her eyes on The Coward while trying to hop to the beat, throwing her head this way and that, and trying somehow not to get too sweaty in the process, which was impossible even with her hair piled aloft into a makeshift bun.

The subject fist-bumped another supersized bartender and then looked around—sizing up his prey, she figured. Within seconds, a supermodel-like, L'Oréal-blessed blonde inched next to him, either to get a drink or to introduce herself. He seemed interested. With every ounce of restraint she could muster, Lottie fought the desire to scramble over and yell, *Run!* In any event, it would have been futile due to the mass of vibrating dancers. Hopefully, he would turn the woman off with an offensive remark sooner rather than later.

Murad seemed oblivious, or maybe he was saving up his gumption for the coming days. She, on the other hand, could not take her eyes off the *kukavica*—or coward in *engleski*—who eyeballed the head turner up and down her tall and well-endowed frame. Looking down at her chest, which hadn't gotten the memo to show up, Lottie instead saw her bank-account-draining Jimmy Choos.

Clearly, The Coward must've blown it as the woman appeared to snarl at him and begin to walk away. He grabbed the beauty's arm, but she was able to break his grasp and get lost in the crowd. *Atta girl.* Lottie smiled. *Atta girl.*

The disco ball spun nonstop. After removing her shoes and hurling them against the wall of the club, after resetting her hair into a doughnut numerous times and after perhaps a total of two exhausting hours, Lottie finally witnessed Murad pooping out. *Yippee!* She thought.

Amen and hallelujah, Lottie thought. *What on earth will tomorrow bring?*

Chapter Twenty-Six
Young in Old Town

Murad's apartment was situated right in the middle of Old Town, so not only did Lottie make a new friend and partner, she would also get to stay in one of the coolest parts of Sarajevo. Thankful that she had switched from screwdrivers to water and Coca-Cola about midway through the night—unlike her looped host—she easily made her way up the winding and narrow stairs to the second-floor living room that would double as her bedroom for four nights. Excitement threatened her sleep but lost to jet lag and the sheer exhaustion from caroming on her feet for a couple of hours.

Murad must've found his way back downstairs, because when she woke up and made her way down in socked feet, he was nestled in his stucco bedroom on the first floor. She tiptoed around until she found what she imagined was the kitchen, then grabbed a copper structure she hoped was the coffeepot. Trying to put it together was like trying to assemble one of those darn 3-D puzzles, which she was never good at.

Lottie had heard about the famous Bosnian—not Turkish!—coffee and was hoping it would wake her up. "What you doing, silly woman?" She heard the sleepy baritone utterance from the direction of the bedroom.

"I'm sorry. Did I wake you?"

"Do you think I am talking in my sleep?" it continued.

"Good point." She placed the copper configuration onto the counter, hoping her exhausted friend would get the hint. "Sorry."

Murad soon emerged and rubbed his eyes, his hair standing up more at attention than he. "No worries, *draga*. I am just teasing you. Besides, we need to get our day started, right?"

"Yes, but first…the famous Bosnian coffee, right?"

"Of course, but I take you to a professional Bosnian coffeemaker, to a place where they make a really big—how do you say?—presentation out of it, you know? And we can breakfast too! Just throw something on, and we can be out the door in a minute." Because her stomach seemed to be eating itself, she agreed and threw on a long-sleeved shirt, turtleneck, and wool cardigan over the entire lot, followed by long wool leggings and boots. Murad—quite bravely, she thought—ventured out in the chilled air in wrinkled khaki shorts and an *I Heart New York* tee.

Only a few storefronts away, they slithered into the toasty cocoon of a *kafana*, or café, which was nestled in the smoothed walls of the ancient city.

She opened her library Fodor's. "What do they call the Turkish Quarter again, Murad?"

"Baščaršija."

"Bas…"

"Baščaršija!"

"Baščaršija. Got it."

The interior of the shop formed a puzzle of colorful rugs, and the coffee wafts immediately invited them in and onto a long cushioned bench on which several patrons sat in their short sleeves also. Murad held up two fingers, and a blonde woman brought over two silver trays carrying several silver vessels on each. One appeared to be a tiny pot, the other an empty cup, the third a small bowl of sugar cubes. Though she desperately desired instant caffeination, she opted to keep her impatient Western mouth shut and immediate-gratification-tude at bay and await instructions from Murad.

"Okay, you are going to love this," he announced, the way he said love convincing her. "First, *draga*, take the little spoon there on your tray and you stir the top of the pot. Gently, now." A brown froth sat on top. She grabbed the spoon and stirred the creamy layer in gentle circles. "Okay, now you pour it into the cup, but be careful. It will be hot." She did as commanded, heady from the exhaustion and exotic environs, inhaling the Ottoman Empire. "Now we let it cool and let the coffee grinds drop to the bottom. Meanwhile, we have a cigarette. It's the true Bosnian thing to do!"

Lottie didn't smoke. Except in other countries. Except when the full experience demanded it. The nicotine demon wasn't an issue for her, a small favor for which she was thankful. He handed her a cigarette and lit it. With great fanfare, she puffed away and donated to the growing cloud gathering on the ceiling. Her lungs felt mad at her afterward.

"Okay, now take your sugar cube and dip it into the coffee, then bite it." Kind of a backward gesture, she thought, but complied, assaulting her taste buds with a sugary jolt of coffee. Her blood sugar would no doubt retaliate later.

They breakfasted on *burek* of meat and cheese, which was a heavy proposition but would fuel them for a long day of sightseeing. Attacking too a cinnamon-roll-looking pastry with gusto, she unrolled, bit, and rejoiced.

Murad rubbed his stomach, indicating clearly it was time to stop with the *burek* nonsense and move on. "What would you like to see first? There is so much to do."

Flipping over to a sticky-noted page, she said, "I would love to go to the Gazi Husrev-Beg Mosque, if that's okay. And maybe the Church of the

Holy Archangels. And maybe the war tunnel. And maybe…"

He held up his hands. "Whoa, *draga*. Take it eeeeeasy." He quirked one side of his mouth, probably proud of his English cliché usage, and she had to laugh at his Western "coolness."

"You're right. Maybe too many. There's just so much to see and not enough time." She must have effervesced but didn't really care as she didn't know when she would be able to venture to Sarajevo again. Murad was the perfect partner with whom to see the unique metropolis, a guide without the threat of attraction. Unlike Afghanistan. *Ahhh, Afghanistan.* "You lead. I shall follow!"

After donating the remaining half of the *burek* to a pair of pigeons, they set off onto the cobbled streets of the Old Town and toward the Gazi Husrev-Beg Mosque. With its sharp minaret and emerald dome, she could see how it beckoned sinners.

"It's so peaceful in here," she whispered, gazing all around at the cool stones and ancient arches. Obviously, Jesus was her guy, and his love and instruction fertilized her fallow life. Yet, the stillness of the mosque, even sprinkled with tourists, settled her energetic heart, and she could see why the searching attended.

"This was founded nearly a thousand years after Mohamed walked the sands of Mecca," he said softly.

"Amazing." A simple and deep respect for the second-largest religion in the world overwhelmed her. Within the hour too, she would hear the muezzin's call, the third go-round of the day, calling the Islamic Sarajevans to prayer, a hymn that always delighted her.

"Do you practice?" It was exactly the same inquisitiveness that had gotten her into "situations" during her Pippi Longstocking-ish childhood. She really should mind her own damn business.

"Do you think they would accept a gay Muslim?" He said it without looking her way as they both walked slowly through the hallowed space. "You know it is *haram*, of course."

"Yes, but…"

Murad turned and put his hands up. "There are no buts, *draga*. It is what it is." Of course, she knew. It was her business—literally—to know. Islam declared it universally to be *haram*—or forbidden—and practicing homosexuality in certain countries could actually result in death.

Yet this was the type of question that kept her up at night. *Didn't God make Murad that way?*

Oh, she'd heard the argument about original sin and how it changed mankind, including gays, forever—that the earth had turned sinful all because of Adam's bite of the apple. Still, it was the twenty-first century, and she knew that she knew that she knew that her gay friends were born that way. Why would God make someone homosexual, then ask him or her not to fall in love with someone of the same sex?

The rabbit hole is calling, and I will answer!

And if Jesus came to bring life to the fullest as he declared—and she believed this—and if falling in love and being in relationships was a big portion of a person's happiness, wouldn't it follow that Jesus would be okay with homosexuality? Because how could he bring said life to the fullest if seventy-five percent of a person's desires weren't being met?

And…if Jesus were so concerned with homosexuality and the like, wouldn't he have said something to that effect?

But, he didn't.

Of course, this was how her Christian mind reasoned. Not knowing the Quran or the Hadith, she couldn't speak to Islam's rationalization or lack thereof.

Murad put both hands in his pockets and leaned backward as though steeling himself for something. As if he'd had the conversation too many times before. A permed and silver-haired lady with stockings gathering forlornly at her ankles tugged her husband violently.

"You have your Lot. We have our Lut," Murad said.

Lottie got it. Well, she didn't get it in the first-person sense, but she had struggled with and finally reconciled the whole Gay Thing within the church, arriving at the conclusion that Jesus was more about love than judgment. She could only imagine Murad's struggle.

Exiting into the cool air of the forty-third parallel, she spooled a wool scarf around her neck and grabbed his arm.

"Where to next?" he asked with a smile—Islamic *haram* be damned.

"Oooooh. The fountain?" Describing it was unnecessary as any visor-strapping tourist knew about the storied bubbler in the square center surrounded by people and pigeons.

"Are you going to drink from it?" As if it was an option. If Lottie drank from it, legend had it that she would return to Sarajevo. It was right up there with kissing the Blarney Stone in Ireland or praying at the Wailing Wall in Jerusalem. It was just something you did. Besides, she wanted to come back, at a time when she could relax and not pursue a tiny righteous act.

They aimed for the famous wooden structure, which resembled a brown buoy in a raucous sea of pigeons and sidewalk cafés. "Watch me. Here is the evidence!" Lottie ran to one of several spigots and cupped the cool water, slurping in the hope of returning. "There, you see! I will return."

He lit another cigarette and waded through a spate of birds. "And now…we must walk down Ferhadija Street in the newer part of town," he declared between drags.

Of course, she could see retail shops and espresso bars à la The Gap and Dunkin' Donuts in her native land, but maybe he wanted to present the complete East-West picture.

Along the way, they passed red splotches embedded into the sidewalks, and stopped at one. "Oh, man. Is that...is that a Sarajevo Rose?"

"Yes, my *draga*. The roses still make me sad every single time I pass them."

They paused out of respect, said nothing, the tobacco smoke like that of the mortars from the war, curled into pure air, invading the still blue.

Lottie bent down and traced her fingers across it. Even before the flight, she knew about the evil, the thousands killed by Serbs in the city alone during the early 1990s, and she read that throughout the town, red resin and paint filled mortar holes and unintentionally created more pleasant images of roses. In reality, though, they were a reminder of horror, solemn memorials one would be forced to walk on. To remember.

After the appropriate heaviness, Murad threw his cigarette to the ground, stomped it with disgust, and looked up at the sky and maybe those horrible days. A second later, he returned to her, full of life, and wove his arm through Lottie's again. "Come on, *draga*. Let's go shopping!" They skipped and tumbled and lost themselves in the joy of the present and the promise of a purchase.

~~

Among the chartreuse and violet pillows, at the far end of the cushioned bench, they plopped. Back in the old village, they would review the plans for the next day. Čajdžinica Džirlo, a popular teahouse, was stuffed with both tourists and non, but they managed to find two seats, sitting shoulder to shoulder with the other sippers. Lottie welcomed any of the many varieties of tea jarred and shelved on the apple-green walls, though thick wafts of cardamom ruled the nostrils. She chose a floral brew and he an orange one.

Privacy was impossible in the crowd and discretion was key. Leaning in closely, she asked, "Okay. Just making sure—are you sure you want to go through with this?" Her maternal side kicked in as it had with Ishmael and Papito. A lot of good that did, though, as they were dancing in the back of her brain at all times. The last thing she needed was another innocent to worry about.

"Absolutely. Two hundred percent!" He took a sip of tea. "How about you?"

"I am ready!" she sang and looked around to see if anyone was looking at or listening to them. Seeing no one, she continued, "But how will you protect yourself from the jerk?"

"Simple, *draga*. Good old-fashioned blackmail." A smile crossed his face that exuded confidence with a dash of naughtiness. "Should anything happen to me, darling, the photos will simply be released to the public."

"But still… What if Rifat tries to hurt you in the process? Or worse?" She needn't say what "worse" was—they both knew.

"Girl," he emphasized with good-ole American slang, "that's why I been workin' out!" and lifted his arms, an act that made his biceps hop to attention. "Will you be safe back in the States, though? I mean, jerks can fly, you know."

"So, I have a crazy best friend back home who has another friend, Mr. Glock." She winked. "And trust me—she won't let anything happen to me." She rubbed her own biceps with vigor, not feeling the strength that Murad exhibited. "Also, I have a few friends in the State Department who have blacklisted him already. There's no way he could ever get a visa to the States."

"I think we are ready, then, my delicious little vixen." He raised his teacup in salute.

They were ready.

Chapter Twenty-Seven
Pretty Girl

"Pretty girl. Pretty girl," Murad's wildly lime-green parrot, Ina, teased, clearly having been appraised fully about Lottie's attempts to achieve Bosnian-style beauty. Oh, how she wished the caged one's comments would come to fruition as she began this new sacrament, as she attempted the Cinderella-à-la-Yugoslav-queen morph. Standing in front of the mirror in Murad's bedroom, with fake nails aflutter and hands a-wobble, she tried to squeeze her wild nest of twigs and feathers into the wig that recalled Cleopatra's glory.

"*Dragi!* Can you help me, pleeease?" Realistically, she just needed a swig of Bosnian booze, something to tame the wild mustangs circling her gray matter, more than they ever had in the past. And El Salvador was a close call with that what's-his-name.

"What is it, *draga?*" Murad sauntered in, snifter in hand, as though it was just going to be another night at the disco. The fruity scent of rakia taunted her, but she would at least attempt to begin the ordeal with a clear head.

"I can't get this blasted wig over my stupid hair." One bundle escaped from the hairpiece in defiance, while the others encamped securely beneath it like good soldiers.

"Stupid hair? *Draga!* There is nothing stupid about your gorgeous head of curls. And women here would die to have that natural color."

"Okay, let's not say 'die,' please. Do I have to wear it?"

"Pretty girl. Pretty girl."

The lights of Old Town turned on one by one and must've appeared glorious to others saner, to others with less cortisol swirling throughout their nervous system. Unfortunately for Lottie, the luminous magic floated way above her, unable to penetrate the swirling mustangs in her head. And Rifat.

"I think it is a good idea. Really." He put one hand on a slender hip, then shook a finger at her. "You need to be very careful. This guy is the *davo*—the devil—darling."

Audio hieroglyphics trickled in from the living room, where the local news screeched. Occasionally, she recognized a word, usually proper nouns—Sony Music. Bruce Springsteen—mid-cacophony.

"Here, let me help you." He put his brandy on the end table, gently took her by the arm, and forced her to sit on the bed. The skintight gold pants into which she had leapt earlier seemed to yelp in rebellion.

"Okay, you know him better than I do, and not for a good reason," she peeped, while Murad's calm shouted at and confounded her. Having had his butt kicked—literally—by the cretin, he was certainly entitled to turn heel and run from the assignment, but he didn't. Had she been in his shoes, she might have cowered away from the task. And from everything. Heck, she might even crawl beneath her bed, never to be seen again—red hair fading, skin yellowing.

"No problems. Ever, *draga*." He picked up the hairbrush, untangled the debacle, and brushed it like a devoted big sister. Gently, he twisted her mess of hair into a swirl and buried the whole lot beneath a black wig cap. "You forgot this. You must put this on first."

267

"Thank you. I'm just not thinking straight." A cue-ball head stared back at her in the mirror, and her eyes blinked soberly. Her temples were yanked back as though she had just paid for a cheap facelift. From the bed, the Cleopatra façade winked at her, and hesitation swallowed her whole. "Can I have a shot of your brandy?"

Returning with another snifter, twirling the liquid magically, he offered, "You know, you don't have to do this. We don't have to do this."

And just like that, there it was. The Out.

Every scenario presented one. One could either accept it or reject it— the choice, of course, forever altering the trajectory of one's life.

Lottie whirled the rust-colored liquid, stuck her sniffer into it, and let the fumes singe her nostril hair. She threw back a big sip, allowing the warmth to burn her throat and mind and allowing herself a brief reflection on the situation.

If she backed out of this elaborate, not to mention expensive, assignment—airfare plus wig plus sequins—she could return safely to the comfort of New Orleans, sit on her porch, and sip rakia from the duty-free shop. But could she deal with having come so close to exacting the sentence on another iteration of evil yet not having achieved it? Would this incomplete justice keep her awake at night?

With not a little fanfare, she snatched the wig and placed it over the cap. "No. Never! This must be done! If the government of Bosnia won't step in and prosecute him, then we will." One sip of the alcoholic grit and she became the Judge Judy of Sarajevo. "We have to do this for Estela. And for you."

Murad lit another smoke, snifter in one hand, cigarette in the other. Again, she joined him.

"Do you think he'll even show up?" Lottie puffed and puffed, though it had been fifteen years (not counting the cheating hours earlier) since she had tried and decided against tobacco products.

"I really do, *draga*. Remember, he answered the personal ad? Imagine? A beautiful American grad student traveling alone, looking for a 'big strong Bosnian man' to take her out for an evening in Sarajevo." He took a long drag and blew it up toward the rickety fan, which dispelled it about the ceiling. "And because you put your gorgeous face on it and described yourself as voluptuous... Well, who could resist that?"

Shifting on the bed, she glanced at the mirror again, then down at her questionable chest. "Don't worry, *draga*. He will look at your blue eyes." The corners of his mouth rocketed skyward, and she revisited her clandestine chest, which sat unimpressively beneath the tight V-neck sweater, and threw her shoulders back.

"Hell with it," she declared, then crossed herself with acrylic-nailed fingers and rose. The requisite spikes stretched her close to the ceiling fan, but Cleopatra would not be decapitated. Not on this day. She held her hand on the wig and filed into position by the doorway. "How about you?"

"Hey, I survived a genocide and a trip to the intensive care unit. I think I can handle this—how do you say—scum bucket?"

Something like that, Lottie thought, and drank up the last drop of brandy and attempted to swallow a lump of trepidation with it.

~~

The auditory blast shot out of the club, bouncing through the two gargantuan doors, past the velvet ropes and the giant bouncer dude, IEDs of bass and treble shaking her bones and rocking her teeth. It traveled up her sparkly polyester attire, through the synthetic wig, and into her already freaking-out mind.

Equivocating, she licked cherry lips, pulled the fake raccoon coat tighter, and looked around for Murad. He hung back with other beautiful and like-minded males, lighting up probably the Bosnian smokes she had seen: Drina Denifine and Auras and Marlboros, the smoke seeping upward to join one huge, gauzy cloud.

Smizing—aka smiling with one's eyes à la Tyra Banks—like a professional, he pointed his chin toward the epicenter of the cacophony. Lottie took a breath, flipped her ID at the bouncer, and charged into the noise and strobes like a Résistance agent in '40s France—fearlessly. Fake fearlessly, but fearlessly nonetheless, chanting all the while, *Fake it till you make it,* draga. *Fake it till you make it.*

Pushing past the statuesque and truly voluptuous women, she headed directly toward the bar, where she witnessed one Coward looking around in expectation. *Here we go.*

She exhaled synthetically. *Psssssssssssss.* Again. Waving like the definitional all-American, she then parted the smoke like Moses the Red Sea and closed in on him. "Why, you must be Rifat!" Excitement was key. Excitement and naïveté. And false eyelashes, of course.

The human telephone pole—both heightwise and musclewise—stood. He towered a good foot above her, or so it seemed. Maybe he was taller than six-five. And, to be fair, metrically, he was probably six thousand meters (though her conversion in this area was never good).

An orange tee hugged his chest much like Simon Cowell's, making solid nipples more visible than she wished. And though Apollo would blush next to this beauty, Lottie knew his heart was full of worms, crawling in and out, choking any remnants of humanity out of him. Wasting no *minutas,* The Coward bent over and planted a wet kiss on her lipstick-slathered lips. *Oh boy, this might be more difficult than originally thought.* She looked over her shoulder to witness Murad wedging into a sliver at the corner of the bar.

"Why, that's mighty bold of you, Rifat! You scoundrel, you!" Scarlett O'Hara had nothing on her, though Lottie wished for a second that she could be back in her own little Tara uptown. Rubbing Frank's chin. Having a beer with Lou.

He gleamed thirty-two unnaturally white teeth. *Lay off the Crest Whitestrips, buddy.* "I'm sorry," he sang in a Bosnian-tuned accent. "I thought that you American girls like that kind of stuff."

"I would love to get to know you first, darlin'." Lottie winked, her false eyelashes flicking like Spanish fans, the glue tightening and itching her lids. "I'm really interested to learn about Sarajevo. I have to write a thesis on the current status. How it has advanced since the war and all."

So dramatic was his eye roll, she swore it rattled seismic waves around Eastern Europe. His chest caved, and he slunk into the barstool. She moved in closer. Poor thing, he might have to resort to his favorite drug. "So... tell me all about your marvelous city. If you can. It's pretty loud in here!"

"Jes, why don't we go to a more quiet place," he snarled. That, Lottie wouldn't mind, but not yet.

"I would love a martini, darlin'. Or, how do you say? *Draga? Dragi?* Can you get us two?"

Evil waltzed in his eyes, she imagined. The Opportunity. Presenting itself once again. Laid at his feet. A golden goose, silver platter, Frankincense, lamb to the wolf. He held up a hand. His bartender pal came and fist-bumped him. The bartender winked and quickly delivered two martinis. Lottie smiled innocently and fluttered the Spanish fans. Murad took a sip of his beer, searing The Coward with his eyes and smiling as though the satisfaction of what could happen had already hit him.

Taking a sip, she then declared joyfully that she needed to go to the *toalet*, making certain to leave her martini precisely in its place as if on an "X" onstage. She treated The Coward to a hard peck on the cheek, threw Murad a look, and pushed through the crowd toward the bathroom.

Moments later, she returned and gave Rifat another kiss, this time letting it linger for effect, then glanced back at her coconspirator. Murad nodded and slammed back a shot of something. The signal.

It was time to fully implement Operation Estela, and in her loudest English, she yelled, "Oh, my goodness! There is Mister George Clooney!" and pointed toward the door, where a nondescript male with salt-and-pepper hair stood. Thankfully, the entire world knew the handsome and unfortunately married Clooney and turned toward the target, Rifat included. When he did, she swapped his drink with hers, making sure to wipe off the lipstick marks. He turned back around and shrugged. "Whoops. My bad." She giggled. "Drink up, *dragi*. As soon as you finish, we can go somewhere quiet and talk." She even whipped out the air quotes like a boss for him.

This last statement caused the abomination to slam back the martini and flash a smile at Lottie that dwarfed the disco ball. She kept staring at him, smiling like an anesthesiologist, waiting, waiting. She dragged him to the dance floor to give the drug time to kick in. After a jig or two, a big slur came out over the din of the crowd and music, "You are *sho* pretty." She stared. She waited. His eyelids opened and closed in slow motion. "Charrrr…"

She nodded nonchalantly at Murad. When the bartender went in the back, Murad moved in quickly. They hoisted the detestation quickly and slung his arms around their respective shoulders. As they exited, they made certain to laugh and roll their eyes to onlookers, who hopefully thought that the three of them had too much *alkohol*.

Murad confirmed the Bosnian version of Uber, and a white Toyota pulled up in timely fashion. He then explained in Bosnian—she supposed—how they had to get his American friend and her drunk date to Hotel Sarajevo stat before the date passed out. This was true as they did not wish to carry Goliath, the telephone pole, complete with tight tee and sparkling teeth, anywhere.

The taxi driver blasted out of the crowd and double-timed to the joint. Within minutes, the driver screeched to a halt in the hotel's semicircle drop-off. Murad slapped the driver on the back, threw out a *hvala ti* at him, and they hastened to get the adorable and now rufied lug to the elevator and up to room 405.

Struggling in four-inchers and blinded by semidetached and dangling eyelashes, she wobbled along with Murad down the hall. He swiped the key, and they tumbled into the room and threw their monstrous charge onto the bed, him falling like a felled redwood.

Yanking off Cleopatra and the cap, she shook out her hair, then scratched her scalp like a speed addict. She ripped off the glue-on nails one by one, then peeled off what was left of the eyelashes. Murad opened the minibar, grabbed two Johnny Walkers, and they collapsed on the sofa, laughing like psychos and toasting like two people who had just climbed Mount Everest. Unfortunately, they still had to descend the mountain, which was inevitably when the adventurers ran into trouble. There was much work yet to be done.

"We can't be too careful. Let's implement stage two after this," Lottie said giddily, perhaps encouraged by the Johnny Walker or just relieved to be wigless.

The Coward mumbled something that sounded like "Mama" and rolled over.

She tugged off his something-like-size-47 shoes, which, of course, were buffed to mirror perfection. Then, she removed his Rolex President and laid it gently on the end table. Why gently? Just because she wanted to destroy a plague on society didn't mean that she wanted to destroy a nice watch. Though it wasn't her taste, still, it would be wasteful to hurl it across the room.

"Look at all these beautiful things," Murad exclaimed from across the space, opening a fabulous tote full of equally fabulous props. Snickering, he pulled out velvet ropes and a pair of handcuffs—both he managed to find at a kinky shop in Sarajevo—one giant yellow-and-black corset, temporary tattoos. "Where did you find this stuff?"

"Some sleezy shop in New Orleans," Lottie replied and continued to disrobe the target, praying along the way for forgiveness. It didn't exactly feel right. Then again, it did. Again, she determined to just do it and talk to God about it later, a habit she had taken to utterly hellish extremes. "I think I need help," she yelped, trying to get his jeans off with one eye closed.

Murad came over. "You pull, and I will hold him by the arms." After much tugging, the designer jeans came off in a *whoosh*, an act that landed her squarely on her butt and made her laugh like a fiend, which maybe she was precisely in the process of becoming.

"Next, please allow me," Murad said and unbuttoned the coward's shirt. Before long, a nearly buck naked and evil goon lay before them.

After much ado and heaving and hoing, limbs flopping this way and that, they ended up with a titan in tights. Or sort of. In the yellow-and-black corset, Rifat lay across the bed like a comatose bumblebee.

Squeezing his Hulk mitts into the handcuffs, they then clipped them to the massive headboard. In celebration of this gargantuan feat, they lifted another pair of mini scotches and collapsed again on the sofa. "This is crazy, you realize," Lottie said, catching her breath, her black V-neck sticking like wallpaper and frothing with perspiration.

"Not so bad," Murad replied and tilted the bottle back. Outside the room, a group of late-nighters laughed and joked indecipherably. A door opened and closed. The smell of scotch and sweat and The Coward's stinky cologne filled the air.

"Come on. This is too much fun. Exhausting but fun." Lottie jumped up and grabbed the temporary tattoo. She peeled it carefully and centered it on his forehead, just above the Cro-Magnon brow and below the sculpture-gone-wrong hair. If pangs of guilt flared, she put them out with thoughts of Estela and the hysterectomy or Murad's trip to the ICU. Besides, the tattoo was temporary. Just enough to torment him and hopefully show him the error of his homophobic ways.

"You got this?" Lottie asked.

"Of course, *draga!*"

Because her part of the mission was complete, Lottie kissed Murad—cherry lipstick faintly leaving a mark—on each cheek and left to return to the relative safety of his apartment. He was the one to finish the act, of course, as he had been forever and personally altered by the creep. It was Murad's form of therapy too, of righting the wrong and hopefully saving others from future assaults. In fact, so horrific were the tales of Rifat's attacks on gays—not just Murad—that it was difficult for Murad to talk about.

She snagged a taxi in front of the hotel, requested the Old Quarter, and found her way back to Murad's. For effect, she lit up another cigarette—

which, of course, had become only a Bosnia-specific habit—and pondered the events of the night. She would await his arrival beside Ina, who was clandestine beneath her blanket.

"I *was* a pretty girl, Ina. You should have seen me!" Lottie looked at her watch. Two or three more hours to go. Sleep, even a short nap, would be nearly impossible with the anticipation effervescing within. Besides, Murad could begin to send selfies at any moment.

And with that thought, her cell ding-donged and flashed a photo of Murad sans clothes and entwined amorously with Rifat. The picture implied much more than actually happened, Lottie knew, as Murad wanted nothing physically to do with the Telephone Pole. More delightful than the obvious implication was the tattoo emblazoned on Rifat's forehead, which read in bold black letters the word PEDER—"homosexual" or "gay" in English. She pressed the phone to her heart, looked up, and smiled. *We did it!*

Still, the giant slept. At some point, he would awaken. And he wouldn't be happy.

Until then and the safe return of her platinum partner, she was entitled to worry. The death stick sizzled as she puffed away and created quite a leaning tower of ashes. It was a new game she would distract herself with, looking to see how long the tube of ashes would grow before it fell to the floor. With each inhale, she crossed her eyes, trying to watch the experiment while it crackled and fizzled and glowed and produced a thin stream of smoke traveling skyward.

And speaking of skyward, she hadn't prayed in a day, and who knows, it might help the whole situation. She didn't know if God would bless it, but she would try. The ashes fell to the floor, and she to her knees.

Dear God,

I realize that I am playing with fire, literally, right now with this unhealthy habit and also with the creep who hurt my friends Estela and Murad. I know that you created the creep, and I will try not to hate him, but it's just so hard. Please forgive me for that and protect both Murad and me as we finish this job.

In Jesus's name,

Amen.

She smashed the butt into the ashtray, swept up the ashes, and sprawled across the bed. The ceiling fan chugged and sputtered, dispelling the smoky remnants. The quilt beneath her felt so soft. She decided to close her eyes. Just for a short while.

~ ~

The curtain rose on the day, and the sun sashayed boldly across its stage. Lottie wiped drool from the corner of her mouth, the foul taste of nicotine violating her tongue.

All was quiet—too quiet. It felt like an ambush of silence. Ina was still in her cage, still covered, still mute. Had her papa come home, she certainly would've flapped and danced and announced, *"Dobrodošao kući, Papa! Dobrodošao kući, Papa!"* or "Welcome home, Papa! Welcome home, Papa!" Lottie's ticker thumped obnoxiously. Where was Murad? The thought revved its OCD motor, and she leapt out of the bed.

"Murad? Murad? Murad?" Lottie howled into the quiet den. Nothing. The sun's rays targeted the apricot wall and multiplied its luminance exponentially, which should have calmed her. Instead, it heightened her nerves and heart rate. "Murad?" she yelped much louder.

Ina woke with a start and began to screech. "Murad Murad Murad Murad." Lottie went ahead and jerked the blanket off her cage.

Just then, the door slammed. Lottie clutched Ina's blanket. Someone lingered by the front door, then stepped softly onto the tile. She held her breath. Ina crowed, "Who is it? Who is it? Ding dong ding dong. Who is it?"

~ ~

The air pulsed. Her brain split. Then she heard, "Rise and shine, *dragas*. Papa is home!"

Did he have to be so quiet, then launch what amounted to a surprise attack? Didn't he know that Lottie's heart couldn't take it? Or brain, for that matter. Hadn't she read so many articles in *Psychology Today* about chronic stress and what it does to the brain? *Damage is the answer!* This zigzagging of adrenaline was carving a crooked path through her soul and almost necessitating warning signs around the curves. Hopefully, this would be the last event before settling into a sedentary life, one where she could sleep well, take a few big clients—like maybe an insurance company or two—R-E-L-A-X.

"*Dobrodošao kući, Papa! Dobrodošao kući, Papa!*" Ina screeched. For the first time, Lottie welcomed the feathered celebration, though it bedazzled her eardrums.

"*Cao bebo! Cao bebo!*" Murad yelled and entered with a bag full of something—full of empty calories, no doubt. He gave Ina a peck and kissed the nest atop Lottie's head too. "I bring *tulumba*," he basically sang, as though he had not just parleyed with the devil.

"I was beginning to worry about you." Significant understatement.

His eyebrows lifted. "*Stvarno?* Really? You look like you just woke up!" He hugged Lottie hard, holding it for longer than normal, as though he realized the danger they both had just encountered head-on. Like they had undressed Milošević himself, only a Bosnian instead of Serbian. Dancing with monsters had its drawbacks.

"I'm sorry. I tried to stay awake."

"I know, *draga*. It's all good, as you Americans say." He flicked a wrist and waved a hand, then yanked her by the arm into the kitchen and opened the paper bag, the smell of sugar and grease presenting an irresistible proposition. Much like churros, the *tulumba* were tubular donuts and appealed to her early morning sweet tooth. "I brought Bosnian coffee also."

If the eating was good, then the debriefing was outstanding. Better than the movies! "Tell me. I can't stand it!"

As he began, Lottie robotically stuffed the confectionaries into her nicotine-bathed mouth. "Around five a.m., The Coward, as you call him, began to stir. With a twitch and a wiggle, he soon realized his handcuffed predicament."

He took a bite and continued with a full mouth, "At that point, I sat coolly on the sofa, cloaked in a towel and nothing more, and puffed away on a cigarette, trying desperately to remain composed. Then I got up and said, '*Dobro jutro, dragi,*' or Good morning, darling."

"And though it made me sick to do it, I went over and kissed Rifat on the cheek. '*Jesi li uživala sinoć?*' Did you enjoy last night?' I asked. His eyes grew as big as—how you say?—dinner plates? and his mouth fell open. 'You were wonderful,' I teased, again trying not to laugh."

While Murad cooed over the jerk, the thought must've occurred to the velvet-tied lug that he had been taken advantage of, and he soon began to boil over, an evil stew bubbling with hate and disgust and fear. Once this occurred, his colossal hands began to jerk in an effort to free himself. The handcuffs and, more importantly, the headboard held up, Murad noted, though both rocked enough to make him nervous. Murad kept his cool, however, and said to him, "By the way, if you try to seek retaliation against me or my lady friend, I will post these photos on Instagram, Twitter, Pinterest, everywhere. I will post it on social media that has not yet been invented. After all, they are already in the cloud." Murad then climbed back in the bed and flashed photo after photo of Rifat in the bumblebee teddy and with Murad wrapped around him naked. At that, the prisoner's nostrils actually flared, and he spat in Murad's face. Murad smiled and wiped off the saliva. "I know that your *prijatelji*—friends—would love to hang out with you after they see it," Murad offered sarcastically.

"Wow," Lottie frothed. "How did he respond to that?"

"Well, I just kept talking. I said, 'But there is nothing to be ashamed of, *draga*—about being a *peder*, that is. Eventually, you will come to terms with it and maybe even be proud of it.' Then he growled like a real beast and writhed. I then said, 'Unfortunately, I must go. You will be okay. A maid will probably free you, if you don't scare her away.' And I got up from the bed and opened the door. Before I closed it, I stuck my head back in and said, 'Oh, I almost forgot. I hope you like the tattoo.'"

Murad then snapped the door closed and headed down the hall. He heard swearing and one big AAAAAAAGGGGGHHHHH. And that was it. Then, he, Murad, jumped into a cab and aimed for the condo, where he found both Ina and Lottie snoozing and ran back out to get breakfast.

"Wow." Lottie said it again, the situation calling for many. "You are amazing." She licked sticky fingers one by one.

"No, *you* are amazing. Thank you for including me in this diabolical plan. I think that I can honestly go on with my life now."

"Well…" She tapped all ten fingers together to emphasize the diabolical part. "Bwahahaha." She could tell he meant it, and just hearing it made her feel good and what else? *Evil? Please, no.* On the other hand, no one had raped Rifat as he had others. No one beat him as he had others. They didn't even embarrass him in public. Not yet, anyhow. That ball was precisely in The Coward's court.

"I mean it. It is true. I couldn't have done it without you." His voice cracked, which instantly made Lottie's nose sting and her eyes get salty.

"Awwww. I hope that you can heal now." She put a sticky hand on his shoulder.

"I feel great, actually." He sniffled and wiped his eyes. "You don't know how much I hated walking around my city…" He poked himself violently in the chest, and his voice cracked again. "Looking over my shoulder all the time, waiting for Rifat to show up and harass me." Then he smiled again. "I feel, I don't know, what is the word?"

Outside, vendors began to say good morning and jingle their keys. The sound of metal shutters opening punctuated the air.

"Empowered?" If so, this was a very good thing and definitely lagniappe.

"*Točno!* Exactly!" He took a bite out of a donut, his nose streaming now like the fountain in Old Town. "Yes, that's it! Em-pow-ered." Between nose wipes and bites of death by sugar, he victoriously raised an index finger.

"Exactly! Exactly!" Ina chimed in from the other room, her little ornithological syrinx reaching new decibels.

"Look, Ina learned a new word!" Murad exclaimed.

"Fantastic." Lottie rolled watery eyes and hugged him again.

~~

After a long nap, necessitated by the physical and mental exhaustion that follows a job well done and from the glorious release of accomplishing it without a hitch, they awakened with smiles and probable cavities.

"It's still relatively early, *draga*," Murad began. "What would you like to do? I shall reward you with whatever you like."

She tapped fingers on the tiny Formica table and thought hard. Sarajevo, nay, Bosnia as a whole presented so many opportunities, both man-made and God-made, that one's head could swim in them.

"Bijambare, maybe?"

"You got it, *draga*!"

Claustrophobia be damned, though it might not have to be. In truth the park known as Bijambare, as Lottie understood it, and according to *Lonely Traveler*, was more than just caves, though that was its main attraction. Flourishing with meadows, conifer forests, and "lost" rivers, it was a hot spot for picnickers and hikers alike. The guide strongly suggested entering at least one cave and embracing the phenomenon, with its stalactites and stalagmites and other ites. This much she knew; however, it would be the only time hopefully that her Timberlands—buried near the bottom of her Samsonite—would touch the inside of a cave. So it might as well be a large one with high ceilings, well lit, and well populated with tourists. Never, ever—not voluntarily, anyway, would she crawl into one.

"Would you mind if I first run into a coffee shop to buy a coffee set to bring back with me? Remember, I leave tomorrow." She could feel her lips dropping.

"Of course not. I will walk you over. I have to go buy a pack of cigarettes from the drugstore."

"Yeah, about that." Lottie looked down at her nails, realizing the necessity of a preflight manicure. "You may want to think about giving up smoking. It will add years to your life, and you'll have fewer wrinkles."

Murad ran his hand through his hair, ruffling bleached feathers. "You're one to talk."

"This is a Bosnia-specific habit." She reiterated this, both to him and to herself. "Besides, I just want you to live a long life and come visit me in New Orleans now and in the future. And it can't be good for Ina."

Ina yapped in the corner. "Pretty girl! Pretty girl!"

"I would love to visit you, *draga*." He kissed her on each cheek. "And I never thought of lovely Ina. I will think about it."

"Pretty girl!"

They exited in Timberlands or some Bosnian equivalent, both looking somewhat uncomfortable and clunky in swaggy Sarajevo. She wanted to leave her American footprint in the caves of Bosnia just as she had in Rifat Turković's misogynistic and homophobic world. If Lottie were a braver vigilante, she might have imprinted her boot on his designer-jean clad rear. But, alas, she only could do so much before she tucked in her tail and revealed her authentic, cowardly nature and scampered back to Leontine Street.

Murad walked her over to the *kafana* and ran off to refresh his supply of carcinogens. The siren scent of freshly ground beans pulled her in, while patrons sipped and chatted on the pillowed benches and stood in queue for the muddy liquid.

The scene proclaimed *Life!* or *Promise!* or *Wake up!* to the world: the start of the day for most and maybe even new adventures for a few lucky ones. She surveyed the sippers in the small shop. Some would certainly run in and out like her, perhaps going off to work or on a trip or to the birth of a grandchild or niece or nephew. Others would meet old or new friends and laugh or cry.

As the spoons hit the metal cups, stirring the top layer of the goodness, she indulged in a second of fantasy, as she tended to in most foreign countries. *Can I live in Sarajevo?* She let the thought swirl around luxuriously. Surely, her talents would transfer. Certainly, attorneys populated the area as they did in New Orleans. What would it take to get licensed here? She shuddered to think. Practicing law was difficult enough in one's native tongue, let alone in one yet to be explored. *Draga* and *zdravo*—hello—were fine. *Your Honor, I submit, blah blah blah,* was another issue altogether.

Next to Lottie on the bench, a middle-aged couple cooed and snuggled, a seventeenish and cologne-doused boy kept his hand firmly on a contemporary's thigh, yet another beautiful Bosnian brunette. The café percolated with friendship and romance.

A saleslady with a warm smile and a red wig attended to the plump man in front of her. Only one more obstacle stood between her and the Holy Grail of Bosnian coffee, which she would use to prove to her NOLA friends that café au lait was not the only game in the caffeinated world.

"*Šta želite?*"

"Me?" She pointed to a displayed silver coffee set. "That, please."

"One moment," the lady replied in English. Eager to present such a treasure to a tourist, she hastened to the back to retrieve it.

As Lottie waited, tapping fingers on the pastry-stuffed glass case and taking in the cacophony of Bosnian and German—hard syllables with many consonants—someone or something yanked her ponytail, which registered in her brain first as pain, then second as trouble.

"Owww," she screeched, but the hand didn't let go. She couldn't turn her head to see who was attached to the hand that was now pulling her out of the shop, out into the ancient streets. Whoever it was had a massive hand and might qualify for some bizarre Slavic wife-toting event in the

Olympics. She didn't have much time to see whether the patrons noticed or reacted or ignored the misogynistic feat occurring beneath their noses.

"You American bitch! I'm going to kill you. You whore! You think you can come into my city and embarrass me?" It was a voice Lottie had unfortunately memorized.

Rifat? Rifat Turković? Of course. Good Lord.

Despite the burning sensation at the pull locus, she contemplated the day's schedule and wondered how The Coward would have been able to escape the ties of velvet and handcuffs. Did the maid release him or run out of the room screaming? The guy must have friends. But how? *How did he find me?*

Though on a good day one might find her complaining about her hair, Lottie wasn't prepared to lose it yet. She twisted like a hooked trout, while the self-defense taught her by Oprah—*Thanks again, O*—began to play in her head: *Go limp. The way a toddler does. Go limp!* Lottie attempted a two-year-old's fit and tried to dissolve into the ground, but he continued to tow her around like a rag doll.

Now she could see witnesses, lots of them. They gasped, their mouths opening, their tongues exclaiming in Bosnian. A mother pulled her child under her coat. An old woman stepped back. Maybe Sarajevo wasn't the place for her after all. Why didn't they help her? She had no idea what they were saying, but from the corner of her eye, Lottie witnessed a congress of locals murmuring. Did Rifat have connections in the town? In the Sarajevan Mafia?

With both hands free but still dangling by her ponytail, Lottie writhed enough to grab the cell phone from her back pocket and hit the last message received. It was from Murad and flashed the hideous source of the blackmail.

"Look, Rifat. Remember, this can go viral faster than you can curse Milošević." She stretched her hand up, behind up, behind her head, hoping he would glance at it. On it, she hoped he could see himself in all his splendor, *peder* ornamenting his fat forehead, Murad naked and wrapped around him.

The Coward dropped Lottie on her rear and attempted a grab at the phone, but she skittered away. Momentum finally shifted in her direction. "That's right. Remember, Rifat!" She spoke it like Marie Laveau putting the gris-gris on him, then added, "It's in the cloud! The cloooooouuuuud!"

After a moment of what looked like sheer terror and dread, he turned heel and ran in the other direction as though spooked by a ghoul. An American one, perhaps? Or worse—a Cajun?

Being dragged into the street in caveman fashion had admittedly stunned her. She rubbed her scalp, assessing the damage. The mane, such as it was, remained follicley intact, still thick, still riotous, nothing falling out. The tender area flamed from the wrenching. An older village woman with a handkerchiefed head approached. "*Jesi li dobro? Jesi li dobro?*" Lottie hoped it might translate to *Are you okay?* and nodded. The teen with the pretty girl asked the same. Pigeons wobbled around her as though offering solace.

She dusted herself off and thanked the do-gooders, retracting any thoughts about their indifference. *Hvala. Hvala.* Thank you. Thank you. Looking around for Murad, she noticed the white head bobbing through the crowd up toward her. "Are you all right? What happened to you?" He looked in the other direction for a perpetrator.

"Oh, nothing. I tripped on your crazy uneven street, that's all. You know how old streets are."

"Well, we should get going to the caves, *draga*. We are—how do you say?—wasting daylight."

Lottie wouldn't tell Murad what really happened. He was in a good place, and she wanted to keep him there. He had slain the dragon, and, judging by the reaction, the dragon wouldn't terrorize the village again, or its inhabitants—in this case, Murad.

She locked one arm soundly around his and made a sweep of the area. They made an interesting pair, the two of them, and woven together could resemble a candy cane, if one had an imagination. "Indeed. Let's go!" They turned on boots and skipped away toward a more majestic scenario. She'd just have to get the coffee set on another trip.

Chapter Twenty-Eight
Farewell, Friend

The departure back to the States was blissfully uneventful—unbelievably, in fact. This time, no enraged lunatic stormed the Jetway seeking Lottie's undivided attention by waving fist or gun. The flight itself, the whir of the Airbus engines, the clanking of the flight attendant's cart, forced her to relax. Of course, the satisfaction of a job well done with the lagniappe of Murad as a beneficiary didn't hurt one bit either. Maybe one day, she would confess to Estela. But not yet. Protection of her sweet friend was paramount to this operation.

Studying her fellow passengers, Lottie couldn't help but imagine their backgrounds and goals and lives. Why were they on the flight? Where were they going? Was the purpose of the trip business or pleasure or a mixture like Lottie's? It was an eclectic mix, probably a few Americans and many Bosnians and Serbians, neither knowing the affiliation of the other without being introduced. It called to mind the stupidity of the war—are any justified? These people had coffee together, took walks, babysat each other's kids. Until the war. How a neighbor could turn on another neighbor befuddled the daylights out of her and twisted her heart until it ached.

Some passengers appeared to be village folks, less fortunate and less professional, with soiled fingernails and stained clothes. Others bedecked themselves with new jeans, high heels, bangles, and makeup. Where the dividing line was, she wished not to know. She simply hoped and prayed—a term she threw around too lightly—they could peacefully coexist.

Were some seeking refuge in the US as Estela and her family had done? Were others flying out for good, leaving the homeland because the post-Yugoslav War prejudice and persecution against them was too much? Lottie had not witnessed firsthand any animosity between the two ethnic groups on her short trip, yet she knew from friends and research that it still bubbled just below the surface like a fetid stew. Like Rwanda or Sudan, it was a frustrating and deadly debacle that seemed to go on forever, the ridiculous eye-for-an-eye tactics of the players stretching back for decades or, in the case of Bosnia and Serbia, centuries.

But there her brain went again, entertaining mental fireworks about war and genocide and injustice. Why did it have to zero in on atrocities so much? For once, couldn't it reap the benefits of sweet revenge?

When the sleek and slender and starched flight attendant came around, exhibiting her own version of the exotic, Lottie ordered a double shot of Grand Marnier and slid into sleep.

～ ～

Pigeons pigeons pigeons! It is a scene from the Hitchcock movie, The Birds. *Pigeons perch on her arms. They poop on her shoulders, nest in her hair. She flails and shoos them. Beneath the slight shelter of the fountain, Ishmael stands, laughing. Once again, he rocks a bundle in his arms. Why are they together at Baščaršija?*

She shouted at him, "You're supposed to be in Kabul with our son!" It's their first fight, but she scolds him as though danger lurks on the other side of the square, as though she knows that a beast waits across the bricks. She

289

runs toward him, slapping pigeons as she goes, felling them one by one like a video game. She immediately regrets harming God's creatures. "I'm sorry. I'm so sorry," she says.

When she reaches Ishmael, she expects to see Frank bundled up as before, but when she pulls back the blanket, a baby appears. The newborn has Ishmael's strong nose, a dollop of red hair, and fair skin. He's beautiful, she thinks, then swirls around to look for the threat. There is a threat; she feels it in her bones, feels it across her skin, which tingles. Feels it everywhere.

Ishmael tosses the baby to her like a hot potato, which, luckily, she catches. Then from well-fitted jeans, he draws a three-foot sword, the kind one would imagine in Ali Baba and the Forty Thieves. *He swings the sword above her head. She screams, "Noooo!" Then notices behind her a three-headed giant marching toward the fountain from the new part of the city. One head belongs to Abdullah, bearded and gruff, with a few yellowed teeth; another to Miguel, knobby scar above his eye; still another to Rifat, PEDER on his forehead in neon, flashing. It growls in three different languages, but in none that she knows.*

The Bosnian war rages. The giant swings its arms at airplanes and helicopters whirring about it like King Kong. Then he aims all three grisly heads at her and the baby (who she named Jake after her father). She begins to run in the opposite direction, jostling Jake along the way until he begins to wail. She stops to comfort him, but when she looks back, she sees the giant scoop up Ishmael, causing him to drop the sword tens of stories to the ground. She freezes, the swaddled baby still in her arms. She can't save Ishmael. Noooooooooo!

⁓⁓

"Miss! Miss!" Lottie felt something pushing on her arm. "Are ju okay? I think you dream. You scary." Lottie looked at the hand, looked at the person attached to it. It wasn't a freaky giant, and, unfortunately, not Ishmael either. Instead, it was attached to an older, village-type woman bedecked in a black head scarf. She sat two seats away and looked as though she wanted to wake Lottie but didn't want to either. The middle seat was empty.

"Yes." Lottie blinked several times and thanked God that it was only a nightmare. "Oh, gosh. Yes, I am. Thank you so much." As the flight continued, her row mate revealed an attrition of teeth, but also a strong and generous heart.

~ ~

When the wheels touched down at Louis Armstrong International Airport, Lottie could sense it. It was ominous—pure and heavy, like the cumulonimbus clouds about to burst over the city. Something had happened. She knew it, could feel it too. Much too afraid to call Lou for fear that someone had died, she made her way sleepily off the ramp of the Airbus, falling in line with the many other disheveled passengers. Glad to have gone through the customs nonsense in D.C., she would only have to grab her bag off the carousel in New Orleans. She would wait until she picked up the bags before calling Lou, and tried to shake off the hopefully misguided notion that something was terribly wrong.

She didn't have a chance.

Just past security stood one Louisa Mae, head down, looking more somber than Lottie had ever seen her. Lou embraced her for several seconds. Even her hug was different, the kind one receives when grief or regret is in the air. "Hey, baby. I want you to know that I did everything that I could. Everything."

Passengers walked all around them, but Lottie began to float. "Oh my gosh. What happened? I knew it! Is it one of my brothers? Is it Ishmael?" And why did Ishmael's name arise as though they were betrothed?

"It's Frankie, Lottie. Frankie."

The words left Lou's mouth, but they seemed to stop at Lottie's cranium, the border, as though ICE officers refused to admit them into the part that registered pain. "Wha— What do you mean? You stayed at the house, right?"

"Baby, I did. Ninety-nine percent of the time. Once I ran to the grocery, like you told me to do."

"So where is he? Is he at Doctor Cat? Can I see him?"

"No, baby."

"What do you mean? Where is he?" She had floated up and out of the airport, up high near the jets queuing for landing.

"Oh, honey." Lou squeezed her again, which really freaked her out.

"Oh my God!!" And she meant it. "Is he…?"

Lou nodded as if she were afraid to. "Yes, baby. He either got into something or someone poisoned him again."

"I've got to sit down." She found an empty seat on a bench next to a couple wearing matching purple-and-gold tees. "I think we both know that he didn't get into something, as you have suggested." Tears formed in her eyes, but she didn't want to cry in the airport and tried to hold back. The couple looked at each other, puzzled. "Come on. Let's go get my bags."

A brass band played "Basin Street Blues" across from baggage carousel 3, where her two bags circled alone. For once, Lottie didn't want to hear it.

~~

Whoever the creep was, Lottie was in no mood to forgive him or her as Jesus instructed. Didn't her God suggest—no, command—absolving seventy times seven? But surely Jesus would have a caveat about that mandate. *Forgive your brother seventy times seven unless and until he or she poisons your fur baby.* A defenseless animal, one who Lottie was charged to protect, had been cruelly murdered. Was there any other kind of murder?

Strangely, anger didn't rule her spirit, tattered as it was. Instead, sadness and guilt tag-teamed and teased her, reminding her it was unconditionally her fault that Frankie died. If she had kept a low profile, done her job staying homebound and helping immigrants and not prancing around the globe avenging acts that perhaps even the avenged didn't care about, she could have protected him. And maybe even investigated it herself.

How could a human be so evil?

Well, of course she knew all about Evil. She studied it, researched it, took notes on it, and if a PhD in Evil existed, she would add more pompous letters behind Charlotte Alice Fornea, JD. Recently, in her ridiculous adventures, she even let herself foolishly think she could avenge it, though now she felt small and futile and weak. And while she used to pride herself on being able to predict Its next move, sometimes It out-crafted her in the little chess game they played.

How could Lottie have been so stupid and selfish? She had to have known this variation of Evil, even in the form of a misguided stalker, might strike again. But in the same manner? And with Lou around?

Now, her most faithful companion, the one with whom she cuddled and whom she adored even more than most humans, was gone, probably charred into dust at the vet, a cup-sized container's worth of ashes to be sprinkled in her garden and raked over by old, obsessive Mister George.

~ ~

Back in her bed, she entombed herself under the covers, wishing the crypt was real, like one of the decrepit ones in St. Louis Cemetery Number One or any of the many Cities of the Dead sprinkled ominously around town.

In other words—she wished she were dead.

The absence of the lavender fur pillow into which she had snuggled was acute, the deficit of down against her chest severe, the silence of no purr audible. But didn't she deserve it? Deserve the punishment she had begun to inflict on others? Wearing the guilt as naturally as her freckles, she wouldn't have it any other way. Failing royally in her charge to care for another creature, she held a summary and emotional execution against herself.

Mostly, though, she just missed her baby.

"I'm tellin' ya, dawlin'. The guy would have found a way." Lou stayed around, got her hot tea, tried to comfort her, but the self-inflicted wound was too great, the bleeding couldn't be stopped. "Crazy always finds a way. Always. There was nothing you could do."

Lottie barely heard her.

~ ~

It would be precisely three days before Lottie would emerge from the self-imposed hiatus from life. Usually, she could talk herself into a better mood, recharge her batteries, fill her tank with premium, though this time would be much more difficult, even more so than when she lost her mom. She wasn't responsible for her mom's death.

She pulled out the most effective pill in her hodgepodged medicine chest: a run in the park. Audubon, with its live oak elixirs and ornithological aspirin, worked faster than any doctor, conversation with a friend, or antidepressants. And on that sunny seventy-degree autumn day, she threw on her New Balances and tattered UNO tee and shorts and set out toward the cure.

I can figure this thing out. I will never get over losing Frankie and might never totally get over the guilt, but God didn't put me on the earth to cave in. Perhaps I can glean a moral from this horrible story.

Step. *I can.* Step. *Do something.* Step. *I can.* Step. *Find a way.* Step step step step. Her sneakers smacked the sidewalks, the mountains and valleys of root-infested cement. Before long, she had looped the park.

Then, as if the Almighty himself whispered, a quiet voice rose up within. *The murderer is closer than you think.*

To that, Lottie quickened her pace and received a small dose of welcome consolation. Could justice against Frank's murderer salve a wound as it had against the three targets in Afghanistan, El Salvador, and Bosnia? Could she assist the FBI better in solving the crimes? And what if he did have larger targets like churches or mosques or the Superdome, for that matter? And what if the aforementioned international pranks in some divine and ironic manner led her to the situation at hand: to exact justice in this case and retract a dangerous person from the public and therefore prevent a larger and more catastrophic act of terror?

The energy deposited squarely in the mourning bin of her brain began to sputter and chug and come to life, then spilled over into the courage bin. The jogging therapy was working. Step. *I can do this.* Step. *For Frankie.* Step. *For our city.* Step. *For our country.* Step. *For me.*

Chapter Twenty-Nine
Keep Your Friends Closer

The murderer is closer than you think. Through the Rolodex of her mind, she hastily flipped. Lou? No way would her BFF do that, and if she did, then the planets would go in the wrong direction, against traffic, the earth slip off its axis. That was impossible, and never would she recover. Just go ahead and put her in a straitjacket. No. No way.

Muslim friends? She had several. Mohamed? After all, he was devout, even had the *zabiba* on his forehead to prove it. Yet the thought of him trying to harm, threaten, stalk her, or get her off her game ran counter to his kindness. The guy was one of the nicest humans she had ever had the pleasure of calling a friend. But couldn't he lead a double life? People did that. Wasn't that the plot of so many NCIS shows? The assailant was always the one least expected. Lottie shook her head and then her entire body, trying to get rid of the absurd.

Who else? Fatima? Dr. Hassan? If she followed the NCIS formula or any of the plethora of other cop shows, she might fancy Fatima a candidate. Her qualifications begged for it. Muslim. Devout Muslim. Hailed from Afghanistan, which was sometimes mistaken as the cradle of terrorism. On the other hand, an Afghan Mother Teresa was what she was, dedicating her life to helping the beat-up people of the world, just like Lottie. She also had tenure at Tulane, for glory's sake!

But couldn't she lead a double life? People did that.

But this isn't a cop show. This is real life! Real people. Real friends. Yes, friends. If they chose another God, that was certainly their business. Did it render them the enemy? Hell no. And devoutness didn't translate into terrorism. *What the hell is wrong with me, even thinking about this?*

Lottie scribbled on the paper, drew a line under the word Suspects. *Suspects!* That the word entered her vocabulary and mostly modest life amazed her. Not in a good way either. Above her, the clock ticked mercilessly. Frank's absence was deafening. If he were alive—*that's right, alive!*—he would be on her lap, kneading, or across from her desk, sinking into his favorite chair, or beneath her, taking one of his famous baths, hind leg lifted over his head.

To boot, shunning protection of any variety left her lacking in the human companionship department. This was particularly acute after evicting Lou for a few days to give herself space and let her clear her head. And though she hadn't officially cut ties—cyberly speaking—with him, Lottie hadn't heard from Ishmael since that eerily suspended conversation on Skype, hadn't asked Fatima about him either, hadn't received an old-fashioned love letter.

On YouTube, she punched up The Meters, attempting to fill the feline and human vacuum and spur herself on to…what? She wasn't NOPD or FBI or any other acronym. She was just Lottie Fornea, Esquire, the immigration attorney, Indiana Jones wannabe, daughter of Bettie and Jake, soldier for the downtrodden. How could she solve the mystery?

She continued to blaze down the list of other Muslim clients—friends, really—placed palms firmly on her temples, then dug uneven nails into her thicket of hair.

Good Lord, am I profiling? The very thing against which she had so arrogantly combated? Perhaps the world had shifted off its axis after all during the Chilean earthquake years back as some had suggested. She chucked the legal pad across the room, pages fluttering in the dead room, her nose stinging, the tears not far behind.

Her cell phone trembled and flashed in exclamation. A quick glance revealed the FBI's number. What now?

"Hello. This is Lottie Fornea."

"Lottie, this is Agent Grant. We have a suspect. Can you come down to the Second Precinct?"

"Thank God." She swallowed. At least this absurd chapter of her life would end. Maybe she would adopt an old cat from the SPCA and semiretire from asylum cases for a while.

Mini Pearl scoffed when she pressed the ignition button. *Not now.* Bells and whistles and little warning symbols lit up the dashboard like angry emojis. What did the triangle mean anyway? Was that an exclamation point? She looked up at the ceiling so close to her nose. *Please God, let it start.* She turned it off, took a breath, then tried again. Mini Pearl spitted and coughed. But started. *Thank you.* She exploded down the street like buckshot, swerving around potholes, dodging pedestrians and bikers on Magazine Street until she reached the Second Precinct.

Hair wild, legs numb in LSU sweats, she slammed the door and flew into the NOPD station, which festooned recruitment ads and maps of the city on its walls. A fifty-something woman beneath a black wad of hair protested not being able to smoke in the building, the smoke remnants teasing Lottie's nostrils as the woman dropped the cigarette to the floor and smashed it out. A young black cop came around the counter and pulled the lady to the side, probably threatening to throw her in the "pen" for the night. Wasn't that what it was called? Or was it a crib? No, that was a pimp's home.

Agents Grant and Ryan Gosling stood in the corner in matching and androgynous suits, offering no clues in their expressions. Grant extended an unadorned hand. Lottie shook it professionally as though her legs didn't totter, as though she were in court, hiding her usual angst. "Wow. I'm so glad you guys caught him. It is a him, right?"

"We'll let you see." They sashayed down a sterile hallway. Humidity occupied the air, and she could feel her hair swelling.

Lottie followed them into a small room with a large window. She definitely cameoed in the cop show now, fully. Stuttering, she tried to speak. "But…" At an unadorned table sat Mohamed, arms folded, body rocking nervously like a dipping bird or praying Jew at the Wall. "He can't be a suspect. He's my friend!"

"They usually are," bragged Ryan Gosling, who suddenly turned Lottie's stomach. "I know it's upsetting, but we talked to several people who placed him at your condo around the time of the crime."

"I'm telling you. He…he is not your guy. It's not him." Tears made themselves at home again in her eyes, where they had appeared so much lately. Soon, splotches would invade the skin, fuchsia confirmation of extreme discomfort, disagreement, you name it. "This will totally kill him! You don't understand… He's been tortured back in…in Sudan! He has nothing left in him to commit the crime!"

Mohamed got out of the metal chair, clutched the table to steady himself, and looked toward the window. His pants displayed a large wet spot in the crotch. Lottie pressed one hand against the window, trying to reach him, then made a fist and slammed the window.

"Bullshit!" Yeah, she swore. *Screw it.* Profanity waited on the edge of the gallery in her brain for occasions such as this. "I want him released immediately!" she shrilled and opened the door to leave.

"I'm afraid we can't do that." Gosling spoke. "Matter of national security. We believe that Mohamed is the one who planted the doll. And we suspect that he might be part of a bigger terror cell." Damn, he was smug, this squirrely agent. As if the future of the nation rested on his puny shoulders. Agent Grant emitted more of a sympathetic vibe. Maybe because they bonded over king cake? Maybe because she really had a soul?

"Release him! Or I will sue the FBI, NOPD, and you two personally." Lottie's eyes were wild, she could feel it. Froth gathered in the corners of her mouth, Al Pacino-style. But she didn't care. Let them lock her up too. She could use the downtime.

She slammed the damn disgustingly gray door and left.

~ ~

When Lottie entered the private, if cupboard-size, space of Mini Pearl, she began to wail. Again. Sure, it was about Frank. But it was also about much more. The tears were fueled by authentic anger, and somehow were different from sad tears. No, angry tears seemed to burn more and not last as long.

Injustice! Again! They arrested Mohamed because he was a devout Muslim. And of course he was! The guy had been tortured grotesquely by his own government. Where else was he supposed to go for comfort? He went to his god. Just like she went to hers. And now, the US government, her government, the government to which he turned for safety, would torture him in its own way. Sure, it might only be interrogation, but his emotional makeup would not allow even for being detained, let alone being accused and questioned.

Fortunately, Pearl graciously and squarely revved up like a sports car. She navigated the gauntlet of Magazine Street, back to the safety of the condo.

From the street in front, Lottie saw what appeared to be letters scribbled on her front door in bright green, though she couldn't make out what it said. As she climbed the outdoor stairs, the word came into focus one letter at a time. T-R-A-I-T-O-R.

She hit her forehead. It figured. The idiot was still at large. As expected. And close. She touched the artwork. Freshly painted, it must have been done within the last hour, which she spent at the station with Tweedle Dee and Dumb. Mohamed was as much of a terrorist as she was. Lottie whipped out her phone and took a selfie, hand pointing to the motif on her door, then shot off a text to Agent Grant. *Fresh threats. I told you. Please release my friend.*

But what if they thought it was a terror cell—one that included Mohamed? All she could do was reason with the agents; they weren't the fiercest weapons in the government's arsenal, if you asked her.

Fueled by newfound courage from her recent trips abroad, she backstepped to the trunk of the Mini and pulled out a crowbar, then ran back up the stairs. The NCIS show continued. Scary music played in her head. Slapping the cold steel onto her palm, she tiptoed through the empty interior.

In the backyard, something clanged. It sounded like a bike getting knocked over. She ran down the back stairs and across the dry grass. The wind had picked up in the last hour and blew her hair around wildly. Approaching on tiptoes, she slowly raised the crowbar. Suddenly, the garage door opened and produced one Mister George in his usual uniform of flannel shirt and work pants.

"Mister George! Geez. I thought you were someone else. I mean, I thought you were...oh, never mind." She laughed and let the crowbar fall to the ground.

"Oh. Hi, Miss Lottie. I was just tidying up is all." He looked a little weird, like something was wrong. "How...how are you?"

"You okay, Mister George? You seem a bit winded."

"Nah, I'm fine. I just came to rake a few leaves. I was just putting the rake back."

Lottie locked arms with him, the paternal stand-in sending automatic comfort waves through her entire frame. Through the carpet of grass and remaining leaves and pine needles, they waded. She had never known him to leave any on the lawn. Age must be advancing in the war against him.

"Very windy today, ain't it? The weatherman says a cold front is coming through," he continued.

Lottie glanced down at her Crocs as they crunched the grass beside Mister George's steel-toed shoes. Drops of green—apple green—dotted the tips of his shoes and shouted at her. She stopped cold.

"What's wrong, Miss Lottie?" In her head, the *Psycho* theme played— or was it *Halloween*?

Reel it in, Lottie. You can handle this. Her eyes began to sting. Not George. It couldn't be.

"Oh. I just have a lot on my mind." She bent over and tried to buy a little time while she thought about the predicament in which she now found herself. "I think I have cramps." Unfortunately, she had become accomplished at lying, but so be it. Well, she would lie to survive. Elemental survival skills. Fight or flight. Or lie. Nothing wrong with that.

"Oh, lady problems, eh?"

Lottie continued to lean over. *It's Mister George.* No, it wasn't Mister

George simply standing there with her. *It's Mister George! The suspect.* She wasn't sure how she would handle it, but she slowly straightened.

When she was upright, she found herself stuffing down a full-blown panic attack as she looked down the barrel of some variety of handgun—which type, she had no clue. Kind, paternal, and, apparently, evil Mister George said, "I'm sorry, Miss Lottie."

"Mister George." She couldn't breathe. "Why? Why me? Why Frankie?"

He paused for a second as though he might be remorseful. "I didn't mean to kill him, Miss Lottie. I really didn't. I was just trying to scare you into staying away from them."

"Who, Mister George? Who? Stay away from who?" *Breathe, Lottie. Pssssssssssss.*

"Them Muslims. You gonna hurt the country." His hand quivered, which wasn't very reassuring. He was a hunter and probably a good shot, even at sixty-five.

Her knees melted, though she couldn't imagine he would really harm her. Then again, who would've thought he would have killed Frankie? A blast of anger shot through her like gunfire. *Bastard! He killed my baby.* Through her brain ran a ticker tape: all the precautions that had to be taken, all the government's resources that went to solving this case, the loss of a beautiful friend.

They stood in awkwardness for what could have been minutes but was probably really only seconds. Lottie sucked it up and pronounced, "Well, Mister George. You know I'm going to have to notify the FBI. I mean, you committed a crime. Several, actually."

He looked down at his steel tips, and, for a second, she thought that he might hand her his gun, not that she wanted it, but wasn't that what the contrite suspect did in the crime shows? She reached into her back pocket and pulled out her own weapon, the mighty cell phone, and began to punch in Agent Grant's number.

"I'm afraid I'm gonna have to ask you to put that thing away, Miss Lottie." The Glock or Smith & Wesson or whatever it was swayed unsteadily, pointing first at her crotch, then her face and then her chest, all valued parts of her body. Bourbon wafts shot out of his mouth like fire. His face had morphed from fatherly to monstrous, and his teeth appeared snuff stained. A crop of gray stubble grew on his face.

Lottie slowly put her phone back in the back pocket, which caused her sweatpants to sag like the dickens. She pulled them up nervously and rolled them at the waist. Mister George's forehead began to sprout fat drops of sweat. She wondered how long they would stand in the middle of the lawn and whether the neighbors would notice the unusual tête-à-tête happening right under their balconies.

"But, Mister George. We're good friends!" It was all Lottie could come up with under the circumstances, her bravado quickly evaporating.

"Were, Miss Lottie. Were. And I'm sorry about that. But I feel called to save this country from the changes that people like you are going to bring about. Called!"

"Mister George, you know God doesn't want you to hurt me. And just like you, I'm a believer too. I talk to him daily—more than daily, actually."

"Yeah, well, you see," he sniffed. "There are two types of Christians in this country: those that want to preserve it, and those who are Libtards"— he clicked his tongue at that and continued—"that want to just give it away. Want to change it!"

"Mister George, I...I don't want to change it. I want to keep it a country that welcomes oppressed people. Send me your tired, huddled masses yearning to be free and all."

"Ah, but Miss Lottie. You and your type are misguided." He wobbled the gun around her chest area, which wasn't massive, but she still wished to keep it, such as it was. "You're givin' it away! Givin' it away on a silver platter, the platter served up by Obama!" She wasn't sure the metaphor worked but chose not to debate him over it.

The wind picked up. The Spanish moss danced a scary tango. And as though defending her, a crow cawed in alarm. Finally, Mister George motioned with the gun toward the back step. "Inside, Miss Lottie!" Stronger than he appeared, the son of a gun then poked the gun soundly into her spine.

"Ow," she squeaked. "But…Mister George. We're friends."

"Not no more, Miss Lottie. You done gone and made me mad! Really mad!" He wiped sweat with the back of his sleeve, gun and all. "Now move!" As she stepped in slow motion, the words of Oprah came to her again: *Never allow the attacker to take you to a second location.* Would the house be considered a second location? Or would being transported to another house be the second location?

"Ow. Cramp in my foot! Ouch ouch ouch." She stopped.

But Mister George was no dummy, that guy, and snarled, "Knock it off, Miss Lottie! I used to like you, but then you got out of control. Representing those people. Bringing them here! Changing our country into a Muslim country! This is a Christian nation!"

"But Mister George. Didn't Jesus say to help the widows and orphans?"

"What the hell does this have to do with widows and orphans?"

"These people are today's widows and orphans." She knew her voice quivered but kept on talking. "You know that Jesus wouldn't turn his back on them!" And speaking of Jesus… *Jesus!* She prayed silently. *Help!*

"Don't you dare mention Jesus! Or I'll put a stop to this right now!"

Fair enough. The gun dug deeper into her back, and her mouth slammed shut like a screen door.

"Now you sit here on this back step while I think about what to do with you." At least death wasn't guaranteed. Lottie complied and sank to the concrete step.

Lord, I don't know if he wants to kill me or not, but please don't let him. This was no time to mess around. She pulled out her spiritual Uzi. *Please don't let him kill me! I'm only thirty!*

"Nah. I just don't see no way out of this but to kill you, Miss Lottie." He even smiled a bit. Had he gone mad? Was this a form of insanity that might be his defense later? And would the government call it white terrorism or just a crazy old guy losing it? "I may even turn the gun on myself after that. I got nothin' left. Don't really feel like going to jail with those hoodlums."

Lottie's momma always taught her never to use the Lord's name unless she was talking to him. Well, she would talk to him now! "Lord Jesus! Please don't let him kill me!" This time, she screamed it out loud. After all, Mister George was a Christian. If nothing else could shake him, that should do the trick. "Jesus!" she called out again, this time looking into the heavens as though he might actually appear. Trancelike, Mister George turned toward her and robotically put the gun against her forehead and closed his eyes.

The crow hovered over them, squawking its own version of madness. The New Orleans autumn—damp decomposition and spicy camellia—breathed on her. The step grew colder and harder. She quaked and braided her arms. In the corners of her eyes, droplets gathered. She squeezed them shut.

From Lottie's left, from the side of the house, she heard rustling.

"Freeze!" Her ears heard, but it translated into angels singing. Hoping it was her cavalry, she instantly regretted swearing at the feds.

And just like in NCIS, Agents Grant and Gosling stood with legs braced and weapons cocked. Mister George dropped the pistol, raised hands to the sky, and looked around cock-eyed, trying to get his bearings.

Chapter Thirty
The First Lady

Eleanor weaved through her panty-hosed legs, her kitty engine opened full throttle. She was mostly deaf and nearly blind and somewhere in the vicinity of fifteen years old, they said, but when Lottie spied her cornered in the cat section of the SPCA, she couldn't resist. "Her elderly human passed away," a teenage boy with greasy blond hair and a patch on his chin said as he placed her into her arms like a newborn.

"I'm going to call you Eleanor because I just lost Franklin." She reached down and scratched under her newest friend's chin.

"Oh, no," offered the patch. "What happened?"

With a boulder in her throat, Lottie spit out, "I'm sorry. I can't really talk about it." And she wouldn't. It was a horrid piece of her life, part of a larger puzzle, which might be fully assembled later. And wasn't life like that anyway? Such yin and the yang, such heartbreak and bliss all working together to form a complete individual.

In fact, she wasn't the greatest poetess, but she could recite the verse of one. Why? Because Emily Dickinson articulated so well the truth about her life, about every man or woman's life: *For each ecstatic instant we must an anguish pay in keen and quivering ratio to the ecstasy.*

To borrow a popular euphemism, there were no free lunches. If you had sad times, you would again have wonderful moments and vice versa. That

Mohamed was released was another weight on the good side of the scales. And, now she had Eleanor.   For the time being, she would honor Frank best by not discussing his senseless death or mentioning the misguided if mentally ill man responsible for it. Instead, she would celebrate Frank's life by transferring all her love onto another kitty, and Eleanor, with her wild tangerine coat and loud motor, fulfilled the role fittingly.

She bent over and lifted the old lady onto her lap and began the transfer of affection, the old girl generously allowing her to hold her without protest and purring at high decibels. Remnants of guilt and grief buzzed Lottie's head like mosquitoes at a crawfish boil, but she would just swat them away. Eleanor was too lovely for any of that. After all, she was grieving too.

Emails formed an ugly ticker tape on the screen again. This time, however, no annoying threats joined them. Lottie leaned back and stretched her arms to the ceiling while Eleanor circled on her lap until she formed a perfect orange pancake. This is good, she thought as she stroked the fur, much fluffier than Frank's. Of course, she would have to detangle and brush, something she knew nothing about. Eleanor was as needy as her, a situation that demonstrated symbiosis at its finest.

Pete Fountain tooted on the radio, the sun dazzled, and autumn generously set her temps around seventy-five. Things were ninety percent right. No, seventy-five percent better. Unfortunately, she couldn't deny one thought as it fluttered around, then navigated the maze of preoccupation and arrived at the forefront of her consciousness: *Where is Ishmael?*

She scanned the myriad messages, mostly junk, some personal. Still, there was a glaring absence on the screen. She checked Skype for messages too but came up empty. Glancing down at her cell phone as she had six thousand other times in recent days produced nothing either.

Though she had internally vowed not to aggravate Fatima often, she shot her a text anyway: *Any word from Ishmael? Any news from anyone?*

Thirty seconds later, her phone blinked. *Lottie Jan, no one in Afghanistan can give news about him. He is all right, Inshallah.*

God willing, that was what she said. *He's all right, God willing.* So, Fatima hadn't heard from him? Lottie knew Fatima was constantly in touch with him, so that if she hadn't heard from him, no one had. She pushed horrible thoughts out of her brain like an obnoxious houseguest and invited better-behaved guests to settle into it. No news is good news, she commanded and resumed focus on responsibilities and Eleanor, who hadn't moved in several minutes but for light exhalations from her tiny pink nostrils.

One email flashed from NO(LA) Justice for Women:

Darling Lottie, could we schedule a meeting soon perhaps?

We are eager to hear about the Bosnian trip and whether you deem it a success.

Best regards,

Isabella Francalangia

Secretary

The board wanted a meeting. What could she report? That the trip was positive? She could certainly assure that the goon would not harm another ever again if the horror on his face was any clue. Yes, Lottie could do that, reassure them that time and money put into the projects had been successful.

What she could not say for sure, however, was that she wished to continue in NO(LA) Justice for Women's quest—or even her own—for justice. Though Frankie's death had zero to do with the folly she pursued, it did take fuel out of her tank, the flame out of her fire, heck, the filé out of her gumbo.

Besides, hadn't she tamed the demons, whipped the tar out of those suckers that instructed her to avenge the crimes inflicted against her female clients? Damn catharsis was what it was. *Yeah, you right! We did it.* That's what she wished to tell them. And that it was time for her to move on, for the board to move along. Sure, the organization could continue to exist and pursue its mission to "support, advocate for, and encourage females of all ages worldwide who have been victimized through violence or cultural or religious traditions." As long as they were within the police tape of that mission, they could pretty much do anything—though the IRS might not be too keen on their recent pursuits. If it ever caught wind of those three little jaunts into other countries, why it would shut them down before you could say *Laissez les bons temps rouler.*

Now reflecting on the burnout of her life's calling—healing the downtrodden—Lottie honestly felt that she had assuaged the weariness a bit and that she might be able to go back to accepting cases. Exacting even a dollop of amends in the world had cleared her pipes a little, had readied her for getting back to more indirect ways of helping.

She wheeled her chair closer to the desk, cracked her knuckles, and banged out a draft email.

Dear Board,

Good gracious, it's been quite the adventure! And yes, I look forward to apprising the board of all the facts and potential consequences. Could we schedule a meeting next Friday night at the Endymion Bar on Rue St. Louis? As you probably are aware, it is attached to Felipe's Restaurant. How about 7 p.m.?

Your humble servant,
Lottie

~ ~

The twenty-by-thirty-ish Endymion Bar was perfect for the meeting, intimate with few distractions, even while the tourists swirled around outside. Johnnie, a handsome waiter in his forties who moonlighted at Felipe's and Endymion, would serve them. Lottie had known him for years and requested him whenever she could. His y'atty humor and impeccable timing put him at the top of the service heap. And though it was Friday, which in the Quarter was a high-revenue-producing night, the board could have the bar—for a small fee, of course—from seven to nine, before the sightseers barged in, drunk and demanding.

Lou and Lottie arrived early to pregame with a cosmo and discuss options. "You sure you want to give up your trips? I mean, I, for one, would be glad to see them go. Then I could stop worrying about you!"

"I'm so sorry, dawlin'. I didn't mean to burden you." She truly regretted the worry inflicted on her buddy, pal, confidante. "Yeah, babe. I think I got what I needed out of the trips. For one, I feel like I satisfied something deep within…a kind of catharsis…"

"Kind of what?"

"Never mind. I just feel like I can go back to helping people again, having gotten at least a little bit of justice out of my system."

A middle-aged man and woman decked out in straw fedoras cupped hands against the window and peeked in. Lottie and Lou waved, performing like orangutans in Audubon Zoo.

"But here's the thing, baby—you do bring justice to them, just by helping people get asylum here in the US. The justice comes by them living full and safe lives. Most of them go on to do great things, and the damn creeps are stuck in the same mess and never become anything but losers. You give people that!"

A sip of the cosmo glided down Lottie's throat, a fine elixir if you asked her, not that anyone ever did. "That's very interesting. I never seriously considered that."

Maybe in a miniscule way, I do contribute to worldwide justice.

The idea had marinated for a few seconds when the door flew open and produced Jezebel and Anna-Maria, jingling, jangling, and giggling. From a crisp Louis Vuitton tote, Jezebel pulled out a stuffed animal, a gray cat, and presented it. "I thought you might like this, darlin'," she joked. But her heart was precisely in the right place, and Lottie gave her a big hug.

Anna-Maria gave her a set of tiny eyeglasses. "For Eleanor—I hear she doesn't see so well."

"Y'all are going to make me cry," Lottie croaked. But cry she would not, as zero tears remained in her weepy reservoir. "Come on in. Tell Andrea the bartender what you want to drink. I'm having a cosmo, me."

Isabella wafted in with the wind and the street symphony of laughter and shouting and the tooting of a trumpet in the distance. Soon, Emile followed in his waltz dance to the "symphony." "Where y'at, dawlin'?" he sang.

Each member of the congregation suppressed smiles with what appeared to Lottie to be mischief and whispered to each other when given the chance. And where was Fatima anyway? She was usually the first one. She missed her peace-inducing friend and hadn't seen her since her return from Bosnia. "Where's Fatima, y'all?"

Each one shrugged but looked like they really knew where she was.

She suspected something was going down. It wasn't her birthday, so there would be no surprise party. Lou gave no clues as to the mystery either. Whatever. That she could feel anything was an emotional step in the right direction. She wouldn't worry herself with their silliness. Instead, she would just plow forward with her "report."

Dressed in crisp white and black, Johnnie brought out trays of oysters Rockefeller and marinated crab claws, which sent tornadoes of steam and spice into the air. Evidently unbothered by Fatima's absence, the group herded together at the bar like pigs to a trough.

Lottie ordered another cosmo and laid off the appetizers. Priorities, right? Examining the deepening creases between her eyes in the wall-length mirror behind the bar, she lifted the martini glass to her imperfectly lined lips and marveled at the tattoo of Extraordinary Pink lipstick on the crystal vessel. The others didn't seem to mind her pity party or aloofness. Whatever. Lou kept swinging by between bites, bounding onto the stool next to her. "You okay, baby?" she would inquire and provoke a weak nod.

The cacophony of the streets tickled her ears again in one unruly *whoosh*, and in the mirror, she could see the door opening again, this time exhibiting her beautiful and veiled friend coming in out of the hoopla. Finally. Fatima waved at her first, then glided toward the group. Her words were too soft for her to hear, but whatever she uttered caused the group to look in Lottie's direction. *Oh, great. I am the object of their pity.* The idea second-lined slowly through her brain as though shuffling down Royal Street. *Whatever.*

Fatima shook hands and hugged the others rather quickly, Lottie noticed, then made a beeline for her pooling in apathy by the bar. "Hello, Lottie Jan! It's been a little while, yes?" Lottie smiled weakly. "Might I join you?"

"But you don't drink."

"Of course, but I will have a glass of Endymion's finest orange juice," she crooned and pulled up a barstool. Like the others, she virtually floated, and also appeared to suppress an unidentifiable something, but Lottie couldn't muster the energy to figure it out. Let them have their fun.

After Andrea the bartender delivered the juice, Fatima ventured, "Might I run something by you before we begin, Lottie Jan?"

It was good to take the focus off herself, so sure. "Of course. Anything."

"I wish to have a guest at this meeting, and I wonder if that will be okay."

This was highly irregular, as their real mission might be compromised. "But this information could be dangerous in so many ways. To me and to the organization."

"I understand fully more than anyone of the potential danger, Lottie Jan, but the guest is also an advocate for the rights of women. It's a new Ph.D. student at Tulane."

"Well, then. Sure. Why not?" There couldn't be too many advocates in the world, Lottie had to admit.

Fatima slid off the stool and walked away, presumably to retrieve her guest. Who was Lottie to deprive someone of enjoying the fruit of the seeds they had sown?

Anna-Maria swung over and kissed Lottie on the back of the head. What was this, Mardi Gras? Why was everyone so happy? Virtually dancing?

Five minutes later, the door swung open, and in walked Fatima and her companion, the figure partially cut off by Emile, who was now kicking his version of the Charleston to Buddy Bolden's ragtime piped in on stereo. Rubbing her hands, recently and miraculously manicured, across her forehead, Lottie felt all at once over the top with her selfish woes, when certainly the world had bigger issues than the death of a cat. Besides, it wasn't fair to Eleanor not to be happy.

A tap on her shoulder lured Lottie quickly out of the pit. The reflection in the mirror behind the bottles of Jack Daniel's and Johnnie Walker Red and amaretto made her jump. Perhaps it was the cosmos. Maybe she was in a dream or another version of the same nightmare. Perchance it was reality.

Lottie turned around slowly, and what she saw both puzzled and pleased her. Before her, in all his bronzeness and beauty, stood one Ishmael. As in Afghanistan Ishmael. As in the subject of her rumination, her persistent obsession.

"I didn't think you would mind my nephew, your—how do you say?—partner in crime attending."

Lottie didn't think she had water left in her, but could feel it pooling in her eyes. "Wha? How?"

Ishmael gleamed, now in a purple button-down Perlis emblazoned with a yellow-and-green crawfish. "How do you like my uniform?"

Never lacking words, this time, she really couldn't speak but managed to burp, "Uniform?"

"Meet the newest PhD in linguistics student at Tulane University," Fatima warbled.

"Oh, hey." Lottie nodded, her eyes wet, her skin sprouting into a field of strawberry patches. Picasso would be proud.

Acknowledgments

How do I acknowledge those who have made putting pen to paper possible and who have helped make this dream come true? With a box of tissues handy, of course.

My editor extraordinaire, Linda Ingmanson, dared to take away my exclamation points and reeled in my new, author drama too many times to count. You, Linda, are my writing goddess. I am immensely grateful for your gentle correction and perpetual patience. You are my Master Po. I am your grasshopper. I sit at your feet and await further instruction.

Andy Bridge, cover designer for this book: Shukran for your patience and for sharing your talent with the world, and, more so, with me.

Kate Rothwell, my prolific, romance-writing pal: thanks for being an impressive role model. I see you, you talented writer. You are out there daily, pounding the virtual pavement and the keyboard. Your dry humor and gorgeous smile kept me afloat many days.

To Joanne "JoJo" Genzale: I can hear our laughter even now from our many adventures, mostly in New Orleans, but also in Kennebunkport (when we ordered *pie*), and in Paris (when we scaled Notre Dame's towers). May there be many more!

To my walking and kvetching girlfriend, Maryann McGuire: much gratitude for getting excited about my many wild ideas, whether it be driving solo to New Orleans, taking groovy, day trips to Woodstock, New

York, or writing this. Your constant encouragement keeps me going. I am forever in your debt.

To Kelley Robichaux, I am grateful for your friendship, your dry humor, and even more so that you moved back to New Orleans. The city is better with you in it!

To my Bosnian sisters, Sani, Sanela and Suada: thank you for accepting me into your Balkan tribe and fattening me up with much *pita*. It is because of you that Sarajevo is included in the book. And, let me just say, Zeljana, is a bonus sister.

To Sue, Angie, Carlos, Milagros, Marirose, Cara, Lisa, Chris, Ann, Danielle, and Martin, my newish forever friends: you are treasures, and I am so grateful to have each and every one of you as kindred spirits with whom I can share *just about* anything.

To all the young baristas at Barnes and Noble in Farmington, Connecticut, Eric, Alyssa, Lea, Hillary, Krizzia & Anthony: you kept me caffeinated with my picky, super strong coffee order, and I am super thankful for that and our friendships.

To my momma and daddy and my four siblings: Walt, Jesse, Judy and Reggie "Bud," we were blessed with loving each other so much! And, I want y'all to know that I carry each of you with me wherever I go.

To my life-partner and husband, Steven Bauman: thanks for loving me, for missing me when I insist on spreading my wings, and for allowing me to be my truest self. I *am* because we *are*.

To the other two men in my life, Zachary and Jake: I am honored beyond words to be your momma. Thanks for always encouraging me in my creative undertakings. Your humor keeps me laughing, and your kindness motivates me daily.

To the asylum-seekers and other immigrants that I have represented, thank you for choosing me as your attorney, friend, sister, auntie, momma, gigi, for playing a small part in *your* story. You are my reason for everything. You are my question and my answer. My inspiration and my family

And, finally. To Jesus the Christ, my radical socialist God: thanks for teaching me to care for those who need it the most.

About the Author

Parker Bauman is an immigration attorney representing asylum-seekers in the U.S. Immigration Courts and at U.S. Asylum Offices. She has a particular passion for domestic violence survivors from other countries. This is her first novel. A former board member of the Connecticut Poetry Society, her poetry has been published internationally and locally in several print and online journals and anthologies. She lives with her husband, two sons, one big black dog, a fat orange cat, and one red-eared slider in West Hartford, Connecticut and New Orleans, Louisiana. Check out her forthcoming projects at www.parkerbauman.net, twitter.com/ParkNet504, and instagram.com/lawyerwriter, facebook.com/parknet504